v11/04

DATE DUE

DEC 03

5-12-04			
GAYLORD			PRINTED IN U.S.A.

The Outside
of August

Also by Joanna Hershon
in Large Print:

Swimming

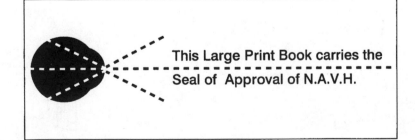

This Large Print Book carries the
Seal of Approval of N.A.V.H.

The
Outside
of August

JOANNA HERSHON

Thorndike Press • Waterville, Maine

Published in 2003 by arrangement with The Ballantine Publishing Group, a division of Random House, Inc.

Thorndike Press® Large Print Basic.

The tree indicium is a trademark of Thorndike Press.

The text of this Large Print edition is unabridged.
Other aspects of the book may vary from the original edition.

Set in 16 pt. Plantin.

Printed in the United States on permanent paper.

Library of Congress Control Number: 2003110051
ISBN 0-7862-5943-4 (lg. print : hc : alk. paper)

for Derek

As the Founder/CEO of NAVH, the only national health agency solely devoted to those who, although not totally blind, have an eye disease which could lead to serious visual impairment, I am pleased to recognize Thorndike Press* as one of the leading publishers in the large print field.

Founded in 1954 in San Francisco to prepare large print textbooks for partially seeing children, NAVH became the pioneer and standard setting agency in the preparation of large type.

Today, those publishers who meet our standards carry the prestigious "Seal of Approval" indicating high quality large print. We are delighted that Thorndike Press is one of the publishers whose titles meet these standards. We are also pleased to recognize the significant contribution Thorndike Press is making in this important and growing field.

Lorraine H. Marchi, L.H.D.
Founder/CEO
NAVH

* Thorndike Press encompasses the following imprints: Thorndike, Wheeler, Walker and Large Print Press.

Acknowledgments

I'd like to express my gratitude to those who contributed to this book: Dan Smetanka, my tireless and talented editor; my invaluable agent Elizabeth Sheinkman; the generous friends who read anywhere from one chapter to numerous drafts — Merrill B. Feitell, Ellen Umansky, Heather Clay, Halle Eaton, Matthew Rooney, Tanya Larkin, and Caroline Wallace; and especially my husband, Derek Buckner, for talking it all out. And finally, for years of good stories and so much more, to Judy and Stuart Hershon, my parents.

Part One

1

Heat, 1977

The house was too big. No matter how many Chinese shoe trees or Turkish prayer rugs, embroidered pillows from forgotten Irish counties, Balinese puppets, Deruta pottery, or African dung sculptures happened to rest in surprising corners of the place, the house never felt quite full. Alice watched her mother notice this each time she returned — the house and its emptiness always appeared to register as sheer surprise. The Greens lived in a large house. They lived in a house on the water, in a cove shared with oysters, glass-green seaweed, broken bottles, and bloated prophylactics. Alice lived with her brother and father and mother in a house sea-damaged and in a constant state of not-quite-fashionable disrepair.

Since the day the Greens had moved in nearly seven years ago, Charlotte hadn't stopped attempting to fill the house with objects. She went away to find more objects, was how it seemed to Alice, who, along with her father and brother, was always waiting for her to come home. That was why it felt so empty to Charlotte each time that she returned. The house . . . it had filled up years ago; they didn't need another thing — and Charlotte knew they were waiting; she had to have known. It was only her presence that was missing. She must have known every time.

In between the afternoon and evening, it seemed to Alice that the world was running out of energy. The sun felt like a legend — forcing people to get things done, day after dismal day. It was cold near the window, even under two sweaters, but Alice still couldn't tear herself away from watching the day fade. The March skies looked like the skin around her mother's eyes, like the dregs of her mother's milky Bengali tea. She found herself standing in front of her parents' bedroom window, watching her breath condense on the windowpane. The sky drained slowly as she anticipated the sight of her father's car coming home from the lab. Alice's father was a scientist, a professor of neurobiology, and he spent days at a lab where he acquired the scent of blood and floor wax, and worked sometimes for hours without so much as a cup of coffee, without a single bite to eat. She wanted to give her father an especially warm welcome, to distract him from realizing the heat still wasn't turned on and that Charlotte hadn't returned. Alice made twenty-three marks in the window's fog, one mark for each day her mother had been gone. Today — her father didn't like to promise — today the chances were good that she'd *wrapped everything up* and that she would be coming home from the airport, arriving before four. The clock said five-thirty. They'd all been wary anyway. Her mother made schedules but rarely did she adhere to them.

Alice turned from the window and sat at Charlotte's table. She bypassed the stamped tin box filled with jade beads and silver, overlooked the crackled hand mirror and the 1920s button rings. She sprayed the Must de Cartier in the air, and then ran through it like a sprinkler in the heat of summer. In the third drawer on the left-hand side of the table, she found the black pearl earrings. They sat on an ivory silk cloth with a purple ink stain, as if they were no more than two good seeds, waiting to be scattered. They clipped painfully onto her ears and she sat for moments trying to imagine having the strength to endure that kind of pain for any length of time. That was how Alice would know she was grown: the black pearls would clip onto her ears and she wouldn't have a thought in her head.

She took off the earrings when they began to burn and put them back as she had always done. Thin sounds of the baby-sitter talking on the phone floated through the door, like a brighter other day. The baby-sitter was cheerful and put on fake foreign accents, which were wholly unrecognizable. Down the hall, the TV was going and August was laughing. She could picture her brother laughing alone, laughing hard and loud, not noticing how dark the room was, or that their parents weren't home. He might not even have noticed the cold.

When Alice heard the tires on the gravel, she almost ran out of the room and straight out the front door, but instead she went back to the window. It was possible that her mother was in the car with him. He might have picked her up at the airport. He might have had the time. Everything seemed to slow down as she looked out the window and watched the car, so small from this vantage, so weak next to the thick and massive trees. The shadows were taking over, going from evening to night, and Charlotte was not among them. Her father got out of the car in three distinct movements. He looked up at the roof and Alice waved but he didn't seem to notice. He went for the front door and Alice ran downstairs when she couldn't see him anymore.

"Hi, Daddy," Alice said from the foot of the stairs. It always felt a little funny calling him Daddy; it made her feel like a baby, but she thought it sounded sweet.

"Hey, honey," he said softly, having hung his big coat on a rusted hook. He wore a turtleneck sweater the color of soil. "How you doin' over there?"

"It's freezing," Alice said. It just came out, the exact last thing she had planned on saying.

Her father didn't come over and rub her arms. "Well," her father said, "put on another sweater then. It's healthier to wear layers than have the heat jacked up indoors. You know that." He ran his broad hand over his face. All he wanted, Alice could tell, was a drink and some sleep. "Where's August?" he asked.

"Gus," Alice yelled.

15

Her father put his hand on her back. They walked toward the kitchen, her father flicking switches, frowning, whenever there was no light, at how many bulbs needed changing.

The baby-sitter, Melanie, was breathless with urgency, a quality many people acquired when talking to her father. He was often distracted and took an unnaturally long time to explain things. "So I have to go, Dr. Green. I'm glad you're home," she said, sticking a slew of papers out for Alice's father. "Um, listen, here are some messages? You should take a look at these; they're from Con Ed — kind of important?" Melanie glanced at Alice before deciding to stop right there.

"Yes?"

"I've gotta go," she said, and, after thrusting the papers in his hand, gave Alice a pat on the head and ran out the back door.

"Gus," Alice yelled. *"Gus."* Her hair was full of static now, thanks to Melanie's hand.

"Shh," her father said, "go easy." He read one message, set the rest down, and poured himself a Scotch. Then he patted her shoulder as he took a sip. Everyone was always patting her. It was what people did when they were lazy, like how her mother left pennies scattered on the floor though they were perfectly valuable coins. Alice began setting the kitchen table for three. She was good at remembering where everything went. Gus always ended up putting out dessert forks and spoons instead of knives, using good linens for a grilled cheese sandwich. There was dinner in the refrigerator that her father stuck in the microwave. They stood there waiting for the beep, waiting for August to show.

"You doing anything new in school?" her father asked.

"Yeah," she said. "War."

He laughed in a kind of grimace, as though he'd remembered a poorly told joke. "You sweet girl," he said absently. She wondered if he'd been listening.

She closed her eyes and willed Gus to come down.

"Get. Down. Here," her father yelled. "Gus." His yelling was like a change in the weather — something you couldn't anticipate, even if you tried. "And no winter coat at the table." From the microwave came the scent of burned butter and something green.

Gus finally came down the back stairs. The parka was on him and zipped up good

17

with the T-bar zipper silver and strong. "Evening," Gus said, imitating someone, but Alice didn't know whom.

"He's just cold," Alice said.

"You want to wear your coat too?" Her father's voice sounded so tight it was almost foreign.

"No," Alice said, and wandered back to the table. Out the bay window in the dining area there was no ocean to see. It was pitch-black, without stars.

Her mother was stealing the brightest light. Wherever she was, Alice knew this: It was still daytime.

Gus came to her side and said, "What are we eating?" It was his way of being nice. She thought her brother smelled like hot cider after you drank it, when you breathed into the cup to get warm.

"Chicken," her father said.

"Chicken," Alice said, and smiled because of the way it sounded, so ordinary and dumb.

She went into the bathroom to wash her hands, waiting for the water to get very hot. Her father started banging some pots around, the way he did when he was looking for something and wanted someone to notice, and she thought of her mother last summer, handing him towels, handing him zinc for his nose. She lay on the beach, the same place each day, squeezing lemons in her hair. She rented everybody bicycles and remembered the return date. There were no overdue books or unpaid bills. Sometimes she was up before ten.

"I just don't see the big deal," Gus was saying. "Why do you care what I wear?"

Her father said something she couldn't hear, and Gus said something back, speaking equally softly, which made Alice nervous. She swung open the door and tried to catch them talking, but her father was pouring two glasses of milk and refilling his Scotch, and Gus was sitting at the table, still in his parka, his dark hair flopped over his forehead. Alice noticed that his hands were kind of crusty and covered in pen marks.

Dinner was chicken with yellow rice with almonds and raisins and broccoli. Mrs. Holterbach made it. Mrs. Holterbach was their piano teacher, who for some reason was always bringing food whenever Charlotte was gone. Alice could always taste when it was Mrs. Holterbach's food; her idea of dessert was baked apples stuffed with peanut butter and raisins. Everything had raisins. Sometimes, when her father

19

was in a certain mood, he'd order a pizza. Once in a great while he'd make steaks. Last week they'd gone to McDonald's, but he had gotten depressed in the car ride home and started talking about apartheid.

Alice sat down, and her father did too. She felt like saying thanks.

"Hand me your plate," her father said. Alice wondered what Gus had said in order to keep his parka on. It really was cold in the house; it had been for days now. Sometimes Alice's fingers pruned and she showed no one. Sometimes she ate more just to keep her teeth from chattering. She wanted to ask her father why it was so cold in the house, but she didn't because she had made a promise to herself. When things were tense, when her mother was gone, she swore that she, Alice, would be good. People had big problems — they were blind, deaf, they had bombs in their countries, they had nothing but pain. Alice would be an easy girl.

"I miss Bo," Alice said, searching for something to sound good, but Gus just shrugged. "Do you think we might get another dog?"

"You never know," her father said, sounding doubtful. "Go on and eat, Alice. Aren't you hungry?"

"She eats so slow," Gus said.

"Don't talk about me in front of me," Alice said, suddenly hot in the face. "I am eating normal."

"I know," her father said. "Don't let him bother you."

"Look at her plate," Gus said, laughing.

"What," she said so hard it was like a cough. She looked down and there were the raisins in a line.

"She's afraid of the raisins, Dad. She thinks they're bugs."

"I do not," Alice said, feeling a warm sob in her stomach. "Why are you wearing that *stupid jacket?*" She forced the sob to remain underground, to not spill over.

"You know what?" her father said, his fork hanging between his fingers like a pendulum. "I have a massive headache that is getting worse each and every second."

There was quiet. Alice tried to think if she ever got headaches. All she could remember was her high fever when her mother fed her and bathed her and sang all of her songs. She wished Bo were alive. He would lick her fingers. He'd eat her raisins and sit at her side, looking up with round eyes. She pictured her whole family as dogs instead of people; it was something she wished for; there was something comforting about the thought of barking all night and never understanding a word.

"Enough," her father said, his voice gravelly and loose. "Take that goddamned winter coat off. This second."

Gus finished the last of his yellow rice. "It's called a parka," he said.

"Take off the fucking coat."

"Dad . . ." Alice felt her face splotching with red. She felt ashamed.

"I'm sorry, honey," he said to her. "But I can't," he said to no one in particular. "Not tonight. I said take it off."

"The heat," her brother said. She was surprised how much like whining it sounded. He never, ever whined. "Maybe if the heat was on I could eat without my coat on."

"It looks stupid," Alice said, trying to help. "You look like some kind of —"

"I'm going to count to ten," her father said, slicing a wing, "and if that coat is not off —"

"What?" Gus asked. "What will be my punishment?" he asked, as if he really wanted one.

Alice wanted to get another sweater, but she was afraid that if she left the table, they would start speaking quietly again, and she'd never know what they'd said. Tonight

22

she'd made sure not to appear bulky, not to wear too many sweaters, because she knew her father would think she was being dramatic or maybe even insulting him. She didn't want to be insulting, so she didn't go get another sweater and she ate the broccoli and rice. The chicken tasted good, but she was so cold it was hard to enjoy it. Her father sipped his Scotch.

Gus put his hood up.

"What is he doing?" her father asked Alice.

Gus looked at her and said, "My ears."

"Please," Alice said, looking straight ahead, out at the dull black night. She pictured heavy waves throwing themselves at each other way out beyond the cove. "Just," she said, "stop."

"My ears are cold," he said; then he snapped the chin flap shut, so there was only a little piece of Gus for anyone to see. The ski tags — there must have been five of them — jutted out from his chin, where the zipper was. He continued eating, neatly stuffing food down behind the chin flap into his mouth. The parka was one of the puffiest parkas Alice had ever seen.

"Alice," her father said, and her stomach shot clear to her knees, "you'd like some dessert, right?"

Alice nodded, twisting her napkin, not sure if she should be nodding. Maybe she should have said it didn't matter to her, that she didn't need anything.

"No one . . ." her father said, and then he lost his steam.

He stared at Gus and Gus stared back. Her father's eyes were low blue flames. Gus had eyes like embers. Alice didn't know where to look, so she returned her gaze outside. But this time she noticed her reflection in addition to the dark. She wondered if it had been there all along.

"Please," Alice said, but the sound just dissolved in the air.

Her father's vein stood out on his forehead. It looked like a little worm. "You don't understand," he said. "You have no idea." The way he said it felt like the middle of the night, when everything seemed dead.

Gus put down his fork and knife. He folded his hands in his lap. Alice thought he'd say "Sorry" but he just kept staring at her father, as if it were the first time he'd really looked.

They looked nothing alike.

Nobody ate more. Nobody spoke. Alice wanted a dog. She wanted her Bo back, his enthusiastic breathing. She wanted dessert and heat and her mother. It was so quiet, with the wind picking up outside, with the unseen trees whipping skinny branches up against the glass.

Her father took his last sip of Scotch, and crunched an ice cube between his teeth, which must have hurt because he sprayed some Scotch across the table and suddenly began to laugh. The air smelled like the nurse's office for a second, like the art-room sink at school. Gus started laughing the way he did when he watched TV, high-pitched and hysterical and shaking so hard that his parka made all kinds of swishing sounds. Alice didn't laugh but she breathed. She breathed so deeply that it felt like laughing. She felt light all through her head.

Her father was shaking his head, laughing through his words: "You're such an ungrateful kind of kid," he said, rubbing his face. "It's okay, what do you know? You don't know. What can I do about that? That's fine." Her father had a big smile on his face and he looked from one child to the other. Gus's eyes were still bright. Her father's face went red, as if he'd just returned from a long walk, and he took a breath through his nose as if he were about to dive off a high board for the very first time. Sound came from him in a short, loud burst, and then, after a few dry inhalations, her father began to cry. And through the hood that Gus had saved up wearing until tonight, the night that their mother Charlotte was supposed to have returned, Alice could see he wasn't sorry exactly, but surprised. Maybe it was enough, maybe it was enough for then, because their father asked Alice to play the piano, and when she said no, when she said that she was cold and that she knew that her mother had screwed up the heating bill, that she always did things like that, her father asked if anyone was going to eat some ice cream or what. Gus unsnapped his chin flap and took down his hood.

"I'll take it off," her brother said.

2

Water, 1979

When Alice came home from school (always before Gus), she'd find Charlotte at the kitchen table, poring over reams of paper or stacks of photos, reading torn-out articles, seemingly shocked that it was three o'clock, and she hadn't even shed her robe. There was a clamshell with a few cigarette butts, an open window, a broken screen, and flies crawling on honey-coated spoons beside cups of half-drunk tea.

"Oh, my God, you're home already. I haven't had a chance to —"

"Did you walk Spin?"

"Did I . . . You know, I think I did. Of course I did."

Her mother's narrow feet were bare, bone white, the remains of some coral polish dotting her toenails. There was no way she'd been outside today.

Alice went running through the house,

calling out, "Spin, Spin!" And the colorless walls took on shades of skin as the afternoon spring light made everything hot, hotter than the actual temperature — all that sunlight and her mother inside, all that sunlight and the stench hit her as she rounded the bend upstairs in the hallway.

Small piles of Spin's crap dotted the area where Alice sat most often, in the narrow corridor where she liked to bounce a neon orange tennis ball off the opposite wall. She'd sit and listen for her brother August coming down the corridor, hoping that he would sit beside her, that he would maybe try to swipe the ball away. But August usually ran by and slid down the banister as he was told not to do, daring the whole structure to buckle. He was interested in explosions.

"Spin!" Alice called. There was a puddle of pee in the guest bathroom. A puddle of pee on the landing at the top of the back stairwell. A stream of yellow (mostly dry) right beside her bed.

Her father was coming home that evening from a conference in California.

Alice stood beside each spot and just looked at what Spin had done. She thought of how badly he'd needed to go, and how he must have whined and whined to deaf ears. Alice yelled out for her mother. She must have yelled for minutes, not moving at all, before Charlotte came up the back stairs, smelling of powder and smoke.

"Look," Alice said. "Would you look!"

"That naughty —"

"*No*," Alice said, with her face burning, "it isn't his fault. It is your fault."

Her mother laughed and then coughed, dryly. It was too warm up here in the corridor but Alice could not move. "Oh, Jesus," said Charlotte, with a small round yawn. "You want to calm down please?"

"It's disgusting," Alice said. "How would you feel if you couldn't go out? No one keeps you inside all day, do they?"

Her mother didn't answer.

"Why don't you walk him?" Alice asked. "It is so easy. You are the one who said so. You said so to convince Daddy."

"Well, love, you wanted a dog, didn't you?"

"So."

"Sometimes it is easy and sometimes it is not. Okay? Sometimes I lose track of time. You two sap my energies and go off to school and I lose track."

"Sap your energies?"

Charlotte looked at her daughter, gave her a half smile that Alice knew too well.

29

The smile was supposed to make Alice feel included in her mother's infuriating behavior. It was the laziest gesture that Alice knew. It was a look that said, *I never need to apologize, not as long as you are mine.*

"That's not normal," Alice said hastily.

"No, I don't suppose it is."

"You just could walk him, that's all. Make a schedule."

Her mother shrugged. Then she reached out to touch the tips of her daughter's hair. "Let me cut it," she said.

"No," Alice said.

Charlotte didn't let go. Her touch should have felt cloying but it felt, instead, like relief. "You won't even notice. I'll give it some shape."

"Why are you still wearing your bathrobe?"

"Don't you like it?"

"Yeah, I like it, but shouldn't you get dressed?"

"Getting dressed is very overrated. Sometimes, sweetheart, I feel like if I'm going to get dressed I want to seriously get dressed. You know what I mean?"

Alice was ten years old and she still couldn't figure out what it was that her mother did with her days. Charlotte hadn't gone anywhere since mid-January, when she'd left for a month while the children were at school, having said good-bye only in passing, as they were headed out the door. On the kitchen table Charlotte had left a folder regarding a program started by a Burmese woman and a man from Boston who imported Burmese weavings and sold them on Newbury Street. He made a killing and spread the wealth to the peasant weavers. Everybody won. The folder was accompanied by a brief note, which said, *Thanks for reading,* as if it were a business proposal for a deal in which her husband and children might have been prospective investors. She'd returned home with a nasty parasite and having taken up smoking again, expressing inarticulate plans about buckling down on "the project." She didn't talk about the project in specifics, but it involved, from what Alice could tell, a great deal of sitting around.

"The project is consuming," her mother explained, as Alice filled buckets with disinfectant.

"I'll be right back," Alice said, and she went downstairs and got two mini seltzers, the kind her father drank straight from the bottle. As she climbed the stairs she couldn't help feeling a little proud.

"Well, look at you," Charlotte said, and

Alice fluttered inside. "When did you get to be such a smarty-pants? Who taught you about cleaning *stains*, for heaven's sake?"

Alice felt her cheeks burn as she shrugged and tried her best not to smile. She tried not to think about how her friend Eleanor's mother, Mrs. Deveau (who taught her about the seltzer), had told Alice with pitying eyes that she could always tell her and Mr. Deveau anything, anything at all.

Charlotte and Alice worked together silently. Alice looked at her mother, down on all fours, and made sure she was scrubbing. Charlotte's hands were like her own hands. They had short fingers and bitten nails and they didn't look motherly. Her hair was amazingly thick, the exact color of a pecan, and it was all Alice could do not to touch it the way she'd touch a horse in a stall — tentatively, with love and fear and a nagging shame for pockets empty of apples and sugar, for the inability to ride.

Even though they were doing nothing more than cleaning, Alice and her mother were together and Alice didn't want it to end. But just as she was thinking about what she could show her mother in her room or what kind of good question she could ask, Charlotte said, "Jesus, do I need a bath." She ignored Spin, who had climbed the stairs again, now that all traces of him were gone, and she touched Alice lightly on the shoulder. Alice watched her mother walk down the corridor, her bathrobe tie trailing behind her like a fallen party streamer.

Alice stood watching the empty corridor and might not have been able to find it in her to move had Spin not begun to whine. She clipped on his leash and set out walking. There were pots of hydrangeas on the front porch and the clay inside them was cracking. The sky was white and the sun shone like a smudge of pale lipstick on a cheek. It was the end of April — warm enough to wear a T-shirt, but just barely. She wondered how far Gus had progressed.

Her brother was in the water. He'd decided to swim out farther than he'd ever gone. There were markers, he'd explained the night before, ones he'd created for himself, before the cove merged with the sound. He intended to hit the very last one and be back in time for dinner. Gus had told Alice that he'd been going farther and farther each Friday, since the last of the snow had melted. He'd bought a wet suit with money he was given for an upcoming school trip to Washington. His ability to know the ocean, to learn what he *wanted* to learn (instead of what he was *supposed* to learn according to some bogus school-time schedule) was more important — *way* more important. There was a man who rowed in a rowboat from Long Island to California just last year, two women who windsurfed to Lisbon. When Alice had asked why he didn't just wait till summer, why he didn't stay after school and swim laps in the indoor pool instead, he laughed and said, "Just don't tell them, okay? That's not what I need."

What do you need? was what Alice wondered. Why would anyone want to windsurf to Lisbon? And why was it, she wondered, that this was the first thought she had: Her mother would not be worried but pleased. Alice could imagine how her eyes would shine at the thought of Gus courting danger. Alice, therefore, tried not to allow herself to be worried. Her brother, she assured herself as she threw a glance out to sea, always knew what he was doing.

She walked Spin out to the end of the long driveway and then back to the house. It was high tide and the marsh was flooded so that it looked as though the east porch always faced not reeds and birds and pattern-making sludge, but only the water. She followed the marsh down the sloping property where Spin drank from a freshwater spring that pooled over mossy rocks. A mass of tall bamboo looked like wheat or sea grass grown to impractical proportions. To Alice's left was where, at low tide, a beach was revealed, along with the detritus of the ocean. You never knew what you could find. Gus once found an egg carton full of golf balls, secured with duct tape. Alice found a dead cat. But now it was high tide and right up to the lawn was the gray-green sea lapping nice and easy.

Nestled right there, between the marsh and the sea, was a wooden shack painted a faded barnyard red. The paint was nearly gone, leaving the drab, salt-stained wood. What was most unusual about it was that there was a tiny fireplace that must have, at one point, gotten a good deal of use, as the chimney bore the scars of thick black smoke. When they moved into the house, when Alice was just five, everybody had plans for the place. Gus and Alice could make it into a clubhouse. Her father could house his bone collection, his jars of gelatinous substances — but Charlotte was going to make it into a poolhouse of sorts, even though they had no pool. Charlotte drew a picture of her vision — an inky, broad-stroked affair — and taped it to the refrigerator, where it continued to hang — frayed corners curling upward, a relic of another time. In the picture there was a chest of drawers, stacks of towels, an area rug on the floor. There was a fire in the fireplace, andirons and bellows. There were pictures on the wall; she'd chosen their frames. There was even a bottle of Perrier idling on a counter and a bud vase with a blue flower — by far the brightest color on the white, creamy page. It was a beautiful picture that Alice loved. It bore so little resemblance to anyplace she had ever seen. Plus, it proved something that was always hanging in the air at any adult function; it was whispered as a rumor, with the same tone that made mention of money or its lack, and of a woman's looks. It was a phrase that smarted with sarcasm or resentment, or else as a kind of excuse: *Charlotte is talented.*

But talented at what? To Alice it was never exactly clear. The picture was lovely but it was a rare effort. She never claimed to be any kind of artist. She never claimed to be anything, except — when she'd had a few drinks — she'd admit to being unusually photogenic. She had been asked to audition for a New York production of *The Seagull* when she was a sophomore at Sarah Lawrence simply because someone had photographed her on a train, looking out the window on a foggy morning. The director had seen this photograph printed in *Life* magazine and had hunted her down, had telephoned the dormitory in search of her. The idea of a director (Alice pictured the low-slung chair, the resonant voice) searching for her mother: nothing but *nothing* could possibly be more glamorous. Whether or not Charlotte had made any impression at the audition was somehow never the point. Charlotte's stories cut off at the precipice of meaning. Her stories weren't so much stories as they were images — nebulous enough that they were always worth a closer, longer look.

But the poolhouse, as it was so called, sat just as empty and shabby as when the Greens moved in. Alice thought of its best and only uses: the hiding place for hide-and-seek (so obvious — no one ever thought to look!), the once or twice a summer that Alice and Gus would sleep in sleeping bags on its cold, dank boards — Alice up all night listening for creatures, on the constant lookout for claws and teeth, while Gus snored. One evening last July she opened the door to find a raccoon settling in for a still-warm meal swiped from the patio table. The raccoon had looked up with a chicken bone in its hands, as if to point out her rudeness.

Alice peeked inside. At first she saw nothing, but then she noticed a neatly folded towel and a Yoo-hoo, a Snickers bar and a sweatshirt. This was where Gus would collapse after swimming this evening. Having seen that he'd taken the trouble of purchasing his own special food for the occasion (Yoo-hoo and Snickers having never seen the inside of the Green household), of planning ahead and even bringing a towel . . . It was impressive. Towels for Gus were an afterthought at best, used after a swim only if someone else remembered. On cooler evenings at the beach, he'd stand beside the comfortably towel-clad, jumping up and down, smiling as his lips turned blue. Someone always offered to share. Usually that someone was Alice.

Spin looked up at Alice and Alice looked out more carefully at the water. Spin tugged her toward the dock (useless without a permit to rebuild), a dock that stood as a testament to a different kind of homeowner, a wholly other life. People at school belonged to sailing clubs and golf clubs, and sometimes it was easy to imagine what the house would have looked like if Alice's parents cared about leisure time the way her father cared for research or the way their mother cared for pursuing her leisure elsewhere.

Now the dock was an eroded gray plank that stretched out into the distance and slid into the water. There was no permit for a mooring and so the wood endured a slow demise — gnawed by the elements year after year. The gulls enjoyed congregating and leaving their white and shiny droppings along the rickety rails. In order to walk onto the dock, you needed to bypass a mound of stones and weeds that were part of a former Indian burial ground. Of this there was no proof, but it was accepted as truth as long as their family had lived here. Once in a great while her father spoke of leveling it, at least trimming the weeds, but nothing was ever done. Alice thought it was beautiful the way the stones made patterns in the bulbous grass; she was certain the mound had powers and that it was the reason the house's former owners had built the little shack there.

Out beyond the dock there were two boats racing, their white sails flush with wind. There was a big yellow barge inching across the horizon. She kept expecting to see Gus, to give him a wave, even if he couldn't see her. It would have been nice to just see him at it, to get a sense of how far he was and how long it would be until he returned. But Alice couldn't see him anywhere. When he'd told her about his swimming, she'd accepted his plan as she accepted all of Gus's plans — fully formed and nothing to question too heavily. If he left at two, Alice thought, he would have been gone two hours already, more than two hours really, as it was nearly four-thirty. Dinner wasn't until seven o'clock though, and Gus said he'd be back just in time for dinner.

It occurred to her that what he was doing could actually be more than a little dangerous.

She tugged Spin and set off running up her family's lawn, under the dogwoods and over the patchy muddy grass. *"Mommy!"* she belted out, before she even knew exactly of what she was frightened. Alice breathed hard and Spin ran fast, and the humid air turned a notch toward chilly as the sun went behind a dense cloud. She pictured Gus waterlogged blue and everyone wondering, *Why didn't you say something?*

Then she thought she heard her mother

yelling back, but she realized immediately that she was yelling at her father. Her father was home! Her father was home; he was home — she could see through the window his white shirt rolled up at the sleeves, his hands on his head, his elbows bent, his fingers clutching his hair. Her father was home and he was yelling too. He looked younger somehow — he hadn't shaved. Her father looked handsome and angry.

From what Alice could tell, listening through the glass, her father was already at a familiar refrain: "What were you thinking?"

"What do you expect?" her mother bellowed.

"Oh, that's rich."

"Alan, it's unfair."

"What's unfair is for me to come home and find dog shit in my shoe because you insisted on getting a dog that you refuse to walk. What is unfair is that our little girl is a nervous wreck."

"Mommy!" Alice was yelling again, but now she was at the window; now she was looking through the glass door, but not going in. She was stuck in one place and she did not want to move. They were talking about her. They were yelling. She wanted her mother to come to her, to come

forward and cover her with kisses, to treat her like a baby. She wanted her father to listen closely and be impressed by her composure. But neither her father nor her mother came forward. Her father saw Alice through the window and made his face into a smile. Her mother pushed her hair off her forehead and motioned Alice to come in.

Charlotte said, "What, sweetheart, what is it?"

Alice ran to her father and threw her arms around him. He smelled like animals — all pelt and heavy musk and somehow so clean.

"Alice?"

"He's out in the water swimming," she said, trying to catch her breath. "He's been planning it for weeks. He's out there in the sound with the . . . the cigarette boats." She heard her own voice and its tone increased her worry. Her voice — weak and breathless — made the idea that much more frightening.

"What do you mean, he's been planning it?" her father asked, not gently.

"Alan —"

"Charlotte," he said, and her name engendered silence. "Alice, why on earth didn't you tell us? Do you know how cold the water is?"

"He has a wet suit," she said.

She told them because she was afraid for his life, yes, but also because she was afraid that her parents would continue fighting, afraid that the conclusion would be eventually drawn that no one, when it came right down to it, knew how to keep everyone together, all in one house at one time.

On a boat, the neighbor's boat, the Mafia neighbor's big white speedboat, they went looking. Alice stood wrapped in a towel between her mother's legs. Charlotte kept saying thank-you to the neighbor, and rubbing Alice's arms and asking if she was cold. Alice wasn't cold but she wasn't exactly comfortable, as her mother's coat was scratchy, but she would have sooner jumped into the water herself than risk losing those arms around her. Her affection made Alice feel thrilled and guilty, as her mother was clearly angry with her father. Not only that, but she knew that when they found Gus, everyone would have more pressing issues of anger. Any affection seemed so temporary.

The Mafia neighbor was small and strong and gripped the wheel with both hands. Alice liked him. His name was Big John, even though he was short. His wife never left the house. His kids were named Anthony and Amy, and they drove fast cars, two separate ones, back and forth from the high school. Alice knew her parents weren't friends with Big John, and it was only out of a dire emergency that her father had phoned over to their house. Her father looked in the water intensely, not saying much of anything. The water was oddly blue — not grayish or green but an eerie cobalt blue disturbed with white as the waves grew the farther out they went. Charlotte wore a too-small camel coat over her robe and a pair of tortoiseshell sunglasses even though there was barely any sun. She was smoking and she smelled like autumn — a trace of vanilla oil in her hair, Merit Ultra Lights — her mother's bare skin when the coat fell open was warm despite the cold.

"John," her mother said, and then louder, "John? Would you mind slowing down just a bit?"

They were creeping along, rocked intermittently by small thumping breakers. They were looking at small splashes, at buoys; they were fraught with false sightings. There were not many other boats around, but the ones that appeared were going gangbusters through the glass-blue water — Ginsu blades whirring on their big black motors — unable to detect that the still-freezing water happened to contain a boy.

"You didn't notice he was doing this?" her father said for the eighteenth time. At this point he didn't even look at Charlotte.

Her mother didn't answer. She gasped, barely audibly — Alice felt the rise and fall of her mother's bony chest against her back.

And then he was there, a few yards ahead, doing the crawl. He was gone and then he wasn't — just like that. Alice recognized this sick understanding, the way a person could disappear and then reappear — unfair and newly possible, made somehow better than before.

There he was. There he was — a shiny black wet suit–clad body, a tawny nape of neck, and pale flashes of cupped hands — perfect.

"Gus!" Alice yelled, jumping from her mother's lap. It occurred to her that she was fond of yelling. It had suddenly become a part of who she was: She was a girl who yelled.

Everyone was yelling. Everyone except her mother. Her mother just stood in her scratchy coat, one pale hand shielding her forehead, the other planted on her high ridge of hip.

Gus swam doggedly, slowly, in a slightly wavering line. If he heard them — and Alice was sure he heard them — he was not letting on. On he swam, even when a wave broke his stride. Big John said, "Good swimmer," and then, "Crazy fuckin' kid." Her father looked annoyed, but Big John seemed to mean it as a compliment. Big John seemed a little jealous. When the yelling didn't work, and Gus maintained his stroke, pretending they simply weren't there, her father said, "Get closer," and Big John got them as close as he could. What her father did then was reach over the side and try to grab hold of Gus, but it was more difficult, apparently, than he had thought; "Goddamn it," he said. The wet suit was tight and slippery.

Unlike her husband, Charlotte didn't seem angry. She hardly seemed riled up at all. In fact, Alice noticed that as her father tried furiously to retrieve Gus from the cold water, her mother merely tilted her face to the sun — as if the sun were a shy suitor in need of some encouragement before going in for a kiss.

"This kid," said Big John, shaking his head.

And August kept swimming, as if he were physically unable to hear their yells or

46

sense their frantic presence.

"Who knew he was serious," Charlotte said, quite clearly.

Her father turned to her, saying, "What?" He was breathing hard, still not giving up on grabbing hold of Gus.

"Will you quit that," Charlotte said. "He'll stop if you do, trust me."

"What do you mean, 'Who knew he was serious'?"

Charlotte sniffed, and brought a ragged thumbnail to her teeth. "He made mention of doing this — this kind of thing. He makes mention of a lot of things to me."

"Ever wonder why?" her father said. He wasn't yelling anymore. He sat on the ledge with his eyes on Gus, but in a different way, somehow. Alice stood apart from her mother. She stood wrapped in the towel, listening. She knew her father meant that Gus was trying to impress their mother. He often made this kind of remark; he had various unflattering theories about Gus's behavior in regard to Charlotte, and Alice could rarely decide if he was right. Most of the time she was certain that Gus was trying to impress no one but himself, and she knew firsthand what a tough audience he could be. "Jesus," her father said, with a certain degree of finality.

"You want me to keep close on him like this, or what?" John said.

The light was starting to fade, casting long shadows on deck. The blue water was no longer so blue. "That's right, John; that's perfect," Charlotte said, keeping her eyes solely on her son, as if she were merely awaiting a testy reply. Her eyes said, *I'm finished; I am counting to three.*

But still nothing.

Charlotte took off her sunglasses and chewed on an end in apparent contemplation. She took a breath and yelled in Gus's direction, "I am so bored!"

Big John laughed.

Gus then veered in a different direction. He veered toward the boat's ladder, and when he stopped swimming, he didn't waste any time getting out of the water. He climbed up on deck without any help. They all knew not to try.

"What were you *thinking?*" her father growled, passing Gus two towels. "Gus? Goddamn it, are you all right?"

"You did a very stupid thing," Big John said. "A very fucking stupid thing, if you want to know the truth."

Gus looked at Big John and said, "I'm fine," and then to his mother: "I only had a little more to go."

Charlotte didn't say anything. She turned from her son, with his blue lips and bloodshot eyes — her son who was twelve years old — and she pulled Alice onto her lap. She could feel her mother's nerves — how her skin was feverishly hot for a moment and how she clutched too hard. Gus looked at Alice with cold wet eyes and Alice looked down at her mother's bare feet. Big John started the boat again. The sound of the motor seemed much louder than before. It was colder now that the sun was gone. It was hard to believe it had, after all, been a pleasant day — one of the mildest of the year.

Gus kept looking at Charlotte, who played with Alice's hair for a few idle moments before settling her gaze on the water, now speeding by.

Alice wriggled out of her mother's grasp. "I'm sorry," she said, tapping Gus on the shoulder. "I'm sorry I told."

He ignored her, shrugging off her finger tap. She couldn't help thinking of that empty corridor, after her mother had walked away.

"Come, Alice," her father said, motioning her up to the steering wheel. "Be careful, now."

And she stood between her father and

Big John, looking out from behind the wheel, all of them silently marveling at how much territory he had covered. But Alice was also watching her mother and her brother and how each of them acted unhappy but somehow didn't look it. They stood apart on opposite sides of the small bow, but they couldn't have looked more similar. Their stances expressed how the world was attainable; they were ready to collect their portion, whatever it happened to be.

But neither of them saw the bird.

It was Alice who gazed up at the sky. She looked up for a moment — if only to look away from her family — the way one looks for any means of escape upon realizing, not without shame, that the love they possess is too much. They know this love is unnameable just as it is unmalleable and that it will, in all likeliness, grow to define them. Alice caught a glimpse of this self-knowledge, but more than anything, she was flooded with wanting. She only knew she had to look away.

But the sky.

But the bird.

It was green and blue and yellow, big as a small dog. It was tropically attired — some flamboyant refugee from a continent away — and it was no illusion. But when Alice yelled (as she'd been wont to do), this time no sound came. She watched the bird as it flew slowly by. Her mouth was open but it was open in awe. By the time the sound came, the bird was gone and no one had seen it but her. Which was sad, when she thought about it, but sad in a way that she would later learn to identify as personal, like touching an old scar on a beloved body and hearing the answer of exactly how it got there.

In the middle of the night Alice still hadn't slept, and she rose from bed. Gus had gone to sleep soon after they'd all wandered inside the house and silently eaten cold chicken. They always had chicken — that fact had become a family joke; it usually made her smile. But her brother had refused to even look at her, which had made it very difficult to eat the chicken, which had made it very easy to cry. She hadn't cried. She thought of the bird, and it helped somehow. She'd asked for a Coke and she got one.

The moon streamed through her tall windows at two o'clock in the morning, casting the room in silvery dark. She could hear the train whistle far away. Their house was close enough to the station to hear the whistle perfectly and yet far enough away for the noise to sound plaintive. Leaving her room, Alice padded through the corridor — imagining riding the overnight train — past her parents' closed door. Gus's door was open a crack, a habit left over from when he was very little, when he was afraid of being locked in.

She didn't hesitate. The day was over now, and she was no longer afraid of losing him, no longer afraid of his judgments. His room was warmer than hers, and he'd thrown off the covers to reveal an old Cosmos T-shirt. He was sleeping soundly. Posters of sharks were pinned to each wall. Every poster had the same black eyes staring out into the room.

It was not by any conscious design that Alice lay down stiffly beside her brother, but she was suddenly there, horizontal in his twin bed, with a wild heartbeat and a ringing in her ears. It was from the fear of sharks and the way their eyes were even darker than these darkly male-redolent surroundings. It was out of dizziness at being displaced and not tired in the middle of the night. And it was also the train shooting off to distant places, of which she had no understanding. The whistle sounded as a kind of reminder that the world was about so much more than houses and trains and the people sleeping in them. *The world is without safety,* was what that whistle said; *the world is without end.*

"August?" she said, and she hated her voice.

3

Distance, 1981

Charlotte's friend Susan was having a barbecue on the Fourth of July and nobody besides Charlotte felt like going. The party was in Connecticut at Susan's new husband's house, a good three hours away. Their father made it a practice not to ever leave the house over holiday weekends. He enjoyed poking around the property, drilling holes — anything to avoid traffic. "You know my position on traffic," he told Charlotte, over breakfast.

"I know, love. Traffic is hell."

"No, hell is other people. Other people at barbecues."

Charlotte smiled with half her mouth and squeezed a tea bag with her fingers. She never used a spoon. "I told her we'd go. The kids will have a ball."

"No, we won't," Gus said. His voice was especially deep because it was morning. Sometimes it seemed as if he had literally grown in his sleep. He claimed his joints hurt from growing, but Alice thought that seemed a bit overboard. He was fourteen and she was nearly his height at twelve, but it wasn't a big deal because she had always been tall.

"There'll be kids your age," Charlotte said.

"Wow," Gus said. "That sounds tempting."

Alice laughed. "We like doing the same thing each year," she said.

"Speak for yourself," Gus said. "I just don't feel like going to Susan's. It's gonna blow."

"August," their father said.

"It's gonna suck moose cock," he said, laughing.

Alice waited for their father to turn. There was always a point where Gus pushed too far, and she suspected that had been it. But he only looked at their mother and said, "Okay, then, looks like we're going. Let us hope it *doesn't suck*. Okay?"

It was too bad. Alice had good memories of Fourths of July at home. She couldn't explain why exactly — they were essentially uneventful times. Her father grilled — that was something. He grilled burgers, hot dogs, peppers, plums — anything you handed him, he grilled it. Once Alice handed him a piece of coconut cake and he grilled that too, maintaining a straight face. Gus and Alice could invite anyone over; they could do what they liked but they had to come hungry — he grilled from three o'clock on. "I'm the grill man," he'd say with a shy grin. No matter how many people were shrieking on the lawn or playing games inside if rain was pouring down, her father grilled. So deep was his concentration that it was necessary to approach from the front so as not to startle him.

So the grilling, Alice thought, that was one thing. Also, her mother could be this certain way: she'd have bursts of ambition to create anything that smacked of Americana. One year she bought a crochet kit and spent the day learning. Sometimes she made strawberry shortcake, or an American-flag cake with at least three layers. And her mother wasn't someone who cooked for the sake of cooking — no, her mother knew how to eat. Alice loved watching her savor each fattening bite. Plus there were Gus's friends. Last year Gus's friend Ezra told her (after an impressive turn at spitting watermelon seeds) that she had a great laugh. It was always nice watching fireworks explode and fall into the water. They were able to see not only the sky's display but also the crowded harbor with all the different boats. "I like this view so much better than if it were just ocean," Charlotte never tired of saying. "It's the boats that make for such a lucky view. Alan? Don't you think?"

It was this reason, Alice finally decided, why she liked the Fourth of July: Her mother usually seemed to realize what on earth she was doing with a family and what it was that kept her coming home.

Susan's party was in the mountains on a pond. There were steep steps built into the lawn that led down to a large deck where most of the adults were sitting. As she followed her parents down the steps, Alice saw a boy about her age dive off the deck into the water. The dive made a big fat splash and two thin women got wet, making brief but sour faces. There were already plenty of swimmers and inner tubes afloat. A grill was giving off smoke, the sooty gray dissolving into the chalky sky. It was a humid day, and the air was thick and hot enough to keep mentioning. The Greens stood for a moment, stewing in the heat, dazed and surveying the crowd. Charlotte kept holding her light cotton shirt away from her body and then, after a moment, letting it slowly fall. Gus took off his shirt altogether and balled it up in his hands. "I'm exhausted," Alan said, "and we just got here."

"Don't be old," Charlotte said lightly, her favorite put-down, while waving a swarm of gnats from her face. "Go get wet."

But Alan didn't go get wet. He continued to hold a large Bloomingdale's shopping bag very carefully — the bag that sat between Gus and Alice on the way up to Connecticut, the bag that contained Charlotte's gift. Charlotte was famous for her gifts, for not only their frivolity and quality but also for their erratic arrivals. Charlotte was a woman who'd forget her husband's birthday and then spend two days making a hot-wax stamp for a friend she hadn't seen in years. She'd send the stamp (or lemon-almond torte or hand-beaded choker) in a sequin-decorated box, and when it was returned with the post weeks later, it would sit — unopened — in the front hall for a good six months. She wouldn't bother to resend it or verify the correct address. She might surprise her husband with a weekend-long apology for forgetting the birthday. There'd be elaborate meals involving quail eggs and oysters, quince, smoked venison, chestnut oil. There'd be quite a bit of "private time," and Alice's father — a man slow to smile — would not be able, not even if he tried, to keep from doing so.

Once, on a trip to India, Charlotte bought a ream of violet silk with which she surprised Alice by transforming her daughter's twin bed into a canopied revelation. A smooth silk canopy, an aerie of purple? Where there was, hours previously, merely blue gingham with a bleach stain? This does things to a child, to a girl.

This year's gift to Susan was a strawberry-rhubarb pie. Charlotte had made it the previous day — a daylong, all-consuming event — perfecting the crust with crushed almonds and hunting down, with Alice in tow, the absolute freshest fruit. Alice's father held the bag out to Charlotte when he saw Susan in the distance.

Susan spotted them while pouring vodka into a large pitcher. She made a big hello face and waved them over to the table. There were bowls of chips and grapes and Red Hots, Twizzlers, platters of cheese and artichoke spread, taramasalata. "I can't believe you got this one to come," she said to Charlotte, while squeezing Alan's arm. "You get big points, Alan," she said. "Oh, my God, will you look at Mr. Gorgeous over here?"

Gus smiled and said, "What's up?"

"And you," she said to Alice, heaving a sigh, "look at you."

Alice was certain she was referring to her breasts, which had appeared quite literally just last week, and over which she was wearing a huge T-shirt that came down to her knees. "What," said Alice, blushing.

"Just look," she said, and Susan ran her hand over Alice's hair, over her shoulders. Susan didn't have any girls and always made her feel just a little bit special.

"I know you probably have enough food here to feed a few overpopulated countries," Charlotte said to Susan, "but here's something to push you over the edge." She handed over the pie. The crust was shaped like garlands of flowers, the top was a complex latticework, and it made Alice sad to imagine it being smashed up at the buffet table later in the dark, no one understanding the care that went into it.

"Oh. My. God," said Susan. She squealed a little and gave Charlotte a pristine kiss on the lips. She kissed nearly everyone on the lips. She was generally very affectionate.

Alice knew that Susan was some high-powered lawyer, but the idea of Susan leading that kind of life — making deals, wearing suits — was completely baffling. Her new husband, Tom, was a handsome urologist who was also extremely affectionate. When Alice met him last year, he took her by both shoulders and kissed her on the forehead. What made people behave that way? Alice toyed with the idea of growing up and being such a person, capable of grand physical gestures. Such a person, Alice imagined, would attract many people who'd spill their secrets and their deepest nagging fears, all out of an urge toward comfort. Alice suspected that was why her mother wanted to spend three hours in traffic — to be petted this way, in this off-hand, almost flirty manner that suggested a deep forgiveness at the same time as it crossed proprietary lines.

There was nothing in either Susan's or her husband Tom's manner that suggested Susan's previous husband gassed himself five years ago in his mistress's garage, or that Tom left his anorexic wife for lush, messy Susan, and that the wife barely let him see his kids — a fact that (Alice had heard Susan tell Charlotte) he cried over daily.

"Your mother," Susan said to Alice and Gus.

Here in Connecticut on the Fourth of July there were kisses and squeezes and pats on behinds. There were kids everywhere, even the ones whom Tom barely saw. Both Susan and Tom had two boys, plus Tom had adopted another son during his *very* first marriage, and *that* son had a few kids, so there were all kinds of halfs and steps popping up everywhere, waving or nodding hello. Within minutes Gus was in the water, having taken off on what appeared to be a quest to swim across the pond. Alice figured it would be only moments before a few others followed. She caught the eye of three girls in cutoff jeans shorts. They didn't smile.

"Susan," Alice said, tapping her shoulder, "do you need any help?"

Susan laughed, "Oh, my God, who raised *you?*" she said.

Neither of her parents laughed.

Charlotte said, "You don't need to be so polite, honey — it's only Susan," and raised her glass to her friend before breaking into a smile.

"Alice, she's right. Get out of here! Look at all these kids. Why don't you go in the pond? Did you bring a suit?"

Alice nodded but there was no way she was taking off her shirt. She backed up and to the side, where the property tapered off into woods. It was cooler in the shade, if more buggy, and Alice was amazed how easily she could fade into the background, close enough to hear certain adult conversations but far enough away that anyone looking would assume she was the type of girl to sit and look at rocks, a weird but harmless loner kid. But she wasn't that kind of kid. She wasn't off in her own world, as she assumed her father was saying to some man who'd just gestured toward Alice. She knew her father liked thinking of her that way, as an inquisitive, if slightly spacey girl. But she was good with groups of kids her own age, good enough, anyway. Right now she wasn't in the mood. She was, if anything, too much a part of everyone else's world, a simple link in a chain, and she wanted to step back and watch the chain swing and grow tangled around her.

Her parents were together, drinks in hand, meeting new people. When her mother was introduced to someone new, Alice played a silent game with herself, predicting all of Charlotte's moves. If the new person looked interesting enough,

Charlotte more than likely would ask for the name again, leaning in a little closer. Her eyes were either on the water, the sky, a tall tree, or else they were directly meeting another person's gaze, almost aggressively so. Though by now she knew her mother's tricks, her father didn't seem to, for as distantly as her mother's gaze traveled, her father's gaze was shortsighted. It rested, for the most part, on Charlotte. He was snowed, thought Alice. He was a man lost in the blizzard of her mother. At this point she almost envied how he was able to walk around even part-time with snow in his eyes, unable to see a thing. And she couldn't help it — she liked watching her parents and was proud of them like this, so clearly together. Amidst all of her mother's smooth moves she always held on to her father's hand. It seemed unimaginable that they should ever be apart, that their mother would feel the need to fly off to distant places the way other moms and other wives went to work or went shopping or sometimes spent a week at a spa. From Alice's vantage, her father looked the way he always looked — a bit uninterested in others but kind, and her mother looked like a more beautiful than average but other-wise normal wife and mother. She could have been a teacher, a journalist, a psycho-therapist. She could have been a pastry chef, a professor of anthropology.

What Charlotte didn't accept was that what she did with her time was take vacations. If someone asked how her vacation was, after her return from any number of stunning locales, she viewed them askance before explaining precisely why she had been to the Philippines or Peru, or Chile or Nepal. It was always something important or essential, each and every time. The overarching concept was that she was doing research for an ever-changing project. She was interested in the local craftsmanship of various provinces in many countries and needed to do extensive research before deciding on the locus of her importing. She had visions of fostering a true partnership with poverty-stricken craftspeople. It was, everyone agreed, a really swell idea. However, the research had been spread out over many years now, and if her father suggested that they really couldn't afford her plane ticket or her lodgings or it just wasn't a good time for her departure, a source of capital (and therefore further proof of why she just *had* to go) would miraculously turn up. She had frequent-flyer miles, a legitimate tax write-off, a nonprofit foundation agreed to provide transportation if she'd write an article for their annual journal.

However, no matter how often these trips occurred and how opaque Charlotte could be about what she was doing and with whom, Alice didn't think her parents would get divorced like some of her friends' parents. They touched each other often (which her friend Eleanor insisted was an important sign of a healthy couple), and they liked to be alone. No matter how far off Charlotte went or how he might have resented her for it, her father issued a kind of unspoken gratitude whenever she returned. Alice made herself consider the idea of her father having an affair, but he just wasn't the type, and it wasn't just because he was her father that she thought so. Alice prided herself on being objective, and besides which, she *could* picture her mother doing it; she was sometimes pretty convinced it had already happened. Sometimes there were strange male voices on the other end of the telephone. They hung up quickly; they never left a message.

It made Alice sick to think about her mother's possible infidelity, but that sickness was given ballast by the perhaps strange notion that it was her mother's love

for her father that seemed the most irrefutable. Alice once overheard two women in a
supermarket, squeezing eggplants, talking
about their sister. "She thinks he walks on
water," one of them said. It was only later
that Alice understood those words as ultimately sarcastic. At the time, though, she
was caught up in the beauty of the phrase
and the surprising security that came with
knowing that her mother's feelings for her
father lay within those words.

There was a peculiar reverence for her
father, and it was always in the air. It
shifted in degrees the way the temperature
shifted with the seasons, but it never went
away. Charlotte wasn't snowed; it was the
opposite of that. Her mother was alert to
his greatness; she paid attention to all that
he was, bringing it to the light if need be.

Alice sat on the ground, letting the soil
touch the backs of her legs, ignoring the
ants making uphill campaigns over her
bare thighs. Up above, crosshatches of
dark emerald leaves weighed down the
long thin branches. She had disappeared.
The adults had willed it so, being more
than happy to believe she was old enough
or smart enough or weird enough to be off
by herself and alone. Clearly no one
thought enough of her to believe that what

she was really doing was spying.

Having procured drinks, Charlotte let go of Alan's hand and her parents each drifted into separate conversations. Her father was alternating between listening to Tom list men's names — "Dan Goddard, Dave Stern, you know Dave Stern, don't you?" — and looking out at the water, keeping an eye on Gus.

Charlotte was shaking a man's hand. He was exceptionally tan and young-looking; though on closer inspection he couldn't have been much younger than Charlotte. He was neither handsome nor particularly tall, but he carried himself in such a way that suggested that he was both.

"What a pleasure to meet you," her mother was gushing. From the way she was beaming Alice could tell she knew who he was. "Your advice has gotten me through most of Southeast Asia."

"You're familiar with my books?"

"Familiar? I'm indebted to you. Oh, and your piece in the *Tribune* on Burmese trade reforms last year was *particularly* good. Not to mention that traveling anywhere, especially alone, you appreciate a bit of intelligent humor in a guidebook. Not to say your books could be thought of as simply guidebooks. They're not easily defined. I mean the section on Chiang Mai, just the noodles alone . . . I'm sure you get a lot of this — I'm sorry."

"No," the man said, clearly enjoying himself, "what?"

Charlotte blushed — a sight so rare it was almost unsettling. Alice felt herself blush along with her. "You know, people feeling like you've traveled with them. I'm sure it's terribly boring for you."

He laughed a low laugh with not much to it. "Come on, I'm pleased. I take it you have the bug."

"Oh, you know, *anywhere but here*," she said, pouring herself more of whatever was in the glass pitcher. Her hair was in a high, loose ponytail, falling to one side. *I hate that expression,* Alice thought, on hearing her say that stupid phrase, at the sight of all that thick hair secured in bright red elastic, a bright red elastic that belonged to Alice.

"Have you been to Burma, then?"

"Mm," she said, sipping her drink. "Two years ago was my first time. There's this project . . ." She was waiting for him to ask another question, but he was the type to nod intently instead. "It's in its early stages, but —"

"It's unusual you had the opportunity to go."

"I put in a request for a special visa in, oh, 1965."

The man laughed. "Tell me about it."

"I figured whenever I got one, whenever it came, I'd just go." She sighed heavily. "It was worth the wait though. My God," she said.

He looked as if he was considering something and then asked, "No kids?"

Her mother bristled slightly, her thin eyebrows working. "Why do you ask?"

"Oh, no, I don't know, the freedom to take off like that. It gets tough," he said, "at our age."

"I have children," Charlotte said, and Alice's heart began pounding. "I have two. A boy and a girl."

"How perfect," he said, with a tone Alice disliked. She knew she shouldn't be listening, she knew she shouldn't be spying, and she also knew that nothing was going to move her from this spot.

"They are perfect," her mother said, finishing her drink. "They are perfect and I am not." She smiled wearily, and for a moment Alice had no idea what she was trying to do. She wondered what her mother was thinking. "You know how it is."

"I don't, actually. I'm afraid I haven't had the pleasure."

"Oh, you should," she said, and then softer, "you really should." Her fingers grazed a stray hair on her neck that had fallen from her ponytail, and his interest — Alice could feel it — deepened.

So did Alice's. She wanted to hear her mother talk about her. That was the whole point. *Ask,* she thought, watching the tan man: *Ask about me.*

Charlotte saw the man look past her, but still she nearly jumped when her husband put his hands on her shoulders.

"Hello, there," Alice heard her father say. "Didn't mean to startle you."

"Hi," the tan man said. "You must be —"

"Alan Green," he said, sticking out his hand.

"J. D. Connor. I've been talking with your wife about her travels." He hesitated, Alice noticed, before saying *wife.*

"Oh," he said, "well, in that case, I'm not sure I should listen. There's too much I probably don't know." He spoke almost innocently, almost playfully. "I'm afraid I don't get away too often." The silence that followed was brief but awkward enough.

"And what keeps you busy?" J. D. Connor asked. He had a way that made Alice think of California. He was breezy and ordered all at once.

71

"Alan's a scientist," her mother said, trying to keep control of this conversation, even if it was veering down the inevitable path of her husband's accomplishments. Alice saw her mother switch gears and get in touch with her seemingly endless reserve of intense beyond-wifely admiration.

"That right? What field?"

"Neurobiology," her father said in his habitually tossed-off way. In a nonscience environment he was used to one of two responses: the conversation stopping there with a banal comment like "Wow," or a series of questions from an earnest individual who asked what *precisely* neurobiology was and what it was, *exactly,* that he did. Her father had mostly nonscience friends, so he assumed no one at parties was really all that interested in his work. He insisted he preferred it that way.

But J. D. Connor said, "Far out."

Charlotte looked irritated with both his interest and his diction.

"Dr. Alan Green?" J.D. said. "You used to teach at Cornell?"

"A long while ago, yes."

"Hey, that was going to be me, man. I was going that route. I was at Cornell when you'd just left for sabbatical, I think. It's too bad. Maybe you would have changed my mind. I fell out of step or something. Never even completed my master's."

"And I'm sure you're losing sleep over it, too," her mother said, smiling. Her cheeks were still flushed with color.

"Actually," he said, soberly, "it was the most difficult decision I ever made. I always downplay it — you know, make it sound like I just was too busy having fun or something. Hey, you do extraordinary work," J. D. Connor said sadly. "You've got the real deal here," he said to Charlotte.

"I'm quite aware," she said evenly.

"What is it you do now?" said her father.

"He's the writer of those books I bring everywhere," Charlotte told him. "He's fantastic," she said with a pale smile. "Would anyone like another drink?"

Alice stood up. As her mother made for the drinks table, Alice eased out from behind the trees, leaving her father and J. D. Connor to talk about science. She felt dizzy and younger somehow, as if she'd woken from a nap. She could see the girls in the jeans shorts lolling in a fading patch of sun, just talking. She could go over and say hello. She could say she liked their hair, the way it was braided in fishtail braids with tiny little strands. She could go ask the only three boys not swimming if they wanted to have a seed-spitting contest. But there was her mother sitting down in a lawn chair with a drink in one hand. Charlotte looked tired, and as her husband continued to talk to the tan travel writer — to one of the people, Alice just knew, her mother most wished to befriend — Alice watched her mother light a hand-rolled cigarette with a huge votive lighter swiped from the grill.

"I thought no smoking," Alice said, after approaching and sitting at her mother's feet.

"Yeah, well, I thought so too," she said. "How're you doing, Miss Alice?" She put a hand on her daughter's shoulder.

"Okay, I guess."

"With these kind, the hand-rolled kind, I do it less, though — the smoking. Don't I?"

Alice shrugged and leaned back onto her mother's legs. She could feel the fine hairs that were growing back from waxing. The mild scent of Lubriderm lotion made her think of petals. "Look," Alice said, "that's Gus. Do you see?" Gus was still in the pond — just a speck in the distance, flanked by two other specks. She'd been right about his followers.

"Where?" Charlotte said.

Alice got up and pointed. She noticed

the sun was blazing through the white haze, announcing a quick descent. "Do you see?"

"I do, sweetheart. He's right there. He's heading our way."

"Can I have a sip?" She reached for her mother's sweating glass of what looked like lemonade.

"I'm not sure you'll like it," Charlotte said. "It's very sour."

Alice — not exactly sure why she wanted it so badly — took a sip anyway. It tasted like etherized bugs. She was coughing and coughing with watery eyes.

"Told you," Charlotte said, rubbing her back. "You okay?"

Alice nodded. "That's not sour. That is pure alcohol."

"Mm," she said, kind of grinning, "there's that too. You want to go get a Coke or something?"

Alice shook her head. She'd get one in a minute. She was hungry for a cheeseburger; it was almost dinnertime. Gus was a bigger speck on the green, dark pond, coming closer. "Why do you think he likes to swim so far?"

After a moment her mother answered slowly. "He needs to know," Charlotte said, after taking a final long sip. "Your brother needs to know what it feels like to be far away from everything familiar, in order to know how to love it. Does that make sense?"

Alice shook her head. The spike of her mother's intoxicated breath heightened her careful speech, and Alice had a growing anticipation for the fireworks explosion. She couldn't help picturing the way her family would find each other — they were that kind of family, the kind who respected these moments like the ball dropping, like the World Series, like fireworks on the Fourth — and they would stand together, their faces upturned like they'd never seen such a show. She couldn't help picturing how her parents would look amazed and in their amazement they would look young — they would look a bit lost. Everyone looked that way, if only a little, when looking up at the sky. Alice could see it all — how in no time the sky would return to mussel blackness, how they'd soon be back on the highway, leaving Susan and Tom and who knew how many kids to clean up the remains of the party. Alice knew instinctively what this was, this seeing the future as a kind of dull past. It made Alice want to crawl onto Charlotte's narrow lap, which was hardly big enough to hold her anymore.

"Do you think he'll always feel that way?"

"I think so," Charlotte said, nodding.

"That's sad," Alice said. She wondered if her mother would call up Mr. J. D. Connor this coming week and ask him all about Cambodia. Or Bhutan. These were the places she'd been pointing out lately in her big world atlas in the living room. "Don't you think it's sad?"

"Yes," her mother said, "I do."

4

Sleep, 1984

Her name was Cady DeForrest. Cady, not Katie, not Kate. She didn't go to their school. Gus met her in October at a party illegally given on a tennis club's courts. The courts were in an old airplane hangar nestled in the woods. They closed at nine p.m., but a burned-out pro (who was leaving the next day for Australia) had the keys, and he'd decided to go out with a bang. Gus knew *him* from . . . oh, who knew from where. Alice had stopped wondering and started accepting that her brother just knew people. He knew plenty of girls, different girls over whom he acted crazy but who were inevitably phased out. She had ceased being surprised.

Cady DeForrest, however, tipped the scales.

Alice hadn't gone to the party. She'd known about it — Gus hadn't hidden it from her — but she had the feeling Gus didn't want her along. Because he actually was great about taking her everywhere without her even having to ask, and because these were places where she was the only sophomore in sight, she thought she'd give him a break. It was Friday night. She went with Eleanor to the movies, drank beers in the parking lot with a couple of boys they'd recognized vaguely from school — most of the time wondering why they'd accepted the impromptu invitation, why they were all just standing around watching cars. Out of not much more than agitation, she gave the taller one a hand job between the stand of trees and the lot. He was big and grateful and smelled like soap, like butter. She liked how he kissed lightly and the way he looked so surprised when she went to unbutton his jeans. He said he'd call her but she really didn't care. Once she had done something like that, once she surprised herself and someone else, the rest felt forced and steeped in obligation, and she didn't trust obligation any more than she trusted good old neglect.

The next morning, from her window, Alice saw a blond girl in a red pilled sweater sneaking out their front door. There were leaves and small twigs stuck in the wool, and her smooth hair was tied in what looked like a bra. She wore a witchy black skirt with an uneven hem, under which were her white bare feet on tiptoe as she hurried out the door. She sat on the front steps and, obviously freezing, tugged on a pair of brown cowboy boots that she'd been holding like books in her arms. She didn't look back at Gus's window. She by-passed the gravel driveway and disappeared into the woods.

Alice went back to sleep and dreamed of the hand job (the odd combination of anxiousness and power, the fear of someone coming and the fear of someone not coming) and she woke up to the smell of bacon. It was the smell of their mother being gone, as she never kept it in the house (a particular vestige of Charlotte's equally ambivalent Jewish upbringing — shrimp okay, pork not okay, skipping Rosh Hashanah barely okay, skipping Yom Kippur simply not). Alice could bet there were also any number of preservative-laden baked goods lying on countertops with their bright cardboard containers torn open, their plastic wrapping cast aside, but not thrown away. She could bet Gus had woken full of restless energy and (after their father left for the lab at seven) put Spin in the car and went to the first open deli in town, picked up the bacon and the packaged goods, chatted with the pimple-faced kid at the counter, chatted with the odd old man. He would be waiting now for his sister to come downstairs; he'd be in the mood for talking. Alice did her best — as she wrapped herself in Charlotte's old blue chenille robe, as she padded down the back stairs — not to be so eager to listen.

"Good morning to you," Gus said.

"You've showered," Alice said, amazed.

"It is," Gus said, handing Alice a cup of milky coffee, "a beautiful morning."

"Are you going to start singing?"

"I might. I'm telling you, I just might."

"So," Alice said, sitting down at the table, looking out at the gray water, at what was, in fact, the blandest kind of day.

"So," he said. Even though she wasn't looking, she could hear that he was grinning.

"All right, who is she?" Alice asked in a bored voice, rubbing sleep from her eyes. "The girl with the boots, the one who left this morning." She still didn't look at him. Spin's big head nudged her hand up and over and she pet him, hard. Outside, a cardinal stood stone-still on a long bent branch: a swath of blood on an arm.

"Oh, man," Gus said, biting a jelly

81

doughnut, getting powder on his face and not bothering to wipe it off. He didn't wonder aloud how Alice had seen her, how she'd known the girl had stayed the night. When you had feelings as big and encompassing as his, Alice assumed it meant you never questioned their importance or their impact on the world. For Gus, the world had stopped. Not just for him, but for Alice as well; and not just for Alice but for everyone. Self-involvement, she supposed, was what that was called. But it didn't feel like self-involvement; it felt like inclusion, like elevation. She wanted to feel along with him. She wanted to lose herself in knowing. She turned from the red bird knowing full well that when she looked again it would be gone.

"Let's start with a name," Alice said, flouting — as she did with nobody else — her expressly practical side.

He told her that Cady DeForrest had been the only one at the party who wanted to actually play tennis. Everyone else had just sat around on the courts doing shots, smoking pot, and she'd shown up with a racket. She had long legs and strong arms and one seriously nice ass. "I'd seen her before," Gus explained. "I'd seen her at the drugstore buying calamine lotion sometime before Labor Day. She'd had a bad case of poison ivy."

"Sexy," Alice said.

Gus, laughing, said, "That's what she said, when I told her!"

"She did? Weird."

"Then she said she had to pee, and I said I didn't want to stop looking at her and I followed her out into the woods, and when we were alone I told her to go ahead and pee. And she did. She peed in front of me."

"Did you look?"

"Yeah, I looked. We were both laughing. She looked so good. I mean, I've never seen a girl look so good. . . ." He piled bacon on a plate, turned off the stove, put the plate on the table, and sat down. "So, you know, I kissed her then."

"While she was peeing?"

"No, Jesus, no. Right after." He was trying not to smile. "She goes to Portbay," he said, suddenly shy. "She's a junior."

"How did she get home this morning?"

"She walked, I guess. I didn't really know she'd gone."

Alice would never understand him. "You didn't know she'd gone? She didn't wake you to say good-bye?" He was not disturbed in the least, not concerned that she left in a state of regret, composing a list of his shortcomings, a state with which Alice herself was so familiar. "Well, are you going to call her?"

"Already did. She's coming over later."

Alice should have hated her. By all rights, she was the kind of girl who had points against her from the start: She was petite but strong, butter-cream blond and actually in the physics club *and* played the guitar in addition to being indisputably pretty. Cady was rich — but super rich — and she looked it, no matter how pilled her sweaters were (she was wearing a green one now, buttoned up the front with two of the buttons missing) and no matter how stained her tan cords. Her good looks verged on the ordinary, and it was their ordinariness that was so threatening; hers was a face you'd see in sepia tones on the walls of restricted country clubs, in generation after generation of well-documented ladies' tennis and sailing competitions. It was a face that barely escaped an upturned button nose. She was from a family that had donated libraries, that had appeared in various biographies of politicians and starlets alike. But her parents had died in their own airplane somewhere over the Indian

Ocean when she was just six, leaving a spinster aunt to raise her, and somehow this fact made Cady seem more real (if sadly more enthralling) to Alice. This brought her down to the same brown earth, the same place where Alice lived, where a mother and a father defined her existence even if they weren't there.

"My aunt is a nightmare," she told Alice in a matter-of-fact tone. They sat together after Gus left them there on the rickety dock; their legs hung down in tacit competition of who could dangle lower without touching her boots to the water.

"Has she always been?" Alice asked carefully. "A nightmare?" not wanting Cady to stop telling about her life. Alice was going for details. They'd already gone through Cady's debacle at boarding school last year, being thrown out for stealing a good deal of Xanax from the infirmary, which happened to be one floor down from her dorm. "My roommate was so sad," she'd said by way of explanation of why she wanted all those pills.

Cady chewed on a pale strand of hair in a way that made the gesture look as if chewing hair were the new sitting up straight, the new way to smile. "My aunt," she said, "she's all right. We have dinner together every evening at six. It's been that way since I can remember. I have to wear a skirt and I have to be on time. If I'm late she eats without me. And she doesn't even particularly like to eat. If it were socially acceptable she'd probably choose to live on Goldfish crackers and gin. We've never been what you'd call a warm twosome." She laughed like someone older, like someone who has already made a new adult home. "People always think I'm exaggerating. You should come over sometime and see."

"Sounds like the house is stopped in time."

"That's about right," she said. "My aunt is eighty-one."

"My God," Alice said.

"There were twenty years between her and my mother. My mother was one of those miracle babies, back when doctors thought it was basically impossible for a woman of forty to give birth, and my parents waited forever to have me, so . . ."

"You don't have any brothers or sisters?"

She shook her head.

"Cousins?"

"A few. But they're all older and awful. They live in the city and piss away all their money on Ralph Lauren and cocaine. I'm from terrible people, I'm telling you," she said. "My aunt smokes, drinks, and eats red meat at least twice a day. She's a savage with impeccable manners," she said. "Although lately the manners have started to go. Her anti-Catholic campaign has reemerged. Most of the staff has quit."

Alice had a feeling she wasn't exaggerating. She was not trying to be funny. "What's her name?"

Cady looked surprised. "I never call her by her name. No one ever uses it. The staff calls her Mrs. DeForrest, her friends at the club call her 'darling,' and I call her Aunt K. Her name is Kippy," she said. "Ridiculous, right?"

"Yes," Alice said, "completely."

"So how about you? Is it always this quiet around here?"

"Our mother travels a lot," Alice said. She wouldn't talk about her mother like some character. She wouldn't reduce her parents to caricatures of themselves. Not yet, at least. *I love my mother*, Alice could say. *I miss her more now than I did when I was little. I have her flight schedule under my pillow. I know her driver Gary's telephone number by heart — Gary, who drives her to the airport and picks her up in case my father has to work, in case he pretends he has to work because he is just so angry she's leaving once more now that we are old enough to be left.* "Our father works all the time."

"You know something?" Cady said. "You're really pretty." She said it in a way that assumed that Alice didn't think so, that she couldn't possibly have heard that sentiment too often before. Cady DeForrest said it as if she were the first person to notice, as if all Alice needed was this older girl's approval.

Well, Alice thought, *I'm flattered.* And then she thought, *Fuck you.*

Cady probably assumed she'd never gotten a hickey, that she had never met a boy at a party, given him a blow job in a closet, felt his eggy cum all over her neck and had him wipe her face with his boxers. Cady assumed she'd never had a boy put his hands down her pants in the costume closet at school, biting her breasts with his big straight teeth, saying "You're so sexy." Or that she could do all of this in just the past month, with all different boys, just because she felt like it. Cady no doubt thought that Alice wasn't pretty enough to do that and not feel used.

Fuck you, she thought. But she didn't mean it. She wanted to mean it, but she didn't. "Thanks," Alice said. "Thank you."

"Do you have a boyfriend?"

"No," she said. She took a breath. "Do you like my brother?" Alice asked, looking her over, feeling an insane need to protect Gus. Cady was a deadly combination of needing no one and wanting everything — everything she felt she'd been denied. Gus was the one who was used to being selfish and elusive. He was the one who showed up when he felt like it, went surfing for days if the waves were good in the very dead of winter. He was the one who didn't call. "Do you?" she said. But Cady had seen Gus coming even before Alice did and she was up and on her feet, running the planks to greet him as if he were back from some great suburban war.

Gus had only run to the house and back to get them all more layers, although Alice was sure that he would have found any excuse to leave them alone. It would be more exciting for him, after Cady left, if he could hear what she was like when he wasn't around. He liked Alice to be informed, or at least give informed opinions about the girls he was with. He was using her, Alice knew, but she didn't mind this kind of use. It meant that, in a way, he needed her more than he did before, when girls had yet to become his means of sustenance, before he needed them like he needed water, maybe even more than water. When there was a girl in the picture (which there had been since he'd turned fourteen), he was like those addicts in the movies: always in phone booths fumbling around for some extra coins to place a call to a dealer. Except, with Gus, his bedroom closet was the phone booth and he'd tug the white cord from the phone in the hall into his smelly closet. He'd call the girls. He'd talk and talk; who knew how they got in a word. He'd tell stories and jokes and muse about his worries, worries that were always about natural disasters or some such looming business. He never worried that he wasn't somehow or other substantial enough to be noticed, or that he felt as if sometimes he could simply evaporate if no one was watching — or even if someone was watching, how he might just disappear. He'd talk and talk and lower his voice so Alice couldn't even hear him, even as she was unforgivably right outside the closet door.

Then they'd come over. They'd come to him. She tried not to picture him being the kind of boy who begged, who made desperate noise, who convinced a girl that if she didn't follow through, he'd just go ahead and die. She tried not to picture this but she failed miserably, because it wasn't like she had to really try — she somehow knew it was true.

And so she didn't mind him using her to talk about the girls, to keep them going in his mind after they'd all gone home. Her brother claimed (only half-jokingly) that he was cultivating her gift of intuition. Besides, she was too damn curious.

With Cady it was different. Cady wasn't merely dashing in and out of his bedroom. Cady asked why the toilet in the front hall bathroom didn't work. She changed a lightbulb in the laundry room when she thought no one was watching. She refilled Spin's water bowl, brought over a bag of Gala apples, a crate of Clementines — dumping them without any to-do in the kitchen's empty wooden bowl. Cady barely went home.

One month later they all sat out on the dock with a thermos of hot chocolate enhanced by rum (prepared by Cady, who insisted they had to have a thermos *somewhere*) and watched the cold sun ease away. They talked about the worst physical pain they'd ever felt, and as it turned out they'd all been very blessed; none of them had broken a bone, been in a car accident,

91

none of them had even had stitches. Pain surely had to be coming, exquisite, torturous pain. As they talked, Alice lit matches and cast the flames down to the water. She didn't smoke but she loved lighting other people's cigarettes; she loved lighting matches and playing chicken with the flame, seeing how long her fingers would hang on before letting fire take over.

"Why do you do that?" Cady asked. She seemed not disapproving but merely curious. She was holding August's hand.

Alice shrugged. "I don't know," she said. "Habit, I guess."

"That's no habit," Cady said. "That's a dare."

"Maybe," Alice said with a shrug, not elaborating, letting Cady think she was maybe a little more mysterious, a bit more dangerous than Alice believed herself to be.

"You know," Gus said, "our mother is coming home tonight."

"How long has she been gone again?" Cady asked.

"Well, a little over one month, actually," Alice said. "Right before you arrived here on our planet. She's been buying rugs in Marrakech. She's selling them to some dealer in the city."

"We think," Gus added.

"I should go home then," Cady said, but she didn't move a muscle. "I really should get going."

Alice looked at her. She got really lucky with that light. Even the dying sun was hitting on Cady and casting only the most luxuriant light and shadows a girl could ever ask for. If it were thousands of years ago, everyone in Suffolk County would have all started worshipping Cady DeForrest right then and there, lighting candles in her honor, sacrificing virgins in her name, convinced she was a human conceived of spun gold, an impossibly valuable woman. Alice wanted to tell her, *Don't even think about moving; even you will never look this way again.* Her skin was warm milk with a splash of rich coffee, and her eyes looked like being underwater on a perfect day, seeing the sky through the surface of the sea. And then she smiled.

Gus seemed to make a decision. "I'll walk you to the car," he said, as if he were saying, *I want to make a baby.* The two of them got up and went to the house.

A few minutes later Alice went too. Cady's decrepit lime-green BMW was still in the driveway. Nobody was going anywhere. Alice had never been so thankful to live in a big house. She went as far as possible from Gus's room, to a room where there was, mercifully, a television. For an hour or two she sat frozen on the couch, as if she were commanded by God Himself to crank up the volume and watch old shows on television. She watched until she could be fairly certain she couldn't possibly hear them doing anything even if she were to go upstairs. Outside was a pitch-black night, a moonless son of a bitch. The phone rang, startling her, and it was their father from the airport saying that he and Charlotte would be home in an hour, what would everybody like to eat? Should they swing by China Express?

"Cady's here," Alice said, turning the volume on the television all the way down, "and I have a feeling she's staying for dinner."

"Whatever happened to that girl with the hair, that Sharon or whatever her name was?"

"Long gone, Daddy," Alice said, smiling at her father, how seriously clueless he was. There had been at least three girls since Shannon, but her father liked girls with reddish hair, girls like his wife and daughter. "How's Mom?" she said, and for some reason she thought she might start crying. Alice looked at the television — as if for consolation — where a pale female hand poured blue liquid on a diaper.

"She's suntanned," he said, sounding happy. "She's right here beside me. Shall I put her on?"

"That's okay," Alice said, swallowing hard. "I'll see her soon enough."

When she hung up the phone, she heard what sounded like Gus shouting. Gus was yelling at Cady. It had been only one month and they'd already fought more than a few times over who knew what. For the first time, Gus wouldn't expound upon his girl troubles. He said it was just very intense and that it killed him, being with her, that it was like ten years in a day. "It sounds miserable," Alice had made the mistake of saying, and Gus looked at her as if he were driving away on a long journey and there was no point in keeping in touch. There was the sound of something landing hard on the floor, the sound of a door slamming. And then there was silence.

All day she'd felt pretty good — even kind of excited — comfortable being included in her brother's wild romance, but now it seemed clear that she'd been only tagging along, that all they'd really wanted was a chance to be alone. They were probably making up from their fight and laughing about it right now — all the times they'd tried to give Alice hints and all the times she'd stayed and stayed. She thought of going out, of having her own destructive passion, but she remembered just last week at Eleanor's club, which seemed like years ago, the way a lanky boy's face changed, becoming more set in his features somehow, when she agreed to "just go for a walk." The idea of passion seemed laughable. It took so little to please them. Each time.

It had started — as most everything she did — as a way to get at her mother. She knew it, too. It was embarrassing, but there it was: two months ago, at a bonfire party on a measly strip of public beach, she'd stayed out later than she had any reason to stay, later than anyone else she knew, because she wanted Charlotte to worry about her just enough that she might go and cancel her trip. Gus was supposed to be back from Montauk, where he'd been working and surfing all summer. He was supposed to have made it back for the party, at least in time to pick her up, but he didn't come and he didn't come, and without her brother there Alice was different somehow. Without her brother pounding that one extra beer, without him being the one who'd have hours ago stripped naked sloshing into the sea, inciting at least five others to follow his lead, Alice's usual quiet self was a different kind of quiet. Lit by firelight and two beers (her tolerance for alcohol being nonexistent), she found herself supplying some dark-haired life-guard with more than enough reason to believe she just might like to go "gather some wood."

"It's cold," he'd said. "I'm Devin."

"You're a lifeguard, right? Didn't you save a little boy this summer?"

Devin nodded, giving a nice heroic squint toward the circle of embers. The fire was — as it should have been at this late hour — dying down. She set off with him with her hands in her pockets with visions of stumbling home, a wrecked picture of teenage trouble, smelling of someone else's breath, someone else's beer. She imagined, she did, crumpling into a ball as her mother screamed and yelled at her, as her father tried *to calm Charlotte down.*

So Alice followed the would-be wood gatherer and they lay down on a stretch of ground that was somewhere between soil and sand. At first it seemed as if Devin the lifeguard just wanted to lie alongside someone and look at the stars, reinstate his summer memories. He'd explained about saving the little boy, how it all went so fast, how his girlfriend became jealous of all the attention and broke up with him but it was, like, so long over anyway. "I'm driving up to Maine tomorrow," he said. "I'm supposed to leave at five-thirty."

Alice, sensing it was now or never, turned on her side and propped her head in her hand as if primed for a set of leg lifts. "You should just stay up all night," she said. "You're more than halfway there."

He didn't say anything, but he kept his gaze on her. He didn't smile and he didn't move. And she felt something drop out from under her, like riding in a sky-scraper's elevator and going straight for the top. There were his eyes, more serious and tragic than she'd noticed before. He'd saved a little boy. He reached out — not to hold her hand or touch her face but to take off her shirt. She let him. It felt like a cross between being undressed as a child and stepping into a sin-red room where she began to understand greed. The air had been warm enough for her skin not to freeze, but cool enough to be alarming. She'd never been shirtless in front of a boy before either, and she was proud she didn't hide herself away, chickening out in the shadows. He kissed her briefly and surprisingly inexpertly (he was a lifeguard, for God's sake) with small hard lips, but he had strong hands, and after a couple of years of being so concerned with stopping their hands — stopping the boys' roving, raging, hormone-fueled hands — she let this one's hands go everywhere, thinking about not much more than getting herself into trouble at home. But she liked it more than she'd planned. She liked the attention and she liked how he actually smelled like the very end of summer, all that salt and suntan lotion being replaced by chill. Sweat coated them both like sea spray, and she did forget the time. She didn't let it go *that* far. He gave her a ride home. No harm done, really.

Except when she did stumble through the front door it wasn't her mother who greeted her.

"Daddy?" Alice breathed, after she saw her father hunched in a chair, sitting in the dark.

He told her he was worried, that he'd had no number to call.

"I'm fine," Alice told him. "See? I'm completely fine."

He looked at her, saying nothing. He ran a hand over the planes of his tired face.

"I lost track of time," Alice said. "I'm sorry you waited up." And she was instantly embarrassed, wholly ashamed, an unconvincing bad girl. Her father was the very last person she wanted to worry. She hadn't imagined his tired face ragged with concern. She'd only envisioned Charlotte and her rage, the rage that Alice craved. She wanted to reassure him that she had stayed out late on purpose — as if that would make it better — and that she was in control.

He asked her to please, please never do that again. He told her it wasn't fair.

"You're right," she said. She nodded. "Is Mom up?"

He smiled, strangely, and told her that Charlotte had been sleeping soundly since shortly after Alice had left for her all-night adventure. "She sleeps like a baby," her father said. "It's funny how well she always sleeps before she goes away."

It's just those French sleeping pills she insists on finishing up, as if they're a roll of film, Alice wanted to tell him. *It's to spite me, don't you see?*

And the days got shorter and Alice's nights became longer, her estimated times of arrival increasingly more difficult to pin down. And her father became angry, and her mother continued planning her trip, taking jaunts into the city to visit embassies and personal contacts, various specialty shops.

On the morning of her flight, Charlotte cupped Alice's chin in her hand, as if Alice were a Czech peasant and Charlotte a busy modeling scout inspecting the local stock. "Sweetheart," she said, "you look tired and a little bloated, are you getting your period?"

Alice shook her head, and her mother's hand fell away. "No," she said, flaunting a yawn. She'd come in the last two nights at three o'clock in the morning and made it to school by eight.

"Well," Charlotte said, taking off her rings and putting them in a Ziploc baggie, ready for the safe, "I think you ought to get more sleep. All this running around, this late-night *drinking* — listen, I can only assume — it'll wreak havoc on your skin, believe me. You can't escape the bloat, even at your age."

Alice looked at her mother, trying her best not to show how shocked she was.

Her mother met that look and tripled it. *Stop,* was what Charlotte's eyes said, *stop this pathetic behavior.* Her mother clearly

101

believed that with matters concerning her daughter she had only to *think* "stop," and that Alice would. Charlotte obviously believed that of all life's complications, her daughter could not be counted among them.

"Gus," Alice yelled, as she got up from the couch and made her way toward the kitchen. "Hey, Gus?" She wasn't going to cower in front of the television all night. "They're coming home soon," she called out, not really caring if he heard. She stuck a piece of bread in the toaster and slathered it with honey. The sweetness hurt, she loved it so much. She dripped some on the counter and didn't wipe it away.

And when they came down the back stairs, they were all rosy and weirdly younger-looking than she remembered either of them looking hours ago. Apparently they'd made up quickly and effectively. Alice felt like the old guardian of a crusty girls' academy.

"How long have we been sleeping?" Gus asked.

Alice shot him a look.

Cady started cracking up. "We really were sleeping, I swear."

"Have any good dreams?" Alice asked with a voice she hardly recognized.

102

"All good," Gus said, putting a hand on Cady's shoulder, as if to steady himself.

Alice thought for more than a second about knocking both of them to the ground.

That evening, Cady's first time meeting Charlotte, they all ate Chinese food and prodded Charlotte to tell stories. It was comforting and sickening all at once, how ritualistic this had become. The taste of mu shu duck would always, for Alice, create the feeling of Charlotte just off a plane. Whether newly skinny or full in the face, smoking new cigarettes or not smoking at all, delighted to be home or desolate (she never hid her feelings, their mother; they had to give her that) — she almost always picked up Chinese food on her way home from the airport. Gary the driver sometimes took some egg rolls in the car so she could immediately satisfy her craving. Even if it was barely eleven a.m., even if she'd just eaten, and even if she'd just returned from China, where apparently, according to Charlotte, China Express could clean up.

Charlotte seemed well rested and had dropped at least five pounds. Her hair was tied back in a yellow head scarf, her fingernails weren't bitten, and she kept touching her husband — his shoulders, his back. She was polite to Cady without being rude or overly solicitous, both of which Gus had previously accused her of being around his girlfriends. Charlotte had tried to pull Alice onto her lap, the way she'd always done when she was feeling affectionate, but Alice felt her face flush with anger as much as with embarrassment and she wriggled herself away.

What Alice wanted from herself: not to get a thrill when her mother treated her like a baby.

As they ate Chinese food on actual plates instead of from the containers (in honor of Gus's guest), Charlotte talked. She'd burn out soon, her family knew, growing cranky and complaining of stomach cramps or else disappearing upstairs, her clothes strewn in colorful piles throughout the upstairs hallway; in the morning she'd be eager to move on, short with answers regarding her trip, somehow depressed by the idea of *describing*. And so they listened to her selective stories and didn't interrupt, hoping to gain at least some understanding of where it was she'd been.

A man called Narouz (a rug merchant? a hotelier? apparently no further description was forthcoming) had given her tea that had smelled like hibiscus flowers, and she'd thrown up for days. She'd seen that French model, the enormous one from the sixties with one name and the square lips (who Charlotte had sworn had long since succumbed to a drug problem) purchasing one hundred small blue bowls. There had been a day spent in search of a Sufi retreat, a night of trying desperately to reach home, a series of broken phones and terrible connections. "I missed my babies," she said, sloppily grabbing for Gus and Alice, grasping for their hands.

"Had you been to Morocco before?" Cady asked. Alice noticed that Cady had brushed her hair.

Charlotte nodded, swallowing a wonton. "Many times."

"You're doing some business there?" Alice could tell, by the way she asked, that Cady had been to Morocco, but she wasn't going to say so.

Their mother shrugged and looked at Alice. "We'll see what happens," she said.

"What does that mean?" said Alice, slipping Spin a scallion pancake — one of Charlotte's very favorite things — under the table. Her mother couldn't just keep doing this, waltzing in and out of this house, this life, with nothing but great anecdotes. Cady had done more in a month in terms of light fixtures and consistent fresh fruit and listening than her own mother had done in years. Alice found herself angry with both of them, with her mother for leaving and with Cady for stepping in so easily as a girl who just knew more. How did she know how to run a house? How to move around like a woman? Servants raised her. She was only seventeen.

"It means she'll see," said Gus. "What do you think?"

"Well," Alice said, "I thought it was an all-important trip for some big, um, *rug* opportunity. What, did something not work out?"

"Alice," her father said.

"Yes?" Alice said. "Oh, am I broaching an inappropriate topic? You've been gone for over a month and we're supposed to sit here and listen to stories about models buying bowls?" She felt like pulling her mother's hair out from under her silly head scarf. "We can't ask what you've been *doing?*"

"Why not ease up?" her father said.

The phone rang and Alice jumped up to get it, seizing the opportunity for escape. "Let the machine get it," Gus and Charlotte both cried out. They had an answering machine now. Her father had brought one home in July, and both Gus and Charlotte loved hearing the things that people said to a machine, how some people clammed up and others rambled on. The whole routine made Alice depressed.

Alice ignored them and picked up the phone. There was silence for a moment after she said hello, and she realized she was essentially terrified of who it could be, how her mother left so many loose ends each time she went away. It could be the bank, a hotel, a man who'd claim he found her wallet, that he'd like to give it to her in person, he didn't trust the mail. "Hello," she repeated in a lower voice.

"May I please speak to Alice?" a voice said.

"It's me," she said. "I mean, this is Alice."

"It's Jeff," he said, "um, from the parking lot?"

"Oh, hi," she said too loudly.

"Hi," he said. She heard what sounded like a small dog yipping in the background. She heard his breath.

God, she hated this. "What are you doing?" she blurted out.

"I was wondering if you wanted . . ." She

107

heard Gus laugh so hard he snorted. She heard her mother: "And then he said, remooove it, *s'il vous plaît!*"

"Why don't you come over," Alice heard herself saying, as if she invited strange boys to hang out at her house, oh, all the time. She saw her mother raise an eyebrow, turn her stupid scarf-head in Alice's direction. "Why don't you come over now?"

Her first instinct after he said okay, after she didn't switch phones in order to have more privacy, and after her family and Cady DeForrest heard her tell him how to get there (no easy feat with her screwy sense of direction), was to call her friend Eleanor. But not even Eleanor knew about the hand job, or that there had been kind of a lot of them in the past two months. Alice told Eleanor that they had just kissed. That is what, for some reason, she always said, even when Eleanor had heard some rumors — especially then. So calling Eleanor was out. She made her way back to the table.

"Who was that?" her father said.

"Jeff. A boy from school."

"And he's coming over now?"

"Is that a problem?" Alice said, prepared to use Cady's presence as a sensible bargaining tool. Gus was playing with Cady's hair, right there at the kitchen table. "It's only nine o'clock," Alice said, "and we'll just be right here." The problem was, she didn't care if he came over. She liked him, she was a little afraid of him, but she was really afraid of herself.

"I just don't see —"

"Alan," her mother said, clearly annoyed with Alice but not enough to take a stand, "just let her."

She'd bring him, Jeff, she'd bring him down to the poolhouse and shock him by not talking. He'd ask her to do things and she would. He wouldn't even have to ask her. She'd beat him to it, doing away with the small negotiations. She wasn't stupid; she knew what he wanted from her. He was too good-looking and too well liked to be calling her for real. She knew she had pretty hair and nice legs and was smart in a strange sort of way, but there were girls who were girlfriends and girls who were not, and she knew herself — she knew which kind of category she fit into.

By the time Jeff made it over, her parents were splayed on the living-room couch, unaware or unconcerned that Gus and Cady were back at it in his room. It seemed they were going for an all-time record; they simply had no shame.

Jeff was even taller than she remembered.

He looked completely foreign to Alice, as if he'd just stepped out of the 1950s — 1955 on a farm. And he was serious. If he'd been wearing a hat, on seeing her parents he no doubt would have taken it off.

"See ya," Alice said to her parents, after a brief introduction.

"Where are you going?" her father asked.

Alice laughed a quick, short laugh. "We're just going down to the water," she said. "It's pretty."

"Well, I don't think that's a great idea," he said.

"Daddy?"

"This time of year the raccoons are staked out down there. Mrs. Craven was actually attacked by one the other evening."

Everyone was laughing, even Jeff, who didn't seem to know where to look.

"Raccoons?" Alice said. "You've got to be kidding."

The way her father was looking at her made her crazy. He was asking her with his eyes if she was okay. He was telling her that she was acting strangely and that he'd show this big blond boy to the door right now, that he'd play the asshole expressly for her sake if what she secretly wanted was to hang out with her parents and watch bad TV. His eyes were saying he had a feeling that this was what she wanted.

Alice said, "We'll bring Spin," and she heard herself force a laugh. "He'll protect us from the evil raccoons."

"I am not kidding at all," he said, his voice on the rise.

"Alan," Charlotte said, her feet in his lap, "don't be absurd. Go on," she said, not looking at her daughter but flashing Jeff a big smile. Her mother was punishing her with that smile and it was working. She left the room pitched out into the galaxy, far outside of her family and its center, her mother the sun. She tried to be lunar, she tried to be a hedonistic creature of the night reveling in outsider status, but on actually stepping outside, all she noticed was that it was colder than she expected, and that she felt disoriented rather than excited with this stranger walking beside her.

He wore a cobalt fleece, the kind of item that boyfriends wore, the kind that girls liked to borrow, and his blond hair and brown eyes were exotic in a way; they made her think of Wyoming, Montana, Christian Science, Mormons. "I brought some beers," he said gamely. "They're in my car."

"Great," she heard herself saying. "That's great."

Maybe she was imagining it, but it

seemed like Jeff was looking at her strangely. Did her breath smell of Chinese food? She'd eaten an orange and drunk a Coke, but maybe he still smelled jade shrimp delight. Maybe she looked different from how he remembered. But amidst all this worry she managed to find her sense of purpose. She was going to touch him. She was going to touch him and it wouldn't matter if she smelled a little like egg roll. Nothing would matter but her fearlessness, her sheer availability. She didn't need love like some girls. She knew better by now.

Gus and Cady, they'd only just met, and bam, they were a couple. They screamed and yelled and threw things. They made up and made out constantly. Last Wednesday Alice had thought that Gus had been smoking pot (which he didn't ever do), but then she realized — to her even greater surprise — that he had been crying. Cady had made her brother cry. He belonged to her now. Alice didn't have to belong to anyone, and it could be out of choice. She could be the wild one, stepping out of her expected self and into other lives. What would her mother make of that? Nobody had to live up to any expectations, because she wouldn't expect a thing.

The dock was empty, no raccoons

prowling after all. There was a stretch of water-watching, beer-swilling silence. "So where do you think you'll apply to college?" Alice finally said, sounding as dull as humanly possible. She was giddy from having nothing invested. She could be as boring as she felt like.

"Maybe Colby," he said, "maybe Bates."

"Those B and C schools," she said, and he nodded.

"So what do you usually do on the weekends?" He didn't fiddle or fidget, Alice noticed. He was calm and smooth as a pond.

"I like to take the train to the city and, you know, wander around." She was going for sounding something like a misunderstood heroine — a girl worth the focus of at least one French film.

He nodded and smiled a nice smile, one that seemed to imply a certain understanding. But "Your parents seem nice," was what Jeff said. "Your brother, he's a really good guy."

Alice didn't respond. Instead she walked toward the poolhouse and he followed. Once inside they started kissing. It was some kind of great relief. They fell upon each other with a force that completely belied their attempt at conversation. She had no idea what he liked to eat, what

113

music he played when he was in his car, if he'd ever traveled outside the U.S., if his parents were still married. But there she was with his tongue in her ear, her hands gripping the ridges of his hips, feeling not much more than in a big rush to feel something more than anger at her mother for thinking she was nobody to worry over. She was taking off his shirt, unbuttoning his jeans, making herself go further. She was a delirious gambler with a recent windfall, through with hedging her bets. He smelled even cleaner than he did the other night, and he was sighing and moaning and he sounded almost worried. She took that as a good sign and moved on. *I'll see that ten and raise you twenty! You heard me, twenty!* Letting her own pants fall to the ground, letting herself fall to the ground with this stranger moving over her. He was so big, so substantial, and this was what she needed, to be pinned to the earth, to be moored by someone else's pressing need. She was a virgin. She was still, if barely, a virgin. She kept telling herself that as she felt him straining against her leg, searching for her the way she knew he thought she was searching for him. Alice watched herself from up above, and there she was, pale and writhing — a vision of desire incarnate. If she were Jeff, she would be doing exactly what Jeff was doing. She would be fumbling around for a condom in the dark and cursing herself for not having brought one.

"It's okay," she heard herself say. "You can."

"Are you . . . are you on the pill?" he slurred, and she didn't answer, only kissed him, brought him to her; she was going going going gone. If she were Jeff, she would be bearing up on those big swim-team arms and thrusting steadily — taking advantage of a story-worthy opportunity. But she wasn't Jeff and she let it happen, let the pain come, let no noise out, and abruptly felt like crying. When he went to roll off of her, she pulled him back on. He was heavy and she could barely breathe, but she told him to just lie there for a moment, if he didn't mind.

The surf lapped up the last of the shore; she could hear the high tide rising. It was this shifting landscape she always pointed out to anyone new to the view. With the tides there was before and after. *Before* was the scraggly, weedy beach, a path to walk under neighbors' docks and on the sand for miles. And *after* was all water and only water clear to their green grass lawn. *You see that buoy?* she'd say. *At low tide there's land straight through to there, a true clean sweep of beach.*

But the night was so dark, even Alice could scarcely tell the water from the land, the difference between before and after. So really, what could she point out at that very moment to illustrate the difference?

Jeff rolled off, and Alice felt naked, paradoxically, for the first time all evening.

"You should probably go, right?" Alice said, pulling her shirt on.

"I guess," said Jeff, his voice looser and louder than she remembered. "Listen," he said, not pulling on his boxers, not rushing to cover up his very beautiful body.

"It's okay," Alice said. "It's okay."

He looked at her strangely, the way he'd done earlier, but this time she wasn't worried about her breath or her looks. She knew it was *her* he was looking at strangely, seeing past her reddish hair and her smallish chest, seeing past her nickel-colored eyes. He was seeing into her distance and noticing how she had given him full permission to treat her badly before he'd given any indication that he would. He looked frightened, and frightened in a way that would never reverse.

He said, "It's my mom's birthday tomorrow, so . . ."

Alice watched him put on his clothes. He wasn't exactly rushing but he seemed to be acquiring a gentle urgency. She imagined him as a husband, accustomed to waking early and dressing in considerate silence so as not to wake his wife.

They walked to his car in a mildly painful silence. After putting the beer bottles in a milk crate in the backseat, he leaned sweetly into Alice and gave her a kiss.

"I'll see you," she said, and he left.

After he'd gone Alice went back down to the water. At first she found it hard to breathe. If only he hadn't kissed her like that — such an open and obvious good-bye. She walked onto the dock and sat down where she'd talked with Cady one month before. *You're really pretty*, she had told her, as if the words were precious; as if they actually mattered. Alice still had matches in her pocket, and she burned a few, singeing her fingers as she cast them off to sea. They actually hurt, the small burns, and she thought of her mother never coming out and saying, *Look, I'm worried about you*. She'd done it with Gus for years now. They'd have huddled conversations about birth control, self-control. They would fight heatedly over his lack of propriety, the way he'd walk around essentially naked whenever he felt the urge. Alice thought, as she rose up and walked toward the house, about how the closest her mother had come to expressing concern or anger toward her was when she told Alice that staying out late was affecting her looks. As if that were all it would take for Alice at fifteen: a quick bit of self-consciousness, a little hit of shame.

She had no idea what time it was, how long Jeff had been there, how long she'd sat alone. Inside the house the lights were out, the television off. Spin was on the kitchen floor, whimpering in his dreams. She didn't care how late it was, or that her mother had just gotten home from Morocco. She didn't care that Cady was no doubt in Gus's room and would hear every hollered word. Alice began steeling herself, preparing to confront her. It was the only available option left to her at this point, unable as she obviously was to keep this kind of anger contained.

She would open the door cautiously, and if her mother was sleeping she would observe her for a while, noting exactly what she looked like before she heard the truth. Charlotte was very particular about how she liked to be woken up, and Alice would break all her rules. She would poke her mother's shoulder. She would turn on the light. She would raise her voice immediately, shattering the illusion of peace. If her father told Alice that this was something that could wait until morning, she would remain calm with him while disagreeing. And then she'd list her mother's shortcomings. She'd list them without saying *like* or *um. You're selfish, you're vain, you're lazy.* And on and on and on. She'd ask her to come to the kitchen, and there she'd detail for her mother what she did with Jeff and what she'd risked, why she did it and how it felt — how it felt to be her.

Only when she arrived at her parents' door, she was humbled by the quiet all around her. She opened the door and was finally silenced by this: the sight of her mother lying so still — head resting on her father's shoulder, pale hand on his chest.

She stood stunned somehow at this ordinary sight, and for the first time all night she felt drunk. She was drunk on disappointment, on knowing she'd behaved foolishly with Jeff, and drunk with the certainty that she wouldn't be telling her mother anything tonight. How could she, when the meaning of her family — the small and glowing white-hot center — was laid out before her right here in a private display? She watched them sleep, her mother and father, and now the room was spinning. Her mother's hand was so much sturdier and plainer than the rest of her. It lay squarely on her father's chest, a nothing-special hand. Alice was dizzy; she became undone by this simple possibility of how her mother's world could be stripped of adornment much like anyone else's. Of how, in her dreams, her careless mother — frivolous, head-scarfed, inscrutable — was possibly more like Alice than Alice had ever allowed herself to believe. But then Alice smelled the very air on her mother's side of the bed; she saw how Charlotte's eyebrows were precise like a fairy's without her ever having to pluck them.

She wanted to crawl between them as she did sometimes as a child. But she wanted even more than that. She wanted to be inside of her mother unnamed and unborn or buried deep within both of her parents, in mere shadows of separate cells. Alice stood watching and wanting and then, when after a while they didn't even stir, when they stayed fused together in a warm tangle of sleep, she backed out of their bedroom and retreated through the narrow and very drafty corridor.

5

Promises, 1985

For one whole year Charlotte didn't go anywhere, at least not by herself. No one mentioned her lack of travel plans, for fear that if
it was pointed out, she might realize she was
bored. For a whole year she made a mess,
tossing her folders of cutout articles and
photographs all over the kitchen table,
leaving bowls of granola and yogurt and rotting apples on the bookshelves upstairs, as if
after looking for a book and having a bite,
she'd been called away unexpectedly. She
still never walked Spin regularly. She
stepped over Gus's wet suit in the mudroom
and walked barefoot over his snack of sugar
cereal that inevitably left a trail. Now that
she was home so much, she refused to employ a cleaning lady on the basis of retaining
her privacy, and when their father finally
stopped yelling and started crying at the
sight of their kitchen, Charlotte went into a

cleaning frenzy, and with the zeal of the converted, took to the high of it, to the simple clarity it provided. She eventually took the cleaning frenzies into the decorating realm, redoing the upstairs guest room, which had hardly ever been used.

Alice loved standing in the middle of the room when it was newly empty. There was much to admire about the original detail work — the low, deep sills that had been obscured by curtains were now stark and freshly painted the color of corn silk, and moldings framed the room boldly, setting off honey wood floors. Alice stood in the room's center and appreciated how perfect the space was in its blankness, like a new unspoken thought. Her mother intended to retain an elegant austerity, but Alice knew she wouldn't be able to help herself. The clutter began with a pillow — one little needlepoint pillow — and within weeks there were piles of excess: framed photographs of a pitch-black night, an antique glove collection, leather-bound books found for a bargain at a local church fair. Collectors, Alice felt certain, were lonely or warding off loneliness with other people's stuff.

Her mother collected with desperation, despaired about the mess, and moved on to a new room. She stopped sleeping late and began clearing out the poolhouse. One day Alice noticed that the drawing her mother had done so many years ago had been taken down from the refrigerator. Charlotte stripped the moldy poolhouse floors and scoured the windows, replaced the broken doorknob with a purple glass fixture, and even oiled the hinges so nothing squeaked. She deemed the poolhouse her office, and declared it off-limits to everyone but her. There were shades hung and they were always drawn. She mostly went there to draw and think; no phone was installed. Having run out of her own rooms, she started designing other people's houses, having lunch with women who had, previously, barely registered on her radar and taking in their goals of midcentury or country classic, Provençal or shabby chic.

"For the first time in my life I'm getting something done," Charlotte said to Alice, and Alice believed her. Alice had to agree. During the week she drove to fabric out-lets, befriended antique dealers, investi-gated the cheapest methods of importing from Java and France. On weekends, while their father worked and Gus went off surfing, Charlotte and Alice hung around the kitchen and watched for the swans' arrival, waited for the babies to come around. Alice trailed after Charlotte with a bag of bread, and spent time watching the swans kick up algae for their little ones and the flurry that followed after they tossed bread ends off the dock. They watched the long elastic slide of swans' necks and the little fuzzy heads bobbing and diving underwater. After an hour or so, they'd do something that required getting dressed. They both enjoyed going to the city on a train. They walked downtown without a specific destination. They went into shops without names, shops with white walls and wood floors, with selections anemically beautiful. Charlotte held clothes up to Alice and inevitably put them back in their place. "With your coloring," she'd say, "you should stick to black or white. Your looks are ornate enough as they are." *What does that mean?* Alice always meant to ask, but she was too taken with watching her mother pick up objects and put them down — earrings, gloves, a transparent blouse — with whatever compelled Charlotte's attention. Alice would try to predict what her mother would notice and was rarely correct.

Sometimes they went to see an exhibit at the Whitney, the Met, always ending up gazing at the Sargent portraits, wondering over what happened to all the costumes and jewelry, imagining what the people were like, how they talked to and treated one another on an ordinary day. Alice stared at the raven-haired girl who went on to be a singer in Italy, who met her death by way of the Nazis, stripped of all her remarkable costumes, stripped of the light in her eyes.

The second Saturday in October, Charlotte was unusually quiet — more romantic than agitated, more spacey than distracted — and as these Saturdays had begun to include stops at hotel bars, they settled into an outdoor table at the Stanhope, where there were heat lamps warming an already toasty Indian summer day. Charlotte told Alice bits about her father: how he used to like nothing better than a whiskey, neat, in a hotel bar; how he'd fixed her cracked teapot on their second date; how he'd worn a coat of chocolate tweed and how she laughed into it, how she laughed and laughed into the wet wool when they were late to the theater after rushing in from the rain. Her mother, in moments of confidence, didn't talk much about Nepal or Jordan or Tibet or wherever — but always of Paris, an impossible Paris, where she'd

125

met their father only weeks after a sea passage in 1966. She seemed somehow sad when she spoke of it, yet she also felt compelled to do so, and only, it seemed, with Alice, and only on these lazy private days.

"You're so lucky," Charlotte told Alice at the Stanhope. She picked almonds out of a nut mix, placed them in a row on the soggy cocktail napkin. They were facing the museum, watching people. The air was heavy with cigarette smoke and the faint salty whiff of pretzels.

"Why am I lucky?"

"Well," she said, "for one thing, you've yet to have anything happen to you."

"How do you know?"

"Well," said Charlotte, "I don't know. You could be living an entire secret life; that is absolutely true."

Alice laughed in a way she hoped was darkly. She wanted her mother to lose some confidence, to waver in her assumptions regarding her daughter just one single degree.

"Your brother should be in the same place. He keeps flinging himself about so hard but all he really needs to do is break up with that girl and go someplace new. It doesn't even have to be college, at least not right away."

"You've never liked Cady," Alice said.

"Well, do you?"

"I *kind* of like Cady, but I definitely wish she'd go home once in a while. I wish they didn't need to have their loudest moments in the middle of the night." *I wish we'd talk about me.*

"She's too serious for him, too demanding."

What her mother didn't seem to notice, it seemed to Alice, was how demanding Gus was of Cady. They seemed to be in a contest of who felt more deeply, of who was more obsessed and more angry and jealous. They needed to fight and make up, it seemed, in order to get through a day.

The only time Gus seemed to be without Cady (besides school, which he attended sporadically these days) was when he went surfing. He'd taken to getting up at five or so in the morning on Saturdays and getting himself out to Montauk. He surfed during the week too, which they all knew except her father. Charlotte didn't confront Gus about it. Alice could tell it gave her a sense of pleasure each time he took off alone with his board, whether in a borrowed car or headed for the train; he looked so insolent and pleased with himself. No matter how often their father came down on him for his lateness, his grades, his ragged and often-ridiculous clothing, Charlotte didn't do much more than shrug when she knew he was sneaking off to do what he felt like doing. His grades were good enough to get him into a serviceable college, should he decide to go, and school would not determine his life, was what Charlotte rather obliquely argued — as if Gus were simply larger than school-as-concept. As if he were, by nature, above it all.

Charlotte was concerned only that her son at eighteen would give of himself freely to someone else, to someone (Alice couldn't help thinking) other than Charlotte.

"What was that, darling?" Charlotte asked her daughter, as she sipped the watery remains of her vodka and lime, as she signaled for the elderly waiter who was perspiring in the heat, wearing white. But Alice didn't remember having said anything, at least not out loud, and she was left with the familiar feeling of realizing she was always asking a question — invisible, soundless — *Do you see me, do you love me* — a refrain like a whisper or maddening chimes drowning out the moment.

"Do you like the decorating?" Alice

blurted out. "You know, all the stuff you've been doing." She still couldn't decide if her mother enjoyed having an actual job. Alice was prepared at any moment for Charlotte to start putting down her clients. She was ready, she told herself, for it all to turn.

"Well," Charlotte said, lighting up a teal-colored cigarette bought at Nat Sherman with the theory that she'd smoke less if the cigarettes were expensive and distinct, "not so much." She inhaled and her narrow nostrils flared. "To be honest it is basically depressing." Alice's heart began beating wildly — beating with the knowledge that she had been right, that this was it and Charlotte would be going soon, that these Saturdays together were mere exercises in killing time. Her mother was about to say it — that when Gus left home, she would leave too. "Other people's tastes depress me, other people's lives. It all boils down to rumpus rooms and powder rooms and office-slash–guest rooms — you know, people creating a sense of a life instead of actually having one."

Alice didn't bother responding. Her mother was angry suddenly, and the glitzy cigarette was burning off into nothing but ordinary ash.

"I don't know," Charlotte said. "I don't

know if I'm quite cut out for it; what do you think?"

"What do I think?" Alice asked. "You want to know what I think? Why?"

"Because you're my daughter," her mother said, as if that could mean everything. "Because you're a smart girl and I love you."

Alice felt a ball of wax growing in her throat, choking on the very words she was always desperate to hear. "I think you should do what you really want to do," she said, not meaning a word of it. "I think you've done — it seems to me — pretty much whatever you've always felt like doing, and I can see no reason to start changing now."

Alice saw that her mother had registered the sarcasm. She saw the shift in Charlotte's eyes, those green eyes that were reddening from smoke and city pollution. She saw the crow's-feet at the corners deepen in her delicate skin.

The train ride home was long and punishing. There was a half hour delay in Queens and they both had to use the bathroom. Charlotte made a few halfhearted attempts at conversation but none of them took. They each read their books and by the time they reached home they were both worn out from keeping quiet. They had that in common. While Gus and her father could keep quiet for days with an ease that seemed almost sinister, Alice and her mother couldn't do it. Neither of them had the will or the stamina. "It cooled off," Alice said. "It was so hot today."

"It was a strange day," her mother agreed, before opening the door and heading up the stairs.

Alice found her father sitting in the library in his big brown leather chair, in the only place he looked small. He looked up when she walked in, as if he'd heard her coming, then took off his glasses and raised his eyebrows, as if to say, *I give up.*

Alice sat on the other side of his desk, the way she did in a doctor's office when she was free to get dressed and ask questions. She could remember being small enough to sit under the desk and play with a paper clip, when her father handed her paper clips. Charlotte never could get over how she sat quietly and happily at her father's feet, needing no more than to be held in his lap at one point or another, not needing more than that. *You never left me alone,* she was fond of telling her daughter. *You just talked and followed me from room to room.*

"Gus tells me he's going to teach you how to surf," her father said.

"Is that right?" Alice said. "First I've heard of it."

"Do you want to learn?"

"I'm not sure," Alice said. "I hadn't really thought of it, to tell you the truth. It's not like we live in a tropical paradise. It seems like so much work just to find the waves and not freeze," she said.

Her father looked at her and smiled. She wasn't trying to be funny and he knew it, and that was why he had to laugh. "How different the two of you are," he said, picking up a heavy fountain pen.

"Not really," she said, wanting it to be so, but on seeing his expression, she turned it into a joke by simply keeping a solemn expression. "Why ever would you think that?"

He smiled and looked at his daughter in the way that children seldom notice. He looked at her proudly as if to say, *I made you.*

He uncapped the fat pen and began scribbling on a yellow legal pad, connecting lines and dots. "Something has been bothering me," he said quietly.

"What is it? What's wrong?"

"I ran into Isabell Donnelly in the hardware store yesterday," he said evenly, stopping to see if Alice was listening.

"Uh-huh." She nodded.

"Married to Bart Donnelly, the one who looks a bit like Abe Lincoln?"

"Yes?" she said, struggling not to sound impatient.

"You know who she is?"

"She's one of Mom's . . . clients."

"Clients," he said, "exactly. Alice, honey, I don't know how to say this — but have you been having some kind of trouble lately?"

"What do you mean?"

"I'm not sure. Like maybe female trouble of some kind, something you didn't want to talk about? Mrs. Donnelly told me that your mother has been . . . helping you out with something. Did you need money for something? Something for which you were ashamed to ask me?"

"I have no idea what you're talking about," Alice said, laughing while her heart pounded out a staccato embarrassment, biting her tongue as she thought about what it was that Isabell Donnelly could possibly have to do with Alice having unspecified problems. Did someone tell her mother that she was having sex? Would her mother even care? Besides which, Alice had stopped her little rampage nearly a year ago, pretty much, with one worthy exception.

Her father still doodled purposefully on the pad. "Alice," he said, his voice tightening, "Mrs. Donnelly seemed to think your mother needed to help you through something lately. She seemed to think you needed money and that it was *her* money, Mrs. Donnelly's, that went toward helping you. That is what your mother apparently told her, anyway." He was trying, Alice could tell, not to ensnare anybody just yet, to let Alice clear up a misunderstanding.

"Daddy, I have no idea what you are talking about," Alice said, and this time she couldn't help but sound angry. "What *are* you talking about?"

He coughed a dry cough and dropped the pen, then clasped his hands together.

"What?" Alice said. "For God's sake, would you please stop doing that?"

He looked confused. "What am I doing?"

"Taking so long to tell me something. It's like torture."

"I think your mother has been not altogether honest with these people," he finally said. His voice sank low. "I think she's maybe been inventing some stories," he continued carefully, "and I think she's been

134

doing something besides going antique hunting with all these people's money." He seemed genuinely mystified. "Do you have any idea what she does every day?"

Alice waited a moment before answering. She tried to be more like him, weighing what seemed like the air around him before giving voice to his feelings. There was a wall of books behind him, all hardcover. There was a picture of Gus and a picture of Alice and a black-and-white shot of Charlotte's profile, somewhere in the desert. "Of course not," she finally said, feeling sweat like a sudden bloom all over her body. Alice looked right into her father's blue eyes and could see that he was afraid too. She had lived with the fear that something like this would happen. There was no way that her mother could be purely going to work and having lunch, picking up the dry cleaning. Since her mother had begun scouring the poolhouse, Alice was afraid to believe. "But . . ." she said.

"But what?"

"I don't want her to leave because of me."

"You've always been too dramatic," he said, not without love. "She won't."

"She will. She will leave. She basically told me today."

"She what?"

"She started going off about her clients and how boring they were, how boring their lives were. What is going on with her? She lied to Mrs. Donnelly about me? What did she tell her?"

"I don't know, Alice. She didn't say."

"Well, think about the possibilities. She probably told her that I was getting an *abortion* or something. Or maybe extensive plastic surgery? Which would be a better rumor to live with, do you think?"

"Alice, listen —"

"No, you listen," she said, and then immediately fell silent with shame. "Daddy," she said gently, "do you *want* to know what is going on?"

"Of course I do," he said. But she didn't believe him.

"How long do you think she's been lying to people? Do you have any idea?" *Sex,* thought Alice, *drugs; drugs and sex together.* Or maybe she was sick. Maybe she was hiding a terrible illness, fleeing home all of these times to participate in experimental treatment. Maybe her mother was dying.

When her father looked beyond her toward the doorway, she knew that Charlotte was standing there. "Alice," her father said, as if an intruder had just entered the premises, "why don't you go in the kitchen.

136

August wanted to ask you something." Alice could hear the blender — evidence that he was in fact there. She almost refused to move, but when Alice looked at her father he was staring so intently that she rose and brushed by her mother's robe without so much as a glance in her direction.

In the kitchen, Gus peeled a banana and stuck it in the blender whole, then dumped in ice and handfuls of berries, a few spoonfuls of protein powder. He looked up when Alice sat on the counter, passing a pear back and forth between her hands. Alice took a bite of the pear and Gus looked at her again.

"You need anything?" he said.

She shook her head, paralyzed, savoring the overripe pear, sucking down its nectar. She could hear the beginnings of her parents arguing in the library. Her father's voice was like the bass on an album — significant but muted, stepping aside for the flashier vocals, the rowdy and anxious guitar. His voice was calm but her mother's was not. Alice remembered the time Charlotte hurled a book in the library to illustrate her rage, and instead of it flying across the room as she'd anticipated, it had landed on her own bare toes, sending her into a fit of tears but thankfully into her husband's care, defusing the argument with a swift if clumsy kind of peace.

Charlotte was yelling at her father, "Are you sure? Because you'd better be pretty damn sure to make an accusation like that."

Gus turned on the blender and drowned out their voices.

"Stop," Alice shouted. "Turn it off."

But Gus increased the power and blended longer than necessary. *I can't hear you*, he mouthed. He wasn't intentionally being hurtful, she somehow knew. He just couldn't stand the tension; he had a surprisingly low tolerance for it, given all his fury with Cady. But before she had time to yell at him further or to pull the plug from the wall, Charlotte came bounding into the kitchen, followed by her father.

"Do you have any idea what kind of accusation you are making, Alan?" Her eyes looked to Alice like flashing green lights. *Go go go*, they seemed to say, *give me my reasons for leaving*. She was heedless of her daughter's terrified expression or her son's defiant blending. "Do you even know what this Isabell woman is like?" Then: "Would you turn that bloody thing off?"

When Gus didn't, Charlotte slapped his face. She slapped Gus and she turned off the blender and he stood up straight, cracking an astonished smile. "You're out of control," he said to her. Alice could swear she recognized in his face the hint of admiration she'd seen her mother have in times of Gus's minor disappearances, his inappropriate attire.

Alice's face was scorching hot, full of flushed silence. There was nothing she could imagine saying. Her father went over to the refrigerator and opened it, contemplating the shelves as if he might like to step inside and stay there awhile.

Charlotte placed her hands over her face for a moment before taking them away. She took a breath and lowered her voice. "Do you," she said to her husband, "do you know what you're suggesting?"

"I do," he said, into the white refrigerator light. "I'm afraid it's very simple." Then he slammed the door shut with surprising force.

"Simple?" Charlotte screeched. "Simple?"

"And I'm only suggesting that if it is true, and you're the only one who knows what's true" — he looked at Alice and then at Gus — "if you have been borrowing some of these funds and not exactly doing things on time, if you've been telling these . . . people . . . that our daughter is having problems in order to provide a false reason for needing money —" He broke off abruptly, as if in weary disbelief. Nobody said a word. The hum of the refrigerator was steady and nearly a comfort. "You ought to apologize," he said. He was winded. After a few audible breaths, he continued: "Just give them the money, Charlotte. Or purchase what you told them you'd be purchasing for them and apologize for the goddamned delay. What — *no,* listen — what is so terribly challenging about that? About any of that?" His voice was low and clear. The wormy vein at his temple was visibly laced with purple.

"And if it isn't true?" asked Charlotte, but something in her husband's face made her stop insisting. Something made her nod and say, "I'm sorry," in a way that suggested she was anything but. "Sweetie," she said to Alice, but Alice couldn't bring herself to look; everything was too obvious and laid out bare like too much makeup or too little clothing on a girl who tried too hard. Her mother had plainly used her.

When Charlotte exited the room, Gus said, "What just happened?" But neither Alice nor her father could answer him. Her father looked at Gus drinking his shake, at the remaining ingredients scattered on the counter. There was something in her father's face — Alice couldn't help notice — that was verging on revulsion. She wanted to assure her brother that her father was just upset, that there was nothing personal in that look. But then her father put his arm around her, stiffly, then looser, and before she'd even noticed he was leaving, Gus was gone from the room.

Charlotte left within a week without warning for nearly a month. And as it turned out, her trip was not spontaneous. She'd been planning and had booked the ticket a good six weeks in advance.

One early evening before Charlotte left, Alice saw her parents standing together on the lawn. They were as close as two people could be without touching. She thought that they might just go ahead and kiss, when suddenly her father sat down on the grass, which must have been damp and cold. He refused to get up, no matter how her mother waved her arms around, and he sat on the grass long after she'd left him there, even after the sun went down. After coming inside and bringing the cold air with her, she told Alice she was leaving on a trip and that it would be the last trip, the last one of its kind.

★ ★ ★

When she was on a plane, days later, Gus didn't come home from school. When Charlotte called from Oaxaca to let them know she'd arrived (*thanks ever so much, how kind of you to call*) Alice could have sworn her mother was mildly uplifted when Alice complained that Gus hadn't come home. "I'm sure he's with Cady," was her response. As if it were Cady who'd lured him away — Cady, who was perfectly happy hanging out in her underwear eating pie in their kitchen, Cady, who wasn't ashamed to admit she wanted a house in a cold climate with at least five children. Cady's influence, if anything, was oddly domestic. "I'm bringing you home some chile-chocolate," her mother said, sounding drunk, and Alice, to her own astonishment, hung up on her. It had felt like no more than an involuntary reflex, and when the phone crashed into the cradle, Alice was flush with pride but also regret. She was this close to finding the hotel number and calling right back.

Each moment of the next day — distracted in class or riding in Eleanor's car with the radio turned up or reading by dim light hurting her eyes — was another stepping-stone on which she couldn't help but walk, leading her from one side of Charlotte to the other. She was stepping cautiously over a gorge but not for one second looking down or backward. She needed to preserve herself, to reach the other side where it didn't hurt as badly and where she didn't live or die by her mother's tenuous and gilded presence.

In the morning Alice waited for the sun to rise. She was up, showered and dressed and ready for school, her chin-length hair in carefully studied disarray. She drank grapefruit juice and ate a bagel before picking up the phone at seven-thirty a.m. and calling Cady DeForrest. When it became clear that Gus wasn't with Cady and that he could be anywhere, Alice admitted she was worried, giving Cady the opportunity to reinstate (as if it were necessary) her undisputed cool. "I'm sure he's fine," she said, yawning.

"Why?"

"What do you mean?"

"Why are you so certain? Are you sure he's not there?"

"What must you think of me, Alice?"

"Why are you so confident that he's fine?"

Alice could hear the rustle of Cady's bedsheets, which were (though Alice had

143

never seen them) sure to be cotton and verging on threadbare, monogrammed with the stitched script of her parents, reminding her of where she came from with the whisperings of the faultless dead. Alice could hear Cady sitting up and focusing, taking her time. "He's fine because he has to be," she said calmly.

"Did you know our mother took off again?"

"I did. He mentioned it."

"Did he, you know, sound upset?"

"No," Cady said.

"No?"

"Not really," she said. "No. What, you don't believe me?"

"Sure," said Alice. "Sure I do." Outside her window the trees were tall and very still, reaching across white sky. Her favorite tree was the one that looked beleaguered by its own lush looks, its ochre and burgundy and vermilion adornments.

"Let me know if you hear from him, will you?"

"Of course I will," she said. "I'm sure he'll be home or in school today. He just needs to do this kind of thing once in a while. Don't you understand that? Alice?"

"Yes," she said. But she didn't. Eleanor would be here soon with a ride to school.

She would go to school. She would listen and pay attention. She wasn't like Gus, above it all. She didn't have it in her — whatever *it* was — a disregard for objectivity, a steadfast faith and self-love.

"Listen," Cady said, "your mother sat me down one day last week. She asked me, *bitterly,* if I was being responsible. She meant about not getting pregnant."

"She did?" Alice said, hating her high voice, the way her palms were stuck to her thighs, the way her thighs were yellowy white like old office paper.

"She threatened me, Alice," said Cady. "She told me I'd better be on the pill. She told me she knew from experience."

"She *what?* What experience? What's that supposed to mean?"

"She's probably just trying to scare me," Cady said. "She likes doing that. Have you noticed?"

"Why are you telling me this?" Alice almost whispered, wondering if she was a mistake and if that was how her parents still thought of her. "Do you think I need to know this?" August could not have been anything besides perfectly planned and eagerly awaited. Of that she had no doubt.

"I'm sorry," Cady said. "It's just that Gus will be fine. You'll be fine. Even if . . ."

145

"If what?"

"Even if she doesn't come back."

"What do you mean by that?"

"Nothing," Cady said, obviously awake now, her aquatic voice of sleep drained away. "It just breaks my heart how you both need her so much."

"I've got to go," Alice said quickly, before hanging up the phone, before opening the windows all the way and breathing hard into the humidity, the stink of warm low tide.

"Why is it," Eleanor said, standing in the doorway, "that your family refuses to install a goddamned doorbell? I'm always knocking and knocking with this fuck of a lion's-head knocker. It's barely eight-thirty a.m. This can't be good for me."

Alice shrugged and touched Eleanor's shoulder, played with the fabric of her flowery shirt in lieu of trying to explain. "Pretty," Alice said, feeling like she might throw up. She couldn't stop thinking of her mother telling Cady about the necessity of the pill, which was a conversation too dark and too easy to imagine. Easier still was the vision of Gus on the side of the LIE mangled by a stranger's car or else as sinking pieces in the Atlantic Ocean torn apart by sharks. Her father would be racked with guilt. Her mother would disappear for good.

Where was he?

"You look exhausted," Eleanor said.

"Gus didn't come home last night."

"Well, there's a shock," she said, opening the car door. "Alice? Getting in?"

Alice sank down into the burgundy leather interior and watched her friend start the car. Eleanor loved to drive and she adored her car a white Cadillac sedan, inherited from her Kansas City grandfather. She loved it without irony; it made her feel secure. Eleanor lit a cigarette after pulling out of the Greens' twisty driveway, while Alice winced, rolling down the window. It took Alice a while to say, "He's not with Cady."

Eleanor exhaled, laughing. "Shock number two."

Eleanor always liked Gus too much to act like it. Alice knew she'd never understood why he hadn't wanted to count her among the many girls with whom he'd spend his time and energy and (at least before Cady) his famous promiscuity. Alice never understood it either, and until recently had spent a good deal of any day dreading how her best friend and her brother would further complicate her life. But the only evidence of what she'd considered serious flirtation between them was their fighting. They fought over any potential issue. If she lit up a cigarette he'd start in with his statistics. She'd pick on his lack of life plans, his affected taste in music, his arrogance. "He's not with another girl," Alice said.

"Look, I know you think Cady is some kind of ice queen who is all-powerful or something, but trust me, she isn't. She's like us."

"Us?" Alice laughed. "No."

"Well, she's not like your mother either."

"Who said she was?"

"You did."

"No, I didn't."

"I'm sure you did, and if you didn't, well . . ."

Alice felt her lack of sleep, and her tireless need to worry eked away slowly. "*Look*, I know you're all into Freud, but do you think you could please quit it?"

"Okay, fine."

They were late. The verdant vineyard to their left allowed for a bigger sky, the downhill slope rolled gently, and there they were on the perfect road — a straight, clean shot with no one in front of them, ideal for blasting music at seventy miles an hour. They never spoke during that one strip of the ride. No matter what the discussion, they both just shut up. After the turnoff they were back to morning traffic, but both a little nicer somehow.

Eleanor broke the silence: "Do you and Gus really talk about her?"

"*Really talk?* What does that mean?"

"I was just wondering. It's hard."

"She's our mother," Alice said, eyes out the window on new houses in ugly adolescence — out of scale, expectant.

"I know that," said Eleanor, sucking in her cheeks, her cheekbones high and prominent. "Believe me," she said, "I know."

Alice tried not to think of what Charlotte had told her not even a month ago. She'd said that Eleanor was boring — "a bore," actually, were her chosen words. She'd been drinking vodka in order to sleep, when Eleanor called after eleven. Charlotte said it with cruel detachment and Alice had cried and her mother had watched her cry, doing no more than sighing a heavy sigh, as if her daughter's tears were additional obstacles on the road to getting some sleep. Alice knew she didn't mean it, and, even at sixteen, she knew that her mother was somehow jealous of Eleanor —

jealous of her looks and her cheerfulness and maybe even her close friendship with Alice, and finally, what it all boiled down to: her youth. Charlotte was jealous of youth, of youthful carefree girls. And perhaps it was no coincidence that Alice took so much care, that she had always appeared a bit older. She could walk alone into the bar near Penn Station and give off not a whiff of innocence. She could order a stiff drink if she felt like it, which always sounded better in theory than in practice because she was, after all, a cautious person who desperately did not want to be so.

When the moon was full and yellow that night and the sky was as dark as it was going to get with a heady scattering of stars, Alice waited. She waited for Gus to walk in the door, she waited for her mother to call, and she waited for her exhausted father to come home. He had a department dinner that evening, which was buying her some time, but Alice knew she had to tell him tonight that she had no idea where Gus was. She was lying on her bed fully dressed, having not so much as removed her shoes, when she found herself waking from a sleep that she hadn't willingly entered. She had no idea what time it was, no idea how long she must have been sleeping, but she realized, after a moment, that what had woken her was a teakettle whistle. In her dream it had been her own scream.

Down the back stairs and into the kitchen; one tiny light was on, and in the muted shadows she came upon Gus, barefoot in jeans, a damp long-sleeved T-shirt, a green down quilted vest. He was watching the teapot whistling and fuming with steam but he was, for some reason, reluctant or unable to remove it from the heat. It was a wailing, unbearable sound. Alice was wide-awake now and short of breath; she swiped it from the blue flame even before switching off the heat. The clock read ten p.m. "What . . ." She trailed off, saying nothing and everything.

He didn't even look at her. His arms drew around her as if clutching a ghost, eager to grasp whatever was there before it faded away. "I'm sorry," he said finally. Alice felt the collapse of the soft down feathers between them, the wet of his sweat-smelling T-shirt. "I just took off," he kept saying, muffled and blurry, into the back of her neck.

Where were you? was what she couldn't say. *Tell me everything you saw, everything*

you did. I'm you but in reverse, can't you see?
He smelled like a ferryboat in the middle
of winter — the briny wind and the waft of
French fries inside the passenger deck.
Alice shook her head, not letting go of him,
her strange big brother.

"I'm sorry," he said again. "You don't
want to know how stupid I've been. Don't
ask me. Okay?"

Contrition she hadn't expected. Tenderness she didn't know quite how to handle,
and serious apologies were baffling. So of
course she nodded. Of course she agreed
to maintain ignorance, which was, in itself,
a certain kind of power and the beginning
of an implicit understanding between
them. She wouldn't say anything to Cady or
to their father. She was his one true keeper.

"I won't disappear on you like that
again," he said. "I won't."

Alice felt grateful, so insidiously grateful,
for a statement she could not even begin to
believe.

6

Riddles, 1985

The phone rang in the middle of the night. When Alice picked up, she heard her mother sobbing and her father saying, "Shh," over and over until the two sounds were nearly syncopated, their voices working within a framework of a composed and trancelike rhythm. Alice held her breath and listened. Her heart sped wildly as she wondered what could possibly come next. "Cherry," her father said. Alice had never heard him ever refer to her mother as anything besides her name. "Cherry, come on," he nearly whispered, "tell me what has happened." Alice didn't know what she was expecting, but it certainly wasn't what came next.

"Nothing," she said through labored breath. "Exactly nothing." She coughed wetly, and tapered herself off in extravagant silence.

"Charlotte," he said, as if he knew

what she was hiding.

"I need to come home right now," she said. "I need to see my children."

Alice thought, Who was going to argue with that?

Charlotte returned from Mexico in time for Thanksgiving — just barely, the night before — with a savage tan and hollow eyes and not one single present. She looked like an actress who'd neglected to put her face on, and she acted almost reserved. Her father and mother sat at the kitchen table late at night. Without realizing they were doing so, Alice and Gus let them alone for a moment, busying themselves with watching water boil for a pot of her new favorite tea. She'd had a carton of *hierbabuena* in her handbag that was tossed on the counter, along with a box of melted chocolate. Charlotte hadn't asked either of them a single question, and her eyes were glazed and unfocused. "I'm sure it's just from being exhausted," Alice whispered to Gus, "from traveling. . . ."

Gus looked over at Charlotte and back to his sister. *Look at her,* he mouthed. Their mother's hair was unwashed, she had a pimple on her chin, sweat stains on her blouse, and she'd lost at least ten pounds from her already slight frame. Spin was sniffing her madly, and she petted him until he settled down. She alternated her gaze from her husband to her surroundings as if the house hadn't quite lived up to her memories, and as if it were her husband and children who had disappeared and reappeared so altered.

"She'll be fine tomorrow," Alice said. Her father was holding her mother's hand in confused consolation. As far as Alice knew (according to her mother's sparse account in the car ride from the airport), Mexico was fantastic, and she had returned for the same reason she'd always returned: because she missed them. And yet here they all were being criminally careful, afraid to upset her mysterious but clearly tenuous balance. It was as if she'd created a household spell that — if broken by curiosity or honesty — would send the walls crashing down. "Mom," Alice said, "would you like milk or no?"

Charlotte looked up at the ceiling. "I need to get to sleep."

"So you don't want any tea?"

"Oh," she said, "no."

"Good to know," said Gus. He turned off the stove and put away the cups.

"Are you sure you're all right?" Alice

asked. Charlotte was looking out the window, past her own reflection at the remains of an early snow.

As their mother nodded, Gus made a face charged with incredulity, a face that was not meant for Charlotte.

Charlotte, having clearly seen his face, walked up to her son. "I suppose you've never been just the slightest bit antisocial?" she said with a dose of recognizable impertinence. Then she shook her head regretfully, maybe even disgustedly, before reaching for his face. She touched her son's stubble, the recent lazy shock of it, with her nail-bitten, sun-spotted hand. "I'm sorry," she said. "Don't hate me," she said.

"You are spewing such crap," Gus said, incredibly. And then he laughed; he laughed too hard. It was because, Alice knew, he wasn't laughing at all. He stepped out of her reach with his shoulders slouching. He laughed into the palm of his hand.

"You poor things," she said to both of them, reaching, as she often did, for their no-longer-children's limbs.

"What are you *talking* about?" he said. "Just stop. Just shut up." Alice looked at her father, whose face betrayed nothing. Gus continued: "We are not poor things. Alice is not a poor thing, and do you really think *I* am? The month *flew by*."

Their father watched Charlotte carefully as if watching an infant, making sure with all of his being that she didn't fall down.

"When you leave," Gus said deliberately, "we are free. We are free to stop entertaining you."

"Gus," Alice said, "no."

"You shut your filthy mouth," her father yelled at Gus. "You —"

"What are you doing?" Gus asked her. "You just show up like this, all dirty and spacey . . . it's pathetic. It's some drama every time. And we — we have to merely wonder at what you *do* every time you go away. What *do* you do to come home looking like this? Why not just tell us?"

Her father growled, "Goddamn it, Gus —"

"Shh," Charlotte said weakly, "no, of course." She looked into each of her children's faces. She retracted her hands and backed away. "I'm sorry," she said, biting her bottom lip, which was chapped and oddly pale. "You're not poor things at all."

"That's not true what he said," Alice stammered. Despite what she envisioned feeling at this kind of brutal, truthful tirade, all she could see was her mother's fear, her weakness. "It's *not*. Mom, *are* you okay?"

"You keep asking me that," Charlotte

157

snapped. "Alan," she started, but then lost the drive she needed in order to finish her thought. She went for the stairs without looking back. Her feet were filthy and barely supported by unfamiliar sandals. Alice imagined her mother picking out the sandals, speaking Spanish in a crowded market or a prim store, haggling over the price. Her other shoes had probably given her blisters from miles and miles of walking. She wasn't a fan of public transportation, and when she did hire a taxi, she consistently overtipped. She wore lipstick. She wore no lipstick. She smoked and drank tequila. She drank bottle upon bottle of mineral water. She sat alone in a borderline café, waiting for someone to talk to. She was lonely. Strange dark men surrounded her. She was nobody's mother.

"You haven't told us anything," Gus said.

"You have no idea," she muttered, "how I missed you."

Alice woke when the sky was an unfiery pink, when the only word that came to mind was *dawn*. It was dawn on Thanksgiving Day, and it had already snowed and thawed, leaving the world a little cleaner. There were still frozen patches along the eaves, tiny corners where the water turned icy, and the snow was caught in the shade. There were no boats on the sound, no trains whistling on the tracks, nothing but a candy haze that would be gone within moments, an unreasonably innocent sky. Alice was hopeful about the day ahead. There was the indisputable relief that came with knowing that her mother was in the house and, to a lesser degree, the state of comfort/anxiety that a holiday can bring, knowing that millions of people across the country are about to embark on the very same questionable traditions.

Alice wanted to cook. There was no shopping done yesterday, and Alice knew that they'd most likely be eating out — perhaps at her father's lab, where the cafeteria prepared holiday meals for the international scientists and students, for those who had nowhere else to be. The thought of going to one of those dinners was so thoroughly depressing that Alice rose from bed and braved the cold floor, scouring the cabinets for anything resembling stuffing or yams, even just one staple with which to work.

What she scavenged: a can of yams, two freeze-dried packets of marshmallows meant to accompany hot chocolate, stale bread, an onion, two carrots, five eggs, two frozen chickens, one can of organic chicken stock, plus an abundance of flour and sugar and butter. It was pathetic or perfect depending on one's attitude, and she thought about the woman she aspired to be, the one who could whip up something nearly spectacular out of a pitiful nothing-much. For was beauty really beauty when presented fully formed? *No!* thought Alice — as she withdrew cookbooks from the backs of drawers, as she found a small tin of plump yellow raisins, a packet of slivered almonds, and look: a perfectly unopened jar of garlic artichoke spread. She, Alice, would create beauty. She would make it happen. And in that hollow where the reserve of her family's unfulfilled wishes festered, where existed a barren and spreading spot of nothingness, there would blossom a minuscule and possibly glorious flower of a meal. She'd slow-roast the chicken with herbs and tea smoke, heat up the yams and top them with tiny marshmallows, use the bread and onion, carrots and almonds, butter and eggs to make a killer stuffing, and try toasting the rest of the stale bread and topping it with the artichoke spread. There'd be sugar cookies; she'd make sure of it, and maybe even a batch of oatmeal raisin, if she could procure some oatmeal. There was plenty for a feast, for a surprise. She'd serve everything on the never-used china with the pattern of lilac butterflies, but only after strewing the dining-room table with crushed shells as if it were a summer wedding. It was not yet seven a.m. She had time. She was sixteen years old and all-powerful; who, if not her, possessed the necessary muscle to create some change?

She'd start small. She'd chop everything first, prepare the ingredients, lay them out in nesting bowls. There was something perfect about the bowls (they were green, a green not found in nature), about setting them out in size order upon a clean wood counter. After consulting a recipe, she began. There was also something deeply satisfying about chopping and chopping with the big sharp blade, until the bulbous carrots and browning onion became lovely and delicate shimmering piles, no less festive than confetti. The perfection Alice felt was a feeble perfection, offset by the recent memory of her unwashed mother, of Charlotte's scrawny limbs, crying out to be fed. Alice was neither scrawny nor unwashed. Alice was not anything, was she? Like her mother said outside the Stanhope, she had no stories to tell. She was as empty as these vacant bowls, and the unexpected mix of rage and pleasure that accompanied this memory disturbed her.

While tearing up the stale bread, she thought of the swans and threw a glance outside, though she knew they were now long gone. It had been roughly a month since the day Alice and Charlotte saw them, and Alice knew that most likely all of the babies had died. The dimpled chickens sweated through their plastic wrap onto the countertop, and suddenly Alice was disgusted and exhausted. Her ambitions felt overblown, her talent for cooking nonexistent. She had never even cleaned a chicken.

Her mother told strangers that Alice had problems. Her mother took money from some local ladies in order to do what? *Cherry,* her father had breathed into the phone, *tell me what has happened.*

There was another world going on. It smelled and sounded different and it was running throughout their world, the Greens' world; it was threaded through this house, and Charlotte had brought it from countries and people far away.

The back door was opening.

When Alice spied a lock of pale hair

escaped from a snug red cap, when she saw the glint of a slim diamond band on an index finger opening the door, she felt an unexpected panic, as if she were about to be caught at something far more illicit than attempting a Thanksgiving meal. Alice held a knife and thought of possibilities. She could ignore Cady and Cady might ignore her. She could shut off the light and hide. Alice dropped the knife on the chopping board, and it made a louder noise than she'd expected. She wiped her hands on her pajama bottoms and breathed.

"Hi, Cady," she said.

"Oh! Shit, Alice, you scared me," she said, shaking, with an angry smile. She whispered, "What are you doing?"

"Cooking?" Alice replied. "Sorry to disturb your path. By all means," she said, gesturing up the back stairs.

"No, no, come on," Cady said, as if she were just sneaking in the back door at dawn to say hello to whoever was up. "What are you making?" she asked, and, still whispering, wandered into the kitchen, shrugging off her coat as she moved.

"Chicken?" Alice said, smiling. "Some stuffing, I guess?"

"Alice, you are so funny."

"What do you mean?"

She shook her head as she picked up the packet of marshmallows. "You're the best," she said, while clearly meaning something else entirely. "I think you'll end up eating out," she said, "no offense."

"I'm not that easily offended."

"Only seems that way, right?"

"That's right."

Cady didn't mean to insult her and Alice knew that; Cady was the kind of person who preferred the easier way — say, if Alice, for instance, could be a shy and possibly worshipful friend. Alice wished, in a way, that she could be that friend and settle in gracefully to a clear supporting role. She'd have fewer lines, less pressure; she'd get a couple of good laughs. But she couldn't quite do it. Instead she felt surges of anger when she sensed she was not on par.

"Want some coffee?" Alice said. She was a person with confidence — a girl who made coffee with a French press, who didn't add milk or sugar.

"Sure," Cady said, sitting down on a stool.

Alice lit the stove and surveyed the kitchen: the paltry ingredients, the knife on the cutting board. Cady's little smile. "What?" Alice asked.

"That's so sweet," she said. Alice followed

her eyes. "You lined up the bowls in size order."

Alice turned up the heat and the gas flame rose.

"Careful," said Cady, and Alice fought not to respond, not to create a challenge where there was none. She *did* line up the bowls in size order. Cady had said nothing untrue.

"So," Alice said, "you're going to Brown next year."

"Well, I have to get in first."

"Oh, you'll get in," Alice said, meaning it. "You'll get in and you'll go."

"You never know," she said, frowning.

"What do you mean?"

"You are truly eager to get rid of me," Cady said, laughing.

"That's not true." And it wasn't, not exactly. She knew she would miss Cady, even if Gus became more available to her, even if Cady's effortlessness wasn't always around as an example of everything that eluded Alice and somehow always would.

"Last summer when I went to visit my aunt in Switzerland, your mother wrote me a postcard and it just said, 'Bon voyage.' I couldn't help but laugh. What else could I do? I don't know what it is with me. Why doesn't anyone actively like me around here?

I mean, I know you don't actively *dis*like me. But . . ."

Alice wanted to sit down but was too surprised. "What's wrong, Cady?"

"Nothing. I'm being stupid. I'm just thinking about how much everything has to change next year. Forget what I said."

"Oh, well, you know . . . change is good. Right?"

"I'm not so sure. I'm pretty happy right here. In your house," she said, smiling, "even though I'm not fully welcome."

"You just love sneaking in the door," Alice said.

"That must be it."

"I don't know why you even bother sneaking."

"What about you?" Cady asked, surprisingly.

"What *about* me?"

"What do you want to do, where do you want to go —"

"I have a whole other year. I'm only a junior."

"Well, yes, I know that, but how about eventually?"

The water began boiling and Alice poured and stirred, waited and pressed down. "I have no idea."

"None?"

"Not really, no. I've never been good at that, you know, picturing what comes next."

"Maybe that's a good thing," she said.

"Maybe not." The sky was no longer pink at all. There was barely a blush to the steely gray. Somewhere, not too far away, a dog was steadily barking.

"You know," Cady said, "you get distracted easily."

"Me?"

"Yeah, you."

"Really?" Alice asked, oddly flattered by Cady's unconcealed annoyance. "I'm sorry. Do you want to help me make cookies?"

"Maybe later on," Cady replied. She lifted her eyebrows to the floor above them.

"Of course," Alice said, trying to look indifferent while pouring two cups of coffee. "Do you want to bring him some coffee?"

"There's not enough."

"Take these," Alice said. "He can have mine."

The stuffing was completed and it sat under plastic wrap in the refrigerator. The chickens continued to ominously defrost. Alice made sugar cookies and ate two, while drinking milk with a touch of brandy just because she could. After sticking another batch in the oven, Alice found that she was wandering with no destination. She was headed for the most impressive and largest room in the house, the living room that no one ever used. A bay window and window seat lined almost one whole wall. The opposing wall hosted a fireplace, with its own cozy assemblage of an overstuffed couch and two chairs. There was a baby grand piano and a tea cart, two shelves worth of photo albums and scrapbooks, boxes and paperweights and pieces of marble. The room was a pastiche of delicate light, in shades of white that were actually blues, browns, celery greens. There were infinitesimal patterns on all of the fabrics. It was a soothing room, its peacefulness interrupted only by the collections: brightly painted warrior masks on shelves and in corners, the ancient carved games from Egypt and Africa that no one knew how to play.

Alice stood looking out the window at the low tide, the hot sun obscured by clouds. She didn't see the figure in the chair closest to her, curled up in a ball. She didn't see Charlotte, nor did Charlotte see her, and for a moment mother and daughter were so similar. They were in need of the same room at the same time. They were part of a larger formal silence. It was not until Alice sat on the couch that she nearly screamed from surprise. "Mom?" she barely had the air to say. Her mother wasn't wearing anything. "Mommy?"

Charlotte wasn't sleeping — her eyes were open — but she also didn't seem quite awake. Her skin was dusted with freckles and — if Alice wasn't imagining it — had come a bit loose from her bones. Her arms were crossed over her small breasts and she looked girlish and older at the same time. "Why, hello, darling," was what she said. She sounded as if she'd been up all night — the center of attention at a party — and the time had simply come to be taken up to bed.

"Aren't you cold?" asked Alice.

"Hardly."

"Do you have a fever, maybe?"

Charlotte shook her head and said throatily, "Can't you sleep?"

"It's — um — morning?" Alice replied. Her mother's hair was still unwashed. She clearly hadn't yet bathed. She smelled musky, but more so, like inhaling deeply from poverty's pillow, the smell relentless and wafting up from an underground windowless room. Alice couldn't help but think of how Charlotte, in a wholly different state, would resent how the built-up filth of her own skin was touching such fine fabric.

"I know it's morning," she said. "I'm not *that* removed, for God's sake." Her eyes were no longer jade but olive green, her skin neither smooth nor flushed. "I just thought it might be nice for you to sleep late. I'm jealous of anyone who can sleep. I keep myself up with nonsense. Someone told me the perfect riddle the other day and not only can I not remember the answer, but I can't get the riddle sorted out either. It's been keeping me awake."

"Don't you take pills for that sometimes, for sleeping?"

"Sure do."

"And . . . ?"

"*And* sometimes they don't really work."

"Maybe you should go back to bed."

Charlotte put her hand out for Alice to help her up. She hadn't shaved her underarms. There was a yellowing bruise on her thigh.

"Maybe you should take a bath," Alice blurted out, having had a distinct whiff of garbage in the sun, and Charlotte grinned as if she'd caught her daughter in a rare moment of truth. "What?" Alice said. "It would help you relax." She helped her mother to her feet and felt how small Charlotte was, how Alice could push her over with hardly any effort at all. "And no, you don't smell so lovely either. That too."

"I remember you used to tell me you loved my smell . . . do you remember?"

Alice nodded, walking her mother toward the staircase, and when the beauty of the living room was gone, Alice felt like a bit of a brute walking with her hand on her mother's skinny upper arm, half convinced that when she took her hand away, a bruise would be imprinted there.

"But you know, it wasn't me — that smell you loved — it was my perfume. *This* is me."

"No, Mom, no, this is everywhere you've been. This is everyone you've spent time talking to, drinking with; this is however long it has been between visits home."

Alice wasn't even fully certain that Charlotte was awake, and she told herself not to be surprised if later in the day her mother denied this entire episode. There was no response to what Alice said, or any kind of explanation. "I'll take it from here," Charlotte said when they reached the top of the stairs, and in the pale

171

morning light Alice watched her mother's bony body fight to stand straight.

"Mommy?" Alice said, taking herself off guard. "Listen to me."

Charlotte placed both hands on the banister and looked at her daughter.

"Why did you take money from those women?" asked Alice, whose arms were folded at her chest.

"What are you talking about," Charlotte said evenly.

"The women, those ladies, the ones you were helping — working for."

"Those women gave me money to buy furniture."

"And did you buy it?"

"No, darling, I did not."

"And why didn't you do what they needed?"

"I will," she says. "That furniture isn't going anywhere."

Alice simply waited.

Charlotte looked at Alice, at her daughter who consistently asked such difficult questions, and said, "All right?"

Why was it that when called upon, a seemingly spaced-out Charlotte could always come up with a clear-cut answer for her selfish behavior? Charlotte's skin was tan and there were, Alice noticed, no tan lines. Where had her mother sunned herself in the nude? What was this naked separate life, the one that Alice could feel slithering through their house, making judgments and humming unfamiliar tunes, even as Alice tried to ask the appropriate question? "What did you need?" was what she finally asked.

Charlotte shrugged, as if there were not, in fact, a choice in the matter of what one could and could not share. "One day . . ." she said, and after clearing up nothing, conveniently began to cry.

Alice waited while she cried, as if perhaps this might clear her head. But Charlotte simply shed fat tears without sound, not coming up with anything more than slim apologies, and then finally ambling away. She was thirty-eight years old, her mother. She was, Alice was somehow aware, essentially still a young woman. Eleanor's mother was fifty-one. But unless Alice was observing with overly dramatic eyes, her mother's month in Mexico had actually aged her. The fine lines near her eyes and mouth were etched more deeply, and her skin . . . there was something deflated about her skin. The suntan afforded her no glow whatsoever. Instead it was as if her mother's lovely coloring had been burned away and replaced with an outer coating, which had taken quite a toll on its texture. While the skin itself looked harder and rougher, it lagged and sagged in places it never had before — her thighs, for instance, her knees.

When Charlotte reached the bedroom door and Alice could be sure her father would take over, Alice returned downstairs. Her mother's manner, as Alice had come to think of it — the particular sway of her narrow hips, the upward tilt of her striking face in search of exhilaration — it had begun to noticeably change when confronted by her husband. When his hand encircled her wrist, her waist, she more often than not demurred to his assertions. Charlotte was adamant about traveling alone; she could fight wickedly, and was, by most anyone's account, beyond independent, but the way she responded to her husband was at times nearly childlike. Alice had begun to notice how her mother welcomed the opportunity to be overwhelmed.

And so, Alice thought, *let him take over. Let him tell her to take a bath, to wash her filthy hair. Let him try to understand just what she says and does.*

The smell of burned sugar was everywhere. The cookies were charred and sinister in their repetitive shape, pointing out the repeated failure in rows of black circles. Alice put one in her mouth and forced herself to take a bite. She knew she'd burn her tongue but she had the urge to taste it anyway. The bitterness was pure, uncut by anything. After drinking water, after drinking juice, she could still taste it. All day long it would not go away.

By midday there was a disagreement about food. Gus and Cady were starving and wanted to eat, but Alice wanted to wait for their mother to wake so they could all eat a real meal together. Her father would do either. He did not feel strongly either way. He decided to embark on a project of insulating the dining-room windows by covering them with Saran Wrap and then blowing them with a hair dryer, which warded off the chill from the bay. He did this every year for as long as Alice could remember and insisted that he found it relaxing. The dryer was on now, and he was deep in concentration.

Gus and Cady were nibblers. They were sneaking a different batch of cookies out from beneath the tinfoil covering. They picked at Alice's hard-won stuffing as if nobody worked to make it, as if food, any food, were an inalienable right for all postcoital teenagers. "Quit it," Alice snapped at Gus, who — standing in front of the open refrigerator — had pinched yet another bit of stuffing from the bowl. "How many times do I have to ask nicely?"

"Sorry," he said, but it was too late. He said it again loudly, as if to be heard over the absurd noise of the blow-dryer, and now they were both laughing, Gus and Cady. Their faces were free of constraint. Two days ago they weren't speaking. Alice had heard Gus tell her over the phone that she was the coldest person he had ever met. After a few seconds, presumably in reaction to her response, he hung up the phone. Now her brother looked dopey with affection; his hand lingered on the top of Cady's jeans, as if he might decide at any moment to pull them down.

"Do you think you can just laugh at me?" Alice heard herself saying to them.

"What?" Cady said, her face unable to be completely smile-free.

"As if you can't hear me," Alice said.

"Alice, there's a goddamn blow-dryer going," her brother said. "It's pretty loud in here. Can't you lighten up?"

"Lighten up?"

"That's right."

"Have you seen our mother, by any chance?"

Gus closed the refrigerator and shot Alice a severe look. "What is it you want me to do? Cower around all depressed like you? Start making home improvements?" He was basically yelling, but with the noise of the hair dryer he could get away with it. "I won't just wait for her moods to include me. And you shouldn't either. If she is going to disappear and reappear on a whim, if she is ignoring whatever depression or . . . or mental problems she may or may not have, then we should play along with her whims. She can't have both."

"But what did she do this time? Don't you want to know?" At this point the hair dryer stopped and Alice's questions hung impotently in the air. "Are you finished with the windows in there?" Alice called into the dining room. "Don't you want to know?" she asked again quietly.

"Nearly," said their father. "I think I'll do the kitchen now — that is, if you don't mind."

"Go crazy," Gus said. "Cady and I are going to take a little ride. I'm assuming Mom will be sleeping for a while."

"I have no idea," their father said, half glancing, as was his way, at Gus. "Alice, would you mind helping me with the Saran Wrap?" And then, "She could sleep straight through to morning, I suppose."

"See you later," Cady said, and Gus gave a loose salute as they headed out the door.

When four o'clock rolled around and Gus and Cady weren't back yet, Charlotte emerged clean in a blue-and-white-striped cotton robe, with her hair wetly combed away from her face. She sat with her daughter at the kitchen table while her husband walked Spin.

"You look much better," Alice said, watching her mother's freckled forehead, her short scrubbed fingers that shook as she lit a cigarette.

"Thanks, love. I always forget how great a hot shower feels. Especially a hot shower at home."

Alice passed her mother the giant clam-shell right in time for the first flick of ash. "How was your flight?" asked Alice point-lessly.

Charlotte nodded as an answer, acknowledging that at this point there was really no appropriate response to such small talk. "I'm, ah, sorry about" — she looked around the kitchen as if to remember where she was — "um, last night? It was

178

last night, right? When you found me in the living room?"

"Pretty much," Alice said. "This morning. It was morning. You were pretty out of it," she said, trying to smile, as if they were no more than two college friends reliving a wild night of debauchery. "You were confused," Alice said, hoping this was true.

Again Charlotte nodded, and in such a way that Alice recognized it as not really a response so much as a new nervous habit.

"Maybe you were dreaming?"

"No," Charlotte said very low, and looked her daughter in the eyes. "No, I remember. I'm sorry."

"I cooked," Alice said. "I cooked us some Thanksgiving food. And there are chickens in the oven — we didn't exactly have turkey available. . . ."

Charlotte nodded and took an imaginary piece of tobacco from her lips. "That's just fantastic," she said. And then, just as before in the grandeur of the living room, her eyes brimmed over with heavy tears, with no warning whatsoever. Her crying seemed purely physical, as if it were no more connected to the inner workings of her heart than sweating or tanning. Her tears rushed on and Charlotte looked down at her own tense hand, gripping the cigarette. When she looked up, Alice saw that she was suffering.

"Don't cry," she said to her mother. She put her hand awkwardly on her shoulder, a deep knot in a spindly branch. "You can tell me what is wrong. It will feel better, really it will."

"Are you mad at me?"

Alice shook her head vigorously.

"I just can't tell . . . I mean I can't remember all the terrible things I've done to you and your brother. I . . ." She was having trouble breathing.

"No, Mommy, shh —"

"I've made awful mistakes." Her eyes were wide and terrifying, her voice rising in panic. "Haven't I? But I never, you know, *abused* you or anything, did I? Oh, please, no, my God, did I?"

"Mom, no, okay, listen, what happened on your trip? What has upset you so much? Because you are scaring me."

Charlotte put the cigarette out in one hard stamp, and she blew her nose into a cloth napkin within reaching distance. "No," she said, "listen, this is no good. This is wrong. I don't want to be this. Let's set the table. Let's eat."

"The table is set. In the dining room. I set it hours ago."

"Great," she said, and coughed. "Good. Let's do Thanksgiving. Did you know I'd forgotten it was Thanksgiving?"

"I can't say that's a huge surprise."

" 'The Pilgrims landed on Plymouth Rock determined they would stay, so with stones and plows and axes, they cleared the land away.' Know what that is?"

Alice shook her head, waiting to see if this transformation would stick, if her mother wouldn't collapse in the next minute, crying all over again.

"Your first-grade Thanksgiving play. I helped you memorize the lines. I helped you make a turkey costume from a bunch of paper bags."

"Really?"

"Yes, *really*."

"Oh, wait, didn't you get in a fight with the teacher?"

"There was that too. I was a little flippant. I added a few lines of my own about the brutal slaughter of Indians and the raping of the land. Your teacher, Miss Jeanie, was not thrilled."

Alice laughed uneasily, remembering being driven home in uncomfortable silence, her mother seeming angry with her more than anyone, angry over having to take part in such a day.

"But it was fun," Charlotte insisted. "You were terrific, so much more mature than any of the other children, so serious. . . ." She rose from the table too quickly and her robe fell open. She wrapped it around herself, drawing herself in, with a sudden burst of modesty. "I'm just going to go get myself together a bit. I'm going to briefly go upstairs again. Then let's eat. We'll have your wonderful meal. Aren't we lucky that you did that."

Alice knew she wouldn't be down for a good while and she sat, waiting for Gus and Cady, waiting for anything to fill the time and the distance growing between her mother and this home. It was as if Charlotte were in a hot-air balloon getting farther and farther away. She had no anchor, no ability to land even if she wanted to. As for her father, Alice didn't have any idea what he was doing, what he knew or what he wanted to know. And as the day grew dark she could not find it in her to move, to call out to her mother to come downstairs again, to even watch television or make a phone call to her one good friend. She watched the Saran Wrapped windows and marveled at the patience and care that went into them. And her father, so exacting, finally found her.

"What are you doing, sitting in the dark?" he said, while turning on the lights.

Alice squinted and said, "Waiting."

"Your mother is asleep again."

Again?" Alice said, making a mental note to search her mother's bags tomorrow. The cabinets wouldn't show anything. The real story would be in side pockets and amidst brassieres, the zipped-in detachable linings. It seemed suddenly clear that her mother went to Mexico, fell in with some bad people with whom she frequented secret clubs and formed addictions. If this was so, it was possible to help her. Addicts went to AA, NA — there was a mandatory assembly at school. A guy named Karl who looked normal enough told a roomful of teenagers how he had, as recently as three years ago, been pimping himself to strangers in Port Authority, stealing from his kids, anything for a fix. Alice would find the evidence to confront her. She felt as though she had been preparing for this sleuthing all along, acquiring the necessary patience and intelligence required to help her mother cope. "You must be kidding," Alice said.

"No, I'm afraid I'm not," he replied, weary, opening the refrigerator and taking out a MacIntosh apple. As she knew he would do, he took the dullest of knives and sliced a piece of apple, then put the rest of the apple back in the fridge. There were at least three already-sliced apples sitting inside the refrigerator, well on their way to rotting. They would sit unfinished until someone finally threw them away. This, as far as Alice could tell, was her father's only vice.

"How do you stand it?" Alice finally said, as he sat down at the head of the table. After years of thinking about saying it, she finally just did. For a moment Alice was afraid she'd angered him by insulting her mother. He was silent for a good long while, but Alice knew not to repeat herself because she was sure he heard.

"Because I love your mother more than all of her nonsense combined," he finally said. "No matter how infuriating her behavior gets — and I admit to you, my own lovely daughter, that it does get beyond infuriating — I still know what it is about her that convinced me I needed to marry her. *Needed* to. I could never put this need in words or . . . or even measure out its value, but it still exists, and just as much and as strongly as the work to which I have dedicated my entire career. Just as my research won't be curing Alzheimer's in my lifetime

— I won't ever see my work come to fruition — it doesn't mean that I'm not fighting for someone's memory every day." Alice paid attention as her father took a bite of the cold, sweet apple, wincing very slightly from the chill hitting his teeth.

"You're patient," Alice said softly. But what she didn't say was that she suspected he was also afraid. She had begun to suspect him of disillusionment, of using this love, so beyond reproach, as a way to avoid his intense disappointment in himself, his failure as a husband who couldn't, for whatever reason, inspire his wife to stick around with any great consistency.

Her father shrugged. "Never thought I'd marry anyone. Did you know that?"

Alice shook her head.

"No, I could never conceive of such a thing. I was already thirty-nine when I met your mother. But you knew that already. . . . You know . . . look, she gave me you. And your brother, of course. I would have never married nor had children with anyone else. Of this I am positive."

"But how do you know? How can you of all people possibly think that?"

"Because I'm so . . . *rational?*" He laughed, finding what Alice considered a strange amount of humor in this perception. "Look,

185

I have, as you might imagine, never believed in the idea of destiny. It always seemed such a preposterous notion, a . . . a child's kind of logic. But with your mother, well . . . I came close to some kind of believing. And now . . ." He looked around him, at the land outside his window, at the bruiser of a November sky and sea, at his daughter sitting before him, basically miserable. "Now I am still on the verge of believing that this is exactly where I belong. Even like this. Is that craziness? You tell me. You're a smart girl."

"You believe we are pawns or something, that there is nothing we can do?"

"No, Alice, on the contrary, and there has been much I have tried to do for her, times I have been far more insistent than you and Gus can ever imagine. You have seen it; you know nothing has improved, and in fact she is more erratic than ever. But I would never, *never* leave your mother. I've never even considered it. It is something beyond infatuation and beyond duty and even love, what I have for her. It is just . . ." Alice waited, but he didn't finish. There were a few moments of puzzled but dazzling ambiguity. Finally he stood and said, "And that is how I stand it, as you put it."

"Okay." Alice nodded, and began to see how her father's sadness was, in a way, what allowed him to come across as a sensitive man. Without his apparent sadness, his reserve would surely dominate and he would seem not so different from the man he might have become had he not met her mother: a man who held up work as the only thing of great value and whose devotion was clearly invested in anything other than people.

"Okay. Now I think you and I should eat some of this meal you've worked so hard to prepare."

"But what about Gus and Cady and Mom?"

"I do not have great faith they'll be joining us."

"And why not?"

"I called over to Cady's house and Gus was there. He said he couldn't handle your mother like this, that he wouldn't be back until tomorrow. He told me to tell you he was sorry."

Alice swallowed hard, thinking of her chickens, her carefully chopped vegetables. "I can't believe this," was all she could muster.

As Alice sat with her hands in her lap, her father began removing her covered bowls from the refrigerator. "I can't help but think that you've gotten the real short end of the stick here. You've always offered more than anyone has known what to do with. You are the best parts of your mother; do you know that?"

"No, no, I'm not. I could never come close. It's Gus who —"

"Don't do that, please," he said almost harshly.

"Do what?"

"Do not put your brother above you. You do this, and I know he's your older brother and I suppose it's natural, but it isn't fair." He stuck the yams and the stuffing in the microwave, the way he used to do for them when they were little. "It isn't fair," he said again.

Alice promised herself to keep together, not to disintegrate into a mess all over the kitchen floor. She'd eat dinner with her father like someone who could handle disappointment. And in silence, she took the overcooked chickens from the oven, put them on colorful plates, and as her father opened a bottle of wine, she set out all of what was her first attempt at cooking a meal all alone. For a passing moment she imagined that she and her father were married, and that she was the consistent, well-behaved wife of his parallel life — the possibility of life in which he didn't believe. She was the woman who didn't leave him to his own well-mannered silence.

"Would you like some wine?" her father asked, seated at the head of the table. Alice faced where her mother would be.

"Yes," Alice said. "Yes, please."

The cabernet sloshed in a deep and delicate glass, and she had such urges — to knock it over, to knock it back, to get so drunk she'd do anything, say anything. She had the urge to learn what she'd say if she were in an altered state, gone hypnotized, and if revealing her hidden self would make the slightest bit of difference in anybody's day. "I'm going to live in a city," Alice blurted out before she knew why. "I can't stand this quiet. I really can't take it. The silence here is making me insane."

But her father merely said, "I can see you living in many places. You have plenty of time." He raised his glass and said, "To your very good health."

"To yours," she said back. "To Mom's," she said softly, as if it were merely an added thought and not in the forefront of her mind. And the dinner was eaten, such a paltry ordinary meal, and night came again. Night came again and Alice had glass after glass of good red wine, which she knew was good only because she'd been told so, and everything was the same but darker, more silent, her father letting her drink more than she ever had before; she drank more than he did, and he was not holding back. The living room was empty of her mother, Gus's bedroom was empty of Gus, and Alice called over to Cady's house, hanging up when a voice said, "DeForrest residence" with a prim Irish lilt. There were dishes bobbing in soapy water, and three empty place settings stayed waiting for her guests.

They'd stay that way — cornflower-blue cloth napkins rolled through painted animals, ivory-handled forks, knives, spoons, and that precious wedding china — all of this luster, this out-of-season optimism would remain for longer than Alice could anticipate. It would stay waiting on this teakwood table, in a way, forever. If *forever* was a word that could be trusted.

It wasn't the smell, as most people assumed, that woke Alice Green at four in the morning. It wasn't the red wine, which later in life would always startle her awake, hours after nearly passing out with exhaustion. It wasn't a nightmare or some nasty

190

premonition. Alice wakes up very relaxed, with the feeling of having had a truly good night's sleep. She feels so awake that she is surprised that it's still dark, and she rises from bed in her T-shirt and underwear and wanders to her tall windows to look outside, which is always what she does upon waking, no matter what the hour. She feels disoriented and always slightly panicked if she can't see beyond her room, as if the outside world could have pulled a fast one and somehow disappeared. And so it is that Alice is up and that she knows she can't be dreaming when she sees the poolhouse breathing smoke, its roof a crown of flames. She knows she isn't dreaming when she hears the monstrous sirens encroaching on the silence — the house's looming silence — stellar, lunar, an absence of sound that she'd earlier despised and would never, no matter how remote the field or how deep down the ocean, be able to hear again. She realizes that Spin is barking in the mudroom, and that his bark might have been what woke her. And there is her father running so fast he's a blue-bathrobed blur, a barefooted lunatic running toward disaster.

Alice isn't dreaming, but Alice is still drunk — she must be — when she finds

191

herself in the downstairs closet, still in her underwear and pulling on the old coyote coat her mother wears to walk Spin, should she ever deign to do so in the cold. Her feet find a pair of flip-flops in the closet and in seconds Alice is outside, doing what seems like a frozen glide toward her father and the raging, burning poolhouse. She can't quite feel her feet. Fire trucks are in the driveway. Big men are racing with ladders across the lawn. They are carrying stretchers and lugging hoses. They are yelling and they use megaphones, and Alice cannot imagine how her mother in her bedroom could possibly be sleeping through this, though Charlotte has slept through a hurricane and a minor earthquake. The tide is high, and in a matter of hours it will look like a respectable attempt at extinguishing the crawling flames. She thinks of all of her mother's papers, the secret boxed-up possessions that Alice had recently begun to suspect of being no more than old movie stubs and random souvenirs. Her mother, so nostalgic, will surely miss what's burning, and no matter how small or seemingly insignificant, its value will grow with hindsight and supply future rainy days with the drama of how her memoirs were destroyed.

Your mother, her father's mouth says, but Alice can't hear above the sound of the flames, the sound of the wind, the sound of the water, the sound of the sirens and men and hoses — she can't hear a thing.

"I know," Alice yells back, "all her things."

Charlotte, he yells, but a rain-slickered man grabs hold of him and steers him toward Alice, who's retreating and choking on smoke. The smoke is everywhere, even when it isn't visible in fat opal billows, the way it looks from afar. Two men hold a fat hose, which sprays water upward in a hard beam reaching the chimney. When her father breaks free from the man, when he punches him hard and with such uncharacteristic sloppiness, Alice takes that punch deep down in her own gut, and — as she feels her brother's and mother's absence — promptly throws up all over the newly ashen grass.

Charlotte, her father continues to yell, and by this time Alice understands.

They never saw her body. Alice remembered the black blanket covering where she was, but Gus had come home to only smoke and absence, the charred expanse of ground and a mumbling father prone to

193

strange articulations regarding, say, the sky. They would move, in their separate ways, through the garrote of seasons without her. They would get through days without answering phones and through nights without much sleeping.

How?

Why? Alice asked Gus.

Gus didn't answer because Gus was gone. He had packed the car and had hugged her with the most absent of all dark eyes. It was suddenly and horribly June.

It was years ago, Alice would whisper in bed, speaking to the windows. *It was a long time ago,* she'd insist, while reaching into darkness. *Really,* she'd say to nothing but shadows, *come here, it's okay.*

Part Two

7

Watch a woman pack in a floor-through apartment, in Brooklyn, midwinter. An old duffel bag sits precariously on a tangle of an unmade bed. The curtain rod beside the bed has broken, and in place of curtains there hangs a tacked-up sheet of printed leaves. There are clothes strewn over the lamp shade and all over the dusty wood floor, but it's immediately apparent, and maybe surprising, that this is an efficient packer. She stuffs socks into shoes, folds T-shirts and underwear with retail precision, even separates clothes by color. Watch how you think you've seen her — this pale blur of a woman packing — you think you might have seen her before. She is tall and not skinny. She is soft and pale, with dark red hair prone to being frizzy, and she wears black boots, a black skirt, and her father's sad smile, inherited pearls and inherited silver; she is the picture of inheritance. She wrote her English dissertation on Anton Chekhov, or at least she might as well have. She is the kind of woman whom other women feel very comfortable calling beautiful, and whose uneven features — most often referred to as "unusual" or "dramatic" — are, in fact, misleading. When she closes her eyes, she is petite and doe-eyed; she is ordinary verging on invisible, but when she faces a mirror she sees a curvy character that attracts men with at least slightly gothic sensibilities, men whose charms — both punitive and extravagant — tend to send her running.

Her name is Alice Green. She hasn't been in her apartment for more than twenty-four hours in the past eight months. The apartment is littered with mail and lists and — like Alice — has the distinct aura of neglect. Her hair (which tends to grow *out* instead of down) hasn't seen scissors in months; her skin is dry, her cuticles ragged, and she's put on an even ten pounds. As Alice packs, she thinks of her mother, whom she never once saw packing even after Alice began to identify all the signs of imminent departure. It is impossible for Alice to simply stuff clothes in a suitcase without invoking the spirit of those hallowed exits and entrances, without having them rise up again and again like the banging of a door puncturing dreams through a windy restless night. Charlotte Green has been dead for fifteen years and it still feels as if packing is something that belongs to her, to the stash of ordinary acts made meaningful because they were carried out away from Alice. Here is a daughter who has not successfully stopped wanting more from her mother, even if — or especially because — her mother is no longer living.

She's packing to see August.

Here is the beginning of a story, a beginning even she can recognize: now it's Alice packing and only Alice, and she's going to see her brother with no clear understanding of why. Here is the middle of a story — the beginning, middle, and end — a move made from fear as much as from freedom. And Alice — she can feel it, even though she is quite lethargic — can feel herself lurching forward and pitching herself through the gray and slushy afternoon. She has always had the vaguely morbid nature of one who can recognize disaster and even name it, but somehow cannot avoid it.

The house was too big. Whatever room Alice found herself in, whatever task she undertook on the long bone-chilling trajectory from the kitchen or study to her father's bedroom, Alice couldn't help but at least once take note of the house's absurdly hollow nature. The collections still maintained authority; no one had moved the Chinese shoe trees or Turkish prayer rugs, embroidered pillows from forgotten Irish counties, Balinese puppets, Deruta pottery, or African dung sculptures. Yet without Charlotte's homecomings, the exotic objects failed to become animated. They sat in corners and on shelves like the molted skins of snakes — now merely colorful evidence of a former life. These carefully chosen objects — having once been packed so delicately between layers of Charlotte's undergarments, or carried on daylong flights along with her bare essentials — were shells of their former selves.

Her family had never grown into all of the rooms, and left to his own devices her father had stopped trying to make the space anything other than what it was — a drafty renovated barn with rooms and additions added on (quite seamlessly, colonial style) up until the 1940s. He'd seemed to embrace the morose nature of his solitude, never (as far as Alice knew, anyway) entertaining any guests besides an occasional exceptional scientific young mind, along with Charlotte's ghost. He was the lonely old genius with the beautiful dead wife. The floors were sagging, the salt air had corroded the window frames, and the roof was caving in. To put it another way: There was no shortage of knocks on the door each Halloween.

As Alice carried a photo from her father's study to his bedroom, she paused at the front hall table where there was still a bowl of mini chocolates that she'd brought out only weeks ago for the eager and morbid neighbor children. She had actually started coming home for Halloween night a few years ago, when she was still living in the city teaching and researching, when she was very much on track and — more important — when such a track seemed like it actually existed and mattered. To make the trip midweek for only one night had seemed like an ordeal back then, but she hadn't liked the idea of her father having to open the door all night long, answering questions from young suburban Wiccans regarding rumors of the house being haunted.

This year, living at home as she was, she'd almost forgotten about the holiday, and although she'd managed to scrounge up some candy, after eight o'clock she stopped answering the door altogether. There was a Goebbels special on the History Channel that she'd watched with her father from the vantage of his bed in a silence punctuated only by the faint sounds of the bronze door knocker knocking and knocking away.

It was especially difficult to care for her father in this enormous and drafty house.

The house was 187 years old. Alice's father had bought it for less than a quarter of its value in the early 1970s from his college mentor — a badly behaved and wealthy cripple by the name of Dr. Norton Flowers. Dr. Flowers was the one dying then, but he'd had no devoted daughter, he'd had no children at all. He loved Alice's father nearly as much as he loved his decrepit house, and he didn't care about taking more money to the grave. All of which was practically unheard-of and very exciting, except that her parents had felt as if they really had no choice in the matter of whether to stay. It was too stunning to sell (even if they *hadn't* promised Dr. Flowers they'd "make a go of it" there), it cost a small fortune to heat, and it was often talked about in the terms one employed when discussing an elderly relative; it was as if Dr. Flowers were living on the third floor, a proud and necessary burden, watching their lives unfold.

The house had, in no uncertain terms, fallen into disrepair. The Historical Society (the Hysterical Society, as her father referred to them) had been fining him for years and pressuring the town to enforce its ordinances on account of the barely maintained roof. There was usually someone who took pity on their family, who referenced poor Charlotte at a meeting, or listed the stellar accomplishments of Dr. Alan Green's career. He was a respected, if puzzling member of the community and a handsome widower, and as such he usually slid by without suffering full rancor, year after year. Even as the area went through the roof on the real-estate market, her father remained steadfast. He quoted his old mentor who sold him the house, his favorite example of a "man of character," and became a kind of mascot for the small band of property owners who, as their area became less of a port town and more of an upscale suburb, shared a renegade sensibility. He was the old and odd exception to almost every rule. *But not dying,* Alice had told him. *You'll die if you don't look after yourself, which you have to admit is much easier in a small and stable environment.*

And because her father insisted on staying, and because his bedroom was far from the kitchen (he refused to move his bed downstairs), once he was confined to his bed, which had been only a matter of time, eating became impossible without someone there to feed him. It was colon cancer that was pulling out all the stops, that — after years of high blood pressure, a low white-blood-cell count, and eventually the onset of diabetes — had finally come to get serious. He'd been in poor health essentially since Charlotte had died, and had made a shocking transformation from an exceedingly youthful fifty-eight to an ancient seventy-three. At some point within the last five years he'd begun to eschew town and everyone in it, insisting with shocking intensity how he'd always thought, all along, that the neighbors — the same neighbors who'd brought him food and conversation for years after Charlotte died — were anti-Semitic.

For a while she'd tried to hire someone to come in and care for him so she could live in her apartment at least part-time, but there was so much running back and forth between the bedroom and kitchen, the kitchen and the cellar (to adjust the hot-water heater, to bang the gas tank), that it was tough to ask anyone else to do it, even for a decent salary. The brokers called weekly, and the brokers made such promises, promises that verged on threats when her father categorically refused to sell. *Believe me,* he said once to Alice when she begged him to take an offer, *I, of all people, know how little I can control anything, but I will do what I can; I simply want to die here.*

And so, after he'd refused the last round of chemo, Alice — having just dragged her feet through the end of her twenties — quit sleeping with a boy eight years her junior, "took a break" from completing her dissertation, and came home. She embarked on bathing her father, on crossing into the underworld of washing soiled sheets and pillowcases and carpets, of mashing tablets into chocolate ice cream and listening to doctors' instructions. She decided whether or not to give him all the whiskey he asked for, and the decision always seemed to be yes. They watched CNN and CNBC and reruns on cable. She heard about his postdoctorate years, an English rose called Polly who liked walking in the Chilterns, the remarkable adventures of old Dr. Flowers, who, before selling him the house, had inspired his years in Paris.

And now it was November.

The last of the warmth had been squeezed out of the landscape, and no matter how extravagant Alice was with the heat, a chill was ever present. It seemed her father held on through his favorite season, when the leaves fell orange into blue water and the summer people all went home.

He'd recently become interested in objects. Two days ago she'd spent an entire afternoon in search of a few missing items — a tennis racket, a painting — which he'd decided with touching insistence that he needed her to have. And her most recent mission, what Alice held in her dry pale hand: a photograph of this house's original owners, a photograph from his study that he'd decided in a panic that he needed to see immediately. The photograph had always lived on the same top shelf in his study, where it was poorly lit and rarely taken down for a closer look. Dr. Flowers had been given the photograph by an elderly neighbor when *he'd* first moved in. The elderly neighbor had become affianced in the house during a Christmas party in the early 1920s and had somehow ended up with the portrait, which depicted a five-member family wearing attire that called to mind the phrase *landed gentry:* the mother and young daughter wore starched white shirts; the father and boys donned suspenders. A black, jowly dog sat obediently facing the camera. *Mr. and Mrs. Frank Storrs and family* was carefully printed on the back of the photograph (now hidden by the frame), *1825*. Alice was surprised that it was this photograph and not an obscure one of Charlotte that her father wanted to see. His bedside table was full of Charlotte: at the beach, in moody profile, with Alice in her arms, with Gus going clamming in the bay. He liked to analyze the photographs, commenting on what made them particularly good.

Alice took the last of the stairs two at a time (she was always in a hurried state whenever she approached his room), and then, having not broken the habit, leaned on the wooden ball atop the banister, which, as the wood had begun to seriously rot, came right up and off in her hand. She rescrewed it precariously, as she'd done for weeks now, and joined her father on his bed once more.

"You found it," he managed, his voice hoarse and low.

"Of course," Alice said, handing him his reading glasses. "No one moved it," she said, forcing a smile. "It was right where you left it in your study. Why did you want to see it so badly?" she asked, smoothing out on his forehead the still-thick unwashed hair.

He didn't answer; he only watched the faces in the picture as if at any moment they might impart some secret wisdom.

"It's amazing to think they all lived here," Alice said, trying to encourage him to speak. Lately he'd fallen into silence for hours at a time. Even his pleas for morphine were muted.

"I've always hated old photographs," he said.

"Why?"

"You're familiar with those old formal photographs of banquets you see sometimes? The ones with a sort of fish-eye lens and everyone in the room is facing the camera?"

Alice nodded.

"I used to detest those especially. I was only able to think of how all those people, so . . . earnest in their black tie and their gowns, so somber and even pretentious for the camera — *they're all dead.* That's what I always used to think about this photograph too. They're all dead. I never thought much more than that."

"And what do you think now?"

"Oh" — he smiled — "oh, well, now I think — they *lived*." And after putting forth a little laugh, he began to cough. Alice propped him more comfortably on his pillows. "Your mother always thought like that. These people in the photograph, they were more alive to her than half our neighbors. She formed stories about each of these people based on the way they looked in the picture. Oh, what was it?" He looked at the picture more carefully, pointing to each person. "I think this brother was jealous of that brother because he was a better athlete or whatnot, while the brother who was athletically superior often came to blows with the father. I can't remember what she made of the mother and daughter. They were no doubt the most interesting ones."

"Certainly the mother," said Alice.

Her father dismissed this with a slight grimace and a shake of his head. "Your mother saw everyone as being alive but in different degrees. I never really understood that."

"Yeah, well, she was a mythmaker," Alice said.

It had been a week of rain — days all like this one where morning, afternoon, and evening melted into one another without distinction. It occurred to Alice that she couldn't be sure what day it was. Eleanor had come on Tuesday, she knew, wearing a bright pink boat-neck sweater and carrying a huge bouquet of gerber daisies that now sat on what remained Charlotte's side of the bed, already dropping petals. Eleanor was still her best friend, the now pixie-chic gamine who was a successful producer for children's television. When in the midst of New York name-droppers, she liked to mention, with a straight poker face, how she had a close personal relationship with Big Bird. So Tuesday had been Eleanor. Was today Thursday? Saturday? With his thin long fingers gripping the Storrs family photograph, her father turned to Alice as if he'd just remembered something important, but when she met his eyes he only returned his gaze to the strangers in the picture sitting on his front porch.

"I need you to promise me something," he said quietly.

Alice swallowed hard.

"No reception here. Not here."

"What do you mean?"

"After," he said. And when Alice refused to understand: "The funeral."

"Fine."

"Fine. Now I need you to get something for me."

"Of course," said Alice, her voice hoarse and unfamiliar. "Anything."

"The attic," he said. His fingers were shaking. His skin was yellowish green. "Two boxes — there are two boxes on the landing. One for you and one for your brother."

Alice climbed the familiar stairs — noting how the temperature significantly dropped and how the wind could be heard whistling through the treetops, rattling the old storm windows. She'd been making trips up here more and more frequently and was surprised, as her eyes lit upon them, that she hadn't noticed the boxes before. Two plain brown packing crates sat side by side: *Alice,* one read, in her father's purposeful hand; *August,* read the other. They were both lined and filled with newspaper, and as Alice lifted hers she could see smaller boxes inside — stamped tin, velvet, carved balsa wood — containing, she knew, her mother's clip-on pearls and costume beads — Charlotte's personal treasures that had been too sad to previously consider. *The good stuff,* as Charlotte had called it, was housed in a bank safe and had been formally passed along to

Alice, but the daily baubles — Charlotte's colored glass, her Lucite bangles — they had seemed *too much* a part of her, and over all these years they'd remained in their little boxes that Alice had so loved. There was more, but she couldn't yet let herself look. She picked up Gus's box and, placing it atop her own, made her way back down the stairs. His box didn't weigh much, and when she peered inside, she was surprised to see nothing more than a framed picture of Charlotte and Gus clearly taken right before she died, and a manila envelope marked *For August* in her father's hand.

"I'm back," she said, and Alice tried to smile, tried not to allow her face to betray how, on entering this room, his weakened appearance still shocked her.

How he sighed then, as she set the boxes down, a wheezy, stilted sigh. "Thank you."

Alice nodded, looking at how carefully he'd assembled these boxes, how their labels were taped neatly with packing tape. "When did you do this?"

He shook his head and mumbled.

She realized they were both looking at Gus's box. Alice was fingering the edges of the newspaper while glimpsing the unfamiliar photograph of Charlotte and Gus. Charlotte was laughing and Gus was not; his arm was firmly wrapped around her shoulders. Their father must have found this picture — maybe even on an undeveloped roll of film — and had it framed especially for him. This gift was breaking her heart. The very nature of such thoughtfulness was painful in light of her brother's long absence.

"Gus is coming Sunday," she said suddenly.

After he was quiet so long she thought he'd drifted off, he muttered, "Is that right?" as if he knew she was lying.

"He is."

"Baby," he said carefully, "I am past pretending."

Oh, no, you're not, Alice thought, glancing at the photograph of a smiling, happy Charlotte, a fun-loving-mother Charlotte, a Charlotte-as-pretty-wife. But what she said instead was, "He called earlier when you were asleep. I didn't want to wake you. He said he was coming tomorrow." There was no need, she thought, to start being truthful now.

He shrugged. "He has his reasons, I'm sure," he said, as he'd said so many times before, regarding Gus's distance from this house, their lives.

"You and your reasons," Alice said, but she said it too softly for him to hear. Her father, as opposed to being made angry or distraught by Gus's absence, seemed nearly cooperative about maintaining the distance. He was always the one who made excuses for why August didn't follow through on his plans to come home. When the plans themselves stopped, Alice had finally decided that how her father reacted was actually quite contrary to being understanding. In truth, he seemed ambivalent.

It's as though you can't handle one more absent person, Alice had said to her father last year. But he'd fixed her with such a meaningful stare, a look that said, *We'll go no further.* Now their discussions of August were no more extensive than what had just transpired. In the face of such dramatic inaction (or *action,* depending on how she chose to view Gus's behavior on any given day) what was there, really, to say?

As it happened, Gus hadn't been home since he'd eked out a graduation from high school and followed Cady DeForrest to Providence. They lived together there in a house cool beyond reproach, a blue Victorian with three housemates and a turret where they slept on a king-size mattress taking up the entire floor. When Alice visited, she had been instantly taken with how many people were always coming by. Gus wasn't enrolled in college and this didn't seem to bother him. On the contrary, he was held up (dangerously high, thought Alice) as a paean to the free spirit — surfing the freezing waves of Rhode Island beaches, learning to cook as a sous-chef, reading *Don Quixote* and Tolstoy, a hodgepodge of social and historical texts, plus some science for good measure. His friends and Cady were reading basically the same material and paying (or having their parents pay) thousands of dollars for a designer degree, was his argument in a less than gracious mood. When Cady broke up with him, when the inevitable finally happened, he left for Indonesia, *naturally,* where from what Alice could gather he surfed big waves, became dangerously promiscuous, and came to believe in animism before finally moving again. Much traveling — the privilege and curse of this shrinking world — ensued, before Gus signed a lease in Santa Cruz. When Cady came to Stanford for architecture school when they were twenty-three, they immediately started up again, showing up at each other's apartments on late Friday nights, turned on and even moved by the increasing unlikelihood of their future as a couple. Since then, for the past ten years, Alice heard about Cady only intermittently. There'd been one other "real" girlfriend named Liz, a social worker in Berkeley who, not twenty minutes after meeting Alice for the first time at a café, asked her (as Alice took a bite of her lunch) if eating a turkey sandwich didn't make her feel generally toxic. There'd been restaurant jobs, construction jobs, and most recently a brief stint as a marijuana farmer on a massive operation up in Humboldt County, which ended when the peaceful hippie landowners pulled out heavy artillery and told Gus that he'd best learn to operate it, because there was no way of knowing when *the shit would go down.*

August was thirty-three and hadn't come home since high school. He'd written letters to their father — long, ponderous letters in his always surprisingly beautiful handwriting, and at first he'd made promise after promise to visit, but never followed through. It was easy enough for the first couple of years when Alice and their father visited Providence, California, even Bali once — he gave them good reasons to travel, and they all pretended as if there weren't any particular reason why

Gus never came to them. But since her father had fallen seriously ill, it was conspicuous and embarrassing that Gus wasn't pacing the same warped wood floors as Alice. He insisted, with his absence, on drawing even more attention to their past — as if, Alice couldn't help but feel, he was staking some claim on sorrow, maintaining distance to prove the point of just how tormented he was. But then again, he *was* tormented. Alice could tell he was angry with himself for not having come home sooner, but the longer he'd waited to come back, the worse his fears had become. He never came right out and said so, but Alice knew that it was elaborate fear that had kept him away, and she knew he had waited *so* long now that his homecoming had, at least in his mind, become a thing of mythic difficulty.

She had done just the opposite.

Alice had gone to college in Manhattan, just a train ride away. She'd gone to graduate school there too. She could have left, at least for a while. Her father had, in fact, given her every encouragement to apply to schools as far away as Scotland. She stayed close by with the same kind of fervor that Gus had stayed away.

Alice now tried to relate to Gus and his

fears, tried to remember how he'd felt in her arms when he came home that morning to Charlotte dead, and how he couldn't breathe as he tried to say, *I can smell her hair.* She tried to relate, she tried to forgive, but instead found herself, not five minutes after she could be certain her father had dozed off with that old photograph still in his hands, going a few rooms away and dialing her brother's number.

Earlier in the year, when Gus had promised regularly to "look into the details" about coming home, most of their nightly conversation time had been monopolized by Gus keeping Alice abreast of what had to have been the most fruitless job search in history. Alice hadn't done too much graphic detailing of their father's demise, as she'd been truly concerned with the magnitude of his debts and his ever-present lack of a job.

But after this past week of her increasingly adamant nightly requests, and after he still wasn't here, Alice cut short any notion of pleasantries. "You've gone to Fiji and Bali and Costa Rica at a moment's fucking notice," she heard herself saying, tears blurring her vision and snot blocking up her nose, "but you can't get it together, you cannot get yourself *motivated* to fly home and deal with your father?" She was yelling and it felt exactly right. She hadn't yelled like that at anyone in a long while. She yelled only at her family; she was invariably polite to doctors and nurses and home-care attendants, with all kinds of strangers and service professionals no matter how rude they were. After hanging up, she gave Gus twenty minutes, and when she called back he had done what she'd requested. He was coming in on the red-eye. She slept in her father's room that night.

At four a.m. her father called out her mother's name while Alice was awake and staring at the ceiling, waiting for the sun to rise. "Oh," he cried, in a voice she'd never heard. His face was painted in pieces of moonlight shining in through the windows, the effect of which was harsh and haunting. "Oh, goddamn it," he whimpered, and crying, crying, "you, you —"

"Shh, Daddy, I'm right here."

He looked at her plaintively, with the eyes of someone who knew the meaning of *finished*, could feel the velvet curtains closing on his face.

"You're dreaming," she told him, as if that were a comfort, as if dreams were inferior or held any less meaning than the stasis his life had become.

"Please stop," he said so quietly and wetly, she almost asked him to repeat himself. "Please . . ."

"What is it?" she said pointlessly. "What can I do?"

"Charlotte," he whispered, his tone suddenly stern, "where are you going?"

Alice was unsure of what to say. Cancer talked; everyone knew this. Cancer had a reality and a language all its own. And then the face of recognition emerged, the look of simultaneous panic and relief, as he re-entered the room with his disturbed soul in tow, accepting the weak and faulty body in the bed as his own.

"I loved her," he said. "I loved her."

"Of course you did."

And her father fixed Alice with eyes that belied his drugged, slackened face. They were eyes experienced in all types of half-truths and justifications and every manner of deception. "She needed me," he said.

By eight a.m. it was over; his surrender was quiet and effortless. Spin the yellow Lab had put up more of a fight, and he was 112. Alice watched her father's last rounds of breathing and thought of how her father had held Spin in his arms and graciously injected him in the paw, ridding him of such suffering. The vet had been unreachable on a holiday weekend, and her father had driven to the lab to get the necessary poison, leaving Alice briefly alone to watch Spin breathe in and out just like her father breathed then. Alice had watched the rise and fall of her father's blue pajama top, the loosened skin at his sallow neck. As the world of her father rose and fell, she saw nothing else; there was no weather, no light. She couldn't have said whether the sky was flooded with sun or pouring rain when he stopped breathing. She couldn't have said whether she was hot or cold when she drew the covers up around her father and herself, cocooning them together. She sat up on the bed, in the space he left next to his body, even after nearly fifteen years. She looked from her father to the insistence of a new day out the window, and she tried to forgive Gus for not coming earlier, for being stuck in mundane Long Island traffic not far from LaGuardia airport, the moment their father let them go.

As she remained beside him, nearly as silent and frozen as he was, there was a phantom car in the driveway one too many times, so that when Gus and his taxi finally arrived Alice wasn't surprised. She rose for the first time and went to the window. She was prepared for Gus, for his sullen and potentially defensive behavior. She was prepared for him to lose it completely, to even take it out on her. What she wasn't prepared for was that he'd *brought* someone.

Staring out the window, Alice saw Cady DeForrest. There was Cady looking offensively appropriate after all these years, her hair pulled back — a study in carelessness just short of austere. They let themselves in and called out through the house. Alice couldn't find the voice to answer, and it seemed like minutes before they finally came upstairs.

"How could you bring someone?" Alice yelled without thinking. She hadn't realized she'd been crying until she tried to speak. "He's already gone," she said; and then more softly, "He's dead."

"Alice —" Cady said, coming toward her.

She didn't want Cady's frosty hug, her practiced line of condolence. She hadn't exactly been coming around much lately. "This is a family situation," she appealed to Gus.

But Gus was kneeling by the bedside with open eyes. He looked more curious than overwrought, as if he didn't quite believe it.

"August," Alice nearly shouted, anxious as she was, thrown beyond any kind of reason at Cady's being present for this moment.

But he only looked up at his sister, offering no response but confusion.

"Do you hear me?" Instead of losing steam, Alice gained momentum.

Cady said, "Alice, listen —"

"My father is lying here dead," she nearly screamed. "Do you mind leaving the room?"

"Have you called anyone?" asked Cady.

Alice shook her head.

"I'll do it," she said, and Alice didn't argue as she watched Cady head for the door.

But when Alice looked down at Gus, who was kneeling at the bedside with closed eyes, she nearly lost her breath. Gus looked as if he was begging for forgiveness, begging for something so much larger than he could ever name. "I'll leave you alone with him," she whispered, before slipping out the door. And as she moved no farther than the dark hallway, she stood consciously breathing, smelling cedar and a puzzling trace of what she could only imagine was Cady's favorite blackberry soap, the same after more than a decade. Alice ran her finger against the splintering molding on the wall, over and over until her finger was raw. The increasingly palpable gap between Gus and her father — she had always told herself there was nothing too unusual about it; sons and fathers, fathers and sons, pairs of them had been reinventing this strained male distance for years.

When Alice reentered the bedroom, August remained kneeling, not having seemed to register her presence. But eventually he stood up, wiped away tears with the hem of his sweater, and said, "Cady and I were married."

"Excuse me?"

"We got married," he said, and — still managing not to smile, not to give away what surely must have been a poor excuse for a badly timed joke — he nodded that yes, it was true.

"She married you?"

"What is that supposed to mean? We married each other. Last week, in Vegas," he said, and finally gave up a grin. "And it was great."

Cady knocked before opening the door. "They're coming now," she said. "They'll be here any minute."

He was buried next to Charlotte on a

beautiful day, a day too beautiful for Alice. She wanted rain clouds, gusts of wind, water seeping through her shoes. A rabbi spoke at length, perhaps buoyed by the cloudless sky. After the list of scientific accolades, after the much-deserved praise, the rabbi spoke about questioning God, how the living had every right to rage. His passion was admirable but it made Alice tired. The sun was so bright she could barely keep her eyes open.

She was grateful to her father for his unorthodox request that the mourners not repair to their home, and Alice was beginning to think he'd made that request entirely for her sake. She knew that the tradition existed to bring the grieving family some comfort, but, for one thing, there weren't enough people, and more than a few of them looked as if they hadn't left a laboratory in years. She didn't want strangers. She knew what to do. After everyone had thrown a shovel of dirt over his terrible coffin and had made their way toward the cars, Alice thanked the rabbi, letting his kind words pour through her. She thanked an old man, a man who was honestly too old to be walking. She let three women hug and kiss her; she was grateful for their softness, for their pliant, powdery skin. Then she remained — in her uncomfortable pumps, in the hard autumn earth — and lost track of time. She found that the air was perfectly still and that she was simply too tired to stand.

With her legs crossed awkwardly beneath her flimsy crepe dress, and her coat splayed on each side, she was sitting on the ground, growing very cold but feeling closer to her father, to the fresh wound in the soil. When she felt a hand on her shoulder she knew he'd been there all along, that he hadn't moved either. "August," she said, without looking. She registered bark, spearmint breath mints, the feral darkness of his hair. When she finally looked up, he was all that she saw; he'd successfully blocked out the sun.

"So strange," he said, sitting down beside her.

Alice nodded and noticed that Cady was leaning against a tree — out of earshot in her slim black ensemble — patiently waiting. Alice was briefly overcome by this lovely display of etiquette. Cady would know what to say to the brainy colleagues, the frightened neighbors — this assorted well-meaning assembly.

"Everything looks the same," Alice said. Then she started to cry.

He inched closer to her. "It's okay."

"I feel like everything's over." Her mother's headstone looked almost mocking in its austerity. They'd brought white lilies for her grave, and the other mourners had also brought flowers for Charlotte — roses, peonies, and a smattering of carnations at which, Alice couldn't help thinking, Charlotte would have rolled her eyes. "Is everything just . . . over for us?"

He shook his head calmly. He did not ask what she meant.

"It isn't?"

"No," he said. "Everything's not over. Nothing is over, I promise."

The sky was too blue, the ground was too cold, and it seemed that nothing would ever feel quite right again. There were bells in the distance — someone else's wedding, someone else's prayers — a trace of leather in the air.

"Come on, Alice, I'm here."

She looked at him then, and for at least one moment her eyes were as sharp as their mother's headstone, as raw as her father's grave. "Finally," she said, "you are."

After the funeral Cady didn't stay long. Her aunt had died years ago; she had no one left to visit and she had to be back for work, so it was three days of her making phone calls in the study, and providing the days with a kind of controlling — albeit appealing — structure. She made eggs. She made waffles. She fixed strong cocktails after five, served with a little something, if only a hunk of cheddar cheese and a small silver knife. She didn't make a fuss over these elegant ministrations, and Alice couldn't help but again admire her efforts.

"Thanks," Alice told her for the tenth time that third afternoon, as Cady handed Alice a dirty martini after placing a bowl of Spanish olives at the center of the scratched and lopsided bay window table.

"It's nothing," Cady said, sipping her own neat glass of whiskey. "I'm just a fool for cocktail hour, the whole ritual; it's in my blood, I guess." Gus was under the table, sticking a folded-up piece of paper underneath the wobbly table leg. Cady looked down at him with a wan and complicated smile before addressing Alice again. "So your father really took shabby-chic to the next level, huh?"

Alice was so used to how the wallpaper was halfway peeled off right there by the kitchen phone, how the wooden floors, which were slanty to begin with, were now giving way in earnest. She was used to the dust in the Oriental rugs, to the moldy saltwater evening smell emanating from upholstered furniture. Alice was so accustomed to the empty hooks and hoops of faded color left where pictures had fallen due to the warping of walls, that taking it all in through Cady's eyes, she became nearly shocked. And it wasn't only decay that marked demise. You had to look a bit harder to see the additions, but they too were there. In the cupboards there were sippy cups, the kind for children and the sick, and there were no children here. In the bathrooms there were safety bars installed on either side of the toilet — the one bit of home construction their father had finally approved.

It was difficult to remember how everything had looked the last time the three of them had sat there.

"So you're going back to work?" Alice blurted — more statement than question.

"Someone has to, right?"

"Poor Cady," Gus said, now standing in front of the refrigerator and looking inside, as if waiting for a craving to declare itself. "I keep telling her to take some time off, come away with me. . . ."

Alice snapped, "She can't exactly take

229

time off whenever she feels like it. Cady has actual responsibilities." Why Alice was suddenly Cady's defender was beyond her, as Cady had never returned Alice's two phone calls, never sent her so much as a postcard after she and Gus had originally split. "Am I right? Cady?"

Cady just laughed. "Look, I like my job," she said, in a tone that suggested that Gus had implied otherwise many times before.

"You're always complaining about the people."

"Yeah, well, my fellow workers tend to take their choice of chunky or wire-thin eyeglasses so seriously that matters of design begin to feel like religious fanaticism, but I do like it."

"You just like the free meal," Gus teased, coming to sit beside Cady with a bag of mini carrots in hand. "In her office," he explained, "lunch is ordered in on the company dime. If you drop in around one there is sushi all over the place."

"It definitely boosts morale," Cady said, opening her mouth.

Gus left her hanging for a second or so before feeding her a carrot. "You have all that fresh fish to consider," he said, his voice softening, his lips by her ear.

"Exactly," she said, before crunching down, hard.

With Cady gone, it was meetings that measured the days. There were meetings with their father's lawyer and accountant, and everyone cooperated to get it all done quickly. The vocabulary was simple and orderly and it bore no resemblance to the mess they were left to sort through. The real-estate agent called, offered her condolences, and in the same breath let Alice know that there were interested parties waiting. For three days people arrived in four-wheel-drive vehicles and didn't bother to conceal their surprise when they saw the falling shingles, the sunken dank floors. Alice hated all of them and behaved with curious charm.

Each night after they'd all gone, Alice and Gus ate pizza and drank beer, and Gus swore he really was married. "We had a really good day," was his explanation as to how it had happened. "Hadn't seen each other in about six months. She was dating a jerk named *Albert*. French. So one Saturday morning she shows up at my place, all flushed in the face and full of plans — you know how she can get — and the day was so good I won't even try to describe it, and the next morning I felt the same way. I wasn't depressed the way I usually feel after spending a good day with her, and so I asked if she'd like to go to Las Vegas. A lot of people talk about that kind of spontaneity but we really did it. I can't help being proud."

"Do you regret it?"

He didn't seem surprised by the question. "Cady is an architect. She works in one of the best firms in the city. She is probably bored with my life, my routines, how everything revolves around the weather and swells and throwing myself around just like I did when I was sixteen. I don't even think she was ever all that impressed with my daredevil shit anyway. That wasn't the draw for her. So . . . it's clear that I know nothing and could not care less about matters of architectural design, and yet I consider myself somewhat of an expert on being interested in Cady. To be honest, I can't imagine ending up with anyone else."

"I'm surprised that you see yourself *ending up* at all."

"You know what I mean."

"Where are you going to, you know, live? Are you going to move to the city?"

"I love her, Alice," he said soberly.

"Good," Alice replied. "Because you promised to spend the rest of your life with her."

"Yes, I did."

"Without even telling me."

"It just happened that way. Would you have said, 'Yeah, go to Las Vegas; that's a great idea'? Of course not. You don't even like her."

"Cady? Come on, I like Cady. She is inherently likable. This isn't about if I like Cady. You married someone who . . . You couldn't even come home all this time, to this house, to us. She's —"

"I know. Move on, right? Move way on —"

"Forget it. May you have many happy years together."

"Could you lighten up on the sarcasm please?"

"I'm not being sarcastic; I just can't get over it. Are you sure she's not pregnant?"

"I told you before — I am sure. This is about the two of us."

"So where are you going to live?"

"Not sure. It's one of the many things we haven't really worked out."

"I see." Alice nodded. "So now you're going to tell me you really do have to head back. You need to sort out living with Cady, starting this life together, et cetera."

"I'm leaving you to deal with all of this. Which you knew I'd do. You knew it. All of these things she brought back from who the fuck knows where. All of the photographs, all of it. And I'm sorry."

"And I'm sorry you never came home until now."

He nodded. "Couldn't," he said, his voice cracking. "Stupid," he said, "fucking upsetting, I know."

"Wouldn't," Alice muttered.

"What?"

"You wouldn't."

Gus finished the last of his beer, pulling on the bottle a little too long. "That was, is, and always will be," he said, "a very fine line."

"Couldn't and wouldn't? Not from where I'm sitting. I'm telling you —"

"Alice, do we have to have this conversation again?"

"I just think you'll regret leaving so soon. I think that you should stay."

"I know you think so," he said. "And I understand; I do. Part of me definitely wants to stay. But Alice, you have no idea what this is like, being here after so long."

"You're right," she said, "I don't." Keeping her eyes locked in his direction,

234

Alice let a question escape: "Do you remember that night when . . . when she locked herself in the bathroom?"

He shook his head.

"Come on," said Alice softly, "the year before she went to Oaxaca when Dad was off giving a paper somewhere. She was in their bathroom and she was . . . well, she was crying. She broke something and I heard it break and I went to the door . . . and she wouldn't let me in. I kept begging her to let me in and she wouldn't. She ignored me and then she yelled at me to leave her alone. Finally I gave up, or I didn't give up but I went to get something to drink. When I came back I realized you were in the bathroom with her. I heard you," she said. "She'd let you in."

"I'm sorry," Gus said.

"I don't want you to be sorry. I don't care. I just want to know."

"Know what?"

Alice pushed her chair back from the table, balancing on the wobbly back legs of the chair.

"Be careful," he said. "What do you want to know?"

"What it was like," she said, exasperated. "What she was like."

"You know. . . ."

"No," Alice said. "I have no idea."

He sighed, and, opening another beer, he said, "We played cards. I brought in a deck and we sat on the floor. Alice, please stop. I don't know why she didn't let you inside. We played cards and it was like . . . it was like nothing. She smoked her head off and didn't say much of anything and neither did I."

She remembered cigarette smoke in the hallway, how she'd listened at the door, how she'd counted to one hundred over and over again. She recalled how everything was as quiet as the soundless high pitch of a scream.

"I'm tired, Alice," he said. And he looked tired. His eyes were bloodshot and heavy-lidded; his nostrils flared with a yawn. "Let's finish this in the morning, okay?"

Each night since the funeral, she'd heard him. She'd heard August in the kitchen, in the TV room, in the halls. She'd heard him in their parents' bathroom, opening the medicine cabinet, shutting it, letting the water run. She'd heard him frying food on the stove, dialing numbers on the rotary telephone. She was already tracking him, as she'd done with Charlotte, the way she hadn't done for years — visualizing her mother from room to room, bracing at the faintest sound. She had habitually guessed at Charlotte's activities during those late-night wanderings; and as she'd listened so keenly for the difference between sleeplessness and restlessness, Alice had tried to discern just what each wandering meant in the context of her mother leaving. And now it was her brother whom she'd grown accustomed to hearing late at night. Despite herself, she listened.

But tonight she heard nothing.

Tonight he was opening a letter. Tonight he was gazing at his father's solid writing on the outside of the envelope. He was splitting open the top of the envelope with uncharacteristic patience and precision. He was sitting on his bed. He was unfolding a letter. He was standing in the center of his childhood room — sharks still tacked up on the walls. Tonight he was reading.

By morning he'd be gone.

8

She started throwing away. There was only so much storage space in New York City. In the house, in a silence broken only by sibilant wind like the inside of a shell, Alice began sorting through it all. There were bags and there were bigger bags and all the bags were full, and then there were trips to the hardware store to get more bags and the garbage did not seem to end. There were blue bags, white bags, and hulking black ones, orange monsters with the faces of jack-o'-lanterns; Alice got to the point where she was alternating colors for fun. The potential garbage was everywhere and she wanted to slash and burn but she also wanted to keep everything, to always have a room or two for this past life, a room she could enter on a whim — desperate or not — and show an unknown someone; she'd lock him in and test whether he was bored, frightened, or merely interested in just what everything was.

A pot made by Alice in ceramics class. A pair of antique snowshoes. A mason jar filled with stones. Bad seventies mysteries. Unused cold cream. She'd never keep another thing in her life.

She was a mistress of another world, a cave of memory where she had to be careful of extending her stay for fear that she'd become disoriented and forget which way was out. She slept hard and the sleep was serious — no easy drift but a dive. Sometimes she clocked twelve, thirteen hours. She ate pots of spaghetti standing over the sink. When a break was needed she put on one of her father's coats and ran as fast as she could through the winter wind, down to the brackish cold water. The dock was now no more than a plank fallen into the sea, no longer sturdy enough to support anyone.

One morning she caught herself picking up a piece of blue beach glass and putting it in her father's coat pocket, only to realize that it too had to have a justification for being kept. The coat would eventually be going into a pile for Goodwill, and then what of the beach glass? It was no longer a charming oddity idly pocketed, but one more item in a pile that was waiting to be disbanded and scattered amongst strangers. She carried the beach glass to the site of the poolhouse, where on occasion a purple or yellow wildflower might pop up, but usually was no more than a thick weedy tangle. There was, in addition, a foot-size piece of dark scarred wood that had somehow staked its claim. Alice had long ago stopped suggesting to her father that they make a garden there or plant a tree or place a memorial bench or *something;* after it was bulldozed, leveling the last of the charred remains, he'd never wanted it touched. As she tossed the beach glass into the choke of green and brown, a phrase rushed through her mind: *If a chimney isn't cleaned over the summer, sparks from the fire can ignite creosote buildup inside the flue.* This phrase had insinuated itself into her thoughts over the course of her life and she never remembered ever having heard it or where she had heard it or who had thought to tell her.

She tried to remember the exact dimensions of the little combustible house. Tiny sparks, even a single spark, had most likely traveled up the chimney. Those devilish embers, they'd risen in pitch darkness and — while seeming no more threatening than Italian cookie wrappers that you burned for luck and floated skyward — burst like bombs into flame.

A café had opened even in this cranky town, and Alice headed there one night, driving around the cove, watching the streetlights come into focus. She stopped in the old bookstore, where she looked at all the books she wasn't reading. She could not browse successfully. She could only imagine putting the books in boxes and sealing the boxes with packing tape. In the cafe there were people she recognized, and she did her best to say hello, but they seemed somehow offended.

If it were a year ago she'd have been in a minuscule apartment on the Lower East Side, being entertained thoroughly, if predictably enough, by one of her students — a twenty-two-year-old fellow named Scotty, whom she'd literally bumped into late one night at one of the bars near the campus. He was tall and gangly-gorgeous, from Corpus Christi, with a shaved head and an always-evolving music collection. No matter what time of night they met up and no matter where, she could count on him having new CDs or mixed tapes strewn along the bottom of his great big Mylar messenger bag. If it were a year ago she'd have spent the day researching and writing, possibly teaching, working very hard indeed, and by nighttime she'd have been allowing herself his shy and mostly physical expressions. Alice supposed, looking back, that she'd been happy enough. However, it had been happiness inextricably linked to impermanence; happiness defined by the assumption that she was working toward a different, more sophisticated future. And she had been working. She'd been a young woman with drive who'd figured that by now her dissertation would have been completed and she would have been applying all over the country for academic positions, convincing herself of how a life in Indiana or Wyoming or Illinois could be a fulfilling existence. She'd pictured that by now she'd have been finally ready to make a serious move.

Instead she was here, consumed with an inertia that seemed to abate even slightly only when she was driving. Not wanting to be back home just yet, Alice pulled over to the side of the road and looked at the coal-dark water. There were small pieces of light caught in the wake, light from the houses across the way and light from a few boats out even at this hour, even in this kind of chill. But mostly it was dark, and in its particular way it was calming. She could imagine driving the car into the water and letting it sink to the bottom, watching all the weeds and small schools of fish rise with her descent. This was why people enjoyed smoking, Alice thought, sitting still in the heated car with the window cracked wide open. This silence wouldn't feel quite as lonely — in fact, it might be just a tad furtive — if there were a little edge of vice on her breath, in the air. She almost yearned for an addiction, for the ability to leave the house untended, to be fined and let the bills accumulate, to let the Realtors call and lawyers call and to say, *I'm sorry but I can't cope.*

When she'd woken in late November at seven a.m., she'd made coffee and waited for Gus to come downstairs. She was going to suggest that they go out for breakfast. She'd waited for forty minutes before she'd seen the note:

Sell this house, tear it down, make a fortune, I don't care. I just can't stand being here. I love you, August.

She could still feel the stillness of the night he'd left, when she was listening and hearing nothing. She'd known he was thinking of leaving soon, but it hadn't occurred to her that he'd actually leave without saying good-bye. It definitely hadn't occurred to her that he wouldn't call. She'd called. She'd called days later and not said a word after hearing his voice. Gus knew where she was; there was no question of that. He'd even written her a missive on a goddamned postcard of the Golden Gate Bridge. He didn't want to talk? No talking then, no more tries. There was a point when even Alice knew where to draw the line.

She drove on now, but instead of going home, she turned around in a private driveway and headed back into town. Alice had no destination but she was awake and the house was not — the tired house and its weary overflow were sucking away at her hard-won independence. She'd been a woman in her late twenties working toward a Ph.D., an apartment-owning, dinner-party-going, participating-in-life sort of person. She'd published an article; she'd applied for grants; she'd had aspirations. The house was killing her urge to be more than what she was, but there was still so much to do and still so much of a private nature — such threads and beads and lists that she couldn't bear a stranger — a friend, for that matter — to see. She was driving a little too fast. The shops were closed; the top floor of a small office building hosted one pulsing fluorescent light, and in an otherwise vacant church lot, one car was parked. Before she knew it, she was on the town's peripheries, the back-road shortcut, the highway.

The house waited up for her; it kept its hall light on. There used to be lights in the massive trees that illuminated the driveway. There used to be a porch swing, a sprinkler, a coat of white paint on the stairs. There'd been a few pots — red terracotta, carved gray stone — pots that, come springtime, could be counted on for color. There was at one time a weeded driveway, an attempt at a mowed lawn. As Alice exited the car, after sitting for who knew how long, she shivered from the cold, clear dark. She watched her heavy breath on the air and remembered how Charlotte would throw open the heavy door before guests had a chance to knock. *Welcome,* she would say. *We're a little shabby today.* She'd said it with pride and a hint of an edgy laugh. The front porch was now covered in slices of peeled paint. Inside the front hall was nothingness. Alice turned on the light and imagined, if she were a real-estate broker, what she'd conceivably say. *One might be surprised to know that at one time this house — this current mausoleum — possessed a subtle feminine grace. Even now* (she'd possibly lower her voice here, attempt a sparkle in her eyes), *during warmer months, if a rogue wind blows through the house there are traces of perfume — Must de Cartier — set free from the faded walls.*

And Alice sees that the house is broom-swept. As she goes from room to room she notes the rugs are rolled up and that the floors and surfaces are free from clutter. There is no clutter anywhere. There are only boxes, waiting. She has been through with packing for quite some time. It is February. When exactly did she finish? It is February, it is a new year, one that arrived without celebration.

She is still in her coat, hat in her hand, when the phone rings. The phone is ringing; it is echoing loudly. The phone rarely rings here anymore. The boxes are waiting, the phone is ringing, it is one a.m., February.

"Hello," she says, half expecting the voice on the other end to be a heavy-breathing prank caller, and she thinks that if it is, she just might invite him over. She goes as far as imagining how his bearded face would feel against her inner thighs. "Hello?" She says, "Hello?"

"It's me, Alice."

How strange, Alice finds herself thinking, that she recognizes Cady's voice so easily. She could be fifteen that very moment. If she closes her eyes she *is* fifteen. She can feel her body changing proportions in the long-distance silence. "Hello?"

"Listen to me, Alice —"

"I'm listening. What's wrong?" *Gus is dead.*

"You've got to get yourself on a plane." Cady sounds so completely unlike herself. She sounds afraid.

"What happened."

"Your fucking brother," she says, and Alice feels a weight lifting — he isn't dead at all. Dead, not dead, any minute this status could change. "Alice, do you know where I am? I'm in Mexico. I'm standing on a dirt road, at a pay phone, alone in Mexico. First we were in Oaxaca. Now we're all the way down the Baja peninsula. I say 'we,' but he is never with me. He is either surfing or off alone, but you know I can't quite believe that. He lied to me. When he got back from New York he made it out like he wanted to take some kind of

247

honeymoon. He was adamant that I get some time off from work, and I somehow managed to convince them. Look, this is no honeymoon. And you know how I love him. I *married* him. . . ."

"I know, Cady."

"He's unreachable. He is hell-bent on not talking to me, and I think he is putting himself in danger. Listen to me," Cady said, her voice on the rise, "something is going on. Alice, you have to come."

She feels for Cady; she really does. But Alice is looking down on this conversation from up above. There is nothing she can do. "I'm sorry," she says.

"You don't seem to understand," Cady responds. There is an undercurrent of hazard built into her tone. "I know what he can be like — have you forgotten how well I know him? Don't treat me — don't treat this like I'm some new person in his life, in *your* life. I know him, I know you all, and this is not part of his propensity to . . . to general strangeness or irresponsibility."

"Cady, he left here without a word. He left me alone to do everything; he hasn't called. I have to return to my life. I have a life."

"No one is doubting that. You have always said that kind of thing to me. I know you have a life, Alice. You're a goddamn interesting individual, okay?"

"I don't need this —"

"It's about your mother," she says, loud and clear.

"Excuse me?"

"Whatever he's not telling me. It's about her."

"What are you talking about?" Heat shoots from her stomach through her throat and now her mouth tastes like blood. She quickly opens the closest door, gulping in cold air.

Cady takes a breath. Alice thinks she hears a truck in the background. "I think there's something going on with him, Alice. And I think it has something to do with your mother. I overheard him talking to someone in Oaxaca. I think that someone here knew her."

Alice writes it all down on the one white pad near the phone in the kitchen. There are instructions; there are names of towns she's never before heard of. There are no telephone numbers, only some kind of post office where she is to leave a message as to what day she is coming and where she is to arrive, no later than five p.m. She looks at the words after hanging up the phone. She commits the words to memory as she calls the airlines. There'll be no sleeping tonight. She turns back around and locks the door. She'll leave it all behind and everyone will wait. This time everyone will wait for her.

On the highway she drives slowly and watches the different trucks, the burned-out buildings and hopeful hibachis on the ledges of housing projects. In the middle-of-the-night darkness the storage warehouses look sinister and greedy for possessions. It's impossible not to attempt an appealing vision of her brother having to do this for her. If he were driving on the LIE in the middle of the night before a last-minute flight, maybe he'd be thinking about nothing but plans, going for miles without noticing a thing, with the feeling that his was the only car on the highway, he was the only person alive. What she did know was that anonymity did not frighten him the way it frightened her. He was like their father in that regard — on good terms with the universe — on better terms with the looming future than with his inner self.

And the streets preserve the quiet she has carried. It is before the sunrise, before the garbage trucks arrive and people move their cars from one side of the street to the other.

Watch a woman pack in a floor-through apartment in Brooklyn, midwinter. She lays out pants on her queen-size bed like linen on a dining-room table. Here is Alice laying groundwork, again, for an impossible family feast. In every family there is usually one, the one who has to believe. Look at her packing. Forgive her. She's a woman possessed with the useless and timeless notion that she is needed somewhere.

9

Pull up your window shade, love.
Pay close attention to the takeoff.
Watch the sky.
Well, if you're going to be that way about
  it, you might as well go ahead and
  have a Bloody Mary.
Believe me when I tell you that you're a
  tense creature, you always have been,
  and I'm only trying to help.

Alice tried to sleep but was invaded by her mother's scratch of a morning voice. As superstitious as it was, she couldn't avoid the feeling of being watched, as she wasn't quite convinced that in going to Mexico, she was making the right decision. But this was about much more than following — Alice had been telling herself since hanging up the phone with Cady — this was about the end of waiting. She'd made the decision to stop waiting and yes, to follow Gus the way she never could with Charlotte. She had, of course, always been suspicious of both of their senses of freedom — suspicious, worried, and *jealous*. Now she could be someone who booked a flight and boarded a plane without planning. She could see for herself how each one did it, how both mother and son could practice such a pure form of selfishness.

Her head hurt from lack of sleep. There seemed to Alice to be a lot of lonely people on the plane. Aside from a jocular bunch of deep-sea-fishing buddies and their wives, everyone seemed single and quietly miserable. Where were the Walkman-clad teenagers fighting with their parents? she wondered. Where were the screaming babies? Alice was one of many lonely people en route to a sunny place, eating an underripe banana and contemplating a cocktail. She was, for better or worse, high in the sky, selfish, well on her way.

Her mother had boarded an airplane many years ago, ostensibly alone, with ideas and expectations. She often spoke about getting the name of a place in her mind (Hydra, Bruges, Elat) and not being able to ignore it until she'd seen the place.

She didn't claim to get the urges from any-where mystical — Oaxaca had come from her gynecologist's office, a framed picture of an outdoor market hung simply on a wood-paneled wall. When Alice had asked her what was so compelling about Oaxaca, why it was that she wanted to go, Charlotte had shrugged, mentioned something about courtyards and cobblestone and that the Aztecs there had been big on ritual human sacrifice. Charlotte had gone to Oaxaca (a nonsense word, a made-up children's game) and she'd come home. She spent the car ride home speaking fondly if a bit too manically of various chiles, of tamales wrapped in green banana leaves, sweet vanilla flan, but she looked as if all she'd done for sustenance was drink nasty mescal, daring the little white worm to go on and poison her. Clearly nothing good had happened there, but death had eclipsed Charlotte's long-ago travels and the mysteries therein. No matter what had upset her so, Charlotte was never coming back to explain anything to her daughter. Nothing too terrible could have happened, Alice remembered thinking, for she'd had the presence of mind to purchase souvenirs — a few area rugs and boxes of chocolate. But the rugs were left rolled up in the front hall, and the chocolates were clearly bought in the airport with the last of her pesos. Nobody in her family wanted to touch them.

Walking off the plane in Los Cabos, Alice imagined her mother hadn't died, and that she was descending onto the tarmac right behind her. She'd whip on a pair of oversize prescription tortoiseshell sunglasses and sigh along with Alice at the feeling of the still-hot early-evening air. She'd be grateful, just like her daughter, for the pleasure of simply being warm. The land was brown, the sky dense blues, and all around were scrubby mountains looking like enormous piles of gravel sprouting clumps of scattered green. Standing still to remove her sweater, Alice noticed the sun. It hovered on the far-off horizon — a magnificent fat lady gazing on the Pacific, wholly consumed with whether or not she felt like taking a dip. As she made her way into the little airport, abuzz with whirring fans, Alice couldn't help the irrational hope that Gus would show up behind the Plexiglas partition, waving a little sign: *Señorita Green*. She couldn't keep up the fantasy, though, because if he were coming he would have been waiting. Punctuality was, surprisingly, one of his

255

better qualities. He would have been front and center with a native tan, unembarrassed about waving.

She was nearly certain, actually, that Cady would never have told him about their conversation. Her presence would be a surprise to him and therefore more effective. Alice began to feel that much more alone, as she was stopped at the random security checkpoint by a plump girl with light eyes who fingered a pair of underwear and spoke in rapid Spanish to her coworker before breaking up into laughter. When Alice finally asked what was so funny, the girl shifted her weight and stopped smiling. She zipped up the suitcase and Alice was free to go, free to think about how her mother would have made a joke, maybe asked to see *their* underwear. Charlotte traveled so often that she must have acquired an indefinable savvy that would have prevented her from being stopped in the first place. Gus would not have been stopped either, or, actually, of course he would have, because those girls would have wanted to see as much of him as they could.

The girl with the light eyes continued to stare at her. And though she told herself she was trying, Alice couldn't seem to look away. For a moment she thought she was having an adverse reaction to the heat or maybe the alcohol on the airplane, as the cacophony of the airport — the sunburns and pale, bloated skin, the greetings and good-byes and smells of crumpled money — everything went slow, silent. The girl's light eyes shone like sunshine on a mirror, and the only place Alice could look was down.

Who knows why she noticed the scrap of paper or why, for that matter, she decided to pick it up, but Alice touched her fingers to the cool tile floor. In old-typewriter font it said: *palmas arriba, ojos abiertos, respirando normal.* She translated for herself as best she could, reaching back to the recesses of her junior high school education. *Palms up, eyes open, breathe normally.* She decided it must have been from an exercise or health manual and stuffed it in her pocket, walking on. But she continued to think of the paper at her side, the girl's light-eyed glare. It took discipline not to look back and check if those eyes could possibly have been that Pernod green.

She was faced with walls of men. The only way to exit the airport was through a sea of them. They were hawking rides and hotels and tours and Alice felt irrationally arrogant as she strode through, convincing herself that hers was a truer and higher purpose than tourism. She made her way to the rental-car counter and agreed to rent a compact car, which was less of a car and more of a red aluminum box with wheels. As the day's heat slightly diminished, there was a definite breeze as Alice drove away. Billboards for Sol and Tecate and promises of condominium paradises stood boldly in reds, oranges, bright yellows, and brighter than the paint were the crimson berries blooming wildly. The signs might have been unfamiliar but the sky issued no singularity. She could have been in Santa Fe, Miami, or Peru; she could have been in Scottsdale. It was impossible to imagine what lay beyond the airport's vicinity, and Alice looked for shapes in the far-off mountain ridge. She thought of the Matterhorn's cocky thrust, the jagged Rockies and her favorite Tetons, with the man in the mountains, his profile sharp against the sky. Here in Baja the heights weren't impressive, but she raised her eyes as far as the land rose; heights had, for some reason, always made her brave.

And bravery was needed, for as it happened, she was not warned sufficiently of how the road down the Baja peninsula was ragged with dropoffs and hosted a seemingly ongoing drag race. The horror of speed was on full display. People drove fast. They drove drunk and fast and in big fat trucks with all kinds of people — children for sure — bouncing in the backs of pickups. Cars drove toward one another from the opposite direction on one thin single lane. Blind with momentum, drivers passed without looking, and there was nothing to do but pray. The highway, to Alice, seemed sufficient explanation for Catholicism's great popularity in Mexico. At this velocity, on this road, faith in a greater beyond seemed absolutely crucial. Besides Bali — where Alice had visited Gus during college and where there were no lanes or any apparent rules as to how many vehicles could drive side by side — this was definitely the worst driving she'd ever seen.

But it was thrilling, too. Though *thrilling* was not the right word. *Thrilling* was not particular enough for how the land was parched beige, and just when she was nearly lulled by its uniformity — out of nowhere, a shock of azure ocean and tall palms stunned her to the spine as she coasted a bend. Alice tried to ignore the little crosses and Holy Virgins lining the highway in uneven stakes, pointing out just how many people had met their deaths right there. There was no radio in the car and there was nothing to distract from the sheer drama of the land. And it was getting darker. Swatches of gray invaded the sky until trees became mere shadows and the mountains blended together. A later flight was the only one she could get on such short notice, and she thought she'd get a room at an inn once she arrived in town. She would sleep and find Cady tomorrow. She was proud of her foresight, pathetically proud to have left as quickly as she had. The highway continued and Alice was going forward, on the lookout for cars. She was so attuned to the distance that at first she didn't even notice what was right in front of her: a plywood trailer being dragged along the highway containing what Alice counted as five ostriches grooving in the wind. Because the plywood came up only to their necks, when they darted from high to low, they looked like performers of that old parlor trick wherein someone stands behind a couch and pretends to descend stairs, creating the illusion by simply crouching down. They were so close Alice could see their long-lashed showgirl eyes alert, and the fine white hairs on their miniature heads. "I wonder what . . ." Alice began to say, but the truck slowed down and she knew she had to pass, inserting the rental in front of the ostriches and behind a huge open semi, the interior of which, Alice saw, was full of gallivanting monkeys. They swung from the ceiling — jumping and landing on the backs of strange-looking horned animals that Alice decided were billy goats. She watched in awed confusion until she had no choice but to pass them too. This was a road, according to Cady, toward a sparsely populated town between the desert and the sea, but sure enough the side of the truck was pastel-painted in a circus advertisement. She was almost laughing when she came around a whip-sharp pass and she saw a herd of cattle, dense and pale against the blackening sky. Alice was in a rare positive frame of mind at a time when frame of mind didn't happen to matter. There was no point in swerving — there was nowhere to go — and Alice simply screamed before slamming on the brakes. As her head hit the dashboard in a surge of pain, the top of the car buckled as if something had fallen from the sky, and she briefly thought something *had* fallen, some vulture or meteor. She did not know exactly what was bleeding but she knew it was her own blood and that it was everywhere — on her white T-shirt, on her jeans, on her unpainted toenails. She saw white flashes before her eyes and was overcome with her heartbeat, her fast and shallow breath. She heard nothing for a moment and then the noise was overwhelming. Cows were baying and moaning and the sound swelled and became so deafening that she barely could concentrate long enough to realize that she should get out of the car.

Outside the air was cool and there were no other cars driving by. Her rental was a pug-nosed mess of red and silver with the roof dipping low. *I am insured,* she thought gratefully. *I am the kind of person who chooses to pay the highest level of insurance. There is something to being that person right now.*

Alice grabbed her one bag and ushered herself onto a rock far enough away, and the cows seemed to follow. She pressed a sweater to her head, grateful for the gentle pressure, as the cows stood like a refugee family together all around her. As the cows kept up their noise level and swung their tails, Alice checked her body for damage, and when she found none she felt tears flowing easily and mixing with her sweat.

Breath was more difficult to come by. Her head was pounding, her hair was caked with blood, but as she searched her bag for aspirin, the blood tapered off. After swallowing some aspirin and codeine without water, she touched her fingers to her forehead, afraid of her own face. While there was tenderness, and while her eyes were wet and hazy, and she hadn't stopped coughing since swallowing the pills, she realized that she had been spared. Her fingers tingled with exalted relief, and, flush with luck, Alice changed right there among cacti and cows, used her clothes to wipe herself off, and left her bloody garments in the dust.

The cow that Alice hit was the color of tea biscuits, and the animal lay on her side, breathing hard and with great difficulty. She was larger and paler than the others were, or maybe it only seemed that way because of her important role in the moment. She, Alice realized, was what had landed on top of the car; this cow, lying heavy on the highway, with huge ballooning udders, had been struck buoyant and had flown right up and over. Alice watched, hypnotized by her glistening flank and blood-encrusted belly, as the cow struggled for final breaths. There was violent shuddering, and Alice wanted to back away, but somehow couldn't bring herself to move. She thought, weirdly enough, of cow farmers, of the bizarre intimacy that must develop between the farmer and the cow. She wondered how she would have behaved if Gus were beside her. Would she be telling him about the farmers and would he be laughing as they lifted the cow off to the side of the highway? Would she be consoling Gus or would she be blaming him or would this never even have happened?

It had been quiet for so long that she'd forgotten that a car could come speeding along at any moment. She briefly forgot she was in Mexico. Everything was smeared at the edges. Alice found herself returning to her sullied clothes, and, with the illicit sensation that she was violating a stranger, she rifled through her pants' pockets and extracted the scrap of meaningless paper.

Palmas arriba, ojos abiertos, respirando normal.

No trace of blood anywhere.

Alice looked up at the stars. The air carried the scent of burned hair and cow shit, which rose from the animal like fetid spirits taking leave of the body. The cow was dead but the others were still loud and boisterous from their stance on the side of the road, expressing through sonorous moaning their big-eyed ennui. Alice realized, for the first time, that they might hurt her. She touched the dead cow's leg, which was wet and hot, much rougher than a horse's. Then she slowly backed up and started walking away.

A horn blasted suddenly with lights flashing and Alice found that the codeine was indisputably in effect, for she was surprisingly calm — her head merely thrumming at a steadily declining rate. She tried to flag the truck down, but it merely steered clear of the cow and sped by, doing eighty at the very least. "August," she said pointlessly, surveying the desolation that was the dark sky, dead cow, and the others still mooing, moving up into the hills. There was a substantial moon, a scattering of stars, and other than that bit of lunar light, there was nothing visible for miles. Her father had tried to explain the desert to her when she was very young. He'd said it was like being out at sea, surrounded by nothing but water. Here, as there was *both* desert and sea, the land blended into the ocean as a seamless spatial expanse. There was not much going for her beyond the fact that she was alive, and she would be riding that high for a very long time. She was alive and walking. The road was as desolate as snow.

A rush of cars. Cars where there were no cars — sudden and inexplicable traffic. Alice began yelling, jumping up and down as best she could, and five passed by before she had the late good sense to try starting the rental car. She ducked low to fit under the collapsed roof, and after a few rounds of gunning the engine for a minute or so, the wreck was inexplicably running. With an attempt to shake her nerves, she pressed down on the gas and felt, with increasing speed, her life flying away. Alice had a flash of her essential self being left there on the highway, a sleepy bovine phantom of a woman, taking a long look around. A chimera perhaps, but there they were: two ghosts, Alice and the cow, stuck in the middle of the road. Their auras issued grassy pastures, glasses of whole milk. They were left for dead but would invisibly flag down cars forever, evoking no more than specks in the distance through a couple of rearview mirrors.

There was nothing in either direction. She felt the precise reason why she'd stayed so close to her careful father and the familiar house for all those years Gus had been elsewhere. It was the letting go she feared — the careening and falling off from some illusive center. As she drove she felt the need to hold tightly to the wheel as if the car might — if she wasn't careful — drive out from under her.

After miles of dark and twisting roads, of holding breath down hills, and after being distracted by glints of whitecaps in the distant ocean, the sight of a gas station was difficult to believe. Clamorous music issued from a small radio; it sounded like a speed-enhanced polka. There was an attendant and a mechanic — two young men with glossy coifs with no real foreheads to speak of (brothers, she assumed), who begrudgingly opened her dented hood and poked around inside. They were neutral enough when she tried to employ her negligible classroom Spanish, but after a few moments she began to wonder if these strangers would turn menacing, if they would take her passport and money and then rape her before leaving her for dead, just like the cow on the highway. It happened. It happened all the time in every country on the planet, so why shouldn't it happen tonight? People tore each other's organs out. People shot each other in the face.

Alice thought about the cow, and how,

before morning, cars and trucks would bump over her lifeless body, cursing the inconvenience. Just when she was considering walking away, perhaps even hitching a ride, Alice noticed, on the other side of the building, two loitering girls — girls whose lipstick was as red and as slick as the original varnish of this rental car. That there were women here made the scene a little less threatening, but not by much. They were in tight-fitting skirts and cleavage-baring tops that stopped above their midriffs. The taller one smoked and the shorter one watched Alice, smiling a hateful smile. It was clear they were waiting for their men, but they also looked as if waiting were something other people did, and they instead were encouraged to pose like rare tropical birds. The taller one indicated Alice with her cigarette while whispering to her friend; they both laughed until Alice looked away. She felt as if this were a seventh-grade outing or a day at her mother's best friend's house. One summer Susan (no doubt in some attempt to quit drinking) held some kind of women-and-their-daughters spiritual retreat at her house in Connecticut, where a pair of girls whom Alice had seen at previous Susan events had apparently had just about all the enlightenment they could take. Every now and then she could recall those exact glares. The secret world of mean girls — it must be universal. It must be programmed in the genes — an intimidation technique that never failed. Alice often felt that if she could just tap into this secret world of indisputable female command, everything would be so much simpler and clearer. Kindness never meant as much when such power was close by; this feminine sway with a touch of cruelty was more elusive and voluptuous and more utterly distracting than a perfect pair of breasts.

Alice tried to picture what her mother would do in this situation. She'd try to communicate; she'd do anything she could to charm. Alice wished Charlotte were here because Alice . . . she was no charmer. She had nothing whatsoever to say. She tried to be inconspicuous as the shorter woman crossed her path, veering in the direction of the mechanic. Alice took comfort in the intimacy between them — a kiss on the cheek, a pat on the ass, the offhand way her long painted nails touched his sweaty brow. With affection so close by, she somehow felt safer.

After they'd properly fleeced her, communicating clearly just how many hundreds of pesos she was to hand over in exchange for the knowledge that this wreck would more than likely get her as far as Santa Lucia, Alice returned to the driver's seat and — white knuckles gripping the wheel — gunned on down the highway.

The car bumped and popped along a rocky dirt road. Her head was pounding and all she knew was that she couldn't drive another minute. She parked among scrub brush, shedding her shoes in the cool sand, and she could hear the ocean long before she saw it. It sounded like screaming, like a crowd going wild. And it looked like the end of the earth. The waves were black and silver and rumbled with the shore. Unlike her home, where the sea was restrained and patient as an old pair of hands, this water was flashy and unrelenting — not allowing for the natural impulse to admire any other surroundings. If you stepped in there was no wading; that seemed perfectly clear. These waves were a date you did not let out of your sight — not unless you were prepared to let her go.

No one would be handing her a blanket. No one but Alice would be seeing that she made good time, that she quit checking up on the sky as if she couldn't quite believe it was the very same one she'd always known. The sky was one thing. The sea was another — everything paled in contrast to this wild face of the ocean. The waves must have been ten feet overhead and breaking right on shore. Alice knew that if Gus were here he would have to create more chaos; he would not, even for a minute, be able to simply observe.

He had told her, when she'd once asked why he loved to surf, that every time he rode the face of a wave, he felt, for those oddly long seconds, all of life's expectations and disappointments simply disappear. He'd said it was all a balancing act, this rush of letting go. If he were here, he would reveal himself to her, and then he would turn around and wave before duck-diving under the massive walls of water.

10

The sky hovered on her eyelids, bearing down on a pounding head. The ocean was going at it, churning away — it was astounding Alice had slept at all. Sand coated her arms and she could feel little grains crunching between her molars. She couldn't have been too far off the beaten path, she realized, as even though the sky still wore its nighttime attire, there were boys — lean, tan boys — taking vanilla colored surfboards off of jeeps and trucks, dutifully waxing them down, and then — with tubelike leashes — tethering them impatiently to their ankles. The air, due to the surf wax, smelled faintly of bubble gum but also of suntan lotion, shells, salt, and smoke, as fires had clearly been burning for a while now. Alice didn't remember there being any fires when she'd collapsed only hours ago. She also didn't remember any trailers or tents. A group of

Mexicans were burning banana and palm leaves on a low cliff, and surf bums were hovered carefully over smaller flames, heating little tin cans. A woman led five dogs through the glimmer of low tide.

Alice took four aspirin and gazed at a surfer wiping out, his thin limbs falling with gravity's force. It would have been nice to think that if her brother were out there she would have known it immediately, but from this distance they all looked alike. You could spend a lifetime with somebody and still not recognize him in a swell of ocean. In Bali, Alice thought she'd witnessed Gus take a spectacular ride and, on running to tell him so as he made his way out of the water, she realized she was about to throw her arms around a total stranger. They all flicked their hair out of their eyes in the precise way that she knew Gus to do; they all leaned on their boards like little kids, looking as slick and optimistic as seals.

As the sun rose, the mountains in the distance became eggplant-colored, with cool plummy shadows falling between the ridges.

You looking for somebody? her mother asked wryly.

"My brother," Alice said softly, imagining

how she'd actually answer that question. "He's about my height and has dark eyes and hair. We don't look too much alike."

He has my eyes, her mother said impatiently. *He has my arms.*

Alice climbed into the car and caught a glimpse of her own face. After expecting to see a swollen temple, at least a few garish bruises, the sight of herself was almost disappointing. She looked fine. She didn't even look particularly tired. It was as if the marks she'd been expecting would have been proof of all that had happened in such a short span of time. Stories carried only so much meaning. Disaster was filtered out by the time it came to the telling, and horror could be rendered as mundane as directions. A scar, blood on torn lace, a lone shoe on the highway — physical evidence was certainty. Her father's death wasn't to be found in the details of his diseases or how he cried out in pain, but in his favorite blue bowl for ice cream, how that ice cream was his only remaining pleasure, and how it sat untouched and melted on the last days of his life.

The car lurched and bobbed heading out from the scrub brush, and the sun rose as she drove once more on those dangerous hills. An egg was slowly breaking over the

world, enclosing Alice in a shock of bright-
ness, and she hoped for what she couldn't
help but think of as her mother's kind of
day, where *everything happens with speed
and ease and you are in the center; you are in
the light.*

Whether it was the obvious and unwelcome thought of the fire's light or the way
Charlotte could (as was said with embarrassing repetition at her memorial service)
light up a room — her mother always visited
Alice in terms of light, the particulars of
which she'd tried to describe in one or two
unfinished personal essays, to a man
named Josh she met in an airport when
they both were stranded overnight during a
storm in Denver. *It was flickering,* she remembered saying. *You couldn't help wanting
to be closer. It drew you in like a castaway to
his own first spark, and still it was cold light, a
mirror that reflected only what it felt like.
Even if the rest of the world was dark and
needed a bit of her glitter, my mother kept it
mostly to herself.* Alice, of course, never
knew if her mother understood this. While
Alice had come to the gradual opinion that
her mother didn't have extensive self-
knowledge, she nevertheless believed that
Charlotte *did* understand, at least half of
the time, how she affected others. She was

inconsistent in her self-presentation, and it was in this unaccountable fashion that she gave and received affection. Because Charlotte was manipulative and had seemingly so much confidence, Alice loved her mother most for her moments of insecurity. There were tender flashes in Alice's memory of Charlotte seriously biting a cuticle, smoking the nasty tail end of a cigarette, holding a hand over her mouth when there was something in her teeth. Alice craved these moments from Charlotte and tended to love the shadows of people, the tenuous impulses and unstable forces that were lost in the face of personality. If someone was shy she'd notice where the boldness lurked — maybe an authority with numbers, decisiveness in restaurants, the tendency to laugh out loud.

The curves in the road intensified. As Alice began to see a few taco stands, a sign for Coca-Cola, she imagined the shock of seeing Cady leaning up against a wall, looking as if she were pinned there by the force of the harsh sun. Cady would look — with suntanned skin and squinting eyes — younger somehow, as if she were waiting for someone to pick her up from an unpleasant day camp and she was, in fact, the last girl waiting. Alice had a sudden conviction that Cady, with all of her sophistication, had been fighting that look her entire life.

When she finally parked the rental wreck, she thanked it for taking her this far. Then she left it sitting in a cloud of dust on one of the unpaved streets. The town was eerily quiet. She looked through barred windows into a few craft shops, a hardware store with barrels of merchandise sitting on a dirt floor, and a number of boarded-up taco stands. Just when she began to think how similar the place was to that town in Greece or that place in Tucson, Alice stepped around a new corner and, like falling off an ocean shelf, became utterly lost in dirt and dust, unfinished houses and garbage. She witnessed an argument between two young mothers whose toddlers stood by their sides. Alice watched with admiration how the shorter woman grabbed her small child's wrist before making a dramatic exit. Besides those women Alice was the only person in sight, and then, rounding a corner, she found herself facing a group of Mexican teenage boys in baggy pants and T-shirts, no doubt taking the slow route to school. There were four of them and they were staring in unabashed silence as the tallest one with the most facial hair whistled, sending the rest into a loud spell of whistling laughter. It was daylight for real now; this was a small farming town with a burgeoning tourist trade, and she knew she was ridiculous for being afraid, but as the shortest one approached her in the middle of the street, her breath became erratic and she kept her hands firmly on her bag.

"Mami," the short one said, sticking out his chin. When she'd made it to the next street, sweating profusely and unmugged, she was faced with a big shirtless man. She was beyond relieved to see that when she smiled at him, nervously, he did nothing but return the favor. Alice kept a smile plastered on her face. She smiled at everyone she passed and was interested to see how everyone — from the old men sitting in chairs in the shade, to the scowling teenage girl — transformed their threatening scowls or else simply ignored her, which made her feel more at ease.

Certain homes were clearly very old and adobe or brick; history emanated from within the wrought-iron windows and rotted wood doors. Mustached old ladies, who swept dust from doorways, yelled at schoolchildren in Catholic-school attire and at mangy, skinny stray dogs. The dogs were everywhere — heaving in the sunlight and lying under parked cars, barking and crying.

When Alice came upon the building where Cady had instructed her to go, the building with the silly name of Casa Communication, it was teeming inside with English-speaking people — but no Cady. Alice bet that Gus would never set foot in such a place, but she checked for his name on the off chance he'd received any messages, which, of course, he had not. She explained about the car and the cow to a Mexican woman working behind the counter with admirable English, an attractive overbite, and a gold crucifix pendant. The woman didn't look particularly sympathetic as she found the number and dialed Hertz for Alice with long red nails, launching into rapid-fire Spanish. "Green," she said, before proceeding to intone a whole lot of *"sí, sí, sí."* People were asking for pens, paper, for names of companies, numbers of operators, names of Cabo hotels. The red nails hung up the phone. "They come pick it up now," she said.

"So everything is okay?"

"You wait too long," she said, shaking her head.

"Are they going to fine me?"

The woman tapped her fingers on the counter and gave a small shrug. "The *judiciale* — you go make report . . ." There were people waiting in line behind Alice, holding nonfunctioning cell phones and useless pieces of paper.

As Alice watched those long red nails dial another number on her behalf, then click on the counter as the questions became tinged with what sounded like flirtation, she saw, right there on the bulletin board, an envelope with her name on it.

The red nails hung up the phone. "You have to wait. The *judiciale* very busy today. Come back tomorrow and I help you."

"Thank you," Alice said, gratefully paying the agreed-upon amount and taking the envelope from her. "Thank you. You have no idea how helpful . . ." but the woman was already ensconced, helping the next clueless American.

Inside the envelope was no note, only a perfect rendering of the surrounding area, including a little arrow beside the Casa Communication. *You Are Here,* it said in architect's handwriting. *August,* it said, beside another arrow pointing to where they were apparently staying in what, at least on the map, seemed to be a hotel. She had Cady to thank for this — Cady, who apparently felt no obligation to welcome her personally.

"Is this a hotel?" she asked, interrupting the woman behind the counter, who, after looking at the map, responded with a blank stare. "Is it?"

"No." She shook her head, then heaved a sigh. "Here," she said quite firmly, instructing Alice where to go.

La Balena, a motel with a sign in the shape of a whale, was attached to a poorly stocked market where kittens played in the potato bin. Flies buzzed around the only available produce — the overripe bananas, avocados, measly tomatoes, onions, and chiles. There was an entire aisle devoted to wrapping paper, ribbons, and piñatas. When Alice opened a door of the glass-refrigerated area to grab a small bottle of water, she saw past the brightly colored grape and orange sodas to what was obviously the meat locker, where carcasses hung from large hooks and two workers heaved cleavers. She'd carried her duffel bag in the rising heat of day, watching the blurs of thatched *palapa* roofs and gray cement. She had planned on finding something that resembled lunch but ended up with a chile-flavored lollipop that tasted hotter than any fireball she'd ever tried to consume and, mouth afire, eyes tearing, seriously pissed off, she ventured next door to see about a room. She was not enthusiastic about wasting her money in an unimaginative rip-off of a roach-infested motel, but she was exhausted, desperate to put her bag down, and she would have gone almost anywhere to lie down on a bed, any kind of bed, before facing her brother and Cady.

A frowning Mexican matron showed Alice to a room — linoleum floors, chemicals masking the scent of human dirtiness, the scent of a cheap holiday. The room overlooked a cement courtyard where no one had cleaned up what was obviously something of a wild night or two. Beer cans and cigarette stubs covered the ground, and a few plastic chairs were turned over. *"Gracias,"* Alice said with a frazzled smile, handing over one night's worth of pesos. The woman trudged out of the room, calling out urgently to a man who was down the hall, apparently fixing something.

With the door closed, Alice felt short of breath, as if the walls — so flimsy and covered with what she realized were smudges of squashed blood-bloated mosquitoes — would close in on her if she used all the air

that was available in the room. The bathroom (she finally brought herself to look)
smelled like eggs and had a drain in the
middle of the floor, a rusted handheld
showerhead. When she ran the water it was
tinted brown, and she watched for a
minute or two before simply turning it off.
She found herself sitting carefully on the
bed, over which hovered fairly decent-
looking mosquito netting. Alice held her
hands in her lap and forced herself to
breathe. There were muffled voices coming
from the right, a broom sweeping the floor
to the left. One of the voices began to
cackle, and she felt as if whoever was on
the other side of the wall was watching her
through a small hole, watching her stillness
and paranoia, seeing her fall apart.

She was fairly well traveled. She'd been
all over Europe, to Greece and to Bali. She
may have gone to college close to home
but she had taken some good goddamn
trips. And she'd stayed in worse places
than this. She'd gone alone on an overnight train from Paris to Rome, sleeping in
a cabin with four strange men who snored
when they weren't hollering in German.
She had, not even twenty-four hours ago,
hit a cow and managed to keep it together
well enough to sleep on an unknown

beach. She should have been fine, just fine. She should not have been jumping at the sight of a roach, the sound of a man's cackle. But she found herself leaving her bag in the room and nearly slamming the door behind her. She was sweating all over, her hair was oppressive, and as she took a second to breathe, to tie her hair in a knot, four beefy men — in tank tops one and all — came bounding down the hallway, carrying surfboards. She looked for the woman who'd shown her the room on the off chance she might give Alice a room *without* rusty water, but no one was downstairs. The beefcakes piled into their well-used Montero and burned rubber toward the waves. *"Adios,"* the driver howled out to her — the utter worst of southern California — and she was left standing, feeling allergic to her own skin. She flinched when a rental car sped into the lot. The driver jerked the car into a parking space and Alice couldn't help noticing how, after switching off the engine, he remained seated. For someone who drove with such urgency, it was unusual — almost alarming — how long he stayed in the car. She got a little closer to make sure that he was all right. He was stocky, with brown hair sticking up and out around his head, and he was wearing a white button-down shirt. She saw him take off the sunglasses and throw them on the empty seat beside him. Then, after a moment, he took a breath, and she was surprised to see how he eased his head out the open window, tilting his face to the sun. His face was sunburned on its way to tan, and his temples were damp with sweat. Sweat fell slowly from his sideburns and his forehead down his neck and out of sight. He had a strong brow — darker than the hair on his head and liberally peppered with gray — plus he really needed a shave, but when his eyes closed and his face fell into repose, he went from looking strictly imposing and coarse to seeming a bit vulnerable. Alice noticed a thought float through her mind: *This is what this man would look like sleeping.* Just as she was thinking how she could relate to him, how maybe they could tell each other stories to pass time over a drink or a meal, he got out of the car and looked at her, squinting without his sunglasses. "Yes?" he said.

"What?"

"Do you want something?"

"I was just — Are you okay?" she asked, which was — as soon as she said it, she knew — the wrong thing to say to this man.

"*You* okay?" he asked sarcastically.

"Fine," she said, incredulous at his rudeness but compelled to keep speaking to him. "Just fine."

He waved his hand in a dismissive gesture (whether he was dismissive of her or himself she couldn't be sure) and heaved a sigh. "You don't know if there are any free rooms in that hellhole, do you?"

"It looked like it," Alice said. "You sure you're okay?" she said, now that she knew how to get at him.

"Perfect," he snapped, "thanks." And he headed into the motel. She watched him walk and it relaxed her to be in close proximity to someone who was possibly more frustrated and inconvenienced than she was. Alice waited a few moments before going back inside and giving the bed another try. Inconsiderate as he may have been, the last thought Alice had before drifting off to sleep was that, under some stress, in desert heat, his shirt was bright white and unwrinkled.

After a few hours' sleep, Alice set out toward the building where Gus and Cady were apparently staying. She could smell garbage burning in the valley below, which wasn't even a valley, really, more like a shallow brown bowl. A steady flow of construction sounds reverberated through the heat, calling out in a stilted pattern of drill, buzz saw, voices. Against the setting sun she saw half-built walls and corroded doors, building wires sticking straight up into the air held together by nothing more than Styrofoam, uneven globs of cement. Garbage was cast at the feet of these structures like gods and offerings gone askew. Undeveloped land lay in tangles of dirt, rocks, and beer cans, and amidst the rubble were interlaced tiny flowers. She was moving toward the ocean. Alice could see a silver sliver in the distance, and there were no longer as many houses. As the dirt road became narrower and dust flew up in heavy clouds, the land transformed into farmlands, into sprinkler-fed rows of what she could only guess were onions, maybe chiles. Past the crops, straight up a huge dune and then, the beach: pale sand, dark waves crashing loudly, no people to be found. Alice turned her back to the sea. From this vantage the path she'd traversed was its own vast sea of palm groves.

Alice walked and walked. The beach was good for walking, and before she knew it she was closer to the rock face that had previously seemed far away. The sand appeared endless, and the shock of such emptiness began to settle in. Anyone could come down off the dune. Who knew what kinds of smart Mexican deviants or perverted gringos would be lurking behind the next rise, waiting for a certain type of American female, schooled on Joni Mitchell and Joan Didion and most of all Charlotte Green; a female who was taught that — forget about the right to choose and glass ceilings and the ERA — *poetic landscapes demanded exploration.* Choosing *not* to wander, in no matter how little clothing, or no matter how alone, would be to forsake one's God-given gift of freedom and wonder. Every piece of driftwood, every pile of rocks — it was all her mother, appearing solid against the sky, apparently fresh from a swim in the dangerous sea. *Now we're talking,* was what her eyes were saying. *Don't you even think of turning back.*

It happens whenever she tells herself she's arrived, that she's come out on some other side. It can be at a party, on a crowded street, in a store making a decision; it can be, apparently, on a deserted beach. Alice is alone and then she is not, as Charlotte walks out from behind a partially closed door, out from a dressing room, or out from the sea. She comes like a swarm of bees and everything disappears into the drone.

Alice shuddered as she nearly stepped on a dead fish the size of a dinner plate. She continued on to see more fish lying in various states of decay. Some were fresh from the sea, still glistening gray and green with fins poked out like little arms, as if they'd died from shock. There were those that had begun to harden and acquire a prefossil look, and others still that were merely masks, their skins hard and leathery as deflated basketballs. Pelican skeletons glowed in the sunlight, their bones picked utterly clean. Curvatures of beaks were hooked like scythes; stark white ribs were patterned with blue stripes of the sky.

There were many times when she nearly turned around but could not help moving forward; her mother's swollen fingertips pushed between her shoulder blades as Alice looked on, staring at the lifeless creatures while fearing the vultures swooping overhead — black, red, and looming. She feared the vultures not only because she couldn't believe they wouldn't take a nip of her, but also because she feared that she was in fact one of them, walking not only to see the beach and the massive shore break and the dried-up riverbed behind the dunes — but also, after all, to see the dead. She watched how many stages these beings endured, and how they didn't simply disappear. And the white dolphin washed up and dried out, with big black holes for eyes? Alice made herself look, forced her breath as her heart sped. Her feet were planted in the sand but her mind was racing in radiant circles to the night before and beyond — to the cow and the speed and the sight of so much blood — her own blood that had stopped just as abruptly as it had begun. She'd only had to wipe it all away. Her mind raced on to her parents underground, as that was, after all, where they were. No matter how many details she retained or voices she heard, she had no doubts as to where their bodies resided.

Alice listened. All around the bloated dolphin, the bugs were having a field day; the tide was pulling back and the waves were crashing — back and forth, back and forth, with light reflecting a kaleidoscopic dance like blown Venetian glass. She could hear the very air crackling around all of its elements, including Alice in this patch of life and its leering opposite.

She'd come to learn that this was called Fire Beach, so called because of the mist from the massive waves, which rose up from a distance like smoke, like a funeral pyre daring any life to come and meet its challenge, as they crashed down right on the shore.

However, five, ten minutes had passed, and no other huge waves took shape. Though she knew better with such an unknown shallow break, she wanted to feel the ocean. Just one little dip, she told herself, just one with her pallid big toe — a splash of briny cold and then of course she'd flee. As she dipped her toe in the bracing water (diamond-pale up close) she expected a force — a warning current — but nothing happened. Only coolness engulfed her, and a mild tug that defined, if anything, how grounded in the earth she actually was. As Alice stood in the wake she glanced around at the beach, and one dead fish just a few feet away looked particularly disturbing. Moving back from the ocean's edge, she stared at the corpse of a creature and then knelt down beside it. The fish was puffed-up — somewhere close to a hollow shell but not quite there yet, as a few vestiges of its slick gray skin were somehow still intact. As she reached out two fingers, Alice realized how its fins were not as paper-thin as she'd somehow expected, and, as if dared by the water, by its previous theatrical display, she picked up the fish and placed it just outside the ocean's reach, laying it out to be claimed again, just to see what would happen.

Alice stepped back. The ocean was still far from rowdy. She closed her eyes and pictured similar offerings on her home's ragged shore. She had stood for hours like this all her life, watching the debris, sifting through her thoughts, grateful to be doing so. There was something oddly consoling about how when the tide was out and the beach was scattered with the ocean's remains, the land — as the host of these often-foul remnants — seemed to expose a component, if only a minuscule one, of the ocean's mystery.

In an instant she was covered with sea spray, eyes wide open. A wave was building, accumulating height, and Alice was running. The fish was long gone.

The sun was now underwater, the moon was being rigged up in the sky, and she could finally see the building from Cady's map while standing at the top of a dune. She would find Gus and they would all sit together at what felt like the end of the Earth — or at least the very last stop past California. Alice headed toward a building that, as she grew closer, was less far along in terms of construction than Alice had originally assumed. In fact, it was a construction site in the initial stages of development. There were domes plastered and painted the color of rust, and the supporting structure was half in brick and half unpainted cement, which looked as smooth as soapstone. It was an enormous building — ugly with an undercurrent of magnificence — with the ambitious sprawl of a hotel, and it was where (although he'd never say so) Gus would dream of creating a surfing retreat, an architect's palace for Cady. Alice leaned, for a moment, against the surrounding tall cement wall. She let herself in and there was nothing but wind. She wouldn't have been surprised if some of the cement was not quite dry. Night had fallen for real now; the sky had gone from purple to black glass cut sharp with stars.

"August," she called, but there was nothing but echoes. It was a shell of a building and, though holy with potential, it was anyone's guess as to whether it was even structurally sound. "Cady?" she yelled. She could make out only shapes and shadows and a staircase without a railing. As she ascended she called out again and again and noticed the air, which was laced with smoke. At the top of the stairs were littered bottles and one wet sandy blanket and what looked like a wet suit, which were no doubt sources of the prevailing dankness. She stopped calling out and stood still. The ocean sounded like a spell of rain with each wave that crashed. The hairs on her arms stood up; a car sped by on the nearest road, popping rocks under tires.

"Shame on you," came out of the darkness. "You really should have called."

11

A small flame was cupped in a pair of hands. Alice saw August light a candle. The room was much bigger than Alice had initially understood; they were only in one corner of it. Her brother had always been thin, but he was now approaching gaunt. His high cheekbones stuck out in ridges, which were clear even beneath an unflattering and scraggly beard. Though his arm muscles were clearly defined, the skin looked shrunken around each tendon; veins were thick as cords. "Alice," he said, "what are you doing here?" His hands were dark against the white of his T-shirt with which he relentlessly fiddled before encircling his sister's shoulders in a quick and pungent hug. Then he backed up, saying nothing as he sat leaning up against one wall, one leg bent and the other flung out in front of him. She could no longer make out his face. "Look up," he finally said.

Alice looked and saw that the dome overhead had an open circle in the middle, as if the builders hadn't gotten around to attaching the center of the roof. It was a peephole to the universe, the size of a small umbrella. "Great," she said, not bothering to sound convincing. "Where's Cady?"

"Cady's gone," he said.

"What do you mean, 'Cady's gone'?"

He shrugged. "She left. I don't know."

"What happened?"

"She went back to work."

"But what about —"

"Believe me, Alice, I don't need your insight on this. Nothing — I mean nothing — is as clear as how it lives in your mind."

"You have . . ." Alice said, swallowing hard. "You have no idea what *lives in my mind.*" She sat down on the cement floor, which was cold and covered with fine wet sand; her legs were worn out. "Gus, what are you doing here?" Alice asked gently, gesturing around the massive hollow space. "What is this place?" she said, not entirely without humor, but the very kind of comment that pushed his buttons. The moment Alice mentioned living conditions or money or working some kind of job, he was raw and complicated and she was polished and simple. At that kind of moment, which sooner or later inevitably arose when she was around her brother for any length of time, Charlotte was silently invoked. Her mother — whether or not in reality Charlotte might have ultimately *agreed* with her daughter — was judging not Gus but Alice. As soon as Alice voiced a negative opinion about Gus, she could feel her mother, languor included, judging the hell out of her. Alice was small-minded and Alice was sanitized, without imagination.

He responded evenly: "I slept outside for a while but it got cold and the ocean kept me up. This I like. And here," he said, as his face was lit briefly and hard by a new match's flame, "here are some more candles," he muttered, lighting a slew of votives. "Let there be light," he said, revealing bloodshot eyes, blackened fingernails, a killer tan.

"Why did you come here?"

He laughed. "You want to know why *I'm* here? The surf is outrageous, the weather is perfect every day, and there's spectacular fresh food to be had for nothing. It seems pretty simple to me."

"And your recent marriage?"

He looked at her blankly and she mirrored him until he finally proceeded. "We pushed it. Maybe I pushed it and she accepted. What's the difference, really? It didn't work."

"The difference is that I don't believe you. I mean, I don't believe you're that blasé about her leaving and I don't believe you about coming here solely for the awesome waves. Come on," Alice said, her voice softening, "you must know that I spoke with her."

Gus got up from his seat on the floor, where he'd hardly even shifted around. He stood up straight and looked at the sky before looking down at Alice. With his baggy pants and small undershirt and wild hair he looked, for the first time, dangerous. Her brother was not a big man — he could appear at times almost elfin — but he was dark and lean, and he'd acquired a recent steeliness that she presumed had come from a dose of hard living and what she could best — though vaguely — identify as inner resolve. "She's never trusted me."

"Have you given her reason to?"

"We all know she's too good for me." His eyes flashed in a way that made Alice uneasy. For the next few days she knew she'd think of his eyes in that very moment and not be able to rid herself of what exactly disturbed her so.

"Gus, why are you here?"

"You tell me," he said, sitting down once again. "You've always been good at that — telling me what I'm actually doing. When I didn't go to college you told me that I didn't go because I felt superior. When I went to Java and didn't call for a while, you told me I was desperate. So I wish you could tell me what I'm doing now. I do. I'm curious what you come up with."

"Are you *that* angry I'm here?"

"Yes. But I'm more angry at Cady for asking you to come."

"She didn't ask me to come. She just called to let me know where you were. She knew I'd begin to worry, and she wanted to let me know."

"Liar."

"What makes you think I'm lying?"

They were looking at each other from a few feet away, each of them seated in a similarly defeated fashion. The dark was muddy with candlelight. "She's not that considerate," he finally said. "Why did you come?"

"I think you've been keeping something from me." When he didn't answer, she wasn't surprised. "Okay, let's start with something easier," she said. " 'How's the house, Alice?' "

"That's fine, just give me the script. It

299

really is better that way. 'How's the house, Alice?' "

"She's a mess, actually — sagging and bulging in all the wrong places, but you know what? She'll survive. Everything's sorted, in boxes. Everything's ready to go."

"That's good, right?"

Alice didn't laugh. "I can't believe you just left like that." She waited, but he didn't seem entirely anxious to explain. "And what was that *note?* If it were all up to you, you'd have sold the house, because we all know you need money, or you'd have asked some buddy of yours to go ransack it and collect on the insurance. All of our photographs and Dad's prizes and collection of articles and Mom's beautiful things, you'd have just as well seen them stolen or destroyed."

He didn't say anything for a while. "You're probably right. I'm not saying I'm proud of it, but I just can't imagine wanting or needing anything from the house. I remember what I remember."

"And what do you remember . . . ?"

Gus smiled as if he were caught in an unnecessary lie. They both knew that she wasn't really asking that question — at least not in the conventional sense — with any expectation of having it answered.

Looking up through the hole in the ceiling to the increasingly starry sky, she surprised herself by saying, "Do you know any of the constellations?" She didn't recognize her own voice. It was the voice of a smart woman stuck with a potentially menacing stranger — that, or a hopeless first date. It was draining — all this talk, the soggy room.

Gus, however, seemed relieved at this banal turn in conversation. He cracked his wrists with a vengeance, as if he wanted to shake his hands right off. "I can still find Cassiopeia, the Dipper, the North Star. I used to know so much more, remember?"

She nodded. "You haven't asked about my trip."

"How was your trip?" He smiled.

"I hit a herd of cows with my rental car and was bleeding from the head. I ended up collapsing on a beach."

He moved forward to examine her more closely and squinted up his face in a way that Alice recognized as something he'd done when they were children — he sometimes seemed as if he'd learned certain facial expressions by imitation and hadn't moved past the exaggeration stage. She could not help but crack a smile. "You look fine," he said. "You're fine." Then he came over and sat beside her.

He took her hand. They sat like that for a long while. It was as if they both knew the quarreling was long from over, and they wanted to mutually prepare; they wanted to tap into their reserves of shared material.

"Since he died," Gus said, "since I went back, I need to be alone more, but I get so sick of myself, you know?" he said, giving a short exhalation that was supposed to pass for a laugh. "The only way I can get out of my head is to talk to total strangers. Do you ever feel that way?"

She nodded. "But I get too involved," she said.

"You've always been too empathic."

"I wish that were true."

"I didn't mean it as a compliment."

"Yes, I know."

"Look, I wish Cady had stayed longer, and I do feel badly that I drove her to leave, but in a way I know she couldn't have stayed, no matter how well behaved I was. I know how it feels when someone's only half there."

"Are you talking about Mom?"

He shrugged. "Mom, me, everyone but you," he said sarcastically, but Alice could tell, for whatever it was worth, that he meant it. "God knows you're always there. You're right there, all right."

"Cady said you met someone who knew Mom," she finally said. And having said it at last, having come to her point, she wanted only to say it again. "Did you?"

"No."

"Just — no?"

"*No*, Alice."

"Why would she say such a thing?" Alice shifted her weight on the floor and waited. "Well?"

"That's totally ridiculous." He sniffed. "She must have said that to get you to come down here and take care of me."

"So you didn't see anyone in Oaxaca who knew her."

He laughed without showing his teeth. "Of course not. She told you that? She's amazing. No, Cady got you on board so she could leave me and still feel like a responsible person. If you haven't noticed, she's big on responsibility."

"Right," said Alice, watching him closely, waiting yet again. Alice thought of Cady, back in her apartment or house — she didn't even know where Cady called home or whom she would call in a crisis. "I don't believe anyone."

"That's too bad," he said. "But I suppose it gives me less reason to worry over you."

"You worry about me?"

"Not really, but you know, I might start. Look at you," he said, "you're a delicate flower." He reached out and gently tugged at a strand of her hair. A moment passed, then: "It's good to see you."

She hated that lift in the back of her throat, the watering of her eyes — the heavy, disproportionate, and welcome relief that inevitably occurred at the softening of his voice.

"Stay here with me tonight," he said.

Alice looked at her brother in this, his personal squalor. She wanted to not be here, not here at all, but ten years old and out in the poolhouse — unrenovated and unburned. She wanted to be holding the big heavy flashlight and watching his hands make shadow puppets. *Do the bunny. Do it again. Do the bird.*

"No," she said, standing, "I'll go back."

"Where?" He grinned, looking up at her. "There aren't many options here. Let me guess: with the Canadian backpackers in a hostel? So you can play backgammon in the *common space?*"

"Where I'm going, there are no nice Canadian backpackers," she said gravely. "There is no common space."

"Don't go. I have a sleeping bag you can use. It's soft and warm. Just don't go right

304

now. It's really late and you don't know the roads well. Please don't."

"Give me the sleeping bag," she said. "Give me a sip of your water."

She curled up in the opposite corner. She blew the candles out as he hummed a made-up song. In his sister's mind there were lyrics about phosphorescence, fireflies, long-limbed selfish children. She wondered if he knew how grateful she was to him each time he helped indulge the small part of her that truly loved not making sense. She waited for him to apologize or to explain; there was a physical space inside her that stayed open and waiting, but as he kept humming those low and infuriatingly relaxing melodies, the space simply faded away.

In the shack that had become the poolhouse where they'd camped out years ago, Alice had remained quiet for hours, and what Gus had done was talk. He'd told her all of his secrets, all of his many plans. Now he was silent, and soon, she heard, he was asleep. She watched the moon, barely a sliver, in the collapsing sky. The stars up above were brutal gossips: *Make a wish*, they said, giggling, so ravishing and mean, so many in number, Alice didn't stand a chance.

12

If she was going to understand just what had happened to Cady and what Gus was very clearly not inclined to share, Alice knew she had to accept, at least for a while, the wide-open blankness of being here. She could do anything with her time right now, and this was completely foreign to her nature. She had never been particularly idle. Besides which, it was certainly not here that she would have chosen to start. The very word, *Baja* — it had always conjured a dusty car mirror, driving forever through endless heat, and the vision, as it happened, was basically correct. It had always been words like *Aix-en-Provence* that, for Alice, inspired lolling around. It was words like *Amalfi, Sienna.* But she'd long been far away from all that she'd considered hers before she moved back home with her father — everything from that life was suspended in time. And her parents' house wouldn't lose its value anytime soon; besides, she liked the idea of it sitting there in the cold, so clean and vacant, waiting.

Idleness as a child had been nonexistent because she was always either pining for her mother or trying to entertain her. She had worked each summer as a teenager, all through college, in between college and grad school in various and thankless administrative positions, and then when friends took time off from research or writing dissertations, Alice never did — although she never finished her dissertation either, supposedly because she was needed at home, but even Alice couldn't maintain that reasoning anymore. She feared being unoccupied or — more to the point — unnecessary. And what could be less necessary than another investigation of the melancholy if perfect Anton Chekhov? *How did I ever let myself start on such an indulgent and depressing road?* she had said to her father, to Eleanor, and it was true.

But what she really feared was this: spending days unaccounted for, living in her threadbare fake silk *shmata* of a robe and turning off the phone and having people believe she was consumed with thought when she was really consumed with the freedom — of what everyone she knew and loved coveted most: choices, an abundance of choices.

Her father got sicker. He saved her.

And now here she was, hot on the trail of not much more than an answer to a question she couldn't exactly name. She needed a response, a definitive one, and Alice knew she couldn't leave this place until Gus gave something up. Alice knew he had something; she was sure of it. She'd spent years reconstructing her last conversations with her mother and feeling perfectly sane in doing so with the aim of possessing some kind of understanding — as if profound thought were all that would be required to comprehend Charlotte's death. Alice, perhaps unfairly, had also wanted nothing more than for her brother to take on some of the burden of proof and insist that she stop. In the last few years she'd achieved a sense of control, an easing away from needing to know why Charlotte met such an untimely end, but this self-imposed grace had fallen straight away with Cady's desperate call. Her innumerable attempts at letting go had ultimately led her here — to this kind of dusty nowhere.

Although she had to admit that in certain lights this town was a reluctant charmer. It wasn't Amalfi, but still . . .

There were a disproportionate number of candy stands. Two were right next to each other, carrying the very same products, and they were both placed precariously on the mostly crumbled sidewalk — *Muy Rico!* was painted boldly on both in the same hand-painted font. Alice handed over a few pesos at each stand, receiving in exchange a few caramels, what she could best ascertain as pudding-in-a-bag, and a cherry-red lollipop shaped like a heart and which was somehow vaguely obscene. Alice knew, like her mother before her, that she would eat them all.

She stopped in front of a locked gate, a caramel melting in her mouth. Beyond the gate was an empty pastel blue-bottomed swimming pool. On the wall inside the gate there was a hand-painted cheerful sign — *Club Aqua Baja* — there were palm trees surrounding it, but the pool was filthy with litter and dead leaves that had most likely fallen during the last hurricane season. It was such a sad sight it seemed as if someone should have thought to cover it up like a corpse, out of respect, protecting its stunted possibilities.

Moving in from the periphery, teeth stinging from sugar, Alice passed men in cowboy hats, men whose bellies hung way over their belt buckles as they smoked Boots cigarettes. There were packs of Boots lying in the street, on abandoned outdoor tables, sticking out of back pockets. The church, painted mustard and crimson, loomed high above the town, creating a beacon for the open plaza, which Alice imagined filled with people and music on occasion but was now as empty as a schoolyard in summer. On the plaza there was an old locked theater, a municipal building of some kind, and an arch that said in black script above it, *Café*. In the arch there was a huge padlocked castlelike door, with its hours of operation on a small tasteful sign. A few signs said *Gallery*, but in two cases the door was locked, and the third was open but clearly not in business, for there was nothing in the empty space whatsoever. It was cold and dark with speckled linoleum floors — not a welcoming venue.

As she walked down streets lined with old brick haciendas, fish taco carts (*Tres Hermanos!*, *Dos Juans*, *Pescado Bueno*), mango stands, frozen coconuts, and a clinic painted bright yellow with an illustration of a huge and blood-filled syringe, each door (even, perversely, the clinic) made Alice want to walk inside. At the onset of a burgeoning compulsion to peer inside people's homes, Alice started to alternate between feeling furious with Gus and also the slightest bit grateful to be out of that big wintry house — forced to focus on objects with eyes that saw beyond their links to irrefutable history and how such objects would ultimately meet the fate of box or garbage.

She missed her father, how he put things in context, how he remembered exactly everything he read. If he were at her side he'd be able to explain just what kinds of marine life were evolving in the nearby ocean, what existed here even before the art deco and adobe. She missed her mother, too, no more than usual but more acutely, as Charlotte still reigned over all foreign places.

On entering a dank dark cement shack (*Feliz Camaron* — the façade depicted a smiling, dancing shrimp), Alice smelled the universally powerful scent of something frying. Lard was in the air and it was intoxicating. She saw that the proprietor was shirtless and sweating, with a cigarette hanging out of his mouth, but amidst the frying smell she didn't care. She would have, she imagined, eaten just about anything at that moment as long as it was fried. The shirtless man was shaking his head at a woman who spoke right on through his attitude, who could have said nothing and still it would have seemed as if she was not only fighting but winning. She had jet-black hair tied in a pink scarf, dangling silver earrings, and her eyes were dark with enormous pupils, which gave her a wild, protesting look. She didn't look like a tourist, but from what Alice had seen, she certainly didn't seem like a local either. Her blouse was loose and possibly from the forties, a dusty-rose short-sleeved fabric that had seen better days. She wore it effectively, over a black bra, paired with faded jeans, and she wore no makeup besides kohl-black eyeliner that Alice didn't even notice at first because her eyes were so dark to begin with. There was something about her carriage that broadcast urban roots. Her Spanish seemed perfect, but what did Alice know? She could have been from Barcelona, Mexico City, Bogotá — anywhere but here.

Alice watched as the woman plunged her hand deep in the icebox, where blue-black shrimp lay in a heap. There were two neon-red snappers with eyes stunned wide open, and layers of green-glinting whitefish lying heavy until the woman reached her small fingers around the top one and separated it from the rest. "No," she said, with a single shake of her head. Then she pursed her lips in dismissal.

The fish man spoke excitedly, throwing the cigarette out back, into the small lot, where what appeared to be a mess of old car parts, fish heads, and tails lay scattered before a stooped lady sitting in the shade, looking not a day older than 110. *"Sí."* He nodded, countering the striking woman's shaking of her head. *"Sí, sí —"*

"You must insist until he lifts the top ones away," she said softly, apparently to Alice, for there was no one else around. Her voice was eerily high and hazy, the effect of which was that of a twelve-year-old girl who'd been a career smoker since the second grade.

Alice found herself nodding a few beats too long, surprised somehow at the woman's perfect English. She had felt somehow sealed off from everyone else, as if nobody could actually see her.

"The best are at the bottom," she continued, taking a cigarette from her purse and lighting up. "The best are always hidden away." She blew smoke in the man's direction as they stood in some manner of a face-off.

The man begrudgingly extracted two

bottom pieces from the icebox after she'd maintained her position, and he wrapped them up for her. As the woman raised her hand to her hair, Alice noticed that she wore, oddly enough, the exact bracelet that encircled Alice's own wrist — a thin silver coil she'd had for years. The silver glinted in the shadows, and Alice tried to remember where she'd bought it, as she heard the woman say something else to him, something that sounded like a friendly threat. "I told him not to be a mean bastard and to give you something fresh."

"Thank you," Alice said. "Look, we have the same bracelet." She held out her wrist and the woman came close to Alice, extending her own tanner, thinner arm.

A birthmark in the shape of a crescent covered the woman's forearm, one shade darker than her skin. She remained silent, staring.

"Why did you assume he'd try to rip me off?"

"You look like an easy target," she said without a smile. "Be careful," she warned, and with a bag of fish swinging from her hand, the woman walked out the door into the light. It took a moment for Alice to realize that this curious woman hadn't paid for her food.

314

★ ★ ★

It was afternoon, the hottest part of the day had passed, and she could bet that her brother was surfing. Fenced-in goats lay still, in a pale herd. The nearby ocean, the fragrant banana bushes and mango trees all tempered the smell of manure and also the faint smell of fried shrimp coming from her. She'd tucked into nearly a kilo, pouring on hot sauce, squeezing limes, and sopping up the grease with buttery tortillas. Alice was now savoring the memory, toying with the idea of seeking out ice cream or maybe a strong cold coffee. A brown and wrinkled farmworker whistled as she walked faster and faster, enjoying — no, loving — the dry heat and wind on her already sunburned face. On the surfing beach, trucks were in the distance; they were pulled up nearly to the lip of the sand ledge, and Alice knew that Gus was out there. As she walked toward the ocean, the hot sun scrambled her thoughts that were spilling at random (Her own silver bracelet, where had it come from? What was the actual fat content of lard?); nothing could be contained in this wide-open space, in this searing Pacific light. Those pale-fire eyes of the girl at the airport, the burned-charcoal stare of the

315

woman from the fish shack — these were female eyes and somehow were seeing right through her, straight into her tenuous hold on just where she was and why.

Alice believed Cady. She believed in Cady DeForrest, in everything she had said, and not her own brother.

The task of prying out information from Gus about their mother, the kind of information they'd *always no matter what* agreed to share, was not only depressing but also daunting. Charlotte had left a good deal of blank spots in her messy wake — vacant lots of questions where her father never wished to venture. Most adults have a secret or two, as their father was wont to say, but Alice and August had always agreed on how their mother had more. She had more of everything and she still seemed to feel slighted, missing out on something vital. She was always hungry, literally hungry, eager to name her cravings, and she was full of secrets; they were stitched into her being, like diamonds sewn into the silk skirt linings of wealthy refugees.

Her children knew this, and it was therefore implicit that there would be no secrets between them; there would never be a reason for it. Alice had grown to feel that, if anything, she had to tell Gus when she *didn't* want to hear his secrets — the extent of the gambling he'd done in Bangkok, the way Cady smelled like sour milk when she had a cold, his postulations of why that turned him on — *Enough,* she'd say, grinning, stretching the phone cord and sitting on her fire escape in warmer weather, picking dead leaves off her plants.

What are you doing, Alice?

How do you know I'm doing anything?

Because you'd never talk this long and not get something done in the meanwhile.

What are you doing?

Since we've been on the phone, I've smoked a joint and been lying completely still, but now I'm clipping my toenails.

There was no detail he'd refuse her if she asked him for it. That was something she used to know.

There was nobody in any of the trucks but an amber mutt passed out in one of the flatbeds, obviously dreaming. His chest heaved up and down, he made sweet whimpering sounds, and his paw reached out and scratched the air. Out in the thick gray ocean, however, in the far-off hills of water, there were surfers. There were about ten of them, all in dark wet suits. Alice sat in the sand near the truck and watched. A young couple with matching mullet hairstyles sat a few yards away in low beach chairs. A few older long boarders were suited up, stretching and taking their time. Pelicans swooped low against the cloud-banded sky, as gulls congregated in darting packs. How small the waves looked from here, how completely misleading. While appearing as rising slopes gently falling away into whitecaps — Alice knew from Gus's years of talk — these particular waves were fast-breaking, and the graceful rides these guys were taking were not about length but speed. Gus had always liked narrating his surf sessions to her, especially when he was first learning, and as far as Alice could tell, the telephone pole was invented so surfers could use it as a measuring stick (*You see that pole?*) when bragging about their latest ride.

Of course she tried to tell if he was one of the surfers, but it was, as always, impossible. She made her way over the mass of rocks in the surprisingly cold water and waded up to her shins, fighting for balance against the powerful undertow. The waves were so tempting, and even as Alice knew she could never make it out beyond the rocks without some type of board, she found herself inching farther and farther

318

until she bashed her toe against one and eventually hobbled back up the sand ledge. She nearly fell asleep, soothed by the sound of the ocean, but there he was, gingerly stepping on the rocks, board tucked under his arm. By the time August made it up to where she was sitting, Alice had made the petty decision to not call out his name. He was out of breath when he said hello, which he said as if she were simply on time for a preexisting plan.

Alice asked, "Aren't you cold?" which came out sounding like an insult.

"Yes," he replied tightly. He took his wet suit off, dried himself with the dirty blanket, and changed in the open air. Standing naked for a moment, he gave the dog in the truck a rough tousle. Gus was one of those rare people on this earth who was truly and completely immodest. He yelled good-naturedly enough, as if he'd jumped into a freezing quarry. The dog did some halfhearted barking. "Cold, cold, cold," he said, imitating the urgent style of little Alice, testing out the bathwater. What an elaborate affair it had been to get her submerged. Gus simply resisted bathing altogether and had to be bribed, but Alice had — weirdly enough for a child — loved taking baths, but they had to be perfect.

Hot, hot, hot. Cold, cold, cold. The adjustments could take a good thirty minutes.

She smiled at his reference as he pulled a sweatshirt over his head and looked out at the water, where the others were perched on their boards. "So, um, you slept okay last night?" he asked.

"Yes, thanks for letting me stay," she said. "You looked good out there."

"Thanks," he said impatiently, "but you can't tell from this far out who's who."

"I can," she said. "I could tell it was you right away."

The silence that ensued was diminished, boring. There was far too much to say. She couldn't yet believe the other possibility, that they'd simply grown apart and whatever urges he'd possessed to confide in her had not only disappeared, but had been all that had kept them so close for so long.

"Why don't we go get a beer or something," she offered. "I'd like to talk."

"Oh, I . . . I can't right now. These guys," he said, "I promised I'd help one of them with his landscaping business. He cuts back palm trees, plants some herbs . . . it's good work."

"Right," Alice said. "So . . ."

"I can meet you later. Around six?"

"Fine," she said. "We'll get dinner. I

think I saw a place or two."

"Oh, well . . . I haven't been doing too much of that if I can help it."

"What, *eating?*"

"I'm broke, Alice."

"Dinner does not need to be such an issue," she muttered. "Let's get a few tacos, okay?"

"Hey," he called to the other guys, heading toward them.

"August?" she said.

"Hey," he called out to the surfers again. "Preston, Javier — my sister, Alice."

"What's up," they each said, nodding, smiling. "Didn't know you had a sister here."

"Me neither," he said. "It was a surprise."

"Nice," Javier said. Preston looked more uncertain. "Come have a beer with us," Javier said to Alice. "No work for us until tomorrow."

She turned to her brother and made sure he saw her eyes, empty of everything but comprehension. "That's okay, thanks," she said in her politest voice. "Gus, I'll see you at five," she said. "Can you handle five? In the plaza?" She made sure she saw him nod before she turned away.

13

The late afternoon had always felt like a lonely time, a type of quiet relenting. For children and the employed it meant going from the public world of school and office to the private world of home, and for everyone else it seemed it was too early to drink and too late to get a whole lot else done. The shadows at five weren't quite long enough, Alice felt, the heat was still at work, but there was no mistaking the time. There was a resignation to the light that was basically the same anywhere. If she wasn't distracted by work, it unfailingly made Alice melancholy.

After a surprisingly drama-free hour of filing a report with the *judiciale*, Alice headed for the plaza, which, as it happened, was empty of Gus. The three teenage girls who loitered on the steps of the church definitely appeared to belong to the secret world of mean girls. They wore pastel-blue school jumpers over starched white shirts, and they looked — with their gold earrings, brown skin, and nonwrinkled scowls — like local representatives from the Dominion of Youth and Beauty. They were selling woven bracelets, and Alice was intimidated into buying one: red and turquoise with one clear bead. It looked like something Alice would have made in grade school, but she liked shedding the silver coil and feeling its weight in her pocket. She was happy to replace it with something new.

Was it possible Gus genuinely thought they'd agreed on six o'clock? They'd agreed on six originally — this was fine; this was better — she could go to the Casa de Cultura, the imposing structure on the main street. She could take in a little culture and thank him for it later.

Alice had expected a gatekeeper, at least a semblance of an organization, given the official town crest on the building and the impressive crimson Deco lettering, but once inside the enormous doorway, she walked straight into a grand courtyard, where trees were overgrown and sun hit the brick like a spotlight. *Oz*, Alice thought vaguely, *this is the light of Emerald City gone languid, imperial entrance included.* There was, however, no welcoming procession; there was nobody around. The wind through the trees sounded like sleep. Labyrinthine hallways surrounded the patio and led into mazes of rooms, cubbyholes, and abandoned desk-lined classrooms. A gigantic papier-mâché woman stood as a goddess of fertility, and behind her were low shelves holding up what looked like artifacts collected from the most obscure corners of town. There was an old ruined typewriter. Alice imagined a gringo writer in the early 1950s, a devotee of John Steinbeck, sitting down in a rented *casita,* set to put his fervor to words. Surely he'd gone mad, Alice thought, driven by the relentless pounding of waves, and had jumped in the ocean late at night, discovering just how cruel those waves really were. His maid, no doubt fascinated by the machine, would have taken it to the cultural center after searching his room for valuables.

There was a tiny Buddha, botanical fossils, and jawbones of what appeared to be whales and sharks. There were two glittery shoes (brand: Neiman Marcus) and a local map from 1957.

There was an assortment of bones.

Alice touched everything. No object was given prominence on the shelf. It was a haphazard pile of the past, chalky and resolute. What made her sick to her stomach was not the familiar faint scent of death and neglect, but of how it could be that she was instantly holding not only her mother's belongings but her father's belongings too — recalling how small a part they played in the sorting out of the house. Besides his papers and clothing (he was a man who would wear one pair of trousers and one threadbare tweed jacket for decades but had a lush array of cashmere socks), there was only his collection of fossils and nests with which Alice was left to contend. She hadn't asked him about it while he was dying because she knew it would break his heart to reexamine each treasured bone. She believed they'd had an unspoken agreement that she should give it to a local school.

With a black feather in her hand, she heard music — thirties jazz — and at first she thought she was imagining it or that it was coming from a nearby house. But she went toward the sound, getting farther from the courtyard, and found herself in an ochre room, its walls covered with sepia-toned photographs. These were pictures of the very building where she stood, and also of squinting farmers in the *huerta*, fishermen in their *panga* boats coming in with the tides. There were fat babies and young beauties, families in caravans, families with horses. The jazz was loud and she could hear the scratch of vinyl.

Gus had to be up in a booth somewhere, looking down and laughing. She pictured him behind a curtain, aware of his limitations but undaunted, invested in pointless illusion. With her eyes closed, Alice could feel her mother's hands on her waist, showing her how to dance. *Pretend you're moonlight,* she'd say, all silky; *you're no longer limited by a body.* The things she'd say to teach them dancing; God forbid she counted to the music, gave them something solid like numbers to fall back on. She was always good at getting people dancing, to shut them up about literature and politics and real estate and simply throw themselves around. Charlotte always started with her children — she was a good and shrewd performer — leading them onto the beaten-down wood, the beer-slicked linoleum, the summer-browned grass. There was one time she'd sweated through her clothing, and delphiniums were wilted throughout her straight hair. Such a scent there was, it must have been one hundred degrees, the air so rich there was no refusing her, there was no such thing as embarrassment. Alice had spun like a dervish, and so had Gus; they'd spun around until she'd held them to her bony chest, all of them laughing from the closeness, from being overheated, from how no one was about to pull away.

When Alice found herself back in the plaza, it was six o'clock, and then six-fifteen, and Gus was still not with her. She pointlessly counted seconds as a mosquito buzzed in her ear and dust kicked up at her ankles. When the smell of candy and cigarettes hit the air, she turned around at once. "Oh," Alice said, on seeing the woman from the fish store.

"Surprised?" she asked.

Alice replied, with a self-mocking grin, "I thought you were someone else."

"*Claro,*" she said. "You're waiting for someone?"

Alice nodded. The woman stood next to her, settling into not much more than staring into space. There were some people, Alice noted, who — no matter how sullen a mood she was in — never failed to make her more of a smiler, someone on a crusade to fill silences. There was some chemistry at work, something in the air that made Alice work harder. "Thanks for earlier, you know, with the shrimp."

"My pleasure," she said. She sat down on a bench and began rolling a cigarette. The lights of the plaza turned on with a flourish, illuminating not only the plaza, but also the surrounding buildings. "Would you like?"

Alice shook her head. "Thanks, though," she said, watching the woman's fingernails. They were bitten down to the point of being swollen and polished bright red. "I'm Alice," she said.

She didn't look up from her delicate task. "Erika," she replied, *"mucho gusto."* Alice realized that Erika was much younger than she'd originally assumed. With her foreign bravado and confidence Alice had placed her at thirty or so, but now, outside, under the stark plaza lights and without the rapid-fire Spanish, she wouldn't have been surprised to learn that Erika was in her early twenties or even younger. She wasn't wearing the pink scarf anymore, and with her thick hair pulled back in an office rubber band, Alice could see dark hair curling at her temples, on her forearms, and on the sides of her face. All that dark hair made her look younger — oddly enough — like a girl who hadn't yet learned to be self-conscious, who hadn't even thought to bleach or pluck or shave a virgin strand. When the cigarette was perfectly rolled, she opened her purse and, in the process of looking for a lighter, she took out a stack of pictures, cards, a key chain, a notebook, a pen, and two lipsticks. There was a picture on top of the stack.

"My mother," she said, having seen Alice looking.

The woman in the picture had narrow, small features, lips in a hard, dark line. "Is she Mexican?" Alice asked.

Erika nodded. "My father was American."

"She looks tough," Alice said, "strong."

"A bitch," Erika said, and then she laughed. She lit the cigarette and inhaled. "A great talent too, my mother, but what a temper. How about yours?" she asked, almost jauntily. Alice heard more than a trace of the accent that until now had barely registered. Erika's dark eyes shimmered under heavy brows, behind pale wisps of smoke.

"My mother?" Alice said.

"Your temper," she said. "You do not have much of one, no?" Her neckline hung low, and Alice couldn't help imagining her leaning over a stove's blue flame, her flimsy shirt dangling, her hair hanging loose —

being careless, daily, with her lighter.

"No?" Alice asked, surprised by her assumption and slightly galled by her strange way of speaking. "I don't know about that," she said, wondering if she should be insulted or flattered.

Erika gave Alice an impish smile. "I have a terrible temper," she said with a laugh. "This is why I am always alone." She picked up the red pen and began to doodle in her notebook with unexpected speed. "You are alone a lot too, no?"

"I'm waiting for someone," Alice said, glancing at Erika's paper, where some sort of acid-sunset church was being frenetically rendered. "Remember?"

"Yes," she said. "You said."

"So what is your mother's great talent?" Alice said, surprised to hear the tinge of sarcasm in her voice.

"Oh, she's a potter," Erika said, still doodling maniacally. Her voice — slowly suggestive — was at odds with her frenetic hands. "She makes gorgeous pots. It's so lucky, I think, to have a talent. As you see, I cannot draw," she said, continuing her endeavors. "What I can do is sell," she said, and, finally stopping, she offered a grin. "That's my talent. I can sell anything at all. I do not have to like what I am

330

selling. I am heartless," she said, laughing, casting her pen aside. "I sell pants too small, bras too big. Last year I sold — I am sure — the ugliest painting ever painted. So think how easy it is for me to sell my mother's pots. I'm going to open my own store soon, my own gallery. She'd starve if it were not for me, my mother; she's such an artiste, you know?" she said.

"Hmm," Alice said, "I have to say, I doubt you're always alone. I have a feeling you must meet people all the time."

Erika shrugged, closing the notebook. "I am a very jealous person," she said, as if it were something she'd been told, many times, to say. Alice pictured her throwing plates at a wall, screaming — a sheet thrown around her — in a multitude of languages.

"You too?" Alice asked, even though she wasn't sure she really was a jealous person. She was more likely to focus for days on comments that no one would remember even saying.

"I once came at a man with my car. I had found some letters," Erika said, waving it off, as if this were nothing at all. "Stupid, I know, but he did deserve it. I broke his arm." She said this lightly, as if it were only possibly true. And leaving Alice

331

to wonder just what he'd done, she stood up and said, "So what about you? Do you have a boyfriend or anything?"

"Or anything?" Alice raised her eyebrows with a grin. It occurred to her that she was speaking with a member of the secret world of mean girls and that this was what it felt like when one of them included you. It felt like secrets, like whispered late-night confessions. It made you want to step up the stakes, to either lie or tell the absolute truth. "I'm engaged," she said, her heart beating at her coy choice of words.

"Engaged?" she said, laughing, as if such a thing were impossible.

Alice nodded slowly.

"Where is the ring?"

"My ring," Alice said, "is at home."

"Is it big?"

Once again, Alice couldn't gauge whether she was serious.

"I bet we have the same taste in a ring," Erika said. "After all, we have the same bracelet."

Alice looked down at Erika's wrist and was speechless for a moment. Erika's silver coil was gone too. In its place was nearly the same homemade bracelet that Alice had bought only an hour ago — the only difference was the color of the bead.

"Where did you get that?"

"What?"

"Were you watching me or something?"

She shook her head, looking confused. "It is a coincidence, no? A double coincidence."

"You could say that."

The sun, Alice noticed, was almost gone, and a slice of moon had risen. Erika picked up a long dark strand of her hair that had escaped from her rubber band and curled it tight around her bitten finger until the skin went red, then white. Alice watched her do so and thought about how her circulation was being cut off, and how she must have been very uncomfortable. Erika saw Alice watching but said nothing. Neither did Alice.

"So, do you love him madly or don't you?" Erika blurted out, vamping now with a line clearly lifted from a movie. She was actressy, Alice decided — a frustrated failed siren.

"What?"

"Your boyfriend. Your fiancé."

"Of course I do."

"Oh," she said, "of *course*. Well, then, I feel sorry for you."

"Is that right?"

"Yes."

"I have to go," Alice said. She suddenly wanted to get far away from this woman.

"Someone stood you up then?"

"It would seem so."

Erika nodded, her small nostrils slightly flared. She smiled. "Bastard," she said.

She was walking faster now that dogs were coming out with the sunset — barking and running alongside her. The faces on the road were not those of August, as she looked around at the blown-out cars and piles of garbage decaying in empty lots, but she was still caught in her brother's gaze — the increasing distance of it, its outside periphery and underlying fierceness that seemed to care for nothing. As Alice made her way to the hotel construction site and when, finding it empty, she returned to the surf beach, she kept expecting August's face to pass, to catch his rare look of surprise, but there were only strangers going their separate ways. When she lived in a city, she could go for days not noticing people, days where faces and figures blended together no more distinctly than leaves. But on some days the faces . . . they'd pierce through the masses as wholly separate — painfully separate — in their startling individuality. It was like that here.

Alice held her breath as she saw a brown woman without legs perched outside a small cement house; the lines on her face were plentiful and weblike, offset by clear brown eyes. She placidly embroidered a stark white sheet and looked up with a smile for the *gringa,* in a rush walking by.

As the sun began to set and the sky swathed itself in lurid colors, Gus seemed farther off than when she'd been miles and miles away from him, when all she'd wanted was to fly across the country and ask him what had happened. Such a thought now seemed painfully naïve. The asking would have automatically led to his telling her, and that telling her would make one bit of difference in his life or hers seemed sadly outdated.

She smelled burning garbage, that sweet strange smell, and prayed for those dogs to be harmless, for the road to carry her along. What she wanted was to find Gus on that beach, yes, but she also wanted to find the very sharpest of knives. She wanted to cut the cheap bracelet from her wrist in one clean slice. She'd throw it in the ocean, but not even that would be enough.

14

On the beach there was a group of women —
thin and fidgety as sandpipers — who were
gathered watching surfers take their last rides
of the day. The surfers looked slight as they
waited for waves, like black dogs paddling toward the dimming horizon. Alice had introduced herself to the women, and after asking
if they knew her brother, August, she became
cause for a small celebration.

There were two Karens: Skinny Karen
and Surfer Karen (who was admirably off
fighting for waves). There was Autumn, a
quick talker, a former speed freak from Orange County, and Christa, the beauty,
quiet in nothing but a crocheted bikini
even though it was really quite chilly, now
that the sun was gone.

"You two are really close?" asked Autumn,
as if needing Alice to verify her credentials.

"He's my only family," Alice replied, not

answering her question.

"That's cool," Autumn nodded, working on a cuticle with her little white teeth.

"What do you mean, 'that's cool'?" Skinny Karen said. "Are your parents . . . dead?" she asked with trepidation, squinting in Alice's direction.

"I didn't mean —" sputtered Autumn.

"That's okay," Alice said, smiling, a little punchy from so much walking, from the off-kilter conversation with Erika. "I know what you meant." They were so young, she realized; they were probably some ten years younger than she was.

A slight shift occurred in the air, and as Karen tossed her hair over one shoulder, Autumn crossed her legs into an insanely flexible position, and Christa did nothing but smile, Alice looked up to see Gus making his way in, stepping over the rocks. She viewed the girls with partial sympathy and partial disdain for their apparent collective objective.

"Oh," Gus said, "hi, Alice. Hey, ladies," he said to the others, flashing them a lazy smile. Christa offered a neatly folded towel and he took it. He couldn't help flirting. Alice knew flirting consoled him and that it had nothing to do with these girls. She felt bad for not telling them so. "What?" he asked, replying to Alice's embittered look. He set his board against a truck with elaborate care, and, as if to point out the imposition, he sighed. He made a vague gesture as if the beach were a dance floor and he was a spoiled young prince, who, at the queen mother's orders, had asked a homely heiress to dance.

"You didn't show," she said.

"What?"

"Um, today? Five o'clock?"

"Oh, I'm sorry," he said. "I got tied up."

"I can see that."

Gus put his hands in his hair and tugged. "Alice, did I ask you to come here?"

"That doesn't matter anymore. I'm here."

"What is it you want?" Gus asked. "Just . . . what?"

"I only want to know what is happening to you," said Alice, her voice as gentle as it was disingenuous.

"Alice, I'm telling you: find your own mess."

"Give me time."

He was, Alice could tell, about to start walking away.

"You do know," Alice said, assuming what she hoped was a judicious tone, "I won't go

338

home until you've talked with me. I don't understand why you can't just tell me what happened there."

"Look, Alice, I promise —"

"What can you promise? Everything is on your terms."

"Right now," he said blankly, "that's true."

Alice followed Gus's gaze, out at the Pacific. The opposing view was nothing but scrub brush, cactus, abandoned houses, and a language he didn't understand. "That's why you're here."

She watched him nod.

"Well," she said, "maybe that's why I'm here too."

"Don't," he said, finally turning toward her.

"Don't what? I bet you can't picture me doing anything besides hounding you."

"You're right," he said, in a tone strangely tender. "I can't."

The motel corridor was even dingier than she recalled. She could bet some of those surfers would be making a grand entrance at any moment. Someone was listening to music in one of the rooms, and the bass was pulsing underfoot. She fumbled with the key, fully prepared to accept the sight of all her belongings having been stolen. As she turned the key she heard a door close right around the corner.

"Turn it down," she heard a stern voice yell, and it was he of course, he of the pissed-off demeanor and clean white shirt, now rounding the corner.

"You found a room," she said. "Lucky you."

"Yeah, well, you gotta sleep someplace, and I'm not a big fan of camping — I've done my share; don't get me wrong — but after my most recent attempt, I'm thinking of starting a toll-free number," he said, smiling bitterly, revealing deep lines around his eyes and mouth. "A preventive hot line — so that, should the camping urge ever come over you, there'd be someone to talk you down."

Alice laughed along with him, all the while waiting for his bad manners to resurface.

He said, "I come down here every year, and I'm telling you every year something goes wrong. This year my rental fell through and no one thought to tell me before I showed up."

"But you come every year?"

"Oh," he said, "oh, yeah, of course. For ten years now, actually." And with that assertion he seemed to relax by degrees.

"I see," she said.

"What do you see?"

"I see someone who's horrified to be staying here." She smiled. "Afraid you'll be taken for a tourist?"

He smiled right back at her; the tips of his ears were red.

"What's your name?" Alice asked.

"Stephen," he said.

In the silence that followed, he took his keys from his pocket and suddenly tossed them to Alice. "First one to drop them pays for dinner," he said.

She tossed them back and they played catch with his keys until finally she said she was hungry, and he let the keys fall.

The café on the plaza — the one with the high-arched wooden door and small tasteful sign — was closed. "Damn it," he said, putting his hand on the beautiful wood. "It's a Monday. I completely forgot."

"I see someone's a regular," Alice said, raising her eyebrows.

"My friend opened this place about ten years ago. He and his wife are actually responsible for bringing the tourists; they put this town on the map, so to speak. The guy is one of these fanatic Italians. He eats in his restaurant every night, and if he's traveling he'll bring a few containers of his pasta, just in case. Every conversation always comes back to what is the best, the freshest, the purest."

"It's an Italian restaurant? Here?"

"It defies classification; it's that spectacular. They're totally self-sustained — their own garden, their own cheeses, local employees. . . ."

"And it's closed." There was a small cluster of teenagers in the plaza, but other than the clicking of typing from an open window in the *judiciale* building, the streets were silent. "So what is this place?" Alice asked.

"What do you mean?"

"This town. I don't understand where I am. I followed someone here on very short notice. I didn't exactly do a whole lot of research."

He shrugged, smiling. "This town . . . let's see. Home to quite a few UFO sightings."

"Is that right?"

"Actually, yes, although the sightings around here were more likely Juarez cartel jets carrying vast amounts of cocaine from Colombia. Did you read about that plane crash a little while back?"

Alice shook her head. "And is that what

drew you here," Alice asked, "an abundance of fine Colombian?"

Stephen laughed a little too hard. "Oh, I've been coming down here since before the drug trade made its cameo appearance. I'm just that old. For the most part — minor tales of the drug trade aside — it's an agricultural town, a fishing village. The old brick homes are from the late nineteenth and early twentieth centuries. There was a real bourgeoisie here, believe it or not." As they crossed a street, he silently steered Alice away from a pile of manure. "What I want to know is who got you to follow anyone anywhere. You seem fairly, shall we say, strong-willed."

"Oh, I don't know, I think you just pushed my final button."

"So you came down here and he wasn't what you thought?"

"Something like that," Alice said.

He smiled sympathetically. "There's kind of a romance to the failed ones, don't you think?"

She couldn't tell if he was making fun of her or of himself. "No," she said, "not really."

"Maybe you haven't had the right kind of failures," he said.

She looked at him and noticed that she

couldn't guess much about him. He was gruff but also refined in a way — his white shirt stained in places but rolled up carefully at the sleeves, the hands a bit gnarled but clean. "Maybe," she said. "Maybe so."

"So are we eating dinner or what?"

"It looks that way, doesn't it? What a weird day."

"Day's not over yet," he said, waving her down a steep unpaved hill.

It was, she had to admit, a relief to do some following. He moved with the gait of someone perfectly comfortable with being not particularly thin. Although he was fairly tall, he appeared even more so, as he had bulky shoulders and there was nothing compact about him. He pointed frequently and half-heartedly to different buildings, not quite finishing his sentences, and this sloppy gesturing made him seem expansive somehow instead of careless.

The last of four dinner possibilities hosted an exhausted-looking woman who intoned, "*solamente* cocktails," while not bothering to look away from a TV variety show featuring two grown women dressed like infants watching a juggling cowboy. Stephen gestured for Alice to exit the doorway. Behind the church, on the other side of the plaza, there was a lit-up street cart, and Stephen did his by-now-familiar pointing. And so they bought hot dogs from a toothless ancient man who piled on so many toppings that Alice was thankful for the dark. Stephen bought a case of Tecate from the market next to the motel, and they sat on the steps of an empty house (he swore it was empty; he promised he knew the owner) and they ate hot dogs and drank beer, while only random cars and begging dogs disturbed the eerie quiet.

He told her about the American couple from the Southwest who began hearing a low-grade humming noise in their town. So insidious was this humming noise, so ever present and soul sapping, that the couple packed up all of their belongings and headed for the Mexican border, although not before convincing many other members of their community that the sound — this "hum," as it soon became known — was some kind of right-wing conspiracy aimed toward wiping out Native Americans once and for all. And now, Stephen explained, the couple lived right here in Santa Lucia in a huge adobe palace with bars on all the windows. They were famous around town for complaining about noise.

"I think I saw a TV show about that hum," Alice said, recalling a phase of conspiracy programs to which she and her father had been briefly addicted.

He looked at her somewhat askance.

"I, ah, watched a whole lot of television this past year."

"Well, they discovered it. They discovered the Hum."

"And," Alice asked, "who owns this house?"

"My ex-wife," he said, taking a swig from his beer. He'd already started on his third beer and she hadn't even finished her first.

"Aha," Alice said. "Is she one of your romantic failures?"

"No." He shook his head. "Unfortunately not. Are you married?"

Alice coughed a little, and took a sip of beer. "Married? No."

"Kids?"

"No, God, no. You?"

"Why do you say it that way? You don't want kids?"

Everything he asked made her feel like he was about to make a joke at her expense, but especially this question, because he seemed so improbably sincere. "I don't know," Alice said. "I suppose I do."

"I really want kids."

"*You* do?"

"Yeah, *I* do," he said, shaking his head,

apparently at Alice's skepticism. "Definitely."

She looked out in the distance; she looked down at her shoe. "Your ex-wife wasn't the maternal type?"

"Which one?" he said, laughing.

"How many ex-wives do you have?"

"Oh, six," he said. And then he shook his head.

"Ha, ha."

"I like to start with a high number, so that in comparison the real number seems insignificant. I have two. I've been married twice."

He cracked open another beer. "I've gotten really good at getting divorced, though. I'm an expert. Both times I've signed the papers, I've come down here, rented the same place on the beach, and watched the whales. Once I get to the beach, once I get out of whatever trouble always seems to greet me, it's really pretty peaceful."

What Alice wanted to know was, *Am I trouble?* "There really are whales here?" she asked instead.

"Don't worry; you'll see them."

"I don't know if I'm staying long enough."

"Well," he said, "you should." Then he

crushed the empty beer can in his hand and tossed it in the paper bag. "For the whales," he said.

By the time they got going, Stephen had put away three hot dogs and six beers. He'd burped out loud. He'd told her that he'd bought a small plot of land for which he was not exactly sure he had the legal title.

"Well," Stephen said, as they approached La Balena, "I got you all wrong. When I saw you I made a snap judgment. I'm usually very astute." He was drunk.

"And what did you think?"

"I assumed you were, to be perfectly honest, like most American women I've met down here."

"And that would mean?"

"Oh, you know, seeing auras, using the last of your alimony, starting a ceramic career or meditation retreat, with prurient hopes of entertaining a Mexican boy or two." He was smiling.

"Good night, Stephen," she said. "I'm going inside now."

"Good night, Alice," he said. "I'm not."

And when she had to step over one of the surfers sitting in the hallway with a blond dreadlocked girl, when she made it to her room and closed the door, she looked outside in the courtyard and there was Stephen, attempting to right one of the plastic chairs. She watched him struggle with it for a moment, and she smiled at the way he seemed loath to put down his beer. When he finally sat in the chair, he didn't pick the beer up again. In fact, he did nothing but stare straight ahead. When he looked up at her window, she'd been watching so long with the curtain wide open, she didn't even try to hide it. Neither of them waved.

15

A coffeepot was set up in the cement courtyard, and after being stirred awake by
honking horns and voices in the hallway,
Alice approached the empty table and
poured herself a cup. She thought of the has-
sled proprietress making coffee every
morning, counting out cups and spoons. As
she looked around, with the intention of
taking a stab at thanking her in Spanish (she
could already imagine the woman's bothered
expression), three girls emerged. " 'Member
us?" one of them asked. "From the beach?"

"Oh, hi," Alice said, distracted by the
plastic chair where she could bet Stephen
had sat last night for long after she'd gone
to sleep.

"We didn't know you were staying here."

Alice smiled politely. She could hear,
from inside the proprietress's apartment,
the sounds of a baby crying.

"How's your brother?" Autumn asked casually.

"You know," Alice said, watching powdered milk surface, unblended, in her coffee, "I'm not really sure."

They all looked at her strangely.

"So," Alice said, "what can you tell me about who my brother's been hanging around with?"

"You don't know?" said Skinny Karen suspiciously.

"I really just got here," Alice said, deflecting. "We haven't had a chance to exactly catch up on everything."

"Well, what we all want to know is whether they're just sleeping together or if it's more than that." Karen, Autumn, Christa — they were blending into a Greek chorus of tan, skinny limbs.

"Blond woman, very pretty?" Alice asked; it had been, as far as Alice knew, only days since Cady left.

They all shook their heads, eager to get down to business. "Not that one."

Alice waited.

"That other one," Christa said, finally speaking up. "You know, the woman with that superblack hair, I think she's maybe Mexican? She dresses kind of . . . I don't know . . . she wears, like, cool *amulets* and shit. . . . She lives here. I know she works in town."

"Where?" said Alice, not believing, yet fully believing. "Where does she work?"

"I don't know," said Christa, recoiling at Alice's sudden intensity. "So do you know who we mean?" she asked. "Do you?"

In town there were more stores and cafés than she'd originally thought. Alice walked the streets impatiently, going in and out of open doors. La Balena's coffee was not fit for consumption, and she was getting light-headed and more than a little frustrated, walking down yet another dirt path and into yet one more brick building. It was dark inside and surprisingly cold, and four tables were covered with flowery oilcloth; a rough-hewn hammock hung from the ceiling and swayed next to an icebox. There was a countertop full of unappetizing pastries, flies buzzing in hovering haloes. Four French-speaking people were sitting at a table, finishing their breakfast. *"Hola?"* Alice called out behind the counter, but no one answered, and she allowed herself to ease into the hammock for a moment, averting her eyes from the bright light eking through the doorway. The deep cool contained between the thick chartreuse-painted walls was in itself a smell; it mixed with the incense burning in a vase that Alice noticed immediately; it was gray with chalk-white veins and had the intentionally unglazed look of something just dug from the earth.

"*Hola, chica,*" she heard — an obviously fake-friendly greeting — and when she saw Erika walk by the hammock with a pot of coffee, ready to offer refills to her customers, she couldn't help but be relieved. There was something undeniably satisfying about finding someone, regardless of circumstance or reason. Alice watched the people sip the last of their coffee. She watched Erika, before they lay down a tip, flash her showy smile. As they walked out the door, Erika wrapped hair around her finger, and as her smile fell, she let the tendril release into a blue-black spiral.

"Is this your place?" Alice asked.

She shook her head, sitting in a high-caned chair. "No, no," she said, "I just work here — not for long though, just until I open my store."

There was something that told Alice that Erika's store had about as much basis in reality as Charlotte's many projects. But Eleanor always said that Alice was too skeptical, and that people also could tell immediately that Alice didn't take their ambitions seriously — all of those various and great urban plans divulged usually after a drink or two. *You're unfair,* Eleanor would say, *talking the talk — that's why people go to parties. If people couldn't exaggerate, all of New York would stay home. Come on, Alice; indulge them.*

"It is shit, this place — the tourists like the coffee, though. He has an espresso machine. So, tell me, what are you doing here? You'd like a decaf cappuccino, or what?"

"I don't need any cappuccino." And of course she desperately wanted one.

"At least take a coffee. Be polite."

"Polite," Alice nodded, "fine. *Café, por favor.* So," she said, *"chica,"* watching Erika behind the counter pouring coffee into a chipped brown cup. "Do you like living here?"

She shrugged her shoulders and handed Alice the coffee, setting a little tray of cream and sugar atop the icebox. Alice could tell Erika hated serving, that even this one cup of coffee was killing her. "I could live anywhere."

"Is that right?" As she liberally stirred in sugar, Erika wandered to the door and fingered a set of wind chimes that Alice hadn't yet noticed. Her mother had hated wind chimes with a passion. Alice could never see why, exactly, but the objects of her mother's hatred had been so clear that it was impossible not to be influenced by them. Charlotte's long list included wind chimes, blush wine, gin in winter, men in V-necked sweaters, and loud public good-byes.

Alice watched as Erika looked around at the walls of this culturally stripped café — the existence of which was nearly a culture unto itself — and then stretched into a gesture of exhaustion and boredom. Her thin arms appeared as ghoulish shadows, liquid dark against the walls.

Alice sat up in the hammock and saw a galaxy of spots in front of her eyes. She drank the strong coffee quickly as Erika came and sat next to her. There was just enough room. Alice knew that she should not let this woman so close, but she found herself sitting immobile. They both faced the doorway and the wind chimes, the bright light just beyond the door. "I know who you are," Erika said finally. "I know you're his sister. August's sister."

Alice attempted not to reveal how unsettled she actually was. "That's right," she said, running her tongue along the roof of her mouth, where the coffee had left a slight burn.

"You are here to force him back to where he came from —"

"No," Alice protested. "No, you don't understand. How do you know who I am? Did he tell you?"

She nodded.

"When?"

She sighed, "Oh, before we met in the fish store. He pointed you out, and —"

"You knew who I was, you've been sleeping with my brother, and you didn't think to point out the connection?"

"We do not sleep together," she said soberly, shaking her head.

It was then that Alice realized that Erika was wearing Cady's shirt — Cady's old blue button-down shirt, soft from countless washings. "Why are you wearing her shirt?"

Erika looked down at her chest, as if she'd forgotten what she was wearing. "This is my shirt."

Alice looked at her, meeting her gaze until she was forced to speak.

Erika insisted calmly, "We do not sleep together; it isn't like that. And this is my shirt. He gave it to me."

"Gus gave you Cady's shirt? I find that difficult to believe."

She shrugged, saying, "He is really something."

Alice now kept her eyes trained on the piece of daylight pushing itself through the doorway.

"He has . . ." Erika said hesitantly, "your brother has some idea about me."

"What kind of idea?"

Erika waved her hand in dismissal and leaned back in the hammock. Alice leaned forward. She thought about getting up. She could see herself putting a few pesos on the counter, saying thank you and moving toward the door, but she couldn't move. She wasn't paralyzed; that wasn't it at all. She felt compelled to stay. "What kind of idea?"

"You ask him," she said. "You should."

Alice had flown here because of a single phone call. Nothing could make less sense. "I'll ask him, but he won't answer me. He used to tell me all about his girlfriends. If this were years ago, I would have known more about you than *you* know about you." She had to laugh. The sense of purpose she'd been lugging around was all but deflating into a sordid little affair. Alice could now keenly smell Erika's cigarette smoke clinging to Cady's shirt — Cady, who could barely be in the same building with a smoker.

Alice herself had grown up detesting her mother's cigarettes, and then one day, in her mid-twenties, found that — surprise, surprise — she'd begun an intense and self-loathing affair with soft packs of Marlboro Lights, an affair that lasted just under a year. It had been nearly five years since then. "Will you roll me one of those?"

Erika barely nodded but began the diminutive motions, slipped into a cadence of performance. "Did you come here from . . . where do you live?"

"New York."

"New York, aha, did you come all that way just to talk with your brother?"

Alice nodded.

"This is fantastic."

"What's *fantastic* about it?"

"Most people just spend their lives wondering, waiting."

"You have no idea," Alice said, turning to her coldly.

Erika nodded, pushing out her bottom lip.

Alice knew all along that she should leave, but instead she found she was accepting a slim rolled cigarette from Erika's nail-bitten fingers. She was inhaling and feeling the good punishing burn, the precise letting go. There were blossoms of smoke through-out the darkness. She took another drag. Then another. "This isn't only tobacco," Alice said. "Is it?"

"Oh," she said, "no, not really. I thought you knew."

Alice hadn't noticed how small the room was. She didn't see another entrance and she wondered where Erika had come from. The room began to smell like burning crayons, and Erika right beside her was a suddenly welcome anomaly — clean and sharp, like plants before they flower. "What do you want from him?" Alice heard herself asking, her voice sounding like the self she knew — strung tight and timid.

"Nothing," she said, "nothing."

"I don't believe you."

"You are such a big beautiful woman," Erika said, and she reached for the ciga-rette in Alice's hand and brought it to her own lips. Alice noticed once again the birthmark that covered Erika's very thin arm. Somewhere out there, Alice was cer-tain there was someone who had run a finger around its crescent shape, or, at the very least, had wanted to. Tales had been spun if not expressed, connecting such a shape with meaning. Erika took her time in exhaling. She reached out and touched the tips of Alice's hair with the same exact pitch and speed as Alice's mother had done so long ago. *Let me cut it. I'll give it some shape.*

She didn't brush Erika's hands away; she didn't even flinch. She said only, "Why are you so hard?" The words — direct and strangely eternal — floated from her careless mouth.

"Inside, I am not," Erika said. "I really am not." *You have no idea how I missed you* came skulking from the recesses of her mind. Erika's eyes were crushed coals, picking up colors like oil slicks on tar where Alice could swear tears were pooling.

Alice felt her breath grow short and her throat begin to close. She never should have smoked again. Smoking now felt like what those waves would do: they'd take her out with their merciless tides; they'd pull her down with a force just like this force until she knew she was drowning.

How Erika looked in this light, in this moment, was nothing if not purposeful. She leaned forward and Alice leaned back, pinned to the bottom of the ocean. Erika's mouth looked smaller, her lips chapped, and when she licked her lips a loose dark strand of hair became stuck there.

When Alice closed her eyes she saw her mother's skin — flaccid, bruised — the morning before she died. "I'm his sister," Alice said, surfacing, her hand at her neck.

"I know," said Erika. "I told you I know." And Erika's face crumpled — a wilted dahlia, her spiky petals gone.

"What is it?"

She was clearly about to cry and then, with a recovery unlike any Alice had ever seen, she took a breath and righted herself, becoming no less than steely. "Today," she said, "I found out I am pregnant."

Erika's breath was hot on Alice's neck, and there was something else now that Alice felt hovering closely, whispering incoherently, and it was Charlotte. Charlotte was making her way forward through the protective crowd in her mind.

You, Alice thought, *are dead.*

I'm not swayed by urgency, that's all. That's really the only difference.

Alice gave the operator Cady's name once again. It was early evening and cars and trucks sped past her toward La Paz. The gas fumes were going to her head as she began to recall her collected stories of disappearance — stories Alice has gathered from bars and from television, hours of eavesdropping on the subway. She's collected these tales to balance out such moments when remembering her mother fills her with a rage so potent it is very nearly exhilarating. *She should be here*, is what Alice could not stop thinking. *She should be here and she should know what to do.*

There's a couple in their early thirties traveling through Europe the year prior to their wedding. They have just visited Anne Frank's house in Amsterdam and they are crossing the street. The woman crosses and the man does not, due to an oncoming car. She waves at him and smiles. Just then a massive tour bus passes, and he is out of sight running. He takes his things from the hotel and leaves her a few guilders. It's years before she hears from him again in the form of a letter, saying little more than "sorry."

Cady was unlisted. Alice had tried, besides San Francisco, every neighboring suburb she knew. She went across the highway to a candy stall. From a hugely pregnant woman she bought gelatinous candies flavored with *jicama,* sugared almonds, *limonada.* There were sticky little boys under the *palapa* roof, a teenage girl chasing after them. A blind man sat with a white dog in the very dark shade.

The father of three small children is driving

home from work one day. He stops for gas and fills up the tank. And then he finds that he is driving without a destination. He reaches the city airport, where he boards a plane to Jakarta. He learns to carve furniture. He gets into massage. His children think he has died in a car crash. Their mother has told them so.

The gelatinous candies were like litchi nuts — an alarming rubbery texture but not nearly as sweet. Sugared almonds were Madison Avenue in the cold. *Limonada* was an alley in Rome. She was eating, consuming; she was her mother's daughter, never feeling full, high from distraction, from the endless possibilities of taste.

A billionaire widow is a mother of four. One day she moves to Hawaii and tells her teenage children she no longer wishes to speak to them. For years they all try to make contact, to introduce her to their husbands, wives, her new grandchildren. She refuses. She has a staff of twenty whom she calls her new family for no apparent reason.

Jangly from nothing but sugar, Alice viewed the promising highway. She could get in the next car that came along and go somewhere else entirely. Forgoing all genuine impulses, she could hop a flight to Los Angeles. She could sit at a hotel bar and meet strangers who'd leave cuff links on countertops, in houses made of glass. Forget about seaweed and ragged tides; she'd swim naked in a Hockney swimming pool, a tame turquoise box where she'd perfect her strokes. She would perfect her timing until she landed in another life entirely. She didn't have to be here and she didn't have to go home. She could leave her brother to the mess he was harboring. She could believe the mess belonged to him and him alone.

If Cady had published her number and if she'd answered, Alice wasn't even sure what she would have said. She might have told Cady about disappearing, about how she, Alice, was beginning to understand how people did it all the time. That reinventing oneself was a kind of pleasure and even Alice could feel it — the beginning of such a pull. She would forever be amazed that her mother came back. She left but she returned and she chose to die at home.

She chose.

Of course it had always been in the realm of possibility, looming as a satellite, a menacing cloud. But Alice had never decided. She'd never felt the right to decide. On the side of the highway in Mexico, with sugar coursing through her veins, with risk in absolutely everything from the speeding trucks to slow conversations, she felt the decision being made.

November was so dark that year — the sky a vacuum, a cancerous space. Charlotte had been lying in bed, thinking about a particular article that she'd enjoyed years ago. She was heavily drugged and tangential, but her mind kept coming back to one single sentence that she felt the urge to reread. Maybe she only wanted to be briefly surrounded by absolutely nothing not hers. Or perhaps she'd wanted to burn all of her old mementos, having had a fairly typical urge of the somewhat middle-aged to rid oneself of accumulated years of dreams and fruitless planning. In any case she was up, in a robe and her old green wellies, heading out into the cold. The moon, she noticed, was no longer lovely. It was a big crude tooth, and it had been for days now. She thought to turn back because being outside felt so ominous, but decided to press on. And maybe when she made it inside the little house, she was cold enough to have the presence of mind to light a fire, but out-of-it enough to have fallen asleep on the ruby red futon, unaware of her surroundings. Her eyelids had fluttered with consciousness and she saw and felt what was going to happen if she didn't act quickly.

She sat up — an unlit cigarette between her lips in utter concentration — watching as the flames licked up the rug, licked up the lines of the shaker chair sitting in the corner. She was so astonished by the fire, by the sheer force of its accident, that she was drawn into it, seduced by the way it accumulated power and colors faster than she could have imagined. She knew her papers would burn — speedy erosion — deteriorating time into rumor, into endless possibility.

Was it then, Alice wondered, that Charlotte realized that she didn't want to move?

The sun was nearly down, and night was slinking in — an aubergine choker cinched too tightly on a neck. There was an implicit sensation of racing against the dark, arriving at her destination before the world was beaten back by black. When Alice came upon the shamble of domes and aborted construction of the incipient hotel, she became aware of her heart beating, though not because it was speeding. Her heart had the cadence of déjà vu or perhaps merely the thump of acceptance. She'd never know what caused her mother to do it, what caused her to retreat so compulsively until she was simply gone. Alice walked as in a dream — not dreamy but *in a dream* — with the knowledge that something was about to happen. There was the imperceptible timbre of stillness; it hummed like bees making honey far away, like caterpillars eating through leaves. Breaking the stillness were the birdlike cries of geckos and the dogs beginning to bark like mad, stirring up a canine chorus. The dog closest to Alice was not barking. She went to pet the skinny creature and saw that its eyes were yellow. As she retracted her hand, she backed up from the doorway. She looked up at the domes against the greenish-lavender dark.

The domes, they were called *bóveda*, and they were laid by hand overhead, all in one day. There were artisans who did this on a ladder — laid bricks in the shape of a dome — and they worked lightning-quick because they had to, quick from the outside moving in, so that the center would hold. Stephen had told her. She tried to remember everything he'd said during last night's strange progression. How the fishermen timed their comings and goings in accordance with the tides. How the fields of chile used to be fields of sugarcane up until the 1950s. How mangoes were his favorite fruit and they flooded the orchards each summer.

There were two people on top of this miraculous *bóveda* roof.

It was evening and fires were burning. A megaphone blared an indecipherable stream of muffled Spanish from the roof of a slow-moving car — an upbeat advertisement that repeated in a loop moving farther away — and the dogs spread throughout the valley were howling loudly, joining in with the loudspeaker.

They sat together on the very top. Gus's legs were splayed out in front, while Erika's were crossed beneath her. Their faces were as blank as two days of dawn. They faced the sea, and though they weren't touching, they may as well have been. They looked close enough to have done away with all formalities: clothing, language, names.

No one had ever impressed upon Alice how shock can feel the same as dulled acceptance. They were together — her brother and Erika — and they looked the same somehow, absolutely right, like a domesticated animal let loose and meeting with its wild doppelgänger — although it was tough to say between the two of them just who exactly was the wild one. Even

Alice could see how they *corresponded*, how the slight movement of her hand through her hair seemed to answer his high, bent knees. They would go inside when the wind came up. Inside would be yeasty and rank, a smell masked only slightly by lingering hash smoke. They would crawl under scratchy blankets and onto a sandy pile of sleeping bags he no doubt referred to as "bed."

To what extent is the future stitched directly to the past? It seemed impossible to believe in an idea as innocent — as fortunate — as *the present*. But seeing them together in their hushed duality, Alice couldn't imagine anything else. The present might have merely been a concept to make life seem more possible, to alleviate, for moments at a time, the sense of perpetual waiting. But gazing on them, Alice felt it.

That night, lying in bed, she looked up at the mosquito net, a spun-sugar cage. There was, for that moment, a bit of rare unbroken motel silence, where she was taken back to years before — gazing up at the Indian fabric that Charlotte had draped over her bed. As she thought of her brother and that dangerous pregnant woman sitting so close together, the netting became a cage and she felt momentarily confined to where grief and silence reigned.

Gus, she knew, was raging against this silent cage of grief. He'd been so keen on raging against it that now he'd gone too far. Alice knew this cage of hollow silence well, and she'd become so comfortable living on its periphery that she'd forgotten it was easy to stay there forever, confusing silence with dignity. It was all too easy to fade, becoming a mere voyeur, to not accept strange dinner invitations, to not wonder nearly enough at another person's audacities and oddities, and it was *all too easy,* she thought, as her heart beat uncomfortably fast, to simply fade as her father had done, safely trapped inside.

16

About a mile down on Fire Beach sat a former turtle factory that was now Stephen's rental; things had worked out for him after all. These days the turtles were protected, were not systematically processed, but instead killed off frequently by illegal slaughter and theft of eggs from the nests (not to mention the unkind forces of nature). From the eggs that did hatch, baby turtles emerged and made a mad dash (turtle style) to the relative safety of the sea, but as seagulls attacked them on their perilous journey, only a select few actually made it.

Stephen imparted this while mixing rum and tonics; he told Alice how he rented this near-ruin of a place for next to nothing. "The industry here was sugar," he explained, "but when the water table dried up, the families that stayed on survived by hunting sharks and turtles. From sugar to meat — quite a narrative."

Alice nodded, imagining those turtle eggs in peril, just like the swan eggs at home right this minute hidden in the reeds, weathering the cold. While the turtles would make a beeline toward the waves, the swans would waddle straight into the marsh, their brown feathers densely tufted, their eyes fogged with sleep. She asked, "Do you stay here every year?"

Stephen nodded, with a look that implied that besides the old factory being in a dream of a spot, near the ocean but set back quite a bit, there was a more abstract reason that he liked staying here, a reason on which he didn't elaborate. Inside was nothing but a big open space with one couch, two chairs and a table, a functional bathroom and kitchen. "It could use a paint job in here, though," he said. "It could use any number of things."

He put a lime in her drink and handed it over with a very winning smile.

"Thanks," she said, not waiting a moment to take a big sip. When she'd ridden up to his door on a rickety bicycle she'd borrowed from Skinny Karen, not twenty minutes ago, she'd been startled by seeing him in the doorway — the way his face changed when she stepped into the room, undoing itself by degrees with a look she'd have to call pleasure.

Alice watched him bear down on a fat clove of garlic with the flat surface of a knife, and she stepped out into the middle of the room, where the cement floor was covered in cracked and dirty paint and the lighting was lambent and heavy with shadow. The sun had just set. Though the ocean certainly made its familiar crashing sounds, the thick brick walls kept the volume down. Due to those walls it was nearly cold inside, which made Alice feel as if she were yet again somewhere altogether different, having entered not only a new house but another country as well.

He ran his hand over his head and said, "Oh, shit, the garlic," rubbing his eyes with the back of his sleeve. He threw the hastily chopped garlic into an already steaming oil-slicked pan and stirred it all around. Smoke rose riotously. With his broad movements came a certain heat, a sensation that was — as much as anything — unexpected. Next to him Alice felt for a brief moment how she rarely ever felt: refined. And not delicate in the way Gus teased about, not easily hurt, but rather someone worth considering carefully. When Stephen looked up at Alice, she could see for a split second what a difficult time he was having, concentrating on cooking. She wondered if he cooked regularly, if he enjoyed it, if he hated it and was trying to impress her — the latter being, of course, the more exciting if ungenerous fantasy. "Are you hungry?" he asked, while pushing fish around in a pan. He didn't look like much of a cook, but at least he wasn't all showy about it.

"Starved," she replied — a lie. She didn't know what she was doing here. While having a qualified charm, he didn't seem like a particularly trustworthy person. He might think that because she accepted his dinner invitation, this meant she wanted to have sex. And he wasn't even particularly attractive. Or he was attractive but she couldn't feel attracted to him. He was too old. He was too divorced. He was too . . . much. And so she didn't want any part of eating, but she was hungry for each moment before it happened, like being hopped up on too much caffeine. She'd increasingly felt this way since her father's death, and though she'd tried to write it off to grief, to Gus, to traveling, even to too much caffeine, she was less sure now how she'd ever felt different, exactly. In order to slow her heartbeat, to keep her anxieties at large,

Alice focused on the layers of peeling paint on the floors, the smell of the salt and burning oil and the way Stephen put the dinner out on the table like a fry cook on speed. "Relax," Alice told him, followed by the crunching of an ice cube between her teeth, the suppression of a cough, a laugh.

"I'm trying to decide if I can," he said.

They ate seared tuna with garlic and sesame oil, white rice, sautéed string beans, arugula and avocado, warm braided bread. Alice kept reminding herself to ask him where he'd found all of the ingredients. The rice and string beans were over-cooked, but the tuna was perfect and the bread was even better. Across the table Stephen was eating his meal with perfect ease; in fact, he was shoveling it in. He dipped bread in oil and the oil dripped on the table, on his shirt. He talked with his mouth full. Alice had barely made any progress. It was a question — as were most meetings of new company and good food — of power. Who was unself-conscious and unrestrained, who could sit still and enjoy more than one thing at a time. Alice took a bite of rice, a garlicky leaf of arugula, and was instantly full. She was losing. She put down her fork and had a long sip of wine. Wine she had no problem with. Wine she could do. "This is good," she said. "This is really good."

He looked as if he was going to laugh. It was the same look that kept passing across her own face, she knew, and she wondered if he was mimicking her.

"So," she said, making a point of eating a string bean or two, "what do you, um, do?"

"When I'm not here sitting on my ass watching whales, you mean?"

Alice nodded.

"I'm a stonemason. Or I guess you could say I have a stonemasonry business. I build walls, fireplaces — I still do some sculpture sometimes, which is what I did before I got sick of being poor, but now I make all kinds of custom pieces for rich artsy-craftsy New Englanders. I get out to northern California — they like me out there — and Seattle every now and then. My crew is a nightmare but not dull. There are twelve guys total who are in and out of each other's rock bands and each other's girlfriends' beds. And getting my stone is like a second job — in the middle of the night on Manhattan piers, in vacant lots off the BQE —"

"You're from New York?"

He nodded. "I've been living upstate, on the Massachusetts border, but it's honestly getting me down, living up there."

"Winter is pretty grim anywhere," Alice said. "Not here though," she said, and was surprised to hear herself say it, to hear what it implied.

"My ex-wife was a cat person. She moved out of the house about a year ago, taking her five cats with her, but it still smells like them no matter how hard anyone cleans. I'm going to need to move, regardless of the winters. I hate cats."

"So do I." Why had she said that? She wasn't wild about cats, it was true, but what she wanted to know was why he'd married both women, who had left whom, and if he thought he was doing the right thing each time. "What I really don't understand are birds and fish as pets," is what she went on to say. "My brother went through a fish phase, then a bird phase for a while . . . they always seem out of sorts and lonely."

He put down his fork and looked at her for a second before casually saying, "And what about you? Are you out of sorts and lonely?"

"What do you mean by that?"

"I mean," he said, his voice all gentle and wrong, "you seem . . ."

"Well?" she said tightly, her face burning.

"Who . . . do you mind if I ask who you followed here?"

Alice looked at this man, whom she couldn't possibly take seriously, a man who most likely cheated on his wives, bought materials for his business off the backs of trucks. A man to whom she couldn't possibly tell the truth. "My brother," she said.

"Your brother?"

"Yes. What?"

"No, I just thought, you know —"

"No, no one like that. I came for my brother. I followed him here — it's a long story, and he hasn't been particularly welcoming."

"Are the two of you close?"

"We were. I still feel like we are. He's . . . you know, he's my brother."

"I have a sister," he said. "Her name is Jill. She's an acupuncturist. I see her once every few years."

"Do you let her stick you with needles?" Alice asked, finishing her piece of bread.

"I have, actually," he said. "Big mistake."

"Not close, I take it."

He shook his head. "But we never were. Siblings are strange that way, don't you think? Some people define themselves so clearly as a brother or a sister, and for others it's always an afterthought. When you were kids did you spend time together willingly?"

Alice nodded. "Willingly," she said, "yeah. Our father worked all the time, and our mother . . . she was often somewhere far away without any of us."

"She went away a lot?"

"You could say that. She was more of an escape artist. But she couched it in all sorts of valiant reasons. There was always some *opportunity* in a warm climate during cold weather, and somehow these opportunities rarely made themselves available during school-sanctioned vacations."

She might not have been able to eat much but she sure could talk; she was on a roll. The time Charlotte told them the wrong flight information, and her father, her brother, and Alice camped out in the airport overnight. The Israeli flamenco dancer whom Charlotte brought to live with them for two weeks who cried every night in her sleep. The night her father was honored at the Pierre Hotel, and the speaker — a beloved dean of studies at a prominent university — forgot every one of his notes and tried to be cute about it, and how Charlotte icily humiliated the dean before the stunned and tweedy crowd.

"She was unbelievable," Alice said, still awed, despite herself, at her mother's command of the crowd, how her rudeness was indeed remembered as righteous when Alice, years later, overheard the story being told by a colleague of her father's.

Stephen nodded, and she was suddenly embarrassed that she'd felt such a need to explain. Her father was fond of a certain expression: *Never complain, never explain* — always said as a joke, but Alice knew that in a way he meant it. He admired those who lived life without making too much of it. His stories were of old men he met at various conferences and tennis courts, men who got up day after day, attended to their work, their property. Stoicism was commended; analysis was not. How else could he have lived with her mother, a person who felt entitled not to explain a day of her life?

"Your brother — he didn't hurt you or anything, did he?"

"How do you mean? Like, is he violent?" she asked. She shook her head with appropriate vehemence.

"He just wants you to leave him alone?"

She nodded, difficult as it was — and it was difficult, admitting the mundane truth.

"Well, maybe you should," Stephen said.

"Right," she said, "of course. You know, that had never occurred to me, thanks."

"You're a pretty angry person," he said. "Do you know that?"

She looked at him. He was a big man who'd exhausted himself cooking a meal; he had callused hands and flat blue eyes that were the color of a five-in-the-morning sky, nothing too drastic about them. "Yes," she said, "I do."

"Well, I have my moments too," he said. "So you can just go ahead and be angry and not pretend otherwise."

"That sounds fair," she said, surprised by her own laughter.

"I have to tell you, I'm less angry by the minute," he said. "You are very good company. Do you know that? You're easy to be with."

"You make me sound like a dog."

"A dog is very far from what I mean to say."

"Well, thank you," she said awkwardly. "Thanks."

"Are both your parents dead?"

She nodded.

Just when Alice began to wonder if he would ever simply react, Stephen looked up into the light and sneezed. It was a funny sneeze, a loud one. He seemed, if anything, guileless.

"Bless you," Alice said, and as she looked at Stephen across the long-since-untouched food, across the two uneven candles burning away, she couldn't help thinking of how he looked like a man who'd had a beard at many points in his life. She couldn't stop the image of how, sitting across from him — her frizzy hair, her gauzy shirt, and her sun-freckled face — the two of them might have been the beachy kind of couple of which Alice hardly ever thought she'd be a part. Lazy people, scandalously mellow. He'd grow herbs and she'd smoke them. They'd have adorable towheaded children doomed to do nothing but surf and fish and end up managing restaurants with names like Café Ole! But change the focus ever slightly and they are exciting — these people sitting in an abandoned turtle factory — they are exciting, private, and impossible to pin down. Her hair is streaked gold from days in the sun; she's an exotic cook, a poet, a goddess of domestic sex. He is fearless, patient; he is forever capable of having a good time.

He stood up from his chair, and when he did he looked as though his body were unraveling, as if those careless arms and barrel chest somehow weren't completely familiar to him. He was a healthy, flush-faced guy, but something about him suggested injury. Alice was so ridiculously certain of this — her certainty verged on arrogance — and she was deep into that kind of abstracted thinking when her heart quit its song and dance routine and her face began to cool down. There was a sense of acceptance when he came over to where she stayed seated in her chair. He knelt down as if he had something to tell her, bone crackingly slow and deliberate. But there was, of course, nothing whatsoever to say. They were going to kiss. He was going to kiss her. She smelled salt and sweat and cotton, the bitter note of garlic on his fingers worn away by limes.

"I should take you back," he said.

Alice almost choked. "Oh," she said loudly. "Oh, I'm sorry."

"For?"

"I've been talking and talking and I've overstayed my welcome," she said, her face burning from shame.

He shook his head. "You must be tired, though."

"You're right," Alice said. She felt about as tired as a stock jock pumped full of coffee hitting the trading floor. She rose from her chair, clearing her plate, and he watched her. "What?" she asked.

"Just leave it," he said, his voice deflated, as if how she'd picked up her dish and brought it to the sink had suddenly broken his heart. She felt herself now enacting her brother's version of Alice-as-delicate-flower. She had been, after all, the type of young girl who read books on blindness, scarlet fever, who preferred playing Hospital to the Bionic Woman. She still admitted to closing her eyes when she went running now and then, just to see how long she could last. She ran the water briefly over her empty wineglass, turned around from the sink, and he was right there. They stood looking at each other for two silent seconds, and those two seconds were enough.

"I'll drive you," he said, and he seemed . . . she didn't know what he seemed. Blood rushed to the top of her head, and as Alice felt the sugar rush of all the world's dime-store candy, the room — with its absurdly sepulchral quality — it softened; it moved.

When he pulled up in front of the miserable motel, neither of them made an attempt to get out. There was something in the car with them, some debilitating seriousness, suddenly, and Alice couldn't take it any longer. "Thank you," she said, opening the door, "for dinner."

"Oh," he said, as if she'd spoken prematurely. "Oh, well, okay then. I hope you're surviving here." He gestured in that same loose way, as if he was unsure what to do with the gesturing hand.

"I am." Her door was ajar and the car was beeping, sounding as impatient as Alice felt.

"Don't go yet," he said. He asked.

She closed the door. They watched a middle-aged couple proceed to the doorway and enter in silence, looking plastered. They watched how, from inside the proprietress's apartment above the market, the glow of a television flickered and changed. "What?" Alice asked, irritated but reeled in.

"I don't know," he said, looking at her.

"Well . . ." she said, and again she felt that sudden rush of laughter. "Let me know if you find out," she said, and, maintaining a half smile, Alice opened the door again and, after inelegantly retrieving the bicycle from the backseat, said good-night. Her back was turned but she could hear that he hadn't yet driven away. Once in her room she changed, brushed her hair punishingly, and drank a bottle of water, all the while jumping at the slightest sounds after she heard Stephen's car drive off. She tried to sleep and couldn't sleep, and when the sky lightened slightly outside the window and she heard trucks barreling by, when an army of dogs began howling at the roosters, Alice rose from the bed and slipped out of her room, out of the sleeping motel.

The streets were still dark when she set out riding. The darkness was unsettling and seemed to last forever, but when she crested the hill, growing closer to the domes, there was no more bluish moon-light, no more night at all. The day was coming, tawny and dry, but she'd stared so long in the distance that the dawn came infuriatingly slowly — finally separating the ocean and the atmosphere — as if the horizon were being sketched in by a meticulous and competitive draftsman. The sky was soft and nearly vacant — the belly of a pigeon, her mother, a dove.

What answers do you think you will get from him?

August? she asked her mother — that muted horizon, that irascible source of light — *or Stephen?*

Her mother was still around. She was still calm in the face of foreigners, finding better places to stay. She was, however, fading.

Alice watched the sun stroking the purple hammered into the sky like one long night of bruises. She heard her mother say, *You're always on the outside.*

Shh, Alice told her mother. Just be quiet and watch me. *Do you think you can do that?*

And she took a matchbook from her pocket. She realized she wasn't moving any closer to the domes as she watched the tip of the sun emerge — a rare blood orange — all the while lighting matches. She dared the flames to crawl up the blond wood, dropping them to the dirt when the fire rose too high. *That's no habit* — Cady had said a million years ago, poor pretty Cady with her blond orphan's glow — *that's a dare.*

Not five minutes after she was back in her clammy motel room, after stripping off her dusty clothing, the door shook with knocking.

"Alice?" What she could swear was Stephen's voice came muffled through the door.

"Hello?" Alice said, pulling back on the shirt and pants with a hard-edged hurry.

"Yes?" She opened the door with too much force, and greeted him too loudly, asking if something was wrong. He took her by the wrist and pulled her outside, closing the door behind her. "You need to see this," he said. They hadn't touched before that — not even to shake hands, not even by mistake.

"What?" she half asked, half declared. She was too surprised and too unsettled to guess what he was doing. The wind had come up outside and everything felt tender. It was still very early morning. She followed him to his car, piecing together just how much time had actually passed since he'd dropped her off in the very same spot, and as he drove in silence — not angry as far as she could tell, not upset — she wondered what he was up to. He wasn't giddy or smiling, and he was speeding. He sped through the *huerta* and up to the dunes, and when they exited the parked car he gestured her toward the waves, getting far ahead. He said something that melted into the wind, but she was too amazed by how the clouds overhead were blowing out their candles, spreading fat, pearly streams through the dawn.

"Would you look!" he yelled, as if he'd been saying it all along. "Do you see it?" he shouted. "Do you?"

It was as stupefying as it was beautiful. A whale was entirely up and out of the water, hurling itself toward the sky by what looked like sheer dint of will. The sky was a wash of faded color photographs — a boxful of sun-bleached days spilled before their eyes. The pigments were not pulsing but spreading out, easing into light and stretching out every step of each possible spectrum. Purple the color of a pontiff's robe blossomed into lilac and burned itself down to a gunmetal rose. The whale's tail flipped hard under its enormous gray body and it fell with a smack, straight backward and under. Just like that, and then it was gone, leaving an immense splash in its place. The air seemed to tremble as if a missile had launched instead of a leviathan, and Stephen looked like a comedic prophet with windblown hair and cartoon amazement for eyes. Alice looked from him to the sky, to the profound absence of the whale. There they were — Stephen and Alice — virtual strangers and mutually proud, as if they'd both given birth to the experience, as if it were really theirs.

"What was that?" Alice yelled, laughing, not taking her eyes off the sea.

"That was the largest, highest-jumping whale I've ever seen."

They made their way up the beach a

little to sit on the cold sand. "That," Alice said, "was spectacular."

"The timing," he breathed. "You know, they're also very affectionate," he said. "They spend most of their time nuzzling up to each other."

"How friendly." She pointed to the wake near the shore, where another whale's back bobbed in the shallows, a coal-blue slope amidst the clamorous tide, rubbing itself on the sand. "Why is it doing that?"

"It's anyone's guess," he said, "but most likely it's for pleasure."

Alice suddenly felt her lack of sleep. Her brother had more than likely gotten a strange woman pregnant. She still didn't know what had happened to Cady. The more she stayed here, the less she knew. She didn't even know this man's last name. "Why do you think it feels this way?" Alice asked.

"What, seeing the whale?"

"I feel almost depressed now."

"Everything tends to feel a little small afterward, doesn't it?"

"But it's not like we did anything. At least I didn't. You, at least, came and got me. I just happened to see a whale."

He smiled. His teeth were a bit yellowed — evidence of what Alice guessed was a vice or two. But with his smile, she realized, came an axis tilting, a cranky gear that settled into place. "You feel lucky," he said.

"Exactly. That and the shock of it, the surprise."

"I knew you'd feel this way. How did I know that?"

Alice shrugged.

"I feel old," he said, reaching out suddenly for the sleeve of her sweater and taking a loose thread between his fingers. "Next to you, of course, I am."

"No, I've always looked older," Alice said, and in a burst of self-consciousness, she rushed to speak up. "I'm getting sunspots, wrinkles, I'm telling you."

"You?" he said, and then his eyes saw past her, as if seeing into another place. "No," he said, shaking his head, "anyone who looks at you and sees that . . . well, they're not seeing."

"I'm thirty-one," she blurted.

He pulled back, looking her over with a clearly appreciative eye. "You'll always look like this. I can tell," he said, and turned away before shrugging. He picked up a piece of dried chartreuse seaweed. He held it carefully in his callused hands, turning it over and over until it fell away.

She could barely breathe. "Thank you," she said, the way her mother taught her to say it, not followed up by any jokes or denials.

"How did your father die?" he asked, and she was both irritated and relieved at the shift in conversation.

Don't go all maudlin now, she could hear her mother say.

"Cancer?" she said flippantly. "Heartbreak?"

"Your mother went first?"

Alice heard the familiar line come out of her mouth: "My mother died in a fire when I was sixteen."

"Where?" he asked. His hand shielded his eyes from the sun, casting a dark, hard shadow.

"Home," Alice said, watching him closely. "At home."

Stephen put his hand on her back — a rock atop paper, no more, no less. The waves beat on the shore, the day was heating up, and at first she thought she was imagining it, that it was the wind or simply her own tired mind, but Stephen's fingers curled out of a fist. They undid themselves in the manner of his long-winded physicality, and they pressed into her back — his palm strong enough to hold her, should she want to let go, should she want to just close her eyes and fall. But she didn't fall.

She didn't move at all. Before she spoke again, before he did either, she wanted to pay attention. She sat almost primly and enjoyed this heady quiet, replete with possibility. Alice knew she had always been too self-conscious, that Gus was often right about that, but she also knew that sometimes there was great value in knowing that life was composed of moments that turned without fanfare, as quickly and quietly as milk.

She turned to him, and when she looked into Stephen's eyes she realized she was no longer able to look at anything else. The same ocean was churning away, and it would, Alice knew, keep on long after both of them were gone. But even the ocean seemed less authentic than his eyes right in front of her, which were more tired than she had noticed before, the blue undercut by ash. She was holding on to the back of his neck, not so much holding on as she was trying to pull him apart and see what she could find. Alice bowed her head and when she looked up she said, "I need to go."

He nodded — less, it seemed, in agreement than as an acknowledgment that she was speaking — and Alice placed his hands on the sides of her face, blocking off her ears; as if the mere touch of his hands could raze her old thoughts and offer up a taste of the freedom she needed so badly. When she kissed him she felt fog burning off, the high-pitched whoosh of altitude and the terror of not knowing which direction was up and which direction was down and even if it mattered anymore. This was not her first kiss; this was most likely not even her two hundredth. She would kiss almost anyone — she was seminotorious for it at certain points in her life. A kiss could always be counted on to take her right out of herself. When she kissed Stephen she *was* set in motion, but now she was running backward, scanning the past for a bearable future — searching while skimming fingers through rough water off the side of a big white boat. She closed her eyes and saw a tropical bird flying through suburban skies. She saw an ordinary hand — Charlotte's hand — those pale, bitten fingers resting squarely on her father's chest. Alice felt the drafty corridor and the long-familiar shadows of a cold moon passing through tall windows. She eyed the empty place settings of her Thanksgiving meal — the lilac butterflies, the ivory-handled knives — waiting for her mother, waiting for her brother, waiting for this kiss, even as it was happening.

17

The base of the domes — the potential lobby where guests would check in and pick up keys — was a poured-concrete foundation with walls stunted at the height of Alice's shoulders. Sitting within the walls during the late morning felt like playing hide-and-go-seek — waiting with excitement for her brother to come claim her. She'd always preferred hiding to seeking because it came with the thrill of being found. During one game, when she couldn't have been more than six or seven, she was the seeker, and when she couldn't find Gus she'd begun to panic, thinking he'd disappeared. *I need you to come out now,* was what she'd said, her voice quavering with tears. This was according to her brother's story — a story told and retold. *I need you to come out.*

It was hot and Alice drank a can of Coke, absorbing the sugary jolt that steeled her against the kicked-up dust settling on her sticky skin. A sense of calm had taken over. She was remembering how — if she was honest with herself — her father never seemed to expect Gus to come home to them. He had shrugged and nodded, nodded and shrugged. She couldn't imagine what on Earth her father had written in that letter. *Don't you care?* she'd nearly cried out, when he'd turned into a sick old man without a visit from his son, but she had done everything in her power not to excite him. She had been good about it, keeping everything — all the questions and frustrations, all those lonely clocked-in hours — she'd been good at keeping things contained.

So when she heard footsteps in the gravelly dirt, not one set but two, not a quiet whistling but a male and female dialogue, Alice kept her head below the walls and listened.

"But don't you want to contact her?" Gus asked.

Silence.

"Maybe she'll give you some money, at the very least."

"Yeah, and maybe she'll tell me I'm a slut like *your* mother," Erika said. "Maybe she'll tell me I'm a stupid slut."

Feet planted in the gravel. Cars passed by, ocean far away — all the sounds were no more than disruption. She wanted to hear every word. She wanted to hear them *breathe*.

"Okay," Gus said, "but if you don't tell your mother? Prepare yourself for when she shows up in a few months and just see what she does then. You think that'll be better? Besides, I want to talk with her again."

"I do not care if she respects me."

"Yes, you do. Erika," he said, "you do."

Alice felt her stomach lurch as she saw herself stand and make herself known repeatedly in her mind. There they stood, right on the other side of these walls, and yet a world away. The minute Alice stood and confronted him, she knew she would never go back. She would never again possess such nagging nostalgia, for truth would become too important. She needed to know why he was hiding from her and why he seemed so troubled, but more than anything she needed to know what had happened in Oaxaca and what had brought him here.

There was silence, and Alice imagined that Gus and Erika were kissing; she stared at gray cement and pictured his hand through that dark mess of hair, her fingers pulling at his T-shirt like taffy — conveying a misleading playfulness that no doubt made him feel free.

She counted to ten and still she was seated. She counted to five and she gripped the Coke can until her fingers ached. Then she stood up.

They weren't kissing. They weren't even looking at each other, and yet they looked oddly comfortable in their obvious standoff. "Alice," Erika said — noticing her before Gus did — which was not, Alice couldn't help thinking, a promising start.

"You need to talk to me," Alice said to her brother, in a voice so understated, so serious, that Gus merely nodded. Although after he nodded, he looked up at the hot blue sky as if to say, *Enough*.

Erika stayed where she was, with her hand twisting a strand of hair around a bitten finger. She smiled at Alice, revealing sharp little teeth, and it made Alice terribly uneasy, like being in a dream where all the colors were off and the people she thought she knew all went by different names.

Alice looked at her brother, who said with surprising diplomacy, "Erika, please. Can we finish this later?"

"I can't stay?" she asked Alice, audacious creature that she was.

"Well, no," Alice said.

"I don't see why not," she said.

"Well, you should," Alice said, and the words weren't her own; they were too confident and too mean. She drew a box with her foot in the dirt and made a mark in the very center. "I'd like to talk with my brother now."

"Don't worry; I'll come find you," Gus said to Erika, who shot Alice a significant look.

"Yes?" Alice asked, looking deep into those kohl-lined eyes.

But Erika was already turning away, walking into the shade.

"Let's walk," Gus said, and they did. They walked through the *huerta,* through sprinkler-fed fields of beautifully symmetrical crops. They walked past a corral of sheep, a truck where men stood drinking beers. There was the ever-present sound of roosters — first one and then an excited call and response, like lost relatives at a disaster site — and dogs, who knew how many dogs, growing noisier before dying down. A woman on a horse came up over the dunes from the beach where she'd been riding. She was fair and middle-aged and looked like she'd learned in an English saddle somewhere on the Gold Coast.

"You think she's the black sheep of her family?" Gus asked, after she passed by with a smile. "You think she married the horse trainer on her family's ranch and stole away to Baja?"

Alice nodded. "I think she loves it here. I think she misses them only during the holidays, when she gets unstoppable cravings for good champagne."

"Once you've had the good stuff," he said, "it's impossible to go back."

"We're walking toward the ocean, I take it?"

He nodded, coughed up, and spit on the ground.

They paused in front of some abandoned construction projects. "Did you know," Gus said, "that unless you build something here — anything — on your property within six months of purchase, the land becomes legally unclaimed?"

Alice barely shook her head.

"And when a house is completed, taxes have to be paid. People scramble to build something just to claim their land, and then they tend to leave their houses *technically* unfinished to avoid paying taxes."

These houses would never be completed. They might never be claimed again. "Dad would really have loved this," Alice said,

400

looking around at the fine mess.

Gus pointed to a few sheep meandering in and out of a freestanding brick doorway without a door. They were livid and sickly and it was anybody's guess where they belonged. When he'd stopped looking at the skeletal houses and the sheep, his eyes rested quizzically on her. When she didn't respond, he seemed vaguely relieved. "When we first got down here, Cady and I went to this resort on the East Cape, where the water's calm. I bet she didn't tell you about that, huh?"

Alice shook her head.

"Every room had a terrace and a perfect view of the sea. We'd lie in bed and pretend we were shipwrecked. The management rang a bell three times a day for meals, and we were, for some reason, the only people there. She loved the bland food and the little hot rolls and, of course, the drinks before dinner. There was an old bartender named Juan who played a mean game of darts, and he could pour an exact ounce of anything — *anything* — without measuring."

"It sounds like a great time."

"It was."

They stepped through muddy tire tracks and onto an unfenced lot, which was littered with cement blocks and empty bottles. Gus said, "But on the way back, after we'd had this really great couple of days, we saw a sign for a town called Santiago featuring a zoo. Both Cady and I were horrified by the idea of a zoo in the desert, but we were also really curious and we made the turnoff. There was no town at all, only two government employees manning cages and listening to Creedence Clearwater on a boom box. There was a tiger, a bear, an otter, a lion, and dozens of tropical birds. They were in boxy small cages; it was seriously hot. It was sad. I mean, I felt unreasonably sad."

As they were about to walk toward the base of the dunes, Alice's calm aspect fell away. Her teeth were nearly grinding. "You know," she said, stopping dead still at the foot of steps leading to no more than a poured-concrete foundation, "you're telling me about poor animals in the desert, and I know my job is to feel like you're this really sensitive person. But I have to tell you: I'm not buying it. I can't. You have been," she said, "outrageous. You didn't come see him — you didn't come see us. You wouldn't help me. And now . . . what happened to Cady?"

"What do you mean, 'what happened to Cady'? She left me, Alice."

"Well, I think it's more than a little strange. She called me and told me where the two of you were, and then just like that, she's gone?"

He said nothing, only kicked at some dirt, which settled in dust over Alice's ankles.

"Ever think about what I was doing while you were off at a resort? While you were feeling so blue over the poor imprisoned animals?" She found she was holding back from kicking dirt in his direction. "You thought you could marry Cady DeForrest and then take up with the first vaguely attractive woman you met? My God, she's *pregnant*." The wind had picked up and they stood on a stranger's unattended land, both of them squinting at the light and the wind. "It's yours, isn't it? Well, isn't it?"

"Stop yelling," he said.

"I'll stop yelling when I feel like stopping. You *don't hear me*," she said, "ever." She shook her head, and deep in her gut a current emerged and drew away her restraint. "You never listen. You never ask any substantial questions and you never really have. You kept our mother all to yourself by never coming home. You played up your devastation so completely that you got away with doing *nothing* for

Dad. When I asked you for help you ignored me. Over and over again I asked and I asked. And then, when you did come, when you finally *showed up*, you hold my hand at the funeral, you tell me not to cry, that you're there, and then you go and disappear again. You left without saying goodbye, Gus. You left and that was it. What are you trying to do to me? It's *humiliating.*" She was breathless but far from finished. "So it's hard, it is very hard not to yell."

Sitting on the cement steps, Gus gathered himself inward like a kid hiding in a closet. He looked up at his sister who loomed above him, parchment and crimson and copper against an invisible house. He looked up in that exaggerated manner, his chest heaving up and down, and he reached into the pocket of his drawstring pants. Alice thought he was reaching for a wadded-up tissue, but he withdrew a few folded pieces of paper and thrust them at her. The thin pages flapped in the wind. She knew it would be a mistake to get greedy and grab for them and so she kept her hands at her sides; the effort in doing so caused her whole body to go slack.

He was crying. At first Alice thought it was only the wind — it had really picked up. "Take this," he said, he kind of yelled.

"Hold on to it carefully. This is what he left me. This is why I left so quickly. Read it."

"Is this a joke?"

"No," he said wearily, "no, it's not." And he rose to his feet and started walking. But Alice didn't even notice, for her eyes were on her mother's violet-black ink, the spare and slanting uppercase letters that had always looked so unlike Charlotte. Her handwriting was cramped and economical — as if the letters themselves bore the full weight of the content they created.

The pages were oily from frequent handling. Unidentifiable colors — maybe wine, maybe blood (a paper cut?) — had left their mark, as well as ubiquitous water stains. Two rips on the first page on the sides, where his fingers must have worn away the eggshell-colored paper. When? Maybe on the sixth read, maybe on the fifty-first, but it was most likely, Alice thought, as her eyes began allowing those letters to become words and letting those words possess their meaning, that those rips were made by Gus during reading number one.

In the upper right corner there was a date. *November,* it said, *1985.*

18

My Dear August,
  I can't sleep. I'm not at home and I miss home. I am homesick so much more than I ever let on. Some stories I told featuring me going out and listening to music or chatting at wild dinner parties were simply not true. Some were true, don't get me wrong, but I also watched television in hotels a good deal. I drank alone and practiced speaking foreign languages with Berlitz recordings. There. That's one confession.
  Where are you now? Do me a favor and look around. What does the room look like as you read these inadequate words? How does the air smell? I wonder if you are still so handsome, still young, and I wonder if I could ever see you any other way, no matter if you were old and decrepit, fat and criminal, no matter what.
  Are you still in love? You were. I bet you

didn't know that I really thought that. I bet you didn't know that I saw you in the poolhouse, the two of you — I know I don't even need to write her name. Don't be angry — I wasn't spying and I didn't look for long — but one night a few weeks ago, a warm October night when Alan and I had gone out to one of those unbearable neighborhood parties, I came home early. I must have assumed that Alan wouldn't mind getting a ride. To be honest, I don't remember. I said I was sick when I was merely very drunk and I drove home drunk, hitting a poor rabbit on the way. The weather has been so queer this year, disorienting and humid, and when I pulled up in the driveway I didn't even go into the house. I walked straight down the lawn to the water and by the time I approached my beloved poolhouse, a light rain was falling. I don't know why I looked in the window. God knows I'm not a tentative drunk, and I'm surprised I didn't just bound right in, but I suppose I wanted to feel like I could look in on my small creation of a room and see what it looked like from the outside. But what I found was you. You and Cady in front of a small, tidy fire. I realized I didn't even know if you knew how to make a fire — Alan keeps such a tight rein over our fireplace in the living room — and I remember thinking, I bet she did it; I bet she stacked the wood and found the news-paper, and I bet that my son was impressed. *Cady was reclining and you were sitting the way I always envied — kneeling, with your legs splayed to the side, the way only children and the double-jointed can do, and you were wearing your father's green corduroy shirt, unbuttoned. The way my view was obscured, I couldn't see Cady very well, but I could see that she was wearing nothing but a pair of boxer shorts. This shocked me, I couldn't help it, and I quickly turned away. I was afraid, I guess — not of being caught looking; I think I almost wanted you to see me — but of my seeing a glimpse of what I wasn't privy to, of what I'd never know, and how this was your life and only yours and you looked undeniably happy in that corny firelight. I saw your face, you see. That's what sent me back to the house, back where I belonged. Your face was nearly unrecognizable. Can you begin to imagine what that felt like? I stared at your face and I had to say your name, the one we had given you; I said it out loud again and again the way I'd done during the first weeks after you were born. I remember being absurdly grateful that I hadn't caught you — you know, in the act. I tried not to think about it and couldn't help thinking about it, and I decided it had already happened that night,* and who knew how many times before. You seemed so peaceful. So I did believe that you loved that girl but I never let you know. I didn't cooperate with you and your devotion, and do you know what's strange? I'm still not sure if I'm sorry about that. You were just so young, and love that young can be brutal. That moment when I didn't recognize your face — I carried it with me up to the bathroom and sloppily into bed, and right before I fell asleep, I realized who I'd seen in your face. And I wondered why it had taken that long for me to really, truly see it.

Did you know that all that time as your mother, I was repentant every day, every single one? You must be saying "who knew?" with an appropriate sarcasm; Lord knows I wouldn't blame you. I'm apologizing now. Do you believe me? Sometimes I convinced myself that you did know, that you knew everything about me and it was our secret; it was what made us the way we were.

I took that money. Do you remember? Of course you do. I took that money from those nice women and instead of purchasing furniture and fabrics for them, I hired an investigator. I asked around and found myself an expensive private investigator. I had basic information and I paid him a not-so-basic fee and he went to work and he succeeded. I had *use of a private investigator. Are you sur-prised?*

And then I went away. His investigation had led him to Oaxaca, Mexico, and that is why I went. That's where I am right now. I'm writing from Oaxaca because it's over. I found who I was looking for and he's dead. He's long gone. I waited too many years to try. I spent those years trying not to think about it and failing.

There was someone. There was someone in my mind all this time, all these years while I have been your mother — your mother and Alice's. There was someone. He was the only truly free person I ever knew, and if mo-nogamy didn't interest him, procreation inter-ested him less. Yet as much as he was crude and wild, he was also tender and very affec-tionate and I loved him, I know I did, and now it turns out he'd gone and done what he swore he would never do: he went and had a family of his own. It doesn't sound unusual and I suppose it isn't; I mean, it is the oldest story in the world. People change their minds, people change, but you see, you never met him. And now I've done what I swore I'd never do: I looked for him.

And so he's dead. He died four years ago in a car crash. He and his wife had split before that. I talked to the wife. We spoke today, out-

410

side, sitting at a café table. It was before noon and neither of us hesitated before ordering a drink. I guess we could have been friends if you were looking in from the outside. She was a little mean like me. But she was honest and funny too, earthy, I think — not that I could really tell. There wasn't a whole lot of room for personality.

I'm going home tomorrow and I'll find you as I left you: a senior in high school — angry, secretive, tough, and beautiful — but first I have to get this down for a someday-unknown you. I don't know when you'll read this but I know that you deserve it.

This is yours.

If you'd show your sister I'd be grateful. She deserves it too. But it belongs to you.

I was Charlotte Fine and I dropped out of Sarah Lawrence College in the spring of 1966. You know that part. You know that I boarded a ship bound for France and that my parents were simply furious. But did you know that I carried a large green valise offered by my roommate, Marie? Did you know that Marie, who had family in Paris, tied a red silk scarf at my neck and handed me a list of phone numbers to call when I arrived abroad? Did you know the term abroad *made me smile with nervousness? Did you ever know I was so young?*

So Charlotte Fine stood on the lower deck,

411

with the hippies and the dreamers and the surprising majority of ordinary families, and she watched New York fade to gray. It was a clear white day. Most of the days on the ship were like that. They were good days to be in transit, to store up reserves of serious attention, waiting to really see. But even independent girls get lonely, and Charlotte eventually met another young woman, whose name and face escape me, who offered oranges and soft yellow cheese, earnest conversation. Joan Baez was in first class, wearing a red sweater.

It's infuriating what we remember, isn't it?

Then the young woman went to the ladies' room, and Charlotte Fine stood up to look at the water below, to watch the way the ship's metal cut through the dark surf. She watched for whales and dolphins; she narrowed her eyes and fruitlessly searched.

"What are you looking for?" a low voice asked — asked me. This is a line that has survived as a whole and perfect entity. This question might as well have been put to me just moments ago, so clearly can I hear the words (ordinary) and their tone (nearly rude). The question is as clear in my mind as the car that is honking right this second just outside my third-floor hotel window.

Night was coming on. He'd stolen tall white candles from the ship's kitchen, and they flick-

ered boldly in the tiny space of his cabin. He'd also stolen chocolate bars. He offered her as many as she wanted — I tell you they were children. He bit into a block of dark chocolate and told her she looked like the devil. "What does the devil look like?" she asked. "Plans," he said. "You look like a plan and I don't want one." Then he kissed her.

That line: What are you looking for? *It might as well have caused the seed, the one that shot through her, straight to her greedy center. There was a whole night stretched out before them. There was, in fact, a row of nights open as windows of summerhouses; nights that were heavy with moon. And the ocean. Don't forget they were still on the ocean. He talked about his dead brother, found shot up at twenty-three, on the south side of Chicago. He raged about his bad leg, the one that prevented him from running fast. He just loved to run.*

His mother was Polish, his father was Greek. He was not particularly handsome. His ears stuck out, he had a weak chin, and his fingers were stained with tobacco. But those hands were narrow — they moved with incongruous, almost feminine grace — and his hair, which grew past his collar, was thick and dark with a smell she would later in life identify (on a trip to Gubbio, Italy, during a late lunch with her husband) as truffles.

413

She didn't know about the seed when they docked in Le Havre. She was young enough to be unaware of just how fertile she was, and besides, she was still hypnotized by the rocking of the ocean, the rough stitching of his low voice. When he told her to have an important life and walked toward the train station near the harbor, his gait was purposeful and frivolous at the same time, and she couldn't stop thinking of how much he reminded her of a ragged animal in heat. She wanted to be an animal but instead she cried for five days straight. She had begged him to let her join him. She had begged a man.

So, no, she didn't know. She had no idea. When she strolled through Montmartre, a zombie girl on pills (S'il vous plaît, monsieur, je suis très nerveuse!), *when she raised her eyes to Notre Dame for the first time, she didn't know about the seed. When she finally dialed Marie's* Oncle Alan, *and was disappointed to hear his American accent, she had absolutely no idea.*

The seed grew inside Charlotte as she learned French, as she worked for various expatriates who were delighted to have an audience to validate just how European they had become. The seed grew as she waited for Marie's uncle at Le Croup Chou, on a rainy day, and it grew as she shook his warm dry hand,

and said what a pleasure it was.

It didn't take long. This you should under-stand. Alan Green was a scientist, a Jew from Scarsdale who knew which wine to drink with a plate of brains or pigs' feet, who had in fact eaten what sounded like every form of traif *and who was currently doing research at the Sorbonne. Charlotte was deeply annoyed that her sea passage devastation did not in fact pre-clude her from feeling anything else. He spoke French and Italian fluently, he had eighteen years on her, and they were years filled with enough ex-lovers and transcontinental confer-ences and exotic meals to make Charlotte be-lieve she'd never again meet anyone so interesting and important. And Alan not only believed that it was high time he married, but her fair face made him — a rigid thinker, a man of science — believe, quite firmly, in the woozy idea of fate.*

But you knew that, didn't you.

Charlotte was heady with travel and the new worlds that were opening to her on a daily basis. It was Alan who could keep her life this high, this full of pure entitlement. He brought her to the opera. He drunkenly carried her up the seven flights of stairs to her rented chambre de bonne, *at the breaking light of morning.*

But how much was her interest and focus on

Alan influenced by the fact that since arriving in Paris — city of romance, city of snails and light — her health had been embarrassingly poor? Had she been able to stay up later than midnight, to rise without nausea at the start of every day — had she not seen herself as disappointingly weak (not to mention knowing that she'd tearfully and unsuccessfully begged a man to let her accompany him absolutely anywhere he wanted; and, oh, yes, that she'd pay both their fares), how much would she have seen differently? Maybe nothing. Maybe nothing at all. But certainly, when she went to the American hospital and learned that she was, in fact, not in poor health, not tainted by heartbreak, but indeed pregnant, Dr. Alan Green, with whom she had not quite yet slept, became even more perfect.

While it never occurred to her that she could maybe seek out and actually find the father of the child, this stranger by the name of Luke Varengis (she was naïve enough never to have questioned whether this was in fact his real name), it also never occurred to her to get rid of the baby, which would have been easy enough to arrange. It also would have been easy enough to sleep with Alan that very night, and to tell him he was the father. But even if she had the guts to go through with that kind of lying, she couldn't do that to Alan.

416

Basically it would have been too messy, and contrary to how she sometimes came across, Charlotte didn't deal well with mess. She couldn't live with that kind of guilt — lying to a man that she sincerely believed she could love.

This part of the story is confusing, isn't it? Because she learned to lie so well later on, didn't she? She — I lied. I lied all the time.

But then again, though Charlotte was no innocent, she was still young enough to believe in the absolution of telling the truth.

Did you ever believe in such a thing?

And so, she told him, and he was sad, but not irreparably so. He was even more handsome in his sadness, and Charlotte no doubt grew more appealing to him with her initial degrees of guilt. There was sex, plenty of it, and it was . . . Well, I don't need to tell you exactly everything. He bought her an emerald-cut diamond from an antique dealer near the Palais Royal, and they married, quickly, back in the States. Her family made the wedding at her grandmother's apartment on Fifth Avenue. You've seen the pictures. She was no longer a Sarah Lawrence girl with a multitude of bohemian possibilities, but a spoiled dropout who somehow managed to land an impressive (if a bit older) man. Alan was dashing and made a toast, thanking everybody. There was ferocity in his voice. Charlotte got drunk. As

417

they danced a quiet fox-trot to a song that neither could ever remember, she agreed to have another baby immediately after this one. It was only fair.

They flew to Greece. Charlotte felt elated and terrified, angry with no one in particular. Alan rented them a dark-wood sailboat, and Charlotte wore a bikini every day. The nausea had subsided, her small breasts were not so small, and her belly was still smooth and flat, but now she could feel that seed, how it swelled within her, fighting for room to grow. She felt Alan watching it while she sunbathed, while she ate, when they walked into ancient temples, and into quaint tavernas. Greece was violently bright, but the seed grew in candlelight; it acquired a low male voice. She doted on her husband, and Alan caught her staring at him with no less than religious gratitude, but the seed was growing, and she would always feel its pull toward a different and inaccessible time.

I'd soon learn, to my immense satisfaction, that it was a boy — a boy who was named by Alan, who knew from the start that you were not biologically his. And he believed, of course, in his beloved biology, but also (he did; he did more than me) in responsibility, in unconditional love. But with your strange dark eyes and olive skin and generally contrary nature, you would never let us forget how strongly restlessness

418

was bred in both your blood and my own.

I did the wrong thing, not telling you. And I believe I never stopped thinking about those long-ago nights on a ship because of the lie that has driven me since then. The lie and how deeply I love you kept Luke Varengis and his selfish ardor always looming larger than life, and gradually I let it take over my imagination. At some point I began to believe in all kinds of notions that I would never have admitted to anyone. I began to believe that I had made a mistake not finding him, that if he had only understood what had really happened, everything would have been different. I could never see him in my mind's eye as a young man simply out for a good time, someone shiftless and restless and maybe even as impressionable as myself. As much as I'm aware that it makes little sense, I'm not sure I'd be telling the truth if I told you I could even see that now. My reaction to you, how I loved you — my first child, my only son — never quite separated from him, or maybe just who I was so briefly when I was with him. Those moments of pure feeling in the middle of the sea, the begging in the goddamn streets — I let it take over my life.

So this is yours now. Now you know. Alan was your father, and we'd agreed to let him be your only father, but I think you should know when we are both gone that there was a missing piece. Maybe you've felt it all this time, and for any pain this has caused, I can only offer . . . well, I can offer you, without any qualifications, all of my love. And I feel very confident in offering up all of Alan's love too. But it's not enough, is it? Nothing will ever be enough. Apologies, in my experience, are rarely much more than excuses.

What would I have done if I'd found him here in Oaxaca, older and alive? I don't know. I might have had to call you right now instead of writing this letter and give you the option of meeting him. But for better or worse I don't have to make that decision. His name was Luke Varengis (you don't, for what it's worth, look much like him), and he's gone, and when you read this we'll all be gone. It's funny how easily I can imagine that.

Being your mother is the best thing about living, because every time I look at you I am filled with certainty, which is, I believe — no matter who you are — a very rare sensation. I know that I made at least one difficult choice that was without a doubt the right one.

Signing off is impossible. You know how I hate good-byes. And I'm sorry, I know, because the blank space of silence is worse.

19

Here was something Alice now knew: She
was born, to be sure, out of fairness. She was
socialism; she was a chore wheel. She evened
out the score.

Looking at her mother's signature, she
felt between her fingers the worn-out
paper and ink. She could smudge the
words into dark blurs; she could tear the
page to shreds. She realized that she was
biting the insides of her mouth and she
had been for a while now — gnawing up
the pink flesh where no one could see. And
just when Alice could barely hear her
mother's voice, when the words on the
paper were very nearly just words, she
could feel Charlotte's hand stroking her
forehead — too soft and not substantial
enough to believe in perhaps, but that was
exactly the way her hand had always felt.

"She's my sister," Alice heard him say

from where he was sitting, right behind her on the poured concrete. She held on to the letter and didn't turn around.

"What?"

"She's my sister," he repeated, his voice unstable and vaguely breathless, referring to Alice for some inexplicable reason in the third person. He came forward and sat next to her.

"Of course I am," she said dismissively.

"And so is she."

"Who?"

"Erik—"

"That woman," Alice said, "is not your sister." But even as she said it, she knew that was exactly who Erika was. And she also knew that August hadn't been involved — at least not in the way Alice had assumed — with her.

"She is," Gus said. "She was born eight years after me. She grew up with him. Do you understand? That man who inspired our mother to lie and cheat and leave *raised her.* That man was my father."

"You had only one father. He raised you, he loved you, and he *just died.* I can't even bring myself to believe this letter is true. How do you know it's true? How do you know she wasn't working on a novel — one of her many unfinished projects — and

422

that the explanation page — the part where she explains that it is all a fiction — how do we know it didn't disappear?"

"When we went to Oaxaca, I met his ex-wife — her name is Elena. She's from Mexico City and she's a potter or a ceramicist or . . . whatever; she's artsy. She met him when he was working in Mexico City, where he'd apparently moved not long after his encounter with Mom. He'd become fluent in Spanish; he managed a popular bar. So Elena was dismissive of Mom's letter — apparently Luke had a serious string of affairs — I could tell there wasn't too much love lost between him and Elena by the time he died — but she was perfectly polite to me. She wasn't warm or anything like that, but she gave me a drink, cooked me a steak. Even though she was pretty skeptical about my story, she told me the basics about him, some medical history — nothing too unusual: my paternal grandfather went blind, things like that — and she told me they had a daughter named Erika. At first she seemed cautious about telling me where the daughter lived, but the more we spoke I got the feeling that she was kind of worried about her. She finally told me that if I tried to convince Erika to return home, if I gave her my word, she would tell me where Erika was. God knows why she thought her daughter would listen to me."

"And Erika?"

"Well, for starters, as I guess you know, she's pregnant."

"By whom?"

"Some guy." He shrugged. "Just some guy she met in San Jose and followed here and he's long gone. Uncanny, isn't it?"

"Stupid," Alice said.

"Well, we know you're so far above anything so sordid."

He had, she realized, the wrong notions about her, but she would let him have them. She wished, in a way, that they were true.

"You're right," he conceded. "It is stupid, and she's irresponsible, among other things. But she's had quite a time. Our father — Erika's and mine — apparently wasn't worth all those decades of dreaming."

"Big surprise. So, what, you're bonding with her now? Catching up on lost time?"

"Something like that, yes."

"How could you do this to Cady? Why didn't you just tell her the truth? Why didn't you just tell *me*?"

"I just . . . couldn't. I couldn't tell

anyone. It was too weird; it was as though my life hit a wall, and every day I'd see Erika and we'd just talk and talk and it was so overwhelming. It was exciting. Don't look at me like that. It was talk, only talk, but I'd lose track of time. She'd tell me anything I asked. Anything. She wasn't shy and she wasn't suspicious — although . . ."

"What," Alice said, her tongue thick and heavy in her mouth.

"Sometimes I got the feeling she didn't even believe me about being my sister. It was like she just wanted to talk. Maybe she'd have talked that way with anyone, but I don't think so. And I knew Cady was jealous, but I just couldn't make it all come out even. I kept thinking that I'd make it up to Cady, that when I told her eventually after I'd sorted things out . . . I don't know; I thought she'd understand."

"Well," Alice said, "that's expecting an awful lot. It's also kind of cruel."

"Maybe I wanted to know that Cady could trust me, that someone actually trusted me. But she became so miserable and angry and demanding that I forgot my intentions. Look, I'm not saying I blame her for being that way. I don't know what I thought would happen. I wasn't thinking past when I'd get the next story from

Erika. It was like hearing about scattered pieces of yourself, if you can imagine, and feeling the pieces come together inside, literally clicking into place."

"Were you . . . Was he like you?"

"Yeah," Gus said fiercely, "he was. But it might be mostly in my head. I'll never know, right?"

"When you look at her, at Erika — what can you possibly see? I mean, beyond the initial impression. She's awful. I mean, really, she is."

"Weren't *you* charmed, Alice — just a little?"

She stared at him, refusing to cooperate.

"You want to know what I see?" he asked.

Alice nodded.

He hesitated before saying, "Well, *Mom,* of course. Alice, she's just like her." He looked at Alice and instantly saw that he didn't need to explain.

"I can tell you one thing," Alice said, letting loose a stone that had grown hot in her hand. "That is Mom's absolute worst nightmare."

Gus laughed bitterly.

"Tell me," Alice said, "have you kept your word and tried to convince Erika to go home?"

He nodded. "She doesn't want to go, so

. . . What she really seems to want is to be chased."

"And you thought you'd fill that position? It's not so easy, is it? Being on the other side?"

"You can't begin to compare it. You know I wanted to come. You know I did. I just, I always felt . . . once I'd left . . ." His face changed just then, going from pliant to stubbornly set. "How could he have wanted me?" And Alice knew he was talking about their father, who would always be sitting in a cold room wearing a few extra sweaters, slowly turning pages. "He had to accept me if he wanted her. I was only part of the package."

"That's ridiculous," she said, but as she said it, she couldn't help remembering how the invisible net her parents cast around their children was, in Gus's case, always larger and looser. If she ever thought of it — the difference in the way he treated them — she'd written it off as nothing to take seriously: a difference between sons and daughters, or maybe a reaction to how Charlotte and Gus often seemed aligned somehow.

"I'm not saying it was —" Gus muttered, cutting himself off, while keeping his eyes on the waves. "He was my father; I know that. And," he said, "I miss him," pressing his right thumb and forefinger to his temples. "But Alice, did you read that?"

"I think she killed herself," Alice said.

Gus replied immediately, in a way that convinced Alice that he believed it too, or at least that he'd considered the possibility. "Don't ever say that," he said. His jaw was plainly clenched. "Don't. She was out of her head when she came home that time. She had a problem with sedatives, she had a problem with lying, but she did not want to die, okay? Okay, Alice?"

Gus was finally looking right at her. In his eyes she could see Charlotte's eyes, still blessedly familiar. She could see how those eyes would have watched the fire, doing no more to combat the flames than engage them in a staring contest. Charlotte would have even possessed the same insistence that all she was doing was passing time while watching the blaze, an act neither dangerous nor strange. As Gus insisted otherwise, Alice believed it now more than ever. "Okay," she said, and what she felt was a surprising relief. If up until now she had blurred the line between her mother and August, this was the moment she'd be able to point to as when that line came clear. She saw that her brother needed to believe — maybe even more than Alice did — in Charlotte's unwillingness to leave them.

"Don't ever doubt that again," he said. He looked panicked and a little strung out. Alice fought not to ask when the last time was that he'd eaten. "I'm serious."

"Okay," she repeated, and she'd never felt closer to her mother than she did right then, as Alice suddenly needed nothing besides her own screwy conviction. She didn't need him to agree. She didn't even need him to listen. "You have to decide who you care about, Gus."

He looked at her suspiciously.

"Why did you have to go and get married?"

"I just did," he said, so solemnly that Alice was uncomfortable for him. "He was . . . dying, and I hadn't been home and I'd left you to do everything and it was too late for fixing any of that. I guess I wanted to do something big, something real. Those urges are the death of me, and look, you know who I am — I seem to have these urges all the time. Usually I disappear while following through on them. With Cady I thought I'd try doing the opposite. But I screwed up," he said. "I couldn't handle it. You . . ." he said. "You're so careful," he muttered, and then shook his head, as if that was not quite what he meant to say.

The ocean, yards away, reflected metallic light. Sunlight thrummed off dusty car mirrors for miles in both directions. She could feel herself giving over to something; her insides turned over and inside out as she finally let herself cry. "What?" she managed, her voice breaking, "what am I supposed to do?"

"I know you hopped a plane last-minute," Gus said, his voice quieting, "and Alice, I know you drove those roads after dark. I'm not talking about any of that. And I'm not talking about what you get up to on the sly. I know you've always gone off and had your little secrets. You must, since, for starters, I've never met a single man — or woman, for that matter — you'd even halfheartedly admit to caring about or even, you know, *enjoying*. I know your life isn't as orderly as it seems. It can't be. Don't look so surprised. I really hate that about you, how you assume that you understand me and I don't even know you, that you're somehow always just below my radar. You *are* careful, or if you're not careful, you're, you know, closed. Besides me, there's Eleanor and that's enough, or at least that's how it's always seemed, in terms of getting out there and getting on with it."

"I don't think *either* of us has been very good at that."

"You think I haven't tried with anyone else besides Cady? I tried. Believe me, I've tried. I loved Cady. I *still* love Cady. But, if anything, I've fought too hard against her being the only one, and I know that's one of the reasons why we've had such a rough time of it. How many people have you told about Mom — really told, not just the winning details — in your whole adult life?"

"You think it's brave to tell just anybody about all that?"

"I'm not talking about anybody. I'm talking about letting someone know you besides your oldest friend. Someone besides me." He put his hand on her shoulder, stiltedly. "How many people have you told?"

"One," she said.

"And who was it?"

It was just hours ago. I don't even know his last name.

Silence crept between them. "Come on, Alice, please. At least look at me."

Inertia was built into the landscape here. In her mind her limbs were sinking into cool sand and she began to crave — the way she might crave ice cream or a drink — the time right before nightfall and right after dusk when the sky took on the murky color that lives beneath the sea. Alice pictured the marsh of home and how there — with the time difference — it was already that hour. She wondered if it had snowed, if the swans were guarding their eggs in the reeds and if any babies would live. She pictured seasons passing and passing and how could she say good-bye to all that — how, before Gus returned? The images played over and over again and then they flittered away like the tail end of a filmstrip. There was nothing to be gained in being able to see such radiance only as a kind of shared past. She looked down at her hand and it was holding the letter, this airmail paper with final words so pathetically revered as truth.

At first she thought she was reaching out to return it to him, but as she extended her hand she saw that she had let the papers go. He went after them at first with a dire reach, just as she'd seen him dive for Frisbees countless times. He pitched himself forward into the dirt exactly as she would have imagined had she given it any forethought. But the wind was up and blowing east, and the papers were flying in the direction of the waves. The papers flew overhead like helium balloons, and they both watched in silence. They walked toward the dunes and then uphill in the sand, stopping at the highest point. They watched the water being combed back by the tide, and Alice felt her hair being combed back by her mother, who used to sing as she worked through her daughter's tangles, softly and off-key. The tides commanded attention; they were as mystifying as Charlotte, as inaccessible as August, but there was no way to fight them, as they didn't fight back. Their effect was constant and larger than intention. Her mother and August — they hadn't intended to chip away at her, stinging her so precisely as they'd both so often done. Like the tides, they couldn't help themselves; and she had offered herself as ballast.

It struck Alice that part of the reason she'd always felt panicked when her mother, and later Gus, would stay away was that she had no idea who surrounded them, and, perhaps strangely enough, Alice could never quite picture either of them truly on their own for much longer than a car ride. They both were people who resembled the light of the moon, and there was no original moonlight; there was only the reflection of the sun. Her mother and Gus came alive through other people, other places. They existed by being seen.

"I'm staying here," he finally said. "In Mexico."

"Oh?" Alice balked. "With her?"

"She needs help."

"Right." And she couldn't help but laugh. She heard her own laugh and it sounded older than she ever imagined she'd be.

"Who is going to help her?"

"Don't," she said.

"Don't?" Gus shot back. "Tell me, who is going to help that *kid?*"

His voice cracked, and she put her hand on his scratchy beard, his thick soft hair, as she finally understood. He was making a choice. He looked at her for less than a second, as if he was afraid, as if the very last thing he wanted to do was what he'd just proposed, and for an instant her anger dissolved. She wanted to tell him that it was okay, that no matter what he did she'd always look to him and always look after him; she wanted to embrace him until both of their ribs crushed. But everything told her not to. Everything told her she couldn't.

And Alice found she was preparing for a crowd, putting on a brave face as she began to walk away. He called after her and her shoulders went up as she tried not to run. Her name sounded embarrassing, irrelevant, and as August yelled she raised her hand, waving backward with the most casual and meaningless of good-bye gestures. But no matter what she did, no matter how she postured, she wasn't yet looking ahead. She couldn't see past what he was seeing — her own turned back and her own foolish wave — trying on the world with his eyes.

20

The morning after Alice walked away from Gus, the waves swelled to fifteen feet. They crashed down on Fire Beach, shaking all and damaging some of the houses built on the dunes. The open window above Stephen's bed would have shattered over both him and Alice, had they not already been awake at four in the morning, and for quite separate reasons, each being the type of person who was quick to recognize danger.

They hurried outside to board up the windows. The night was blustery, with an overcast prune-colored sky, and as she watched Stephen disappear around the front of the odd building he liked to call home, her breathing grew faintly labored. Sand blew around her ankles in a prickly mist, and she tried to find a suggestion of even the gauntest moon. Palms lashed overhead, though not quite violently enough that she might fail to see their grace. The ocean was deafening, of course, but she ignored her surroundings in order to focus on keeping the window shut. If she was in immediate danger she wouldn't have been too surprised, but there was also nowhere else she would rather have been. This was not entirely different from how she'd felt twelve hours previously, when she'd opened the door in the late afternoon and Stephen had been in the midst of a nap. He was under mosquito netting, sleeping on his side, and she had walked right in.

Now it was the middle of the night and he was out of sight, and Alice couldn't see much of anything. She had no clear understanding of windstorms — about any storms on this coast, for that matter — and what did or did not count as a reasonable fear. Stephen had handed her a flashlight before they'd rushed outside, and she remembered to turn it on now, but the yellow beam clarified nothing but spinning sand.

She could keenly feel Stephen's absence and he was anything but ghostly. He was all too substantial, a fairly hulking mass, and without him beside her there was developing — in addition to the increasingly rasping wind — an unexpected and frankly disappointing hollowness. And here came the vague feeling of dread that meant nothing other than having something to lose. Alice entertained walking away right then, escaping such inevitable damage.

But his hand was on her back. "You okay?" He was coughing and gesturing her toward the door.

"Feels like rain," she said.

"One thing at a time." He smiled, shaking out sand from his hair. "Come on," he said, "let's go inside."

They kept the lights off, as the electricity was already waning. He poured tall glasses of water, encouraging her to drink, as he gulped down glass after glass. She sat on the kitchen table, her sandy feet resting on his thighs.

Alice hasn't left the turtle factory since the winds began, and now she's finally emerged to forage for this evening. It's the first calm afternoon and she's biked into town with the bicycle she took from Skinny Karen in exchange for most of her clothes and the silver coil bracelet. Alice wants to cook. Alice wants to cook for Stephen tonight, as she is leaving tomorrow. She's going home. With the bicycle basket full of provisions, she's at the bottom of a steep dirt road, and as she looks up toward the mountains, she's faced with a sight she's certain must have been created by the glare, or at the very least by her profound lack of sleep, a deficiency delicious and three days old.

But when Alice's eyes adjust to the angle and the sun, she sees that her vision is just fine. Her brother is on a motorcycle. He's gunning the engine and he has a little boy not five years old seated in front of him, a chestnut-brown boy with shiny black hair; a boy small enough that, as he leans back, his head barely reaches Gus's chest. Alice nearly screams out to stop him, to prevent Gus from endangering this child, when she realizes that the motorcycle isn't running, and that without a key in the ignition the cycle is only a toy, a big, muscular, metal toy with which these two can play. Gus surrounds the child, leaning down and talking in his ear, pointing out buttons to push and switches to flick. He is laughing along with this thrilled kid; he even puts his bearded chin on top of the boy's small head. He looks relaxed and loose, and Alice realizes she hasn't seen this August in a very long time and that *this* is the version of her brother that she has always and only chosen to see. Chasing down this version has meant neglecting herself, but it has also meant neglecting who he was all this time — who her brother was in the process of becoming: someone she didn't know as well as she thought she did, someone who based decisions on letters and stories, on a misguided responsibility.

But it is good to know that, after all, this August still exists. It's good to know he's still in the world, even if she can't be included inside of it.

She hasn't been too careful, she thought, remembering how Gus had searched in vain for the right description of his sister. But while she's been extravagant with Gus — inflating his better qualities without realizing it half of the time — she has been sparing with herself, dwindling her details, paring herself down. She'd made the mistake of acting on the notion that after Charlotte had gone she could not afford, not at any cost, to lose him. But there was no way to control so profound a loss; she tells herself she knows this now. She knows she can't hold on to him whether she stays or if she goes.

Alice knows that the minute she calls out to him, he'll be different, he'll be changed. When she calls his name, when she explains how all she wants is a proper good-bye, this very Gus — the one guiding the child's hand to the rearview mirror, the one pointing, laughing — he'll be gone. It will happen immediately, and Alice is sure that the child will start crying, howling; it is he who will have felt the change perhaps most acutely.

She rides toward the beach as fast as she can. Fixed in amber — in a place that is permanently late afternoon — are her brother August and a boy. They're in the desert; they're on a motorcycle. With the sun on their faces and the wind at their backs, they are going nowhere.

Part Three

21

Inside, 2001

The doorman posted outside the Upper East Side apartment building was idly spraying the sidewalk with a hose while sweating in his too-heavy suit. As Alice passed by him, she gave what she hoped was a sympathetic look and recited the apartment number she had scrawled the night before on a scrap piece of paper. The doorman came inside with her and called upstairs, dialing while asking for her name. "Alice?" he repeated back to her, and then, "Yeah, Alice is here?" He hung up the phone, and Alice had an irrational feeling that she'd be turned away, after having taken the train into Penn Station and traipsing uptown on a brutally hot day, worked up for nothing at all. Just as she was debating on whether to spend the day in the frosty reliable Met or get a cheap pedicure and head back, the doorman said, "Go on up."

"Oh," she said, "oh, thanks."

"You all right?"

"Perfect," she said.

"It's a scorcher today; you'd better be careful."

"I'll do my best," she said, nearly stepping on a little bichon on an extended rhinestone-studded leash, while making her way to the elevator. When she'd entered the building there had been sweat gathering at the base of her neck and dripping down her chest, but the lobby was filled with whirring fans, and by the time she was in the elevator she would have been quite cool had she not grown dizzy and flushed with another very internal heat wave spurred on by the nature of this appointment, its incongruous surroundings and formality.

In the short elevator ride, Alice looked up at the mirrored ceiling, which offered no more than what seemed appropriate — an exaggerated version of herself. She should have been wondering what to say and what not to say, but she was too busy acquiring a phobia of elevators, and when this one stopped with an alarming dip, she nearly pried the doors apart. Alice looked in both directions down the fluorescent corridors, nearly running through the blur of powder-blue walls and black Art Deco moldings. The door opened before she could even knock. "Cady," Alice said, out of breath. And without a word Cady put her arms around her. Her neck was a quick refuge from the impersonal apartment, the stultifying city heat. There were no traces of the expected blackberry soap, but instead fresh-cut grass. Alice pictured a glass bottle of scented lotion next to a porcelain sink — a bottle falling from Cady's cool hands, crashing to the floor. Cady held her at a distance for a second or two. She was, Alice had forgotten, so much stronger than she looked.

When they let go they were shy with each other; they were all about their surroundings. "Swank company pad," Alice said, looking around the duplex apartment, done in hues of gray. The air conditioner hummed lightly. "They must love you at work. You must be doing really well."

"Better," she said. "I'm doing better." Her voice revealed a little fury and a lot of pride, and Alice guessed that it had been sheer ambition that had gotten her through these past few months. Cady was in New York for business.

"Good," Alice said, "that's good. You look good — beautiful," Alice said, and it was true and not true at the same time. Even though Cady's hair was cut in chic layers and her complexion was as lovely as ever, Alice had never seen her this thin; she supposed Cady looked more elegant, but she also looked hollow, her even features verging on stern — like a woman literally just off the *Mayflower* — except this Pilgrim was also wearing well-applied makeup, good leather shoes. She didn't know if Cady ever wore stockings or tights in California, but Alice could imagine her pulling them on — one leg after the other — trying to keep balanced. What she looked, Alice realized, was older. It had been only seven months.

"You too," she said. "Are you . . . working?"

Alice nodded. "At the bookstore — basically my old summer job — which I suppose should be embarrassing, but I honestly just really like it. I'm running the place now; you wouldn't recognize it. I even started a reading series."

"Fantastic," Cady said with unfiltered pity.

"It's not forever or anything; it's just that I decided to fix up the house before I sell it," she said, in what she hoped was a practical tone.

"I would have thought you'd be long

gone by now. I was sure you wanted out."

"Well," Alice said, suddenly parched, "I'll be able to get . . . I thought there'd be more money this way, if I do most of the work myself. Right?"

"That's a pretty big job."

"Yeah," Alice said, "it is. So I'm living there," she said, beginning to cough a little. "I'm living back at home. Do you think I could have some water?"

"Oh," Cady said, her cheeks deepening a shade. "I'm sorry." She went into the kitchen, and Alice watched her pour a glass of water, taking surprising comfort from how familiar it was to see her move around a kitchen. Alice remembered hiding her awe when Cady would search their cabinets for ingredients — Madeira, capers, mint jelly — items Alice didn't even realize that they had in their pantry or, for that matter, even existed. When Alice finally asked her one day who taught her to cook, Cady admitted that she'd grown up idolizing her aunt's servants, and that up until not so long ago she'd spoken with a slight Irish accent and wanted nothing more on Sunday mornings than to attend Catholic Mass, which of course horrified her aunt to no end.

While Alice drank a full glass of water,

she flinched briefly from a score of persistent little splinters (casualties of a recently stripped windowsill) as she gripped the cold glass too hard. She wandered to the window looking out on Third Avenue, where a woman pushing a stroller stopped to talk to someone she knew. A yellow parasol shaded the child from the sun, the smog, from unwelcome attention. Alice couldn't stop the thought of how Erika was probably enormous and sure to be screaming in childbirth not too long from now.

"Look," she said to Cady, "look at that parasol." And she pointed out the window at mother and child.

"Let's go to lunch," Cady said in a virtual outburst. "Let's go have a real lunch like ladies," she said. "I can expense it."

"If you're sure," Alice said. She went to put her glass in the sink.

"Leave it," Cady said, almost critically. "Just leave it. Let's get out of here."

They ate in the kind of restaurant that Charlotte would have disdainfully described as Fake French — the label reserved for any establishment that served *steak frites* and did not allow smoking. But the place suited Alice just fine, as it wasn't smoky, it was very dark and air-conditioned, and she

450

could order a glass of wine. Cady's thinking must have traveled along similar lines, for before they even saw menus, she'd asked the waiter for a bottle of Sancerre. There were wine labels laminated to the walls that served as wallpaper, and an alarmingly old couple were the only other patrons; they ate dessert and drank coffee in faint wheezy silence. Alice could imagine the chef and the cooks sweating in the kitchen, wondering who the hell would want food like this on a sweltering day like today.

"I think I'm too hot to eat," Cady said. But when the menus came she seemed to forget her discomfort, and when Alice ordered a salad, insisted it wasn't enough. They ended up with a beet-and-goat-cheese salad, an endive-Roquefort salad, mussels and french fries and duck pâté, two cold soups.

"We have too much food," Alice said.

"Come on," Cady said, smiling sharply — her smile containing a small shard of glass. *Help me,* was what she was actually saying. *Be loud and keep talking. Pretend that you and I have in fact had lunch alone before.*

"You're right; this is no time to hold back," Alice said, not knowing what exactly she'd meant by that.

Cady described a project she was working on in an Oakland loft space, something about poured wax and the way it looked like water, the functionality of metal as opposed to wood. She could have been speaking Spanish as far as Alice was concerned, for though she recognized most words and could basically glean Cady's meaning from facial expressions, that was the basic extent of her understanding. "Did you think you'd ever see me again?" Cady finally said, after a long, prosaic review of this current client's demands.

"Did I? I didn't know. I mean, how could I know?"

"You could have called."

Alice nodded.

"But you didn't."

"No," Alice said, "I tried. You were unlisted."

"And you couldn't have asked your brother?"

Alice pierced the plump meat of a mussel and pried it out of its shell. "We haven't spoken."

"You mean you had the conversation — that conversation you told me about — and you left and that's that?"

"Well, I hope that *isn't* that. I hope he comes around sometime."

"Yes, well, I have to find him," Cady snapped back. "I have to do something about getting his signature." She briefly touched her napkin to her lips as if she were ashamed. "I can't believe he stayed there with her."

"I can," Alice said.

Alice wondered what Cady would make of the fact that in the past five months (after learning his last name: McAlistair) she had spent nearly every weekend with Stephen — meeting his friends, his crew, his dog — in upstate New York, and she had not let him once come to see her. She wondered what Cady would say if Alice told her that each time she saw Stephen, the last thing he always asked was, *When can I come see where you live?* She'd made countless excuses of why it was better for her to come to him. They had started to argue. *What I'm really after,* he'd yelled, *is taking over your house. You're right* — he laughed, a truly caustic laugh — *goddamn it, you've figured me out.*

Alice said, "I know for a fact that Gus still loves you, and —"

"No," Cady said, taking a determined sip of wine, "just stop. I don't want to talk about him. Okay?"

"Okay," Alice said, "I didn't know."

"I can't," she said tightly.

"Fine," Alice said, "that's fine."

"I'm seeing someone," Cady said, brightening. It was impossible to tell if she was lying, and Alice hoped — to her surprise — that she was. It was impossible to believe that she was really and truly finished with Gus. "And I might want to marry him one day. Or if it isn't this person, I would like to have the right to marry someone, which I can't do, obviously, if I'm still legally August's wife. I mean, it's good to see you and everything, but I am trying to take care of some practical matters, which have been holding me back. It's all so ridiculous that we got *married*. How did you not laugh in our faces when we told you?"

"Well," Alice said, "if you jog your memory a little harder, you might recall that I did."

"Being with him felt as close as I ever want to come to living under an anarchy," she said with a joyless laugh. "Anytime he hurt me in any way, it was always, according to him, outside of a context — he'd get furious if I ever referred to how 'normal' people behave or I dared to analyze our relationship. He would barely let me name it. I can't imagine what possessed him to suddenly want to become included in the rest

454

of the world's standard of commitment. And I can't believe I went along. Being with him," she said, her voice close to a whisper, "it was *all feeling all the time.* I can't imagine how I managed to get through college, let alone high school, when I barely ever slept. I was either waiting up, wondering where he was, or I was . . . People should not be allowed to feel that good when they're in high school, for Christ's sake. It's punishing."

Alice looked at her and saw that it was in no uncertain terms that Cady firmly believed what she was saying; she was not being wistful. "I thought you didn't want to talk about him."

"I don't," she said.

"You were so confident whenever he took off. You always told me I should be more understanding."

"Well, obviously I didn't know how else to make myself believe it without preaching it to you."

They ate and kept quiet; four men in suits were seated, and the elderly couple was trying to stand. The man took the woman's arm in what looked like an ingrained attempt at chivalry, but the force of his hand appeared to be holding her down. As she saw Cady eating with small, eager bites, she became heartened by the knowledge that Cady had actually needed her. "So what's he like?" Alice asked. "The man you're seeing?"

"I'm so sorry, Alice," Cady said in a sudden flooding, betraying what she now knew. "It must have been awful for you, finding out like that, in a letter."

"It seems so obvious now, doesn't it?"

"You can't let it color everything; not everything."

"I'm stuck on having something make sense after all of this."

Even right this moment Alice couldn't help but think of how, in the house, the sun would be hitting the kitchen's newly finished floors, showing off the honey-colored wood. She'd found the lumber with the help of an old boatbuilder she knew from the bookstore and it was . . . sumptuous — a word she'd certainly never have imagined relating to pinewood flooring. She envisioned how the old brass light fixtures and moldings were the house's only current adornments, and how every single *thing* was boxed beneath the stairs. She tallied the furniture in her head: dining-room table and chairs, single living-room couch, heavy desk and thirties club chair in her father's office. Upstairs there were beds and lamps — no curtains, no photos, not yet.

Eleanor: *You've been living in it like this? It's kind of . . . you know . . . empty,* she'd said, before laughing, if a bit worriedly.

Alice hadn't mentioned how sometimes she could swear she heard the swish of her mother's robe, the cutting of a cold red apple. But she also knew she hadn't *needed* to mention how when the sun was down and the moon was up the sky was a fine dark blue — a blue that was free of everything, including heritage, which enclosed the land and water, bringing them closer together.

Empty, was all Alice had said. *Exactly.*

Alice now looked at Cady, who was dragging a spoon through vichyssoise with the stony concentration of a toddler. "Do you know," Alice asked, "do you know what I mean about claiming? Maybe that's what he thinks he's doing — only he's . . . well, he's going with a different past."

"A stranger's past," Cady said. "A stranger he has decided to call his sister, if that is what he's really calling her."

"Cady," Alice said, but she lost steam. By now the sharp, hollow Cady, the all-business woman — she was long gone.

Gus had always warned Alice not to bring up Cady's dead parents in conversation, presuming it would only upset her to dwell on their absence, and that speaking of their foibles or even their merits would only cause her more grief. But Alice would never forget the few details that had, for whatever reason, come up: Cady's father could stand on his hands for minutes at a time, and he detested catsup so intensely he refused to have it in the home. Cady's mother was tiny and plain, with absolutely perfect ears, hands, and feet. It hadn't occurred to either Gus or Alice how asking might have made it easier for Cady to remember, and how most people need to remember if only to understand where it is they think they are going and how to recognize when they have arrived.

Alice hadn't asked, not once in all these years. "What . . ." Alice began. "Cady, what were your parents' names?"

By four o'clock, the restaurant had hosted a handful more people, and was now completely empty except for Alice and Cady, who was barely coherent after drinking most of the second bottle of wine and had insisted on ordering raspberry sorbet, most of which lay melted in a deep white bowl. After the chef had come out and made an introduction and after he sent them two glasses of Poire Williams, Cady took out her wallet and rubbed her eyes with her knuckles — smudging gray eyeliner — before fumbling for her credit card. "He once told me he'd never be able to fall in love with anyone as long as he knew I was around. Like I was an inconvenience, or . . . a curse."

"I understand that," Alice said, and having stopped expecting anything to change from mere conversations with her brother, after having stopped believing that it was through August that a bit of their mother might emerge, she'd begun to actually see differently: how, while driving, Stephen's arm inevitably went up in front of her if he made a sudden stop, how, when he laughed hard he nearly always involuntarily cried, and how the tears deepened the flat smoked blue of his eyes.

Since she'd walked away from August, she began to welcome anger — inviting it in for coffee and hours of mindless television, for all-night wine drinking and long, pruning baths until they'd ended up parting ways. She'd noticed, while driving to see Stephen on Friday afternoons, that she'd begun to feel progressively lighter — nearly stripped not only of her mother's voice, but also of the chronic expectation that she'd inherited from Charlotte.

Last Sunday morning she'd woken early in Stephen's bed and she'd looked at him breathing big and easy underneath incongruous flowered sheets. She'd felt protective of Stephen, of his mistakes and his misgivings. He was a flawed man, she understood that, but for whatever reason he seemed to turn her upside down inside, like a child with a head rush after compulsive handstanding or spinning, fulfilling an irrepressible urge for a change in perspective. He was not going to change her life. This she somehow knew. But what she'd started to consider, what Alice had begun to allow, was that she might just change his.

"*He's* the curse," Cady said, "August," her blurry eyes coming into focus.

The two women walked down Third Avenue linking arms, a gesture somewhere between affection and an attempt to keep Cady on her feet. "I see," is what Cady kept saying, as Alice pointed out cars and people in a rush, sidewalks of broken and glittering glass.

On the short drive from the station back to the house, Alice fought not to get lost in the early-evening sky, which was unusually pallid. Her exhaustion was tempered by the ease that came with driving, with the mixed-up scents of brine and bloom. She loved it here, and she let herself think it, allowed for a silent admission that the only reason she'd sold her apartment, the only reason she was still living in the too-big house — the house where her parents died, the house nearly *given away* by a man with the last name of Flowers . . . it was not even close to practical; she was living there because she wanted to. She was living there because — at least for a while — she could. Which wasn't to say that she was enjoying the house exactly, because it was, at best, disorienting, waking up there all alone.

One day — a day not today, not tomorrow, nor next week — Alice will walk down to the site of the former poolhouse, and — without knowing she'd come to do any such thing, without having brought gloves or bags or shears — rather than poking around in the choke of endless weeds, she will grab onto one weed and pull. One day the sky will be yellow with haze, the morning neither warm nor cold, and Alice will feel with her own pale hands the surprising strength of roots — the assertion and resistance from the very earth when faced with sudden change. Though her fingers will grow raw from digging and stung by wild nettles, she won't feel much of anything, because on this particular day in the future, resolve will override discomfort; it will briefly demolish nostalgia. And when the weeds are piled high as a hay bale and the sun burns overhead, Alice will finally wrench the remaining piece of charred wood from the ground. In the soil where it sat for so many years, slugs and worms will be squirming, and she'll have the unexpected desire to flatten every last one. But with the wood in her grasp, Alice will be drawn to the ruined dock, and she'll step out and throw it as far as she can into the outgoing tide. By the time she heads back to the house, the wood will still be floating, loitering in the shallows and of no particular interest to two passing swans, so imperious and cold.

And there will be other days, better ones. Maybe she'll plant a fruit tree, a birch tree, a spruce. Perhaps there'll be a neighbor offering a spare slab of limestone, an extra wrought-iron chair.

The details won't be these — not these exactly — but the days, they are coming; they're rattling the bars of their cages; Alice can feel how they're restless and edgy, almost set to explode.

Now, late at night, when Alice gazed out at this mild Atlantic cove, it was still wild dogs and burning garbage that seemed to surround her, and she didn't, oddly enough, want any of it to subside — not the persistent barking, not the haze of dust, not even the unfortunate and very smelly remnants of smoke — she wanted to hold on to it all. It was June again — never her favorite time of year, fraught as it was with comings and goings — but it was also Thursday; she had packing to do; she was driving to Stephen's tomorrow.

As she hugged the turn and saw the cove to her left, she thought, *Gus will show up one day.*

Stephen has told her this; Eleanor has warned her; but it was only after her daylong lunch with Cady that she began to not only believe them, but also to allow herself to see it. She could see it as if she were dreaming, but she was completely awake and speeding. She could see August walk into the house. He'll just walk right in — in the middle of a party, maybe — into this house where he never wanted to return, a house he knew she would have sold long ago had he bothered to call her, had he bothered at all. She could see him so clearly wearing his tan like a scar, wearing a lightly battered windbreaker, in — let's just say — the month of March, having not remembered exactly just how cold it can get back east. She could picture how he'll be clean-shaven with close-cropped hair, having brought the crisp air inside with him, and she could imagine how he'll seem smaller somehow, how his eyes will shift from the unfamiliar furniture to the new paint colors, new art on the walls, new people.

Come inside, is what Alice will say, is what she will always say. She'll have to introduce him because he won't know a soul. And as her guests filter out into the night, they'll whisper about him — maybe a newer friend or two in hushed low tones: *I didn't even know she had a brother. . . .*

But inside, Gus will admire the new stone fireplace and sit by the fire, flinching ever so slightly when the fire pops and sparks. He'll eat a meal prepared by his sister and he will not leave a crumb.

There'll be just enough food left over from the party. It's as if — he won't be able to stop himself from thinking, *conceited bastard* — it's as if she's been waiting all this time, all these years, as if Alice has known all along that he was coming home.

About the Author

Joanna Hershon is the acclaimed author of *Swimming*. She received a master of fine arts in fiction from Columbia University. She has been an Edward Albee Writing Fellow and a twice-produced playwright in New York City. She lives in Brooklyn with her husband, Derek Buckner, a painter.